Anne Melville, daughter of the author and lecturer Bernard Newman, was born and brought up in Harrow, Middlesex. She read Modern History at Oxford as a Scholar of St Hugh's College, and after graduating she taught and travelled in the Middle East. On returning to England, she edited a children's magazine for a few years, but now devotes all her working time to writing. She and her husband live in Oxford.

By the same author

The Lorimer Line
The Lorimer Legacy
Lorimers in Love
Lorimers at War
Lorimer Loyalties

ANNE MELVILLE

The Last of
the Lorimers

GRAFTON BOOKS

A Division of the Collins Publishing Group

LONDON GLASGOW
TORONTO SYDNEY AUCKLAND

Grafton Books
A Division of the Collins Publishing Group
8 Grafton Street, London W1X 3LA

Published by Grafton Books 1987

First published in Great Britain by
William Heinemann Ltd 1983

Copyright © Margaret Potter 1983

ISBN 0-586-06612-8

Printed and bound in Great Britain by
Collins, Glasgow

Set in Times

For
JEREMY
who has lived with the Lorimers
for so long

Contents

THE LORIMER LINE

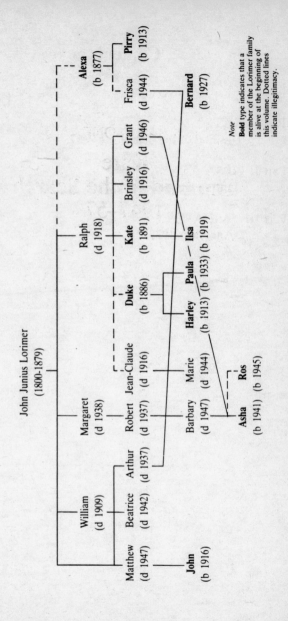

John Junius Lorimer
(1800-1879)

Matthew
(d 1947)

John
(b 1916)

William
(d 1909)

Beatrice
(d 1942)

Arthur
(d 1937)

Margaret
(d 1938)

Robert
(d 1937)

Jean-Claude
(d 1916)

Barbary
(d 1947)

Marie
(d 1944)

Asha
(b 1941)

Ros
(b 1945)

Harley
(b 1913)

Duke
(b 1886)

Paula
(b 1933)

Ilsa
(b 1919)

Ralph
(d 1918)

Kate
(b 1891)

Brinsley
(d 1916)

Grant
(d 1946)

Frisca
(d 1944)

Bernard
(b 1927)

Alexa
(b 1877)

Pirry
(b 1913)

Note
Bold type indicates that a
member of the Lorimer family
is alive at the beginning of
this volume. Dotted lines
indicate illegitimacy.

PART ONE

Kate
The End of the Search
1947–57

Prologue

Exhausted by starvation and despair, the woman sat patiently in the corridor which served as a waiting room. If she had been forgotten, it would not be for the first time. She tried to work out the meaning of the initials stencilled on the door of the office, but without success – for she was thinking in Russian and this building was in the British sector of occupied Germany. What was happening, she wondered, on the other side of the door, where a single official stamp, or the refusal of it, would change the course of her life. Early in the spring of 1947 the search for her daughter had come to an end. Would she now be allowed to search for the family she had not seen for more than thirty years, and discover whether there was any place for her within it?

At his desk inside the office Major Ryan made a quick preliminary appraisal of the latest batch of files sent over from UNRRA. His finger pointed, ready to reject.

'Katya Belinska? Last fixed address Leningrad! What's this one doing here? The Russians can have her.'

'She claims to be British, sir.' Private Ingram had been seconded to refugee liaison work on the strength of his languages.

'You mean she was born in England?'

'Well actually, sir, she seems to have been born in Jamaica. Her father was a missionary there. But he came from a Bristol family, she says. All her ancestors are British. And she may have relations in England, if they're still alive. She mentioned a Lady Glanville, her aunt.'

11

'No documents to prove it, I suppose.' But Major Ryan was sufficiently interested to open the file. 'What was she doing in Russia, then? Have you interviewed her yourself?'

'Yes, sir. It's quite a story. She's a qualified doctor – trained in London. She went out to Serbia with a medical unit in 1915, retreated with the Serbian army and arrived in Russia just in time to get mixed up with the Revolution. As to why she stayed – she married a Russian and had a daughter.'

'So what brought her here?'

'Her daughter was taken off to a concentration camp in 1941. The woman's been searching for her since the war ended. Tracked her as far as Bergen-Belsen and then lost the trail. As far as I can tell, applying for a British passport is an admission of defeat. She's given up.'

'I suppose I'd better see her, then. Get her sent over.'

Private Ingram flushed. A National Serviceman, only six months out of school, he had not yet learned to remain detached as he interpreted the personal tragedies of Europe's homeless and bereaved. 'She's here now, sir. I thought you'd probably want to interview her yourself.'

'Hm. Very well, then. Send her in.'

Major Ryan studied the information in the file as the woman came into the room and sat down. 'Your name is Katya Belinska: is that right?'

He spoke in English because if her story was true it was her native language. But no doubt her previous interviews had been in Russian. He was conscious of the struggle it cost her to understand him and frame a reply – a struggle as much physical as mental. As he waited, he looked at her for the first time. She was a big woman, shabby and tired and ill. At first glance there was little to distinguish her from any other refugee whose only address was a camp for Displaced Persons. But her appearance changed in front of his eyes. As though she was casting off the hardships of her past life and becoming a new woman, an Englishwoman, her shoulders straightened and her tired green eyes, looking across his desk, steadied into an unexpected forcefulness. Pronouncing each word slowly and carefully, she gave her answer in the language of her birth.

'No,' she said. 'My name is Kate Lorimer.'

1

The past is dead, Kate had told herself as she signed the papers which buried Katya Belinska and saw Kate Lorimer reborn. But of course that was nonsense. There was no real sense in which she could begin a new life at the age of fifty-six. No way, either, in which she could escape from memories of her youth – especially here, at Blaize. She had been here before.

The old house was just as she remembered it from the time when Lord Glanville was still alive. Two wars and the passage of thirty years had done nothing to disturb its serenity. Kate stood still for a moment, gathering her strength for the meeting with her aunt. Then she tugged at the bell chain.

The door was opened. How typical, thought Kate, that Alexa should have held on to her butler through all the years of war and austerity. She checked the inappropriate thought. Had it not been for her aunt's guarantee of support, Kate herself would still be in the Displaced Persons' Camp. Gratitude must be the order of the day.

And here came Alexa now, not waiting in the drawing room for her guest to be announced, but approaching with outstretched arms. In a moment they would embrace, murmur the first words of greeting. But Alexa paused, unable to conceal her horror at the first sight of her niece. The two old ladies stared at each other in silence.

As far as years were concerned, only Alexa was old. Kate, as she travelled towards Blaize, had calculated that her aunt must have reached her seventieth birthday in the spring of 1947. But ever since her marriage to Lord Glanville she had been wealthy. As a young woman, a prima donna, she was a beauty and it was clear that since her retirement from the stage she had used her wealth to preserve both complexion and figure. It seemed unlikely that even Alexa could have survived two world wars without unhappiness, but whatever anxieties she might have suffered had left no visible signs. The pale skin was tightly stretched over the fine bones of her face, giving her an imperious expression. She was handsome now rather than beautiful, but still recognizably the same person who had wished Kate Godspeed thirty-two years ago.

By contrast, the sufferings which Kate had endured were all too apparent. Although fourteen years younger, she looked far older than her aunt. In the course of the Channel crossing earlier that day she had caught sight of herself in one of the saloon mirrors and studied her appearance dispassionately for the first time in many years. Alexa, she knew, had cause to be shocked. As a young woman Kate had been sturdy rather than slim and later, during the food shortages of many Russian winters, a badly-balanced diet had made her fat. By the time she was forty she was overweight and, but for her height, would have looked as dumpy and dowdy as most of her neighbours. But during the past two years, while she searched Europe for her missing daughter, she had learned what it meant to be not merely hungry but starving. As her weight and size diminished, the skin which had once stretched over her flesh became loose and wrinkled. She was still tall, of course, and big-boned. But her face, her neck, her arms, her legs were all scraggy – and the shapeless clothes which covered the rest of her

15

body were of the kind donated to charities and issued to refugees by people who had already recognized their shabbiness.

Her face mapped the history of her life. As a child in the West Indies she had never bothered to protect her complexion from the sun; as a medical student she had scorned cosmetics; and during the years since then her skin had been weathered by the harsh Russian climate. The pain and desolation of losing all those she most dearly loved had etched two deep lines vertically from her nose to what should have been her hairline. Stress and an inadequate diet had played her one other trick. Within the past year her thick tawny hair had fallen out, coming away in handfuls whenever she combed it. Like some grotesque figure in a circus, Kate was completely bald.

It could be no wonder, then, that Alexa hesitated, perhaps not recognizing her guest, certainly appalled by her appearance, possibly even nervous that the woman she had rescued from a devastated continent might be bringing with her all the diseases of deprivation.

Alexa's reaction had a surprising effect on Kate. During the past few months – ever since the moment when she had forced herself to accept the fact that she would never see her daughter again – she had become lethargic and dispirited, not caring what became of her in a life which could have nothing good to offer. But her missionary father and her doctor mother had brought her up to be polite and considerate, and that upbringing came to the rescue now. Alexa had saved her from spending the rest of her life as a refugee. She had a duty in return to give Alexa pleasure in her role of saviour. She must present herself as someone who was glad to have been rescued and willing to be helped.

16

Yet, wishing to reassure her aunt, Kate discovered that the right words would not come. For many years in Russia it would have been so dangerous for her true nationality to be discovered that she had forced herself to think as well as speak in her adopted language. As a refugee in Berlin she had painfully reverted to English in the attempt to prove her identity, but had found it almost a foreign tongue.

The effort must be made. She smiled – but kept her distance, so that Alexa need feel under no pressure to touch someone whom she might find disgusting. 'Alexa,' she said, 'this is very good of you.'

Once the ice was broken, Alexa swept on towards her as though nothing had interrupted her progress. Kate felt herself being hugged and kissed, more warmly than she would have expected from the woman who before would merely have offered a calm cheek or pursed her own lips formally at the air. 'Kate, my dear – I can't tell you – when the news came that you were still alive I could hardly believe it! It's been so long since we even had news of you. Let me take you straight up to your room. Thompson will bring your luggage.'

Kate could not resist a smile, and saw Alexa successfully translating it.

'No luggage? No, I suppose not. Well, I hope you'll find everything you need here to start with. Oh, I ought just to explain about Blaize. Nobody these days can afford to keep up a house this size. This socialist government – ' Alexa checked herself. 'Well, anyway, most of the house is being used as a school. For musical children. I live entirely in the west wing now.'

'It was the same when I left,' Kate reminded her. In 1914 she herself had helped in the task of equipping the main part of Blaize and the little opera house by the

17

river to receive convalescent soldiers. She recognized the rooms to which she was shown now as having been her aunt Margaret's suite at that time – a large bedroom which had been refurnished as a sitting room, with its original dressing room proving quite large enough to serve as a bedroom. Light and spacious, the rooms overwhelmed Kate by their luxury – and, above all, by their atmosphere of security. For three years she had been on the move, with no permanent home. Even before that, a single room in the orphanage just outside Leningrad had served her as bedroom, living room, office and laboratory. Alexa now was apologizing that to reach her bathroom she would have to go a few yards down the corridor. Kate sat down on the edge of the bed, uncertain whether to laugh or cry, and her aunt left her alone to relax and adjust herself to this remembered but unbelievable way of life.

After she had bathed, Kate was forced to dress again in the same clothes. Alexa, waiting in what had once been the library but was now the drawing room, made no attempt to be polite about them.

'I'll get my dressmaker round tomorrow to measure you and run up a few basics,' she said. 'Did they give you any clothing coupons?'

'Yes. Sixty.'

'That won't go anywhere. You'll need to spend them on shoes and stockings and that sort of thing. Never mind. You remember I had a little opera house down by the river? It had to be closed in 1940, but fortunately the wardrobe was well stocked with fabrics for the next season's costumes, and they haven't all been pillaged. We should be able to find something suitable. And I've just bought two surplus nylon parachutes. With a little embroidery they make quite tolerable underwear.'

Kate didn't know what nylon was. It would not be enough, she realized, to recover the language she had not spoken for almost thirty years – she would need to learn a new vocabulary, to catch up with everything which had been happening during those years in a world from which she had been totally cut off.

'I'll make one or two skirts and blouses for myself with anything you can spare me,' she said. 'For the dressmaker, may I wait a few weeks? I'm not usually as thin as this.' The words were coming back to her now. An English lady was pouring tea from an English silver teapot in an English drawing room and Kate, absorbing the atmosphere, realized that she would soon be English again herself.

'We shall have plenty of time to talk,' Alexa said, handing the tea-cup. 'But do give me an idea of your life, Kate. Just the bare bones of what happened after 1915. From your letters we learned how your unit had to retreat with the Serbs and re-group in Russia. But the only message we've had from you since 1917 was the one which your friend Sergei brought us after the Great War. He told us that you were married, but he didn't say to whom. He said you were in charge of an orphanage, but he wouldn't say where. And he said you had a daughter. All that was in 1920. Since then we've known nothing – nothing at all until the man from the Control Commission called to say that you'd turned up in Berlin.'

It was painful for Kate to talk about those days. But to answer Alexa's direct questions was the best way to avoid more probing of the past. 'Do you remember that in 1917 you sent me a letter of introduction to a friend of yours, Prince Paul Aminov?' she asked.

'Yes, of course. I sang for him once in the theatre of one of his palaces.'

19

'That palace became the orphanage which was my home for twenty-odd years. I never met your friend: he was killed in the revolution. But I married his brother, Vladimir.'

'So! You became Princess Aminova!'

Kate shook her head. 'By the time we married he was travelling on false papers. I became the wife of Comrade Belinsky.'

'You are a princess,' said Alexa firmly – and Kate could not help smiling, guessing how the story would be embroidered as it travelled the circle of her hostess's friends. 'What happened to Vladimir?'

'He was forcibly conscripted by the Cheka. Then they discovered that his papers had been stolen. He was – ' the word was hard to say – 'executed. It was a long time ago, but I wasn't told at the time. So many people in those years were taken off to Siberia but came back in the end. So I waited, hoping.'

'I'm so sorry, my dear. So very sorry. But – ' Alexa hurried on – 'before he was killed, you had a daughter?'

'Ilsa. Vladimir never saw her.' Kate paused, trying to phrase what she needed to say in a manner which would be definite without giving offence. 'I can talk about my husband, Alexa, and the revolution and my years in the orphanage, because that's all past history now. But Ilsa – I will tell you once and then, please, I want never to speak of her again. It's too close, too painful.'

Alexa nodded her sympathy.

'Ilsa was a musician. Right from childhood – a prodigy, like yourself. A professional pianist. Before the war, before she was twenty, she was giving recitals. The orphanage was occupied when the Germans invaded Russia in 1940. They came very quickly. With two thousand children in my care, there was no time to escape.

Some of the children were Jews. Ilsa hid them – stayed with them in the cellars for three months. They were discovered.' For a moment Kate could not go on. This was the moment which had haunted her nightmares for years but which she could not bring herself to think about in daylight.

'They were all sent to Auschwitz. The children were killed at once. But Ilsa wasn't a Jew. She had to work like a slave, but she lived. When the Russians began to advance at last she was moved to another camp, Bergen-Belsen. Again, although thousands starved, she survived. I know all that from visiting the camps, reading the lists there and at the Displaced Persons' Commission. After the liberation she left Belsen. She must have gone home. But the orphanage had been mined and completely destroyed. The whole village was ruined – abandoned. Nothing there. And at that time, in 1945, I was a thousand miles away with the orphans. There was no one to tell Ilsa where I was, or even that I was still alive. When I got on to the train with the children, nobody knew its destination. Where did Ilsa go? No one knows. There were millions of refugees on the roads of Europe. Did she leave a message somewhere? Is there some place she thought I would look for her? As soon as I was able to leave the children I tried to find her. I traced her to Belsen. I went back to our old home. I have left messages in offices, with friends, nailed to trees. She may not still be alive. I saw some of those who were in Belsen on the day of its liberation and I knew that they would not survive for very long. But even if she *is* still alive, I have lost her. For ever. I've had to make myself recognize that.' Kate's voice trailed into silence as she sat, crumpled, in a corner of the sofa, as though dead herself.

'Did you never tell her about Blaize?' asked Alexa. 'About your family – *her* family – in England?'

At last Kate stirred herself and shook her head. 'At the time when she was born the British had sent troops to intervene in the civil war, supporting the Whites against the Reds. There was anger in Russia. And the British blockade was blamed for the food shortages. Thousands of people starved in the famines after the revolution. Except for Sergei, whom you met, I never allowed anyone there to suspect that I was not a Russian. Especially not a child, who might chatter without understanding the danger.'

'But as she grew up?'

'Then I was planning to escape. Ilsa was to be my passport to freedom. I intended to go with her on her first foreign tour, to break away with her and never go back. If she had known of the plan, she might have shown guilt or nervousness. As it turned out, by the time she was first sent abroad, Germany was our ally and England our enemy. I'd left it too late. But I went on hoping – as sometimes I still hope now that she may take up her career again. Perhaps one day I shall read of her performance in a concert review or hear a musician praising her. But until then, Alexa, I don't want to speak her name or hear it. I shan't ever stop thinking of her. But when I asked to be sent back to England, it was because I'd given up the search, accepted defeat.'

'I understand,' said Alexa. For a moment she was silent, and then sighed. 'What more can I say than that I'm sorry?' She left the room, perhaps to give Kate time to bring her feelings under control, touching her niece's hand in sympathy as she passed. When she returned she was accompanied by a six-year-old girl, a slight child with a pale complexion and hair so fair that it looked almost white. The child looked at Kate as she came in – at first curiously and then with some alarm, clutching Alexa's hand for reassurance.

'This is Asha,' said Alexa. 'Asha, this is your Aunt Kate. I told you she was coming. She's going to live with us at Blaize.'

'Hello, Asha,' said Kate. She did not attempt to embrace the little girl or even hold out her hand to be shaken. Children, she knew, were frightened of freaks. 'I look very odd, don't I? I've been ill, you see. But I'm better now, and I expect my hair will grow again quite soon. What shall I do to cover up my funny head until then? Do you think I ought to wear a hat? Or a scarf?'

Asha stared at Kate with wide blue eyes, but did not answer. For a moment she stood still, rubbing one foot up and down her other leg. Then she let go of Alexa's hand and – still without speaking – ran out of the room.

'Your granddaughter?' asked Kate. She too had some catching up to do. At the time of their last parting, Alexa had had two young children – Frisca, blonde and bouncing, and Pirry, heir to the Glanville title and estates. Asha might easily be the child of one of them – but Alexa was shaking her head.

'No. Asha is my great-niece. When I introduced you as her Aunt Kate, I wasn't giving you a courtesy title. Her father was your brother Grant.'

Kate was startled by the statement. Her younger brother had been a late addition to the family, born fourteen years after herself, with a badly deformed body. Kate had left Jamaica at the age of eighteen to start her medical training, and remembered the boy only as a whining cripple. So the first surprise was to learn that Grant had not only survived into adult life but had found someone prepared to marry him. A second shock was contained in the tense of Alexa's verb. 'Was?' she queried.

'He was captured by the Japanese in Malaya and spent most of the war as a prisoner. By the time he was released his health had been so badly affected that – well, he died a few months ago.'

Kate had never liked Grant. But throughout the past ten years, years of bereavement and fear and hardship, her strongest support had been the resolve to return to her own family as soon as possible – to become a Lorimer again, surrounded by all the other Lorimers. Every death in the family deprived her of part of the reassurance she needed. 'And Asha's mother?' she asked.

Alexa sighed. 'She died as well, only a few weeks later, although not for the same reason. There have been too many deaths in the family. Too many altogether.' She sighed again. 'Margaret is dead, of course. You remember my sister Margaret?'

'Certainly I do.' Dr Margaret Scott had treated Kate like a daughter throughout the time when she was studying in London. But Margaret would have been ninety by now, so this piece of news could come as little surprise.

'And you'll remember Margaret's son, Robert. He must have been about your age. He died as well, working out in India. But he left one daughter. She married Grant, and Asha is their daughter. Very much alone in the world, you see, except for me. So she lives here. She's a bright little girl.'

Kate was still thinking about Margaret, who for many years had been the mainstay of the Lorimer family. In those days Alexa had been withdrawn, too busy with her own affairs to concern herself with the needs of others. It was a surprise to see her obvious affection for the little girl.

24

Asha returned carrying an armful of hats. She first of all dropped them on the floor and then silently handed them one at a time to Kate. Her own school beret brought the first smile to the little girl's blue eyes as it lay flat on the top of her aunt's head. 'Too small,' said Kate.

The next was a wide-brimmed straw which perhaps Alexa kept for hot days in the garden. 'Too scratchy.'

Number three had clearly been discarded from normal use long ago and handed down to a dressing-up box. Battered out of shape, it was still drunkenly decorated with feathers and veiling. 'Too grand.'

The last was a printed silk square. Kate folded it into a triangle and laid it firmly along her missing hairline, knotting it at the back of her head. 'Very Russian,' she said. 'Just right. Thank you very much, Asha. Do I look better now?'

Asha nodded solemnly. 'Will you tell me Russian stories?' she asked. 'Aunt Alexa's run out of stories. She said you'd have new ones for me.'

When Ilsa was a little girl, and before such subjects were denounced as decadent, Kate had often soothed her to sleep with tales of bears and woodcutters and magicians in dark forests. She did not wish now to be reminded of Ilsa. But Asha, no longer afraid, was slipping a small hand into hers, offering friendship.

'Yes,' agreed Kate. 'I'll tell you Russian stories if you'll tell me English ones in return.'

Once again Asha nodded. Then she looked from Kate to Alexa and back again. A smile of satisfaction spread over her pale, thin face. 'So now I have two aunts,' she said.

Kate had received a second welcome to Blaize. She was truly home.

2

'Who am I?' Every morning, in the moments which came between awakening and the full consciousness of her surroundings, Kate found herself asking the same question. She was not so much a guest at Blaize as a dependant and, living on Alexa's charity, had lost her identity.

Over a period of thirty years she could have answered the question precisely. 'I am the doctor in charge of this medical unit. I am the medical superintendent of this orphanage.' Whether or not it was right to define personality in terms of occupation, she had been accustomed to do so without hesitation.

Now that certainty was destroyed. Nothing could alter the fact that Kate was a qualified doctor, but for the time being she had lost the confidence which would enable her to apply for work in England. For far too long she had been out of touch with modern medicine. There had been no point in trying to keep up with all the new discoveries which had been made in the years when it was impossible to obtain enough of even the most old-fashioned, standard drugs. No competent medical authority in England now would trust her to give advice and Kate, all too well aware of her own limitations, saw no point in exposing herself to rejection.

There had been a few years, even while she was still in Russia, when she had answered the question of identity differently. 'I am a mother.' In a society which she saw at last as corrupt, based on terror instead of on the high ideals which she had once shared with the Bolshevik

26

revolutionaries, her daughter Ilsa not only represented Kate's hopes for the future but defined her status in the one enduring entity: the family. It was no longer of any relevance to Kate that she was the daughter of Ralph and Lydia Lorimer, but to be Ilsa's mother had seemed important. Even when Ilsa was snatched away from her and sent to Auschwitz it was possible still to feel herself a parent. But now she must accept that her daughter – even if still alive – was lost to her for ever: it was necessary to search for another answer to the question which distracted her mind. 'Who am I?'

Well, she was Asha's aunt. That at least was a fact, although it could hardly be regarded as a career. Kate tried to attach the six-year-old to herself, but only with limited success. Almost alone in the world after her mother's death, Asha had accepted Alexa's guardianship with a fiercely possessive loyalty. While welcoming the widening of her family to include Kate, she made it plain that she was still Aunt Alexa's special girl.

The first snow of winter fell two days before Christmas. To Kate, after so many years in Russia, it hardly ranked as a snowfall at all, but merely as a decorative gesture, like a dusting of icing sugar sieved on to a cake and promptly tapped off again. But Asha, on holiday from school, had long ago forgotten all about the previous winter. Bouncing with excitement, she ran out on to the terrace to feel the snowflakes settling gently on her upturned face. Kate went with her. Reason told her that Asha was safe enough in the part of the garden nearest to the house, but the memory of too many partings made her uneasy, reluctant to let out of her sight the little girl who represented the youngest generation of the family.

For half an hour they threw crumbs to the birds.

Then the sound of a car crackling over the frosty gravel distracted Asha. She tugged at Kate's hand.

'I expect that's Bernard. Come and see.'

'We'll give him a moment to say hello to his grandmother first.' Kate knew, of course, that Alexa was expecting her twenty-year-old grandson for his Christmas leave. As a result of spending the war years in California, Bernard had started his period of National Service later than most of his contemporaries. From the letters which Alexa read out over the breakfast table, Kate could tell that he was enduring rather than enjoying the compulsory interruption of his studies and looked forward to being pampered for a few days over Christmas. Her intense interest in the family from which she had been cut off for so long made her anxious to meet him, but it seemed proper to wait until he had greeted Alexa. She did her best to restrain the urgency with which Asha pulled her back towards the house.

'Bernard's an orphan like me,' said Asha as Kate was helping her off with her coat and gloves and wellington boots. 'When my Mummy died I used to cry sometimes, and Bernard said I mustn't, because if I cried for being an orphan he'd have to cry as well because his Mummy had died too. So we have to cheer each other up and we don't cry any more. Well, not very often, anyway. Bernard's a very cheerful sort of orphan. Are you an orphan as well, Aunt Kate?'

'Well, yes, I suppose I am. Most people are when they get to my age.'

'But not when they're only six.'

'No, not so often then. That was bad luck. You'd better go and cheer Bernard up again then, hadn't you?'

Kate watched the little girl run off as she followed more slowly. Meeting new people was still an ordeal. It

28

was not her appearance which worried Kate. She had never been vain, and even on the first day of her return to Blaize she had been able to foresee the shock which her appearance must cause without feeling upset by it. In the past weeks she had begun to put on weight and had lost something of the scrawny, haggard look with which she had arrived – for although food was still rationed as stringently as during the war, Alexa's tenants and the manager of the home farm made sure that Blaize was never short of fruit and vegetables in season, eggs and chickens, rabbits and piglets. So rest and a healthy diet had filled out Kate's sagging skin, strengthening her muscles and bringing life to her green eyes. To complete the transformation she had acquired a wig to cover her hairless head – though she could tell from Alexa's guarded comments that it might have been wiser to choose a mousy, inconspicuous shade rather than specify the tawny redness which had been her natural colour once. It looked artificially young, emphasizing the lines on her weathered face. She recognized that Asha thought her even older than Alexa.

None of that was important. What bothered Kate was the problem of conversation. She guessed that Alexa too had anticipated trouble before her arrival – had even feared that they might quarrel. Alexa, who had married a wealthy nobleman – and who even before that had made her way to the top of her profession with nothing to help her but ambition and talent – must be expected to believe in the virtues of aristocracy and meritocracy. She had never disguised her wish to see power and influence remaining in the hands of the élite who could use it wisely, nor her scorn for those politicians who – unable to secure equality of happiness – seemed determined to achieve equality of misery.

How deeply she must have expected her niece to disagree with her views! Kate had left England in 1915 as a bright-eyed idealist, out-spoken and often tactless in her criticism of privilege and inefficiency, determined to change any society which condemned some people to lives of inescapable poverty while others lived in luxury. It was these views which had persuaded her to support the revolution in Russia and to remain in that country as a citizen of a communist society, hoping to see her own youthful ideals put into practice. What Alexa could not have known was that thirty years of fear and suspicion, hardship and corruption, had disillusioned Kate long before she was able to leave. There was never any danger that the two women would quarrel about communism.

The real difficulty of conversation had proved to be something less easily foreseen. Kate found it impossible to chat to Alexa because they had so little common ground. It was as though they had been living for thirty years on two different planets. Kate thought herself well-informed on political and military affairs, but soon found that her history books and newspapers had described a world which Alexa did not recognize. They were no more likely to quarrel about this than about communism, but it made serious conversation difficult. Instead, Alexa chattered about people whose names were household words in England, or so she claimed: artists, writers, playwrights, sportsmen. Kate had not read their books or seen their pictures or their plays or their films: she had not even heard of their names.

With Alexa herself it didn't matter too much. But in front of strangers Kate felt awkward, humiliated by her ignorance. It would have been easier if she could have been introduced as a foreigner, a Russian, who might be congratulated on her grasp of the language but would not be expected to express any profound opinions in it.

As a subject of common interest only the family remained, and here too Kate found herself floundering. Having known Alexa's two children before she left England, she naturally asked for news of them. Herself robbed of her only child, Kate was quick to understand the pain it caused Alexa to describe how her beautiful daughter Frisca had been killed in an air raid. The son, Pirry, had inherited the title of Lord Glanville when his father died in 1918 and had come into his life interest in the Glanville estate in 1934, but it appeared that he had chosen not to make his home at Blaize. For almost the whole of the Second World War he had been a prisoner of war in Germany, and since then had lived abroad. Speaking obliquely, Alexa indicated that there was a special reason why Pirry had decided not to return to England, but she seemed unable to explain precisely what it was. Perhaps he was ill, Kate thought, and needed a warm climate. She continued to puzzle, but did not like to press for elucidation.

About Bernard, however, whom she was now to meet, there seemed no mystery. Only the demands of the army had prevented him from seeing her before. He was the son of Alexa's daughter Frisca, who had been a star both of the London stage and of many Hollywood films before her death in 1944. And Frisca had married her cousin Arthur, whom Kate remembered well – for she herself had received a proposal of marriage from him in 1914. What a very different life she would have led had she accepted! Instead of enduring the hardships of the Serbian campaign she would have been the mistress of Brinsley House, the Bristol mansion which the Lorimers had built in the eighteenth century from the profits of the slave trade. And later, when Arthur became a baronet, she would have been Lady Lorimer: rich and well-fed and safe.

Well, Frisca had enjoyed that life instead, but now was dead. Kate opened the library door and went in to be introduced to Frisca's son.

Alexa performed the introduction casually, trying to work out the relationship. 'It must be first cousin once removed, mustn't it?'

Kate should have made some equally casual friendly remark, but her face had frozen into an incredulous stare: it was unpardonable but uncontrollable. Seeing Alexa frown, she struggled with her manners, answering Bernard's polite questions. Only when Asha nudged her way back into the attention of the adults could Kate retreat into silence and try to discipline the confusion in her mind.

Alexa had told her, surely, that Bernard was the son of Frisca and Arthur. Could she have remembered that wrongly? No, of course not. The memory of the proposal which she herself had received in the conservatory at Blaize would have been irrelevant unless the name mentioned was Arthur's. And she remembered Alexa reading out a request from Bernard that he should never be addressed by his title on any letter sent to the barracks. To be known as Sir Bernard Lorimer, Bart., was to invite sarcasm from sergeant-majors, he pointed out. No, there was nothing wrong with her recollection of what Alexa had said.

Why was it, then, that the sight of this boy recalled not the thought of Arthur stiffly inviting her to be his wife but a quite different moment on the same evening? On that occasion in 1914 when Kate's brother, Brinsley, had celebrated his twenty-first birthday at Blaize, a telegram had arrived summoning him and his young friends to fight on the Western Front. Kate remembered that she had been dancing with one of her young cousins. He interrupted the dance to lead her into the library – the very library in which she was standing now – to ask whether she thought his mother would let him join the army like Brinsley. That young cousin, twenty years old, with tousled red hair and a smile abruptly made earnest by the summons to war, was Robert Scott. And this young cousin, twenty years old, with red hair whose curls resisted the military cut and with a serious, pleasant smile, was Bernard Lorimer. But the likeness was so complete that for a moment Kate felt faint. Was this the library of 1914 or of 1947? Was this Robert or Bernard? Was her hard-pressed mind playing tricks with her?

Alexa recognized her distress and told Asha to take her fellow-orphan up to his room to change out of uniform before lunch.

'So you noticed.' She poured herself a large whisky. 'Bernard doesn't know, of course. He was only nine or ten when Robert died in India. They never met.'

'I don't understand. What happened?'

'What happened was that Frisca fell in love with Robert. They were going to be married. Then, without telling anyone why, they broke it off. Robert went back to India, Frisca married Arthur, and Bernard was born seven months later.'

'And no one ever told him?'

'What would be the point? He never knew Robert, and Robert is dead. Frisca did want him to know the truth one day. When she was dying, she asked me to tell him. But the baronetcy is a complication, you see. Bernard was born in wedlock and has inherited his title from the man he believes to be his father. He's a very earnest

33

young man – very moral, you might say. If he learned the truth he might feel compelled to renounce the baronetcy. It would be a ridiculous gesture, of course. After all, who really cares? It would simply cause a scandal. But he might try to do it. And that would be a pity, because it meant such a lot to poor, sterile Arthur that he should have an heir. He knew exactly what he was doing when he married Frisca. I'm sorry to have sprung it on you like this, Kate. I didn't want to tell you the truth unless I had to. Secrets are best kept from absolutely everybody. But I could see how startled you were.'

'They're the same age, you see,' Kate explained. 'Bernard now and Robert when I last saw him. That's how I remember Robert – exactly like that. But of course I won't say anything.' If she had learned any lesson from the years of terror and purge in Stalin's Russia, it was how to keep a secret.

Bernard, when he returned alone, wearing different clothes, had something different on his mind. 'I need advice,' he said. 'What am I going to do about Brinsley House, Grandmother?'

'Why do you need to do anything about it? I realize you can't live there until you've finished with all this army nonsense – '

'And all the Cambridge nonsense which will follow. Shall I *ever* live there again, that's the point. Do you remember Brinsley House, Kate? Did you ever stay there?'

'Yes. I came to England from Jamaica when I was eighteen and spent my first few days in Brinsley House.' The home in which she had spent her Jamaican childhood was a simple building – a single storey with a wide verandah all round, raised on blocks so that the island's torrential rains could rush unobstructed to the river. She

34

still remembered her amazement on entering the Lorimer mansion which dominated the Avon gorge between the port of Bristol and the suspension bridge at Clifton – the mansion in which the Lorimers had lived as merchant princes for more than a hundred years. Even after the collapse of the family bank they had managed to maintain the old house in something near the style to which it was accustomed.

'It's ten years since any of us lived there,' Bernard told her. 'Mother let it when she went to Hollywood before the war. And during the war, part of the BBC was evacuated to Bristol; they took over the house for their staff. For the past few months it's been empty. It's shabby and damp and – well, neglected. Putting it to rights will be a full-time job for somebody – but not for a chap in the middle of his National Service. And now someone's made an offer.'

'To buy it, you mean?' asked Alexa.

'Yes. Bristol University. For a new hall of residence. In the house itself they want to have common rooms and a library and kitchen and dining rooms, with a few students in the bedrooms. Then they'd build two complete wings of bed-sitters on the upper lawn.'

'What, spoil that beautiful garden!' exclaimed Alexa. Kate, not feeling it any of her business to comment, watched as Bernard put his arm affectionately round his grandmother's shoulders.

'The garden hasn't been very beautiful for some time; but I don't want to upset you, Grandmother. I know this was your father's house. That's why I wanted to discuss the offer – in case you feel sentimental about keeping it in the family.'

Instinctively all three turned to stare at one of the pictures which hung on the library wall. It showed an eighty-year-old man in sombre Victorian dress: John Junius Lorimer, Alexa's father and Kate's grandfather.

'It's true that my father owned Brinsley House,' Alexa said thoughtfully. 'But – perhaps your mother never told you this – I was only an illegitimate daughter. He was almost eighty when I was born, and he didn't acknowledge me during his lifetime. I did spend a few years in the house after my sister adopted me. But they weren't happy years. I was glad to leave. So no, I'm not sentimental about Brinsley House. If you'd spent more of your own life there, I'd say that it might be a mistake to cut yourself off from your roots. But you left there when you were twelve, didn't you? If you're sure of your feelings, then let it go.'

'Thank you, Grandmother. I like people who advise me to do what I already want to.' Bernard's smile was mischievous as well as affectionate. It was Robert's smile: for a second time Kate felt her breath snatched away by the resemblance.

'And what about you, Kate?' he asked. 'Are you going to look for *your* roots? Do you plan to return home?'

'This is Kate's home now,' Alexa reminded him severely; and at the same time Kate, perplexed, said, 'I have no home.'

'Your birthplace, I meant. I thought you might be interested in a holiday in Jamaica, to see whether it had changed.'

'I hadn't considered – ' The years of childhood in Jamaica were far away, in a different world. Living a lie in Russia for so many years had made it dangerous to remember her origins, and so in the end she had genuinely forgotten them. Bernard's suggestion startled her now, at the same time tempting and alarming. Was it wise to return to the place of one's youth, the scene of childhood

36

happiness? Kate was still pondering the question as they moved towards the dining room for luncheon. Abstracted, she did not join in the conversation but interrupted it when her mind was half made up. 'Would I find relations there?'

'Where, dear?' Alexa had been talking about Bernard's choice of a subject to read at Cambridge when his army service ended.

'In Jamaica. If I went back to Hope Valley, would I find any of my family still there?' Alexa would know what she meant. Two of Kate's brothers were dead, and both her parents. But before he died her father had acknowledged one other son; the intelligent, brown-skinned boy with whom she had played as a child.

'Duke Mattison is still alive, if that's what you mean,' Alexa told her. 'And he has some money for you. Your father insisted that a fund must be set up for the day when you came back. Duke will want to settle with you. It's a good idea of Bernard's. The sea voyage will provide a rest, and if you go soon you'll avoid the worst of the winter. A month or two of sunshine would be the best possible tonic.'

Kate did her best to hide her amusement. Dear Alexa, so generous in her hospitality, was still not quite able to conceal her enthusiasm for a suggestion which would give them both a break from the strain of living together. Kate, whose gratitude was as sincere as Alexa's generosity, felt in no need of rest, and it was unlikely that an English winter could discommode someone who had endured temperatures so low that it was painful to breathe out of doors. Nor was she interested in money.

All the same, Bernard might be right. Perhaps somewhere in the island which had been her home for the first eighteen years of her life she would re-discover her identity and be able to answer that nagging question: 'Who am I?'

3

Kate Lorimer's father had spent the whole of his working life as a Baptist missionary in Jamaica. He was a man of strict religious beliefs, but what chiefly moved him to devote his life to the people of the West Indies was a sense of guilt. The men and women to whom he ministered lived in Jamaica because their ancestors had been carried there as slaves, and his own family was one of those which had made a fortune from the buying and selling of this human cargo.

It was in the 1880s that Ralph Lorimer had come to his pastorate of Hope Valley to preach and to teach. Both these duties he performed meticulously, and still had energy and ability to spare. So from early in his stay, care for the bodies as well as the souls of his congregation became his concern. He found his people largely without employment and unable, from the small areas of land allocated to them by the government, to feed the children who were born with such unwise frequency. Within ten years he had brought them good health and a measure of prosperity by appropriating the adjoining Bristow plantation – abandoned ever since the emancipation of the slaves had made its working uneconomic. He organized his congregation into an agricultural labour force, bullying them to work and using the profits of the enterprise for their common benefit.

So under Ralph Lorimer's direction the men and women of Hope Valley provided the labour needed to clear and plant and maintain the Bristow estate. At first they were paid with a share of the food they grew and with the provision of community benefits – a church, a school, a hospital; later with money. But the land itself became the property of Ralph Lorimer personally; and when he died it was bequeathed to the man he had chosen as his heir. This was Duke Mattison, the child of an unholy liaison between the hot-blooded minister and one of the village girls, and it was Duke who was to be Kate's host during her visit to Jamaica.

He was waiting on the verandah to greet her as she arrived at the plantation house, and the meeting was not an easy one. It was because she had feared that she and her childhood companion might fail to recognize each other – and that the failure would be hurtful to them both – that Kate had asked him not to meet her off the ship at Kingston harbour. But although she had realized that he was bound to have changed as much as she had, she had still not been able to think of him as anything but the young man, clever and athletic, who shared with her brother Brinsley a passion for cricket and used his flair for mathematics to help their father with his business accounts.

At that time the colour of Duke's skin had been markedly lighter than that of the other village boys. Now his curly hair was grizzled and the effect was to make his skin, which had once been so smooth and shining, appear darker as well as rougher. Prosperity and the passing years had thickened his body, and there was a stiffness in his movements as he came down the steps from the verandah. Was this elderly coloured widower her half-brother and the friend of her youth?

They did not even know how to greet each other. Duke was smiling but waiting for his visitor to reveal how she wished to be treated. Uncertain of her own feelings, Kate held out her hand.

'Duke. I'm so glad to see you again.'

'Welcome home, Kate.' If he was as startled by her appearance as she was by his, he gave no sign of it as they shook hands. 'Come inside. Living so long in Russia, you must feel the heat.'

He stepped aside, and Kate led the way in. Bristow Great House had never been quite as grand as its name suggested. In the old slave days the homes of all the plantation owners were called great houses, but because of the danger from hurricanes they were never built more than two storeys high, and because of the heat and dampness their inner rooms were not as many, or as elaborately furnished, as in an English stately home. The wide verandah which went right round the house, offering shade both morning and evening, would always have been the place for most of the family activity. Nevertheless, Kate clearly remembered that when she played there as a girl, this Great House had been almost a ruin. Storms had ripped many of the shingles from the roof, so that the bedrooms on the upper floor were made musty and rotten by the tropical rain. Windows and jalousies had fallen away from their hinges, allowing birds to nest and mess in the downstairs rooms; and exploring goats had fouled the verandahs. The three children – Kate and her brother Brinsley and Duke – had adopted the abandoned building as their secret house, but they had never managed to make more than one room habitable.

Kate paused as she passed the door of that room. It had been a gentleman's study in the eighteenth century and now was Duke's office. Once upon a time Brinsley had made unsteady furniture for it out of broken banana boxes, but this had been replaced by a fine mahogany desk which matched the shining floor and the heavy carved doors and the panelled walls.

The whole house bore witness to a miraculous resurrection. Once ruinous beyond hope, it had been rescued and repaired. Roof and floor were sound, walls were dry, furniture glowed with polish, and sparkling paint had not yet had time to blister in the sun. From the ceiling of the spacious drawing room a fan was suspended; its silent revolutions disturbed the air, giving the impression of coolness merely by movement. Kate could hear the throbbing of a generator in the background; when evening came it would be possible to turn a switch and enjoy electric light. She could not control an exclamation of astonishment. 'What a transformation!'

'It wasn't right that I should live in the pastor's house after Father died,' Duke explained. 'That belonged to the church. Why he never chose to live in the Great House himself, I can well understand. For a white man to take the home of a slave owner – that would make him the boss, not the minister. For me it's different. I'm one of them, the lucky one. I'm proud to live here – and the others, they're proud for me as well.'

'So am I,' said Kate sincerely. 'And glad to see that the old house is a home again. I used to think it sad that it should be so neglected.' She walked through the drawing room and looked out across the rear verandah. The garden had been restored with as much care as the house. The rising terraces which protected the building from stormy winds were grassed and mown. Stone steps and balustrades were in good repair, hedges of poinsettia had been neatly trimmed and the huge specimen trees – flamboyants and ackees, tulip trees and cottonwoods – had been freed from the twining cages of creepers and vines which Kate remembered.

The state of the house and garden made it easier for Kate to reconcile herself to Duke's changed appearance. He was a landowner, a prosperous businessman, someone of standing in his community. But one question had to be asked, and she turned back to face him. 'Duke, do the people here know who your father was? I want to go into the village soon, of course, and see whether anyone still remembers me, but I wouldn't like to say anything tactless.'

Duke shook his head. 'They think he left me the land because I knew how to run it and because all his children were dead. I didn't ever say the truth. It would give a bad name to a good man. When I spoke the word Father to you back then, it was the first time since the day he died.' He paused. 'Soon you're going to meet my girl Paula. She doesn't know that you're her auntie. She can't know, d'you see?'

Kate fought to control her disappointment. Until the day of her arrival she had taken it for granted that Duke would have publicly claimed his position in the Lorimer family, that he would openly welcome her as his half-sister, that his daughter would have been looking forward to meeting an aunt. To fit into these relationships had been part of Kate's purpose in coming to Jamaica, and most of her pleasure in anticipating her arrival. She had needed to remind herself some months earlier that aunthood was not a career – but had not, in spite of the reminder, anticipated that she would be welcomed by this niece as merely a guest.

Duke called for Paula to join them now, and she came at once, carrying a tray of iced drinks to refresh the visitor after the tiring journey up from Kingston. Doing her best not to stare, Kate studied Paula as the girl distributed the glasses, acknowledged the introduction with a smile and handshake and sat down, very much at ease, to join in the conversation. Both physically and in personality she was more mature than an English four-teen-year-old was likely to be, and more attractive than a Russian adolescent. Tall for her age, slim and straight-backed, she held her head proudly and moved with grace. The tight curls of her black hair were closely trimmed so that her head appeared small and neat. Her skin was darker than Duke's at the same age, but a little of her English inheritance revealed itself in her features. Ralph Lorimer's nose had been long and his lips thin, and these characteristics were displayed in Paula's most un-African face. Mixed blood was a recipe for beauty and here by any standards was a strikingly good-looking girl.

Her dark eyes, too, were lit with the same intelligence which had marked her father out from the other village boys from an early age. Kate waited until Paula, after chatting politely for half an hour, excused herself on the grounds of homework to be done; then she commented on this.

'You have a clever daughter, Duke. I remember how bright you were at the same age.'

'When I was fourteen I knew cricket and I knew figures. These children of mine, they have half of me each. Harley used to be the best cricketer in Jamaica, the best Jamaican cricketer ever, maybe, but except on the cricket field he's got no sense, no sense at all. Paula's clever. You're right there. With words, not figures, but clever. She can't play cricket, though. Can't hardly catch a ball.'

Kate laughed sympathetically. 'I hope I shall meet Harley as well while I'm here,' she said. She had learned from Alexa that Duke had a son by his first marriage as well as Paula, the child of his second.

'I don't know about that. Harley, he's drinking himself to death. I don't see him so much nowadays.' He sighed. 'When he was twenty-two, twenty-five, every man and boy in this island worshipped him. Cheers wherever he went. Put a bat in his hand, he ruled the world. Like our father, Kate, when he was a young man. Father told me, in his last days, about those times. At school, at college in England. When he stopped playing cricket, he found something else to do with his life. But Harley – one moment he's a hero, a god. Then the war. He joins the army and he's just another black man. And after the war he comes home and he's thirty-three. He sees boys of eighteen playing in teams where he thinks he ought to be. Too old at thirty-three. It's hard, I see that. But there was a place for him here if he'd have taken it. He could have learned. As it is, who's going to look after Bristow when I'm gone?' He sighed again. 'Tomorrow, Kate, when you've rested, we must talk business. I've something to show you. They told you in England, perhaps, there's money for you here.'

Kate opened her mouth to protest, but decided to wait until the next day. If Duke had gone to a great deal of trouble to preserve an inheritance for someone who might not even have been still alive, it would be ungracious to turn down whatever he had set aside without even giving him the chance to offer it.

'And I'd like to walk round Hope Valley,' she said. 'Would Paula come with me, do you think?'

'No school Saturdays, so she'll take you any time you like. You just ask her.'

Over breakfast next morning Kate asked, and was offered an immediate walk, before the sun should become too hot. The hundreds of acres of the plantation were on a plateau, lying between the mountains and the sea. The

45

Great House stood almost on the boundary of the estate, and only a short walk brought Paula and her aunt to the quite different terrain of the village which had been Ralph Lorimer's pastorate. The unproductive soil of the steep and rocky ground showed that a hundred years earlier Hope Valley had been allocated to the emancipated slaves without too much generosity. A stream rushed down the centre of the village, cutting the land away so that it sloped from the sides to the middle of the area as well as from the hills toward the coastal plains. The paths which linked the village houses had been steep and slippery in Kate's time, and they were much the same still.

Also unchanged was the number of children of all ages. Babies were tied to their mothers' backs or literally to their apron strings, toddlers scrambled around on the ground, girls helped their mothers round the cooking fires while boys carried water or played with balls or chased pigs and chickens. Paula shook her head disapprovingly.

'Too many babies!' she said. 'When I'm grown up, I shan't have babies. All these women, they do nothing all their lives except bring up babies.'

'And what would *you* like to do when you grow up?' Kate asked her.

'I'd like to be queen of England,' replied Paula promptly. 'I know I can't, but you asked what I'd like. I'd like to be able to *do* things, to get rid of all the muddles. And there'll be a queen of England one day soon, won't there?'

'I'm not sure that she'll be allowed to do much except look regal.'

'Well then, I'd like to be a prime minister. In Jamaica, you know, Dr Lorimer, the women have to look after the

46

families – get the money, do all the work. The men make the babies, but then they go away. And yet it's the men who make all the laws and the women just have to do what they're told. I don't think it's right. Is it like that in England as well, Dr Lorimer?'

'Won't you call me Kate? Your father and I are such old friends.' She saw the hesitation on Paula's face. 'Or if you find that awkward, you could say Aunt Kate. Young people in England often do that when a grown-up is a friend of their parents – think of her as a kind of honorary aunt.'

Paula's smile revealed her pleasure. 'That's nice. Aunt Kate.'

Kate was pleased as well, but she came to a halt at the sight of a building which she remembered as clearly as the Great House. 'My father built that church,' she told Paula. He had replaced what was little more than a wooden hut with this substantial stone building, set in the centre of the village on an outcrop of rock too hard to have been worn away by the stream. 'So our own house must have been – ' She turned to find the spot and at once, as though she had spoken a cue, was formally welcomed back to Hope Valley by the present occupant of the pastor's house. The minister now was a Jamaican, with a black skin and a beaming smile. He had been told of Kate's arrival from England and was anxious to be hospitable.

On the verandah of her old home Kate's mind began to whirl and her body to chill. She felt her hands shaking as she accepted food and drink. Her speech became hesitant – as though the language she had only recently salvaged from the back of her mind was slipping away again. Immensely old ladies were introduced, ladies who claimed to remember her and her parents. They had prepared for the meeting by rehearsing to themselves anecdotes of forty years ago or more – but Kate, taken by surprise and unable to recall the trivial events, found herself struggling for words in an attempt to be polite. She was aware of Paula watching her, critical and sympathetic at the same time, not prepared to rescue her until the old ladies had enjoyed a full appreciation of their reminiscences.

That moment came at last. Kate, trembling, could not have spoken for herself, but Paula reminded the minister that his visitor had arrived only yesterday after a long journey; she had chosen to come to Hope Valley as soon as possible but now needed to rest. Kate felt Paula's hand taking hers, leading her away. She allowed herself to be guided until they were out of sight of the pastor's house, but then held her niece back.

'The Baptist Hole,' she said. 'I'd like to go to the Baptist Hole.'

Paula turned without speaking and together they climbed the steep slope to the head of the valley. Beside the path the stream had cut a deep ravine, clothed by Jamaica's luxuriant climate with creepers and trees whose roots seemed able to survive on a bare inch or two of soil, trapped on the narrow ledges of the vertical cliff. The spray from the tumbling stream was caught on the foliage and converted to steam by the probing sun, making the atmosphere even more humid than on the plain. By now, too, it was very hot. Kate found it hard to breathe and was forced to sit and rest for a few moments after they reached their destination.

This was the point at which the stream fell from the mountains in a sparkling waterfall. Over the centuries it had worn a deep hole in the rock, which accepted the water from the fall and allowed it to pour downwards on

48

the far side through a narrow and more controlled channel. When the slaves were first brought to this part of Jamaica they gathered in this place whenever they could to indulge in the dancing and singing which they had learned in Africa. Ralph Lorimer did his best to subdue the pagan associations of the pool by using it as his baptismal font and its rim as the pulpit from which he delivered some of his most fervent sermons. But the atmosphere was too strong for him; in this place Christianity had never been more than a veneer on the depth of a rich and very old heathen culture. As a little girl, lying awake, Kate had heard in the night the distinctive music which had descended directly from the slaves – sometimes frenzied and joyful, sometimes heartbreakingly sad. It permeated her childhood and later, after her own child was born, she had hummed the syncopated melodies to Ilsa as she rocked her cradle.

Today, though, there was no sound but the splashing of the clear water over the rocks and into the pool. Paula waited, understanding that her guest was upset but not knowing why. It seemed important to Kate that she should explain, although not sure of the reason herself.

'When I was your age, I lived here in Hope Valley,' she said abruptly. 'I wanted to get things done, just as you do. I wanted to be a doctor. Not as impossible as being queen of England, but not easy, either. I left here when I was eighteen to study in England. I said goodbye to my parents and never saw either of them again.' She paused, overcome by sadness at the memory of that farewell. 'They seemed very old as they waved goodbye.' They had been about fifty, Kate reminded herself – younger than she was now, but old. 'Shabby and tired and somehow disillusioned, unhappy. Perhaps I was only imagining that. Perhaps at heart they were satisfied with

49

what they'd done and the unhappiness was only in losing me. It upset me, because once upon a time they must have been eighteen like me then, ambitious young students, knowing what they wanted to do to make the world a better place. I saw them as two people who had been defeated, and I promised myself that it would never happen to me.' She could not go on. In the past few years she had suffered too much to have any tears left, but she was unable to speak.

'And did it?' asked Paula.

Kate nodded. At eighteen, a medical student as her mother had been and an earnest Christian like her father, she had vowed to devote her life to the relief of suffering, and perhaps that was one vow she had managed to keep, at least until recently. As a young doctor, she had hoped to do far more than that – to change society, to abolish poverty. The ideals of the Russian revolution had matched her own and for several years the excitement of building a new world had been enough to sustain her. But just as her faith in God had been killed by the horrors of war, so her hopes of a utopian society faded. Love for individuals sustained her for a little, but one by one she was robbed of those she most cared for. One hope alone remained – that through her descendants she could look for some kind of continuity. The disappearance of her daughter had broken her last link with happiness.

'Yes,' she said. 'It happened to me.' She forced herself to smile as though it were not important. 'So now you look at me just as I looked at my parents. You're young and clever and ambitious and you see this old woman and vow that this will never happen to you. And you must go on thinking that, and I ought not to say anything to make you doubt it.'

'Are you feeling sad for me or for yourself, Aunt Kate?'

'I don't know,' Kate said honestly. 'I'm confused. Going back to that house, remembering myself at your age – ' She began to tremble again.

'I shall go to England,' Paula told her. 'When I'm eighteen, just like you. I want to go to Oxford. If I stay here all my life, no one will ever have respect for me. But if I go to England for my education, I shall come back different, more important.'

Kate might have argued, questioning the girl's assumptions. But instead she found that by giving thought to Paula's plans she could control the unsteadiness of her own emotions. Her niece was still much in her mind later that day when Duke explained how he had interpreted the wishes expressed in Ralph Lorimer's will.

'Every year I set money aside for you from the plantation, like Father asked. Your cousin Arthur, Sir Arthur Lorimer, Bart., he was trustee while he was alive. But after twenty-one years with no news of you, the money came back into the estate. I used it to build one special thing. We grow sugar again here now, as well as bananas. Two crops, it makes the risk smaller. I built a sugar mill. It's called Kate's Mill, so everyone knows. It's yours, you see. Now you're alive again, I can buy it off you, if that's what you'd like. Or you can keep it, and then the plantation must pay you the milling fees. So you should choose, to have the big piece of money or the income every year.'

'I don't deserve either,' said Kate. 'I've done nothing – I don't believe that people should be rich just because their fathers were.'

'Rich? This won't make you rich. It's been a bad time in all the islands. But Father wanted you to have something. He was very serious about this. So that you'd be independent, he said. I want you to have it, too. It's here, waiting. It's yours.'

During all the time of travelling to Jamaica, Kate had been resolved to refuse anything that Duke might offer. But now that it came to the point, she hesitated. Her half-brother was making it clear that he did not think of the money he was giving away as his own, and the mention of her father affected her. Kate could understand how sincerely he would have hoped that one day she would re-appear to take up her inheritance, because she could think of nothing she herself more desired than that Ilsa's disappearance might end in the same way. She reminded herself of her vow never again to hope for something which was impossible. Whether her daughter was alive or whether she was dead they would never see each other again. If Kate were not to drive herself mad, she must stifle the smallest temptation to say 'If . . .' So she told herself now that Ilsa was not likely ever to take advantage of her grandfather's hard work – but there was another granddaughter who could benefit.

'Paula,' said Kate abruptly. 'Paula was telling me this morning that she wanted to go to England one day, to a university there.'

'Not just any university.' Duke was smiling. 'The University of Oxford. All her teachers tell her, even for an English girl, that's hard. For a coloured girl, so far away – ' He shrugged his shoulders. 'But Paula, she wants to set the world to rights one day, and she's made up her mind, Oxford is the key to her kingdom.'

'Would you let her go?'

'If she can win a scholarship, she can go and no problem. If she only wins a place, we have to think harder. It would be expensive. But if it can be managed, yes, I'd let her go. I'd be proud. Father was at the University of Oxford.'

'I want to help her,' said Kate. 'While I was on my way here I planned to tell you that I didn't intend to take any of my father's money. But now, I'd like to accept your offer of the milling dues, so that when Paula is ready she can come to England. I'll make a home for her and pay her fees. It would give me a lot of pleasure. Will you let me do that, Duke?'

'A young girl, she'd need a home in England,' Duke agreed. 'I've thought about that, worried about it. It would be peace of mind for me to know you were there. Not for the money. Just so there'd be someone to care. There's time yet, of course. Three, four years.'

Not for many months had Kate felt so happy. She had something to look forward to, a new relationship to explore, the prospect of a life in which she would have her own interests and not exist merely as a dependant of Alexa. Ilsa might be dead, and her place could never be completely filled; but Paula, who had no mother, had as much need of family support as Kate herself. They could help each other.

And Kate saw that she could make good use of whatever income the mill provided even before Paula's arrival. There would be no need to wait until then before finding a home of her own and preparing for it to be shared. Duke was offering her independence, just as their father had hoped. Since her return to England she had behaved as though her life was over, yet she was not really an old woman. She could move away from Blaize and find some kind of employment, something which might be useful to the sick but would not demand too close an acquaintance with newly-discovered drugs or treatments. In any medical service there was always some speciality which was less popular than the rest.

Duke smiled as though he recognized the change which had taken place in her attitude. As for Kate herself, she felt as though she had stepped into a new world, breathing a new atmosphere. She had travelled to Jamaica thinking that she would be making a journey into the past. But the past was dead and she had been offered a future instead. In friendship and gratitude she smiled back at Duke.

4

The mood of hope and energy in which Kate returned from Jamaica carried her with surprising ease into a new life. Before leaving England she had been so sure of her unsuitability for employment that she had made no attempt to look for work, but on her return was offered the first hospital post for which she applied.

It did not take long to discover why no one else had wanted the job. Alexa, visiting her there just once in three years, made no secret of her horror at the conditions under which a hundred and eighty geriatric patients and their resident doctor were expected to exist. But Kate herself, aware of the difficulties of finding accommodation, was grateful to have a living-in post. Feeling herself to be useful, she hardly noticed the passing of months and then years – and was surprised to be told on her sixtieth birthday in 1951 that she had now to retire.

Alexa again came to the rescue, inviting her to spend the summer at Blaize while she searched for a flat of her own. Kate smiled to herself as she accepted. Had she continued to stay at Blaize after her arrival in England, no doubt her aunt would long ago have become heartily sick of her. But she was no longer the drab, resigned refugee to whom Alexa had originally offered shelter, and there seemed no reason why they should not enjoy a few months in each other's company.

On only her second morning at Blaize a letter arrived from Jamaica. Paula was coming to England in September! She had won not merely a place at Oxford, not merely a scholarship, but two – one from the college whose entrance examination she had taken, and the other a special award for a Commonwealth candidate of outstanding ability.

'What's a scholarship?' asked Asha when Kate read out the news over breakfast.

'Well, you know what an examination is.'

'Of course I do.' Asha was scornful of anyone who could doubt it. 'We have them at school. I came top in English.'

'The examination which Paula took is more like a competition. Being allowed to go to a college for three years is the prize. There are far more girls trying to win places than places to be won, so most of the girls – even if they're quite clever really – are told, "Sorry, there's no room." The rest are allowed to come, and just a very few of them, who get the most marks, are given some money to help pay the college fees. That's the scholarship. I don't think it's a great deal of money. It's really more of an honour.'

'So is Paula very clever?'

'Yes. And she must have had good teachers as well.'

'Would it do if I won a scholarship, Aunt Alexa?' asked Asha seriously.

'Do for what, dear?'

'For being good at something. You're always telling me I ought to be best at something, and I'm no good at anything but exams.'

'You've plenty of time to find your talent,' Alexa assured her. 'And you need something which will last you all your life. But yes, a scholarship to Oxford would do as well as anything, for a start.'

The two adults laughed together. Later, when Asha

56

had slipped away from the breakfast table, Kate commented on the conversation.

'You haven't changed, I notice.'

'In what way?'

'When Frisca was a little girl, Asha's age, I remember you were always saying to her, "Nothing but the best will do." I gather Asha's being brought up on the same principle.'

'It's the only way to be happy,' Alexa said firmly. 'To know what you're good at and to do it. Do it well. The hardest part is finding Asha's talent. It was never a problem for me or for Frisca – I can't remember a time when I didn't sing, and Frisca danced from the moment she left the cradle. Asha doesn't have that particular kind of vocation. But there'll be something, I'm sure. It's just that she hasn't yet been exposed to whatever it is that will strike the spark one day. But speaking of Paula has reminded me, Kate, there's something I ought to have shown you long ago. I'd completely forgotten about it.'

She left the room and returned to hand across the table a crumpled envelope which had already been opened. The note inside was in the handwriting of Margaret Scott, Kate's aunt, who had died more than ten years before. Puzzled, Kate read it aloud.

'In 1878 a nursery governess, Claudine, who had been employed for a time by my brother William, gave birth to a son in France. He was christened Jean-Claude and brought up on a farm called La Chalonnière half way between Sarlat and Les Eyzies in the Dordogne. Claudine's husband agreed to bring him up as his own son, so he goes under the name of Grasset. But his father was my younger brother, Ralph. Jean-Claude is a Lorimer. Someone ought to know.'

'Margaret fastened it to her will and then put it away,'

57

explained Alexa. 'It was only found on the day of her funeral. There were some pointed comments from the younger generation about the habits of Victorian missionaries, I can tell you. We'd known about Duke in Jamaica, of course, but not about this earlier escapade. Your father seems to have sown quite a few wild oats in his time.'

'I'd like to meet him,' said Kate. 'The boy, I mean. Jean-Claude.'

'Hardly a boy if he was born in 1878. That means he must be – what? – seventy-three by now. And it sounds as though he's never known who his father was.'

'I wouldn't say anything. But – ' Kate found it hard to explain her need to know that her branch of the family was still alive and would continue to exist after she was dead. Her father, she was convinced, had shared the feeling – Duke's description of his rage and anguish when Brinsley was killed on the Somme reinforced her belief. It added to the sadness of her memories that Ralph Lorimer, who had fathered so many children, should have so few descendants. The existence of a whole new family in France would cheer her up.

'Paula won't start at Oxford until October,' she said, thinking aloud. 'I've plenty of time yet to find a flat, somewhere she can join me for the vacations. I can take a short holiday in France. It'll be easy to invent an excuse for visiting the farm.'

There was nothing to stop her. The travel allowance permitted by the government was meagre, but Kate had learned how to travel with an even emptier purse. She left in July with Margaret's note, a French dictionary and a map of France. With their help there proved to be no trouble in finding the farm for it was still owned by the Grasset family. Clumsily Kate explored relationships in stumbling French. Many years ago she had spoken the language well, but her vocabulary had faded from lack of practice and she was hard put to it now to ask questions which would not seem unpardonably abrupt. She was interested only in the descendants of Jean-Claude, not of any later children of Claudine's. Her father, she told the surprised and suspicious peasant family, had been a benefactor, a kind of godfather to the one-time governess's eldest son. The story was accepted, because it was remembered that the farm had originally been purchased with money given as a dowry by a rich gentleman in England. Now it was Kate's turn to be surprised – by this confirmation of a story she thought she had invented. Presumably her grandfather had acted generously to avoid any scandal in England.

Jean-Claude, she learned, was dead – he had been killed, in fact, in the same battle as his half-brother, Brinsley, more than thirty years ago. But before he died he had married and fathered a daughter.

'And has she had children of her own?' asked Kate.

'Five children. Two boys and three girls.'

Kate smiled with satisfaction. 'What is her married name? Where can I find her?'

'She married Pierre Bedouelle, from Limoges. They went to live in Oradour-sur-Glane.'

'May I have her address?'

There was a curious silence. At the beginning of the interview both the Grassets had been surly, not prepared to answer questions until they knew the reason for them. But since hearing her explanation they had spoken more freely and in a friendly manner. Kate did not understand why a shutter should suddenly come down on their smiles.

'You know of Oradour?' asked the farmer.

'I have a map. I can find it. But I need to know where her house is.'

'Excuse me.' Mme Grasset left the room without explanation. Her husband also rose, bringing the conversation to an end.

'When you reach the village, you will discover. Anyone will tell you.'

Kate was forced to accept her dismissal. Not until two days later did she discover the reason for it.

The bus from Limoges set her down at the edge of what seemed to be a building site. There was a cluster of prefabricated huts, apparently being used as temporary accommodation while more permanent homes were under construction nearby. She called to a small boy who had just run out of one of the huts and asked whether he knew where Madame Pierre Bedouelle lived.

He shook his head. 'Not here.'

'But this is Oradour?'

'This is New Oradour. Wait.' He ran up to a schoolmistress who, surrounded by other children, was emerging from the same hut. To Kate's relief, she spoke good English.

'May I help you?' She listened gravely. 'Yes, I know of Marie Bedouelle. She was the dressmaker for the village.'

'She was? Do you mean that she's dead? Then why didn't her cousin tell me? Is there some mystery?'

'No mystery, alas. Has no one told you, Madame, what happened at Oradour?'

Kate shook her head. She was angry at what seemed to be a waste of her time, but the general reluctance to give a direct answer to her questions made her uneasy as well. The teacher was offering to show her the way to something and Kate followed, perplexed.

The path led them through two fields and over a stone

bridge beneath which the River Glane flowed. It seemed a peaceful enough country scene. A few steps more brought them into the main street of a large village. 'This is Oradour,' said the schoolmistress.

Kate looked in bewilderment from one side of the street to the other. The walls of the houses were of thick grey stone, but they were blackened by fire and the rooms they enclosed were bare and roofless.

'Was it bombed?' she asked. In her wanderings across Europe immediately after the war she had seen the effects of fire storms in Dresden and Berlin. For one horrified moment she even wondered whether perhaps the British, rather than the Germans, had bombed the area after the occupation of France.

'No,' said the schoolmistress. 'It was not bombed. There was nothing here that needed to be destroyed. A village in the countryside, that was all.'

They walked up the street beside the metal tracks of a disused tramway. The silence of the dead village was intense – but in a curious way not a silence at all. Never before had Kate found herself in a place with such an oppressive atmosphere. It was as though the stones of the abandoned shops and houses were trying to speak, and their message was audible to Kate's heart although not to her ears. She found herself breathing faster, needing to control a horror for which she still had no explanation. They turned aside from the central thoroughfare and came to a standstill. 'This is the church.'

Like every other building the church was a ruin. The signs of fire were stronger here: it had destroyed not only the roof but part of the walls, leaving only jagged fingers pointing to the sky. Where the altar should have stood, two sticks of charred wood had been bound together to form a cross. Lists of names, the writing protected by glass, were propped on either side of the cross. Kate stepped forward to see them, but her companion held her back. 'Now I will tell you what happened in Oradour,' she said.

Even after this promise, the same emotion which had sent Mme Grasset hurrying from the room kept the teacher silent for a moment longer. 'The village was visited by the German SS in June, 1944,' she said at last. 'They called all the inhabitants to assemble on the Champ de Foire.' She pointed across the main street towards an open space. 'At first, I believe, there was no alarm. There had been such assemblies before, to check on identity papers and search for deserters. The children were led out from school by their teachers, the men came from their work, the women from their homes – even the babies had to be carried out. The women and children were brought to the church, here. The doors were closed.

'The men were taken to other buildings in the village – barns and garages. Then they were shot. Not all of them died in the shooting. The buildings were set on fire while some were still alive. The women heard the shots, the cries. They began to scream. But not for long.'

The schoolmistress paused. Kate understood now what she was about to hear.

'The church also was set on fire. First there was an explosion, with smoke which suffocated many of the children. Then machine-gunfire against those who rushed to the doors. And finally the fire. They were all burned, all but one woman who escaped. That is how we know.'

'The children!' whispered Kate. '*All* the children?'

'There was one boy who ran away when the assembly was called. He was already a refugee, from Lorraine, and he had learned to be frightened of Germans. He was the only child to live.'

'Marie Bedouelle had five children.'

'They died with her here. Two hundred and forty-six children were killed. Six hundred and forty-two villagers altogether.'

The bones of Kate's body seemed to turn to water. She staggered and would have collapsed if her guide had not caught her and helped her to sit on one of the fallen stones.

'This is why your friends did not want to tell you the story of Oradour. It is too terrible to say, as well as to hear.'

For a long time Kate could not speak. 'Where are they buried?' she asked at last.

'There are no true graves. The women and children were burned together, in a heap, scrambling on top of one another to escape. Later the Germans threw many of the bodies down a well. It was not possible to separate them. A new cemetery is to be built soon. For now, the bones have been buried in consecrated ground, all together.'

'May I see?'

There were photographs, in the French fashion, around the area where the burial had taken place. But not, as normally, of old men and women or soldiers in uniforms. These were family groups, which might include both a baby and its grandmother. Kate found the photograph of Marie and Pierre Bedouelle and their five children, one of them only a few months old. The eldest, a boy of ten, had a lively, intelligent face. Kate searched his features for some resemblance to her father. But what difference did it make if she found one or not? The boy was dead. This unacknowledged branch of the Lorimer line had been most decisively cut off.

'Their house?' By now Kate could hardly speak.

It was a little way away, on the edge of the village. The family had been prosperous, it seemed, owning an orchard and large garden round the house and a car in the garage. The car was still there, sunk on the rusting metal rims of its wheels. In the garden, equally rusty, a pram stood untouched since the day when Marie Bedouelle had picked up her baby to carry him to the assembly. Inside the house Kate could see how the rooms had been used. There was the sewing machine to show where Marie had carried on her trade as a dressmaker. The stove was still in the kitchen, the iron frames of bedsteads had fallen from the upper rooms as the floors burned, a bicycle hung on a wall with spokes tangled like knitting wool.

'But why?' asked Kate.

'Nobody knows. There is another village called Oradour – Oradour-sur-Vayres. It was a centre of the Resistance, the maquis. Perhaps there was a decision to punish the Resistance, to make an example. And then a simple mistake. Who can say?'

'Thank you for telling me,' Kate said. 'I'd like to stay here for a little while by myself now.'

'You should not remain too long,' the schoolmistress warned her. For the first time she needed to search for a word. 'The ambience, the atmosphere, is not good. No one comes here now except to weep. When you are ready, return to where we met before and I will give you coffee.'

'You're very kind.' But already Kate had withdrawn into her own thoughts and was hardly aware of the moment when she was left alone. She needed no warning about the atmosphere. From the moment when she reached the church it had chilled her, driving the blood from her head and at the same time sending her thoughts into a whirl as though by their confusion she could reject what she had been told and so in some fashion make it no longer true.

The abandoned pram in the garden made such a fantasy impossible. A live baby had lain here on a summer morning; a warm, soft baby, kicking and gurgling; a great-grandson of Kate's father. Marie Bedouelle must have believed, as she bent to pick him up, that he would be safe in her arms. Instead, she had carried him to his death. Well, at least she had not lived to suffer the grief of her bereavement. It was better to be dead than to suffer such a loss, the loss of a child.

Ten years had passed since Kate saw Ilsa snatched away from her. The building of Auschwitz and the destruction of Oradour were all part of the same horror. War might provide the occasion for such atrocities but could not excuse them. Marie Bedouelle, burned to death, was fortunate. She had suffered pain but had been spared the long-drawn-out anguish which Kate had endured. Parents should never outlive their children. Kate touched the pram with her finger and began to cry, because she had lived too long.

For more than two hours she wandered through the ruined village, sobbing noisily and without restraint, shouting aloud to the ghosts of the murdered villagers, who seemed to press upon her from every side. She wept because everything in her life was dead – her God, her ideals, her loved ones. She had known all that before, but realized now in addition that even a family could die. Marie Bedouelle would have no grandchildren, nor would Kate herself. The only thing which did not seem able to die was Kate's useless, worn-out body. Her pain at the death of Oradour was transformed into rage against her own continued life. By the time the schoolmistress

65

returned anxiously to look for her, Kate was too distracted to remember why she had come to this place or even who she was. She could not live with her thoughts and so she had closed her mind to them. Like a drowning woman she felt herself pulled down into silence and blackness.

Time did not stand still. In the outside world, minutes and days and weeks continued to pass, but Kate was not aware of their passing. She had withdrawn for a little while from the pain of living.

Even after she had in a sense recovered from her breakdown Kate remained in bed, refusing to talk or to read or to show interest in anything she was told. She had no recollection of the hospital at Limoges or of Alexa anxiously bringing her back to Blaize. Occasionally she ate some of the food which was brought into her room: more often she allowed the tray to be removed untouched.

At some point during her illness Alexa's son, Pirry, arrived to spend a month with his mother. Kate was once or twice conscious of him standing beside her bed, a good-looking man in his late thirties, elegantly dressed in a white suit. During those first visits he was sympathetic, but the moment came when he must have decided that brutality would be the greater kindness. He came to her room one morning and spoke far more firmly than usual.

'Paula is due to arrive this afternoon, Cousin Kate. You must get up and prepare to welcome her. The doctor tells me that fresh air and exercise now will do you far more good than staying in bed.'

Kate turned away, but Pirry would not allow her to evade the conversation; he came round to the other side of the bed.

'You're behaving very selfishly towards Mother. Do

66

you realize that? She's done her best to help you. She's allowed you to regard Blaize as your home whenever you need one. She doesn't begrudge you that – and nor do I.' He was reminding her, Kate supposed, that he was Lord Glanville and the real owner of Blaize. 'It's not much of a reward for her hospitality if you cut yourself off from everything like this. She worries about you, naturally. I don't see why she should be made upset just because you won't make the effort to behave normally. Don't you think it's time you showed her a little more consideration?'

'You're a fine one to talk about selfishness.' It was the first time Kate had spoken for more than a week and her voice, low and rasping, startled her by its unfamiliarity. 'You leave her to manage all the property which should be your business. You refuse to give her grandchildren, although you know how much that upsets her.'

'My mother has never been one to coo over babies.'

'It's nothing to do with babies,' said Kate. 'It's knowing that you won't be completely alone in the world as you grow older. It's being able to feel that you're part of something, a family, that will live on after yourself. You don't understand, do you, how it feels to long for that kind of security and not to have it?' She sat up, her strength surprisingly restored by the need to communicate her anxiety. 'A family can die, Pirry! Don't you realize that? Even a family like yours, that's been in the history books for a thousand years. The Glanville family will die if nobody cares to keep it alive. As for the Lorimer family, it's almost dead already.'

'What about Asha?' asked Pirry. 'Or Paula, if it comes to that. I know that you've had a lot of bad luck in your life, Cousin Kate. I know that you would have liked to have grandchildren yourself, and I'm sincerely sorry that

67

you have this unhappiness. But you mustn't project the same feeling on to my mother. She has one grandson, after all. Bernard may not be a Glanville, but he's certainly a Lorimer.'

'It's not enough. You know that she needs *you* to have a son – she needs to know that Blaize is safe.' Soon after her first arrival in England, Kate had learned from Alexa the details of the entail which tied Blaize to the Glanville title. If Pirry should die without an heir, it would all pass at once to a cousin. And if Alexa were still alive she would have to leave her home, for there was no love lost between the two branches of the family.

'That's not really any concern of yours, is it?' Pirry's voice was still pleasant, but the firmness in his eyes made it clear that he was not prepared to discuss the matter further. In any case, Kate could hardly have expected to argue him into changing his way of life. Another of the family secrets she had learned in the four years since her return to England was Pirry's reason for not residing at Blaize. She had thought at first that ill-health kept him in a warmer climate and had only later and gradually learned the nature of his relationship with the man he described as his secretary. Should they attempt to live in such a manner in England, Alexa had confessed one evening when she was tearful with whisky, the two men would find themselves liable to long terms of imprisonment.

'No,' Kate agreed. 'It's not my concern.' She allowed herself to sag back into bed. 'And perhaps you're right. What's the use of having children when people kill them? The world is full of murderers. Five little children, burned to death. All five at once. A mother should be able to protect her children. Five little children, screaming, and no way to help them. My daughter called out, and I couldn't help her. They took her away. I had to watch.

68

You're right to be selfish. It's better for the children that they're never born. Never to be born is best.'

She turned away from Pirry again; his sigh of exasperation was audible but did not dispel the lassitude induced by her despair. Nor did Paula's arrival in the bedroom later that day rouse her to anything more than a mumbling apology.

'I promised to have a home for you. I'm sorry. I've let you down. You'll have enough money. But I can't – I'm sorry, Paula. I'm not well.'

'I see that.' Paula's voice was soft and sympathetic. Kate turned her head. Her dark-skinned niece, eighteen years old now, was even prettier than at their last meeting, tall and slim, straight-backed and graceful. Kate could feel proud of such a niece. But she remembered in time that for the sake of a dead man's reputation she was not allowed to claim the relationship. If Duke had permitted her that pleasure, she would have made more effort now to keep her past promises. Instead, she continued to mumble what was intended as an explanation of her illness.

'It was like Pompeii,' she said. She had spent a fortnight's holiday in Italy the previous year. 'Oradour was like Pompeii. Silent streets and deserted shops and abandoned objects lying where they were left. But then, not really like Pompeii. Accidental death is horrifying, but there's no malevolence in it. Different from murder. At Pompeii I saw fear lying in the ash. But at Oradour I could hear the screams trapped in the stones.'

She raised her head and found that she was alone. Just outside the door Pirry, who must have led Paula away, could be heard apologizing on her behalf.

'You see how it is. It seems to have unhinged her

mind. I'm sure she'll be better soon. But for the time being – it's hard for you, when you were relying on her.'

'I don't need her.' Paula's voice was clear and self-possessed. 'In Jamaica she was kind and interested – and it made my father's mind easy to know she was here. But he doesn't need to learn any different, so he'll go on feeling easy. There's a room waiting for me in college. She's not obligated to help me, after all. I'm nothing to her. Just the daughter of someone she knew forty years ago.'

'I'm your aunt!' called Kate. Why should she care what anyone now thought about her father, who had been dead for so long? But already Pirry and Paula had moved out of hearing. Unsteadily, because it was so long since she had had a proper meal, Kate left the bed and began to search for clothes. Someone had put her wig away in a cupboard; it took her a little while to find it. By the time she had dressed and packed and made her way downstairs, Paula had left.

'Pirry's driving her to Oxford.' Alexa made no attempt to conceal her disapproval of Kate's behaviour. 'Why are you carrying your suitcase, Kate?'

'I'm leaving. You've been very kind to me and I've taken advantage of you. I'm grateful for all you've done, very grateful indeed. But I mustn't impose any more. It's best for someone who's lonely to be alone. I'll keep in touch with you, of course. And with Paula as well – I know I've behaved badly. But you won't have to put up with me here any longer. May I phone for a taxi to take me to the station?'

'Certainly not,' said Alexa. 'You can't possibly leave. Where would you go? You need company until you're feeling better again. Put that down and take off your coat and have a drink.' She poured her niece a whisky almost as large as her own.

Kate had no choice. She accepted both the drink and the instructions because she did not feel strong enough to cover the distance to the railway station on foot. But very early next morning she came quietly downstairs to call a car for herself, and by the time the rest of the household assembled for breakfast she had gone.

5

Kate Lorimer knew well enough what Dr Morley's patients thought of her. They sat in rows in the surgery waiting room with nothing to do except stare at the receptionist until their turn should come. There was plenty of time for them to study the frown-lines of her face, her dowdy clothes and the auburn wig which was not only too bright a colour for a sixty-six-year-old woman but refused to stay in its proper position.

Her own hair had started to grow again: that was the trouble. More than ten years had passed since the end of her long period of semi-starvation during and after the war. It was more than ten years, too, since she had accepted the fact that her daughter was lost to her, that she would never see Ilsa again. Probably it was the shock and grief of that certainty which had caused her hair to fall out – but now, in 1957, for no reason that she could understand, a white fuzz had made its appearance all over her scalp. In a few months' time perhaps she would be able to do without the wig. Meanwhile, reluctant to discard it but no longer able to fit it snugly on to a bald head, she found herself tugging at it like an ill-fitting hat under the contemptuous gaze of the neat young women with their sniffing children on their laps.

The patients were frightened of her as well as contemptuous, especially when they wanted Dr Morley to make a home visit. Kate knew that her manner on the telephone was too brusque. She found it hard to conceal her impatience with the triviality of most of the illnesses

72

which the doctor was called to attend. In Serbia and Russia during two world wars she had seen so many people die, and in such pain, that she had little sympathy with anyone who could not endure a small discomfort until morning. Sometimes the patients complained to Dr Morley, telling him that it was none of Miss Lorimer's business to decide whether or not their need was urgent; and sometimes, uneasily, he mentioned the complaints to his receptionist, making it clear that he would have to take the responsibility for any misjudgement on her part – but at the same time assuring her that she had never yet made a mistake.

Kate knew that he would not press the criticism too far: she was too useful to him for that. As soon as he discovered that she had few friends and rarely went out, being content to sit all evening in front of her television set, he had offered her a flat in the basement of his own house, rent free in exchange for her almost permanent availability to answer the telephone. She was expected to take down details of what were claimed to be emergencies and to pass them on to him.

Occasionally Kate wondered whether she ought to reassure him by revealing that – on paper, at least – her medical qualifications were as good as his own; but on the whole she suspected that he would be embarrassed by the discovery. In any case, it was because she no longer considered herself competent to practise as a doctor that she had applied for this humbler work after her breakdown at Oradour.

On Saturdays Dr Morley held a surgery in the morning only, so for once Kate had asked for time off from her telephone duties for an August afternoon in 1957. It was Paula's wedding day.

The wedding was to be at Oxford, where bride and

73

groom had first met during their undergraduate days. 'In Laker's college chapel,' Paula had said laughingly, pressing Kate to come – and Kate, still in many ways a foreigner in England, did not realize until she arrived that the chapel of this particular college was actually a cathedral. This was a smart occasion: the men were elegant in grey top hats and cutaway coats, the women not so much elegant as showy in an excess of frills and flowers. Kate wore a hat, but it was the wrong kind of hat. She sat alone in a back pew, knowing her appearance to be eccentric and not wishing to let Paula down by linking herself too closely to the bride.

Paula had made good use of her university years. She was the only coloured girl amongst the undergraduates of her generation and this fact attracted not prejudice but a kind of stardom. Almost without effort she became the girl who knew everyone and everything worth knowing at Oxford, and used her information to begin a career as a journalist even before she graduated. This was perhaps the reason why she failed to achieve the First which was expected of her; but it certainly helped her to move straight into Fleet Street without the usual provincial apprenticeship. And now she was marrying James Laker-Smith, who came from a good family and had been to a good school and had just been adopted as a Parliamentary candidate for a safe seat. That was not quite the plan which as a girl of fourteen she had outlined to Kate. But since the moment of her arrival in England no more had been heard of her intention to return to Jamaica.

The reception after the service was in one of the college quadrangles. A marquee had been erected to shelter the buffet tables, but the afternoon was hot and Kate, like the other guests, took her plate and glass on to the lawn. A social occasion of this kind gave her little pleasure and

74

she would have liked to slip away. But Paula had proved to be remarkably understanding about the chaotic lack of welcome with which she had first been greeted in England. She had made a point of keeping in touch with her father's old friend, although still not knowing that Kate was her aunt. Nor had she ever been allowed to learn that Kate existed solely on her tiny receptionist's salary because all her income from the Bristow plantation went directly to provide Paula with an allowance.

Alexa and Asha had been invited to the wedding as well. Alexa, appalled by the pokiness of Kate's basement flat and worried by the manner of Paula's arrival in England, had been generous with vacation invitations to Blaize, and Paula, no doubt, was anxious that the bride's side of the church should make some attempt to balance the rows of her bridegroom's well-bred relations. Making her way across the quad, Kate was shocked to see – what she had not noticed in the cathedral – that Alexa had taken to a wheelchair.

'Don't let this worry you!' Even in old age Alexa's eyes still sparkled with mischief. 'Policemen these days won't let you leave a car anywhere convenient unless you're absolutely decrepit. You'd think it was enough to be eighty, but no, you have to be lame as well. So I am, when it suits me. Ah, Paula my dear, how beautiful you look! And what a lovely wedding! I'm glad to find there's a little style left somewhere in England.'

Paula did indeed look beautiful, in a high-necked cream dress whose cut emphasized her slenderness. Her eyes were shining with happiness as she thanked them for their presents.

'Are we allowed to ask where you're going for your honeymoon?' enquired Kate.

'To Bristow. I've had news that my father is ill. He's

had a stroke. In Jamaica, to be seventy-one is to be an old man. I want to see him again before he dies, and my brother writes that that may not be too long. I'm sorry, Aunt Kate. I ought not to upset you with bad news on a happy day. I know he was a friend of yours from a long time ago.'

'He's my brother,' said Kate. Why should she keep somebody else's secrets any longer? Except for Duke himself, there was no one still living who cared about her father's reputation. 'My half-brother, at least. My father was his father as well.'

'Pastor Lorimer my grandfather?' Paula's eyes and laughing mouth revealed her pleasure and amusement.

'Don't let your father know I told you,' Kate begged her. 'He's never wanted anyone in Hope Valley to find out, in case it hurt a good man's name. But for a long time I've wanted you to know.'

'Thank you, Aunt Kate!' exclaimed Paula. 'I'm glad you're a real Aunt Kate, not just a courtesy one. I've always hated not knowing about my family. It's not an unusual thing in Jamaica, not to know the name of your grandfather, but all the same . . . And so Asha is my cousin! What a joke! Do you mind, Asha? Will you accept me?'

It was indeed hard to believe that the two young women were related as they stood side by side, laughing, with their arms round each other's waists. By Jamaican standards Paula was far from black, but her skin was a dark shade of brown, while Asha was as white as could be. Kate had never known any other girl whose complexion was so translucently fair, and the ash-blonde hair which had inspired her christening seemed also to be almost without colour.

'Of course.' Asha blushed and smiled her pleasure in

the newly-discovered relationship. Like her unexpected cousin, she was clever and admired Paula for winning an Oxford scholarship. It was her ambition, Kate knew, to do as well herself one day.

Still laughing, Paula came across to grip Kate's hands. 'I won't tell my father what you've said,' she promised. 'Nor Harley, because he's always drunk and can't keep secrets. But it's a second wedding present you've given me today, Aunt Kate. The present of a family. Thank you very much. When we get back, you must come and visit us in London. We shall have so much to talk about, now I'm a Lorimer too.'

Her unaffected pleasure was infectious. Preparing to leave, Kate felt a contentment such as she had not known for years. She had little in common with the other members of the family and would never again try to make her home with any of them. But they were all Lorimers, and she retained her place in their tangle of relationships. If only – but she banished the memory of Ilsa from her mind. This was a day on which she must think only of Paula, and be happy.

Kate had promised Dr Morley that she would be home by half past seven, and punctually at that time she reported her arrival and switched the telephone through to the basement flat. She took off her hat, put the kettle on to boil, and turned on the television set. It was an old set with a small screen and, because it offered no choice of channels, Kate never bothered to discover the programme in advance. She left the set on all evening. If there was anything of interest, she watched it: if not, she still watched it, but knitted at the same time.

Tonight she had arrived home, it appeared, in time for the beginning of an orchestral concert – one of the Proms. The work to be performed had presumably been

77

announced before she switched on; by the time the picture appeared on her screen the players were tuning their instruments. There was a second's silence and then a burst of clapping from the audience as the conductor appeared. Kate went back into the kitchen. To watch a concert added nothing to the pleasure of listening to it – the cameras would move fussily around, picking out individual players and their instruments and distracting attention from the balanced orchestral sound. She heard the quick double tap with which the conductor demanded attention and silence, but remained in the kitchen, waiting for the kettle to boil. The wedding reception had provided her with quite as much food as she ever ate in a day; a cup of tea was all she needed for the evening.

The music surged into the little flat, overflowing from the dark basement sitting room into the even darker kitchen and illuminating them both with a sunlight of the spirit. The sound enveloped her in comfort in exactly the way in which, as a child, she had felt herself wrapped and comforted by the balmy warmth of the Jamaican climate. So close was the texture of the music that it seemed to transform the humidity of her island birthplace into this other medium, heard instead of felt. Presumably it was only her imagination, but could she not hear beneath the swirling strings a faint syncopation, as though drums were beating in the distance? It added a jungle rhythm to a motif as familiar, though long-forgotten, as a hymn tune, and reminded her of the lullabies which the women of Hope Valley sang to their babies in the darkness while Kate and her brother Brinsley lay awake, listening. Kate had passed the same tunes on to her own baby, although she was careful only to hum them, recognizing from the beginning that it would be dangerous for Ilsa to hear any English words. By now Kate had forgotten the words herself, but she was not mistaken, surely, in recognizing some of the themes. She found herself humming again, remembering – for once without bitterness – the day when she had left Jamaica as an eighteen-year-old. It had been a day when her eyes were bright with hope and enthusiasm, her step firm and springy and her heart filled with a passionate determination to help those less fortunate than herself. Briefly now, as the music swelled, her heart swelled again with it.

The kettle was boiling. For the next moment or so Kate busied herself with the making of a pot of strong tea. It would need to brew for five minutes. While she waited, still in the kitchen, she returned her attention to the music.

The first movement must have ended while she was rattling the lid of the teapot, and now the mood had changed. Drumbeats and syncopation, comfort and jollity, were replaced by the melancholy notes of a single violin, at first plucked in sad half-tones and then soaring heart-breakingly upwards as though the music were stretching itself through the darkness of night to touch the stars. It brought back another memory, as distant and unexpected as the first and just as poignant – the memory of a night in 1916 when she huddled in a blanket on a high pass of the Albanian mountains, wondering whether she would live through the cold of the night, whether she could survive another day on the march.

Sergei had come to sit beside her, filling her mug with slivovitz. It was the night of Christmas Day – although she had not been aware of the fact until then. And from beside a camp fire higher up the pass, one of the soldiers had drawn his bow across the single string of a gusle, using the same poignant half-tones as the violinist at this concert. Every man on that retreat had known that he might never see his country again: the music expressed the heartbreak of them all.

Not until twenty years later had she become Sergei's mistress, but on that Christmas Day the mournful Slav music had been fixed for ever in her memory by the intensity of her love for a man who was not a lover but a friend. What she was hearing now was not the same tune, but unmistakably it expressed the same mood.

She had been sad on that evening, expecting never to see Sergei again. Her life, when she looked back on it, contained too many departures, too many farewells. But in the end she and Sergei had been reunited, just as in the end – although too late for her parents – she had returned to Jamaica. At least, thought Kate as she poured the first cup of tea, this composer who had so unexpectedly touched her memories with his music was not likely to penetrate the privacy of the two separations from which she had never recovered. She raised the cup to her lips but, before she could take the first sip, the mood of the music changed once more.

It was not possible, she thought. Her eyes widened unbelievingly as the plaintive note of the single violin faded away and the whole orchestra, in a dramatic crescendo, swept her in sound out of the tiny, dark basement flat and into the limitless Russian countryside. She felt herself flying over snowfields and forests. But no, she was not flying, she was in a train, travelling on and on, and it was night again, and all would be well as long as the train did not stop. She willed the music to continue, pressing it on as it whirled like a snowstorm, with each wild flurry embracing more and more of a landscape without horizons.

Kate's heart beat fast and noisily, thumping the blood against her eardrums so that she could hardly hear the music. It could not be a coincidence that a symphony should run so exactly parallel with her life. A single flash of recognition, one familiar theme to recapture a mood, would be usual enough. That the same work should contain two such encounters of musical memory was unlikely but not impossible. But three! How many people in the world could there be who had absorbed the music of Jamaica and Serbia and Russia?

Kate searched for an explanation and gave herself a choice. It was possible that she was, at last, going mad. Ever since her Oradour breakdown she had been conscious of the danger. It was to avoid the risk which complete solitude would have held that she had applied for the job as Dr Morley's receptionist. Or could it be that she was dying? The pounding of her heart suggested the possibility. Perhaps it was not only a drowning man who relived his whole life in its last few seconds. Some other physical change, unheralded and less dramatic, might have the same effect.

There was a simple enough test. She had only to move, to step from the kitchen into the sitting room, to see whether the orchestra was still playing and to concentrate on listening to the sound. If what she heard was only in her head, then she must look also to herself for the explanation. But if, against all probability, her life had in some extraordinary manner been set to music, there must be a rational explanation. She did not in fact move, but waited for what she knew was coming. It was certain that she had never heard this work before, but with an equal certainty she knew how it would end. Whether she was hearing the music or imagining it would make no difference to that.

It came exactly as she had expected. The symphony had opened with one lullaby, which Kate had known once but almost forgotten. It approached its end with another, which she would never forget. As the orchestra faded to a whisper, a balalaika began to play the tune which Prince Vladimir Aminov had composed during Kate's pregnancy, ready to welcome the baby he had never lived to see.

Ten years had passed since Kate last allowed herself to indulge in hope. Tears flooded her face as she allowed the unfamiliar emotion to overwhelm her. She did not notice that the untasted cup of cold tea slipped from her hand, shattering on the floor and splashing her ankles. All her concentration was directed towards the moment when the symphony would end and she would hear the name of the composer.

The sound of the balalaika died away. There was a single shrieking chord from the whole orchestra. A moment of silence. The enthusiastic applause of a young and generous Prom audience. Pressing against the wall for support, Kate made her way back into the sitting room.

The conductor was bowing. He shook the hand of the leader of the orchestra. He waved all the players to their feet. And then, with one arm outstretched, he hurried to the side of the platform. When he returned, he was accompanied by a woman.

It was too much to bear. Kate's head was spinning and dizziness forced her to stand still in the doorway. This must be the composer, and the composer must be Ilsa. No one else knew the tune of that last lullaby. And yet for a moment Kate could not be sure. The daughter who had been snatched away from her sixteen years before was a sturdy twenty-two year old, strong and healthy even after three months spent hiding in the cellars with the Jewish children. The woman who moved forward now, tall and elegant in her long evening dress seemed older than Ilsa should have done. The extreme slimness of her figure accorded with contemporary standards of beauty, but to Kate she seemed unhealthily thin. Her hair – it was impossible on the black and white screen to tell whether it was a dark chestnut colour – was strained sleekly back off her oval face to give her the look of a ballerina: beautiful, but remote. It was not so much a beautiful face as a beautiful mask, of pale skin stretched so tightly over high, strong cheekbones that the cheeks below seemed hollow. Kate's first reaction, in fact, was that of a doctor rather than a mother. This woman, whether she knew it herself or not, was ill.

Now the camera offered a close-up – only brief, but long enough for Kate to recognize the high cheekbones and slightly tilted eyes which Ilsa Aminova had inherited from her father. There could be no doubt about it. Kate had found her daughter again.

Above the continuing sound of the Promenaders' applause came an announcer's voice. 'You have been listening to the first performance of the Cradle Symphony, by Ilsa Laing, played by the BBC Symphony Orchestra in the Royal Albert Hall.'

It was a miracle, Kate thought, struggling like a swimmer to keep her thoughts clear above the maelstrom swirling within her head. A miracle that Ilsa should be alive. A miracle that the discovery should be made in such chance fashion. Through the more familiar miracle of television she was actually looking into her daughter's face. And soon, very soon – although it seemed unbelievable, she could not doubt it – they would meet again.

The programme was ending. In the Royal Albert Hall the audience continued to applaud and the players to bow, but the camera was withdrawing, retreating backwards as though from the presence of royalty. The figures on the platform became too small and too blurred to see. In a moment they would disappear.

Kate's rational mind knew perfectly well that she would have no difficulty in making contact with Ilsa. She could telephone the BBC, the hall, the orchestra. But there was a moment as the picture faded in which her thoughts were no longer rational. In the darkest hours of her years of loneliness there had been more than one occasion on which she had feared that despair might unbalance her mind. She hardly had time to recognize in these last few seconds that her reason had snapped at last, because it was not misery which overwhelmed her but bliss, the redemption of a lifetime of hardship and much sorrow by a single experience of pure happiness. Her daughter was alive, and so Vladimir Aminov lived on as well and Kate herself would never completely die. She flung herself at the vanishing picture, her arms stretched wide to clasp it, to embrace Ilsa and hold her back. Beneath the weight of her unsteady rush, the television set staggered and toppled, and they fell together to the floor.

At the coroner's inquest three days later Dr Morley gave evidence that he had identified the body of the old lady in the ginger wig as that of his late receptionist, Miss Lorimer. But an even more elderly lady in a wheelchair intervened, announcing herself to be Lady Glanville and desiring it to be put on record that the dead woman was a doctor and that her correct title was the Princess Aminova. The young reporter from the local papers, doing his routine round of the courts sniffed a good story but found no one willing to provide more details.

Nor were the facts of the princess's death any clearer than those of her life. Neither the firemen who had carried her out of the blazing basement nor the doctor who had examined her body could say whether she had died from electrocution, from suffocation or from burns. So the coroner certified that death was due to misadventure and left it at that.

He was wrong. Kate Lorimer, mother of Ilsa Laing, had died of joy.

PART TWO

Ilsa
Letting Go
1963–65

1

Ilsa Laing had so often, as a little girl, begged for the story of her birth to be repeated that the scene was as vivid to her as though she had been a spectator. On the morning of her birthday in 1963 – as on every previous anniversary – she recalled the circumstances and remembered her mother with love.

It was in February 1919 that Katya Belinska, heavy with child and weak with starvation, had collapsed in the snow on a windy ridge outside Petrograd. A peasant couple, discovering her there, had taken her into their cottage. After the old woman had delivered the baby, she wrapped Katya in blankets and laid her on the ledge above the wood-burning stove in an attempt to raise the temperature of her body. But so sure was the old man that the young mother would not survive the night that he carried the new-born child to the home for war orphans which had been established in the one-time palace of the Aminov family. Ilsa could imagine her mother's anguish when she returned to consciousness to find her baby gone; her joy when they were reunited.

Sometimes Ilsa felt as though the biting cold of her first few hours had put a chill on her life from which she would never escape. Perhaps that was why – far from Russia in both time and distance – she liked both to begin and to end every day by lingering in the warmth of a deep bath. Or perhaps her later experiences provided a more direct explanation of that habit. The years of filth and freezing conditions which she had endured as a young woman were a long way behind her now, but might still explain her obsession with cleanliness. On this, her birthday, though, it was not her years of imprisonment which she remembered, but the orphanage – and her mother, who had kept hundreds of sick and half-starved children alive in it, while bringing up her own baby.

The water was cooling. Ilsa reached out to turn on the hot tap again.

'Ilsa! Ilsa, you're going to be late!'

The anxiety in Michael's voice came clearly through the bathroom door. Ilsa smiled affectionately at the sound. The sixteen-year-old boy was almost as obsessive in his regard for punctuality as she was in her need for hot water.

'The interview is to be recorded,' she called back. 'It's not going out live. So the time is not too important.' Nevertheless, she stretched to release the water and began to prepare herself for her morning's engagement.

Michael was staring out of the window as she came into the bedroom, took off her robe, and stepped into the dark red dress which she had already laid out. To be wearing evening dress at half past nine in the morning felt strange; but the televised interview would be shown in the evening, immediately before a concert to be relayed from the Royal Festival Hall.

'Will you zip me up, Michael?' Esther, who could normally be asked to help, was at this time of day busy with her responsibilities as a housekeeper. As careful in this task as with the scientific experiments which absorbed him at school, Michael put one hand underneath the zip as he drew it up, to be sure that he would not catch her skin.

'You're getting thinner,' he told her. 'This dress was tight last time I helped you.' He fastened the hook at the top of the zip. 'You should eat more. You didn't come down to breakfast.'

Ilsa laughed at the accusing note in his voice. 'I never come down to breakfast.'

'But it's your birthday. Had you forgotten? You should have come to be given your presents.'

Ilsa never forgot the date – and because tonight's performance of her third symphony was billed as a birthday tribute, there had been more reminders this year than usual: but she had long since ceased to think birthdays important. Now she was dismayed at hurting Michael's feelings. She set down the mascara which was to add the last touch to her make-up. Even if it made her late, she must not rush any gesture that he wanted to make. But he was holding nothing in his hand: nor could she see anything unusual in the room. He smiled as he saw her eyes searching.

'Richard's checking his lecture notes in the study and mustn't be disturbed before lunch,' he said. Richard – Michael's father and Ilsa's husband – was shortly due to leave for a medical conference in the United States. He had arranged to stay on after it for three months, studying developments there in his special field of allergy, and then to give a series of lectures in Australia before returning home. 'But my present's outside,' Michael added. 'You can see it from the window.'

The front of the Laings' house, an expensive portion of a Nash terrace, faced directly over Regent's Park. But Ilsa's bedroom was at the back. It overlooked a small private garden in which the housekeeper's husband, combining the duties of gardener with those of handyman, struggled against problems of excessive shade and air polluted with exhaust fumes. She looked out of the window. The bitterest winter of the century still held

91

London in its frozen grip, and the sheet of snow which had covered the lawn six weeks earlier had been disturbed only by birds scrambling for the crumbs which Michael threw out. Above ground, nothing but the brave golden stars of a winter jasmine gave any promise of a spring to come. But at the far end of the garden was a black mound which had not been there the previous day.

'It's municipal sludge,' said Michael. 'Happy birthday!'

'Municipal sludge!' For once Ilsa did not need to affect astonishment. 'What is municipal sludge?'

'Well, you see, my first idea was to buy a climbing rose and plant it for your birthday. But Rundle said that it would never do, because the soil was too tired. From being used over and over again for a couple of centuries, he said. Then I read about this sludge. The council makes it by turning refuse into a kind of manure, and it reacts chemically with the soil – so if we dig it in and leave it for a bit, I may be able to give you the rose for Christmas.'

'Michael, I adore you! Has any other woman in the world been given such a marvellous present. Municipal sludge!' They fell into each other's arms, laughing. 'Thank you, my darling. As soon as I get back, we'll go out together and smell it. And now I must get the interview over.' She grimaced to show her distaste for the prospect.

'Why are you going to do it?' asked Michael. 'I know you hate talking about yourself.'

Ilsa gave a wry laugh. 'Would you call my music popular, Michael?'

'Well – '

'No need to pretend. Most people who listen to concerts care only for three or four old favourites. Beethoven, Mozart, Brahms, Tchaikovsky. A few have moved into the twentieth century – for Mahler, perhaps. If you ask a man in the street the name of any composer alive in England today, he may possibly be able to remember Benjamin Britten. But no one else, I promise you. "Ilsa Laing? Never heard of her."' Ilsa had been dialling the number of the local taxi rank as she spoke and now asked to be picked up at once.

'And you see,' she went on, 'this is a problem which faces every composer now that princes and patrons are out of fashion. If an artist paints a picture, that picture exists as soon as he has finished it – even if he never finds a buyer. But although I can create a piece of music on paper, the music doesn't come alive until it's interpreted, and to pay the musicians there must be an audience. If I'm to think of my music as a form of communication and not merely as a self-indulgence I have to use every means I can to interest audiences in my compositions. Most people, unfortunately, are more interested in the composer herself than in her work, so that's where I have to start.'

'What are you going to talk about, then?'

'The interviewer will ask me about my childhood – because if he has done his homework he will know the answers already. And I expect he will ask how I physically set about the task of composition. People are obsessed by the mechanics of creative work. Do I rule the staves myself, use pen or pencil, sit at a piano, play before I write? Very few people are capable of talking intelligently about contemporary music. If he proves to be one of them it will be a pleasant surprise. A *considerable* surprise.'

There were to be no surprises. So much was made clear in the preliminary chat before she was taken into the studio. Ilsa waved away the sandwiches which represented standard BBC hospitality, but accepted a cup of coffee

93

and drew on a cigarette as her host leaned forward in his chair to discuss tactics and provide reassurance.

'This won't be an *aggressive* interview, Mrs Laing. My intention is to give you the cues, in a sense, so that you can tell the viewers what you think will interest them. We'll come to a discussion of your music – and how you see your place in British musical life – in the second half of the programme. I plan to start with the history – ' he glanced down at his notes – 'the very *dramatic* history of your life. If there are any private areas . . .'

'My husband is a physician. A specialist. He has his own clinics – the Laing anti-allergy clinics. I'm sure you know about the silly doctors' rules which regard any public mention of a speciality as advertising. I can talk about him at the time when we met, when he was in the army, but not about his work now.' Richard had been at pains to impress this on her when the letter from the BBC first arrived.

'And in your own life? For example, I know that some ladies don't care to specify their age . . .?'

Ilsa's laughter lightened her low, husky voice. 'I was born during the Russian Civil War. I first composed music during the siege of Leningrad. I said goodbye to a career as a pianist when I lost two finger-tips in Auschwitz, building a railway in below-zero temperatures. Every event of my life is tied to some event in history. If the matter of my age is important to them, it will not take your viewers very long to do the arithmetic. In 1963 I am forty-four years old. You may ask me the question directly if you wish.'

She had already noticed that the fluency with which she spoke English came as a relief to him. After seventeen years in the country only an occasional intonation or slight formality in her choice of words betrayed her

94

foreign origins. Now he relaxed even more obviously. 'I was told I might find you reticent,' he confessed.

Ilsa leaned forward to stub out her cigarette. 'The time to be shy was when the invitation arrived. It was not possible to half-accept. I made the decision, so – ' She gestured the whole-heartedness with her hands. 'I'm fortunate: there are no skeletons in my cupboard. Misfortunes, yes, certainly – you have them already written on your little cards, no doubt. If you press too hard, perhaps you could make me cry. But not blush.' She knew, though, that she would not cry. For very many years now her emotions had been wholly under control.

That did not prevent her from feeling a stab of annoyance as – face powdered and chair adjusted under the hot studio lights – she listened to the musical extract which had been chosen to introduce the programme. She thought of herself as a composer of atonal music. The Cradle Symphony was untypical of her work: it was sentimental and old-fashioned. But she saw that it must have seemed a useful lead into the story of her life, and answered the first, obvious, question without any indication of resentment.

'Yes, my own cradle, you might say. It was based on the tunes my mother hummed to me during my childhood. I wrote the symphony as a kind of requiem for my mother – although for all I know she may still be alive.'

She saw his eyes flicker as he wondered briefly whether to explore that hint of mystery; but he was not a man to take risks. He continued to work chronologically through his notes.

'You were born in Russia?'

'Yes, in a village outside Leningrad. It's called Pushkin nowadays.'

'Were your parents musical?'

'I never knew my father. He died before I was born. My mother was a doctor. Not musical in any professional way, but valuing music. I was brought up in an orphanage, because my mother was its medical superintendent. But the building had been a palace once, belonging to a family of the old nobility, and one of her triumphs was to preserve a piano – a very good piano – through a time when anything which would burn was being chopped up for firewood. She wanted me to be a musician. But she never had to force me. It came naturally.'

She allowed the questions to lead her ploddingly on, past the early recognition of her talent as a musician, her training at the Leningrad School for Musically Gifted Children, her first recitals, her first foreign tour. But when they reached the invasion of Russia in 1941 she became uneasy about the bland pace of the questioning.

All her answers were true. When the Germans over-ran her village and occupied the orphanage, she had hidden in its cellars for three months with those of the orphans who were Jewish, and it was in that silent darkness that she had first known the urge to compose. But there was something else about the smoothness of question and answer. The interviewer – because he was facing her at this moment, knowing that she had survived – did not seem to understand how unlikely survival had seemed at the time. She had expected execution when she was discovered in the cellars, and reprieve had condemned her instead to years of slave labour. Sickness brought her to the very brink of death in Auschwitz; and later, after the retreating Germans transferred the inmates to the camp at Bergen-Belsen, starvation had taken her for a second time almost past the point of no return. It was difficult now for Ilsa, expensively dressed and speaking out of a prosperous background into the comfortable drawing rooms of her viewers, to give a true impression of how it had felt to endure those years. Looking back on them, the interviewer might suggest that her story had had a happy ending; but at the time it had been impossible to imagine any ending at all except that of a squalid death.

'And after the liberation, did you return to the Soviet Union?'

'I tried to go back home, to look for my mother. But the whole village had been destroyed. The Germans exploded mines under every building as they withdrew. I was told by an official that my mother and all the remaining orphans had been killed when the orphanage was blown up. I'm not sure now that I was told the truth. The Germans who were quartered in the orphanage showed no mercy to the Jewish children, certainly. And they were harsh to me, although by their rules I suppose I deserved it. But they had seemed to respect my mother – and I can't believe that they were such monsters as to murder so many innocent children. There were many such horror stories told, and at that time it was easy to believe them because our hearts were filled with hatred. Later on, I had doubts, and tried hard to find out what might have happened instead. But it was impossible. No one had records of possible evacuations during a time of chaos. And the Soviet Union is a huge country. It's easy to become lost. My mother may at this moment be caring for a new generation of orphans somewhere in the east, in the new lands; but I have no way of finding out.'

'So how did you come to live in England?'

'You could say that was a romantic story . . .'

'You could say that was a romantic story.'

In the drawing room of his Nash home that evening,

97

Dr Richard Laing stood up abruptly. 'It's time we left, Ilsa,' he said.

Michael turned his head only briefly to say goodbye, before returning his attention to the television screen. Ilsa knew that nothing she was about to say in the recorded interview would come as news to him. He had heard many times the story of how his father, arriving with the British troops to liberate the prisoners at Belsen, had stared in horror at the skeletal figures inside the electrified fence. By his medical care he had saved the lives of hundreds of them, but one in particular he had picked out from the first moment – guarding her from the dangerous generosity of the soldiers who were shocked into distributing their personal rations, and gradually building up her strength until she was able to assist him as an orderly. No doubt Michael did indeed believe what followed to be a romantic story; but Ilsa understood why her husband was not prepared to remain in the room while she lied. She followed him out to the car without speaking. The concert – to be transmitted live from the Royal Festival Hall – would follow immediately after the recorded interview.

Four hours later Richard drove her home again in silence. Ilsa was excited by the evening. It was not just that the audience had applauded and that the conductor, over a celebratory drink afterwards, had been enthusiastic. Before every first performance she suffered from a kind of stage fright – a terror that the music she was about to hear in the concert hall might not be the same as the music she had originally heard in her head. No amount of trial recording or attendance at rehearsals could reassure her. Only a full-scale performance could provide the electric certainty of success. At the end of the symphony she had been certain. But Richard did not speak.

'You didn't like it,' she said as he unlocked the front door and stood back to let her go in. She went straight up the first flight of stairs to the drawing room.

'Technically it was very good.' Richard poured himself a brandy and soda and raised his eyebrows interrogatively in her direction.

Ilsa shook her head. 'But?'

He frowned over a choice of words. Lighting a cigarette, Ilsa watched his restlessness.

'There was something missing. There was no feeling, no heart. You're growing very cold, Ilsa.'

'Myself, or my music?'

'Are they different? When you wrote the Cradle Symphony – '

Ilsa made a gesture of annoyance. 'That was years ago. I felt the need then to express a particular emotion. I used an old-fashioned romantic style because it seemed appropriate. It was a side-street, a tributary, which has nothing to do with the main flow of my music at all.'

'Perhaps that's what I'm complaining about. Perhaps I'm just an old-fashioned romantic who likes to have his emotions touched. I understand what you're trying to do with your atonal music. I can even appreciate it in an intellectual kind of way. But with every year that passes I find it more difficult actually to *enjoy*.'

'I'm not writing for anyone's emotions. My music – except for the Cradle Symphony – comes through my head. I don't *feel* it. I'm a channel of communication, that's all. There's a sense in which the music exists already. My work is to organize it, to write it down.'

'I'm not sure that's a wise attitude. You're cutting yourself off from life, Ilsa. I admire your dedication, the

99

hours you spend at your music. But you ought to spend more time with *people*. You should have more friends.'

'I have Leo.'

'I sometimes think that your affection for Leo is directly related to the amount of time he spends outside the country.'

'And Michael. And you.'

'Yes?' Richard, still prowling, glass in hand, turned to face her. 'Do you expect this way of life to continue for ever, Ilsa?'

She glanced up at him, wondering whether she should be alarmed. 'For Michael's sake – '

'Michael's nearly seventeen. He's experimenting with his own relationships. We may be doing him more harm than good to live a deception. Do you want him to believe, on his wedding day, that this is how married people live?'

'He's never seen anything but affection between us.'

'You mean that he's never seen us quarrel. Do you think he doesn't realize that it's only because we don't care. I need more warmth in my life, Ilsa.'

'I think from time to time you've found it.'

'Because I've been driven . . . I don't regard myself as a philanderer. What happened three years ago was because I was tired of being – well, tolerated instead of wanted. And since then, you haven't so much been punishing me, have you, as indulging your own taste for privacy? It can't go on.'

Ilsa waited in silence to hear what he proposed.

'I shall be away on this jaunt until June. Plenty of time for us both to think about things. You must decide what you want. We'll talk about it when I get back.' His voice dismissed the subject for the time being and he sat down, his restlessness assuaged by the attempt to clear the air.

100

As he set down his glass, he glanced at the notepad beside the telephone. 'A message for you,' he said, tearing off the top page and handing it across.

As she took the sheet, Ilsa was still considering her husband's ultimatum, and a moment or two passed before she looked down. But what she read brought her to her feet, her eyes widening with an even greater shock. Unable to speak, she handed the paper back to Richard.

At the top of the page, carefully printed, was an unfamiliar telephone number. Michael had written a message underneath.

'Ilsa, someone called Lady Glanville phoned. Says you don't know her. Sounds pretty old. Will you ring her back as soon as poss. She wants you to come and see her at Blaize (her stately home, I rather gather) tomorrow morning. She's just been watching your TV interview and says she can tell you what happened to your mother.'

2

'Ten years!' repeated Ilsa incredulously. 'For ten years we were both living in England, and didn't know it!' Had she been alone, she would have cried her anguish aloud. As it was, she could only fumble in her handbag for her cigarettes. 'Do you mind if I smoke, Lady Glanville?'

The old lady on the sofa facing her made an almost imperceptible movement of her shoulders, which Ilsa interpreted as indicating sympathy but disapproval. Breathless with the shock, she took two or three quick pulls on the cigarette and then threw it into the fire.

What she had just learned tempted disbelief. Yet Lady Glanville had been too definite in her statement to permit of any real doubt. On the telephone she had refused to do more than promise information at a face-to-face meeting, but she had wasted no time after Ilsa's arrival at Blaize before making her announcement.

'Your mother was my niece. When she came to live here in 1947 she told me all about you, and how she had failed to find you after the war. Everything you said in that interview agrees with her story. There's no possibility of mistake.' With the meticulous memory of the very old, Lady Glanville had detailed Kate Lorimer's life story from her birth in Jamaica until her loss of contact with the family after 1917; and then again through the last ten years of her life.

She had explained, as well, why it was that Kate had felt her British background to be a danger to herself and her child – in turn because of the Intervention, the purges, the Nazi-Soviet Pact and the German invasion. 'At first it was because she had great ambitions for you. It was necessary, she thought, for you to be a good citizen, with nothing unusual in your background. And later, when she began to plan a return to England, she was afraid that if you knew of her intentions you might show anxiety, which would alert the authorities. Afterwards, of course, she was angry with herself on that account.'

'The last ten years, in England, was she happy?'

The old lady's delicate hands gestured her inability to give any assurance. 'She felt in need of a family when she came here. You could say, perhaps, that she was looking for another daughter. She found two nieces with whom she tried to develop a close relationship. But I don't believe, really . . .' The frail hands fluttered again. 'She wanted you, and she had lost you. She had the satisfaction of knowing that she did useful work. But no, I can't say that she was happy.'

The television interviewer had not been able to make Ilsa cry, even when he probed the most terrible years of her life. But she was near to tears now – tears of frustration at a missed opportunity as well as of distress. For a moment she had to struggle for breath as the realization of her loss overwhelmed her.

In an attempt to calm herself she stood up and crossed the room. Between two long windows, a console table was covered with photographs in silver frames. Ilsa bent down to study them, expecting them to represent members of the family and hoping to see her mother there. But the first to catch her attention was the face of a friend of her own, who could not possibly be related to Lady Glanville. Later she would ask why Leo Tavadze should have been signing his likeness with love and gratitude, but for the moment there was only one question she wanted to put.

'Have you a photograph of my mother, Lady Glanville?'

'I'm your great-aunt, you know. You could call me Aunt Alexa. But I expect you find that rather a sudden relationship. Well, your mother would never allow herself to be photographed in those last ten years. But I guessed you'd ask that question. I looked through my old albums last night. At the end of 1914, just before she left for the war, Kate had a picture taken to send to her parents. She gave a copy to my sister, Margaret. I kept the photograph after Margaret died.' It was ready on a table beside the sofa: she held it out to her guest.

Ilsa's last sight of her mother had been of a distraught woman, screaming aloud in an unknown language – it must have been English, Ilsa realized now – at the sight of her daughter being dragged away to imprisonment. Even before that, bereavement and responsibility and an unbalanced diet over many years had made her mother's face heavy and lined with worry. Now Ilsa found herself looking at a handsome young woman in her early twenties, with a clear complexion, shining eyes and a wide, smiling mouth. Her long, thick hair framed the strong features of her face and everything about her expression proclaimed her confidence in herself and in the work she was about to undertake. It was the face of someone who expected to be happy and who could have no conception of the hardships which lay in wait for her.

As Ilsa stared at the photograph, her heart seemed to tear painfully apart, as though it were breaking not metaphorically but in reality. The emotion which flooded her body robbed her of breath; or else the room had been suddenly drained of air. She felt herself suffocating and, as she gasped for breath, her head began to swim. Like someone clinging to the end of a twisted rope she fell, spinning dizzily, into blackness.

She awoke – but it was not a usual kind of awakening – to find herself lying on a chaise longue in an empty room. For a few moments she coughed, trying to clear her throat, and the sound must have acted as a signal, for the door of the morning room opened. The elderly gentleman who came in spoke with a polite, almost tentative voice; but Ilsa was accustomed to look at the hands of strangers and saw firmness and competence in his.

'Mrs Laing. I'm Dr Mason. Lady Glanville asked me to have a look at you.'

'She shouldn't have troubled.' Ilsa sat up and managed to control her cough. 'It was stupid of me to faint. But I had had a shock.'

'Alexa told me. Not the details, but the fact that you'd had news to upset you. This is no trouble. Not a professional call. I come to have lunch with her every Sunday. When she telephoned, it was to suggest that I should bring my little black bag with me.' He was unfastening it as he spoke, and hanging his stethoscope round his neck.

'There's nothing wrong with me, thank you very much.'

'Then I hope you'll allow me ten minutes so that I can pass that reassurance on to Alexa. She was worried.' He wound a wide band round Ilsa's arm as he talked and pumped air into it to check her blood pressure. She opened her mouth to protest, but was overcome by another fit of coughing.

'Nasty tickle. Does it bother you much?'

'Only when I wake in the morning, as a rule. My husband tells me I smoke too much.'

'He could be right. How many?'

'Oh, forty or fifty a day.'

'He *is* right. Could you not cut that down?'

'If I saw the need.' A few moments of coughing a day, a slight breathlessness, had always seemed a small price to pay for the comfort which smoking brought her. A cigarette was part of her routine of concentration when she was working. It gave her something to do in company and prevented her from feeling lonely when she was alone. The habit formed in the chaotic months after the end of the war, when cigarettes were the currency of friendship, had become part of her way of life.

'May I look at your hands?' He studied her fingers without making any comment on the mutilation which had been caused by frost-bite. 'Now would you slip off your blouse? And cough? And again. And breathe deeply. More deeply still, if you can.' Ilsa felt the small cold circle pressing into her skin. 'Have you always been as thin as this, Mrs Laing?'

'Not always, but for a long time. As a girl I was quite plump. "Sturdy" was the word my mother used.'

'And since then?'

Ilsa heard the question, but did not answer it immediately. The casual mention of her mother had upset her again, but this time she was determined not to let her emotions affect her. During the war she had been starved. And afterwards, when it might have been expected that she would eat voraciously, the self-control that Richard had taught her in the first days of liberation had become another habit. She had found herself regarding food almost with disgust, and ate in order to stay alive, but not for pleasure. 'I haven't much of an appetite,' she said.

'Let's hope that Alexa's cook can change that.' Dr Mason put the stethoscope back in its case. 'How long is it since you last had a complete medical check?'

'Many years. I'm never ill. And my husband is a doctor, so –'

'From my own experience I know that doctors recognize illness everywhere except in their own families. Unless it falls into their speciality, and then they see it where it doesn't exist. I think you should let someone look at your chest, Mrs Laing. Take an X-ray, I mean. I'll give you a note to a hospital. Or you may prefer to go to your own doctor. And if you could cut down on the cigarettes in the meantime, that would help you to find out whether the coughing diminishes as a result. Now, then, I'm to ask you to come and have a drink before lunch as soon as you feel up to it.'

Ilsa returned to the drawing room just as Alexa was accepting a generous glass of whisky from a good-looking man of about fifty. His stylish, although casual, outfit of pale blue slacks and polo-necked sweater, with a navy-blue blazer, covered a trim figure, and only the thinness of his carefully-combed sandy hair gave a clue to his age, for his sun-tanned face was smooth and unworried. He smiled at Ilsa with a mixture of friendliness and curiosity as he waited for Alexa to introduce him.

'Ilsa, my dear, this is my son, Pirry. Pirry, your new cousin, Ilsa Laing.'

Ilsa had not yet come to terms with the discovery that she possessed an English great-aunt. No doubt it followed naturally enough that she must expect to find herself part of a complete family; but her bewilderment must have shown on her face, for Pirry laughed sympathetically as he raised her hand lightly to his lips.

'I stayed out of the room while Mother was breaking the news, so that you wouldn't feel completely overwhelmed by unexpected relations,' he said. 'But I couldn't wait any longer to tell you what a privilege it is to find myself connected with you. I'm a great admirer of your work.'

Ilsa gave an astonished laugh. 'It's almost as unusual for me to meet someone who admires my work as to find myself with a new cousin.' Warmed by Pirry's open charm, she accepted a glass of sherry and felt her strength flooding back after her brief collapse.

'You and I share the same birthday, it seems,' Pirry told her. 'Not the year, but the day. Yesterday's concert was a birthday tribute, wasn't it, for you? And the reason why I was in England and able to listen to it on the television was because I always visit Mother for a few days when it's *my* birthday. So we're both Pisceans. Both creatures of water. Generous and sympathetic and self-sacrificing. Talented in music or art and philosophic about accepting the ups and downs of life. Naturally I'm only emphasizing our good points.'

'You surely don't believe in all that nonsense about the stars, Pirry?' said Alexa accusingly.

'Certainly I do. What can be more satisfactory than to learn that one's character has been fixed for ever at the precise moment of one's birth, so that there's no point in making the slightest effort to improve and all one's imperfections are the fault of one's mother. If you think that my consumption of champagne is over-enthusiastic, you should have given birth two days earlier, to make me a reserved, intellectual Aquarian. Now, Cousin Ilsa, if you would turn round, you have yet another cousin to meet. But this is positively the last – for today, at least. This is Asha Lorimer.'

Asha was a tall young woman in her early twenties, with a transparently pale complexion and straight, shoulder-length hair so fair that it seemed almost colourless. The severity of the spectacles she wore contrasted strongly with the luminosity of her skin, becoming almost a disguise; but behind them her blue eyes were as lively as Pirry's.

'Like Pirry, I kept out of the way,' she said as she shook hands. 'You can't have the faintest idea who I am, can you?'

'Let me explain.' Alexa was drawing wavering lines on a sheet of paper, but broke off to point to an oil painting of a sombre Victorian gentleman which hung above the display of photographs. 'That portrait there is of my father, John Junius Lorimer. He had four children. I was the youngest, by many years. Your grandfather, Ralph Lorimer, was my brother. He went out to Jamaica as a missionary and had three children. One of them – Kate – was your mother. Another one was Grant Lorimer, Asha's father. So your mother was Asha's aunt.'

'And are there more to come – cousins, I mean?'

'Not many,' Alexa told her. 'Not enough. But I have a grandson, Bernard. And a great-nephew, John. Both of them Lorimers, not Glanvilles.'

'You're forgetting Paula,' Asha reminded her. She turned back to Ilsa. 'Paula Mattison, the journalist, is a relation of yours as well. When Aunt Alexa said that our missionary grandfather had three children, she was thinking only of the white ones. But he had black descendants as well.'

'I'm impervious to shocks by now,' said Ilsa, seeing that Asha was watching for a reaction. 'When I woke up this morning I had no blood relations anywhere in the world. And now, without warning – '

'But too late for the only one you wanted.' Ilsa found herself being hugged in sympathy. Undemonstrative herself, and averse to being touched, she was unable to respond with any movement of her own, but she warmed

109

to the girl who so quickly understood how much more important was the beloved mother lost than the strange relatives gained. Asha proved equally sensitive to her dislike of embraces, and moved away without fuss. In any case, the sound of a gong drew them all to the dining room for lunch.

Ilsa spoke little as the meal progressed. When she had had time to collect her thoughts there would be many questions to ask, but she had still not recovered from the shock of discovery. Alexa, however, would not allow her guest to isolate herself. She posed a fighting question.

'Do you believe in mixed marriages, Ilsa?'

'Oh really, Aunt Alexa!' protested Asha, while Pirry grinned at her sympathetically and Dr Mason looked down at his plate with the concentration of a man who did not propose to get involved in what was coming.

'My own marriage could be described in that way,' Ilsa said cautiously. 'My husband is British.'

'Well, so are you.'

'Not by birth. Not by upbringing. I'm Russian. I can't alter that at a moment's notice simply because I learn I have an English grandfather.'

'But neither you nor your husband is black? And you share the same religion?'

'Ranji is not black,' said Asha. 'And you know perfectly well, Aunt Alexa, that if he hadn't come from a Christian family he would never have been sent to my grand-mother's mission school. I love you very dearly and I was delighted to come here for Pirry's birthday – and to meet a new cousin – but if you're going to keep on at me about Ranji I shall start making excuses next time you ask.'

Ilsa saw the old lady draw breath to continue what was clearly a long-standing argument, so she came to the rescue with a question of her own.

'Since my mother was born a British subject, her marriage as well as mine must have been of mixed nationality,' she said. 'You never met my father, I suppose, Aunt Alexa?' She did not find it easy to use this form of address, but was rewarded by the success of her change of subject.

'I knew his brother. In my youth I was a prima donna. I sang for Prince Paul once in his theatre palace outside Leningrad – of course, it was St Petersburg then, before the revolution. That palace became the orphanage in which your mother worked. Perhaps she never told you that? Your father was Prince Vladimir Aminov, you see, and to be the daughter of a prince was dangerous, I suppose.'

Ilsa set her coffee cup back on its saucer, aware that her hand was trembling. Her father had been a soldier named Belinsky, a hero of the Civil War. Or so she had always believed.

'I'm more grateful to you than I can express for what you've told me,' she said. 'But I don't think I can listen to any more news today. It's not just news, you see. It's discovering that nothing was what it seemed. Having to abandon all the certainties of my past life.' Suddenly she could not even speak, but buried her head in her hands, struggling to control herself. Once again it was Asha who reacted with quick sensitivity.

'May I ask you for a lift back to London, Cousin Ilsa? When I came to Blaize last night for Pirry's birthday dinner, I planned to leave straight after breakfast. Naturally I couldn't resist the chance to stay and meet you. But I ought to get back as soon as possible.'

'Of course.' Ilsa managed to recover her composure sufficiently to thank her hostess, her great-aunt. 'I hope

111

you'll allow me to visit you again. There are so many questions – but I need a little time.'

'I quite understand, my dear.' Unlike Asha earlier, Alexa did not force embraces on her visitor, but remained seated as she said goodbye. Pirry's touch was light and cool, as though he understood Ilsa's dislike of being tightly gripped, but his eyes were still bright with a sympathetic interest. Dr Mason, standing a little apart from the family in order not to intrude, held out an envelope.

'I took the liberty of scribbling this note,' he said. 'I've addressed it to John Simpson because I happen to know him and respect his work. But of course you could give it to your GP if you preferred.'

'Thank you very much.' Ilsa was polite but uninterested as she put the envelope into her handbag. Her brief collapse was the least important incident in a dramatic day.

Outside the great house, she lit a cigarette, sighing with satisfaction after she had inhaled. The driver of her hired car – for Ilsa had never learned to drive – held the door open; but she paused to study her surroundings. The day, although bright, was still very cold. The rhodo-dendrons which lined the long drive between Blaize and the river were weighed down with snow, and the pale sun of the afternoon was not powerful enough to melt the frost on the woodland trees. The thick white carpet which covered lawns and terraces isolated Blaize in silence and stillness. Stepping in the tracks which the car had made, Ilsa moved to the side of the house and looked down over the gentle undulations of the parkland. Beneath an old and beautifully-shaped oak tree, fallow deer clustered round a bale of forage which had been thrown across from the boundary of the home farm to keep them alive. Nothing else in the landscape moved.

'In Russia, too, we knew this silence – the silence of the snows,' Ilsa said. 'You know – ' she turned to face Asha – 'the grounds of the palace which became our orphanage were laid out in the style of an English park. It was fashionable amongst the nobility at the end of the nineteenth century to clear part of the evergreen forest and to landscape the area like this. Almost every evening my mother used to stand outside for a few moments staring at the trees – the English trees. Perhaps they reminded her of Blaize. Perhaps she often used to think about her life here. Yet she never spoke of it. Never.' She sighed again, gesturing Asha towards the car. 'Well,' she said as they drove off together. 'Tell me about Ranji.'

'Nothing to tell,' said Asha. 'He's just a friend of mine. Indian – from the south. I always fight Aunt Alexa when she says he's black, but it's true that he's quite a dark brown. He's terribly clever; especially considering his background. I have a step-grandmother who's the headmistress of a mission school in Tiruchirappalli. Ranji was one of her pupils, and because she realized how outstanding he was, she got him into a good secondary school. When she heard that he'd been offered a place at the LSE she wrote and asked me to help him settle down in England. I was glad to do it. It must be pretty daunting for someone who was born in a tiny Indian village to cope with London. I can see that he needs someone to make him feel at home. Anyway, I like him.'

'And this is not approved?'

Asha gave an exaggerated sigh. 'Aunt Alexa brought me up. She has the right to fuss over me as though she were my mother. But she doesn't understand how things have changed since she was young. She's ambitious for

113

me in a way that I'm not for myself. I'm a teacher – and in her book, teaching's a second-rate profession. And if I have to do it, I ought at least to get a job in some classy private school, teaching the daughters of the upper crust, instead of in a multi-racial comprehensive. Then, no doubt, I could marry the wealthy brother of one of my pupils and move in the right circles for the rest of my life.'

'I didn't have the impression that Lady Glanville was a snob.'

'No. Sorry. I shouldn't have put it like that. You're right, really. She's not a money snob and she's not a title snob. But she *is* an achievement snob. An élitist. She was immensely famous herself when she was young. All the Lorimer women for the past hundred years have been high achievers – and now you come along, and you're a high achiever as well! Because Aunt Alexa's so old, everyone she likes has arrived at the top already. She doesn't realize that young people may need a little time to get there. If she'd let herself get to know Ranji, she'd realize that he has all the ambition that she'd like to see in me. He's determined to be rich and successful one day. But you're not interested in Ranji. Nor in me, more than to be polite. It's too late, isn't it, for you to accept us as your relations?'

'My mother was older when she came back to England.'

'Ah, but she was *looking* for us,' explained Asha earnestly. 'Everything else had let her down. Being part of a family was tremendously important to her. What she really wanted was to find you, of course, but as a second-best she needed aunts and cousins and nephews and nieces. She hoped too much of us sometimes, and perhaps we didn't always live up to it, but there was never any doubt about what she wanted. It's different for you. Of

114

course you must be curious about what happened to your mother, and sad at not seeing her. But as far as the rest of us are concerned – yesterday you didn't even know we existed. You haven't emerged out of nothingness as Aunt Kate did. You've got your own family, your own life.'

Ilsa glanced at her young cousin's serious face. It was tempting to protest, to express interest, to make some gesture as spontaneous as Asha's own embrace earlier in the day. But many years of controlling her feelings had left her unskilled at forming new relationships and she could not easily throw off the habit of restraint. Besides, it seemed to her that Asha had spoken the truth.

'Yes,' she agreed. 'I have my own life.'

3

'I'm here on business,' said Asha, calling on Ilsa without notice in the Easter holidays, a month after they had met at Blaize. 'Educational business. I could have done it over the telephone, of course, but when I saw where you lived, I couldn't resist the temptation to come and snoop. I've always wondered what these houses were like to live in. They look so grand from outside.'

'Someone who was brought up at Blaize is surely not impressed by this. It's different for me. My mother had just one room for living and sleeping and working, and as a child my only territory was a bed in an alcove off that room, with a curtain to draw across.'

'It was in a palace, all the same.'

'When a palace is occupied by two thousand people, it ceases to be palatial. Would you like to see over the house?'

'Yes please.'

Ilsa laughed at her cousin's frankness and gave her a conducted tour of all except the housekeeper's basement flat. 'As you see,' she pointed out when they returned to the drawing room, 'a large part of the house consists of the hall and stairwell. Our heating bills are astronomical.'

'Is your husband very rich?'

'Yes.' Ilsa did not resent the inquisition. At Blaize she had been given information, and no one had spoiled the occasion by asking questions in return. But it was natural that her relations should be curious. 'He's a specialist in allergies, and he owns two clinics. One is in the country:

patients come from all over the world, sometimes for very long stays. Everything in their diet and environment is controlled – even the air. The other clinic is in London: for consultations and tests and diet control. It may take a long time to discover exactly what is causing an allergic reaction, but Richard always succeeds in the end. That's satisfying for him, and satisfying for the patients as well, so they don't seem to mind paying high fees. Of course, the expenses of running the clinics are very high. And the tax bills also. But after all that – ' she waved her hand round the elegantly furnished drawing room – 'there is enough.'

'Lucky you. Well. To business. For my sins, I have to help with careers at school. I don't deal with the individual interviews, but every week I have to find someone to give a talk to the children who are in their last year. Once a fortnight I'm producing a thoroughly useful person to talk about the sort of job which most of the children will in fact end up doing – someone from a bank, or Marks and Spencer, or the army, or a secretarial agency, or our local furniture factory, or London Transport – you can imagine the sort of thing. But on alternate Thursdays I try to introduce some new idea. And I wonder if I could persuade you to give a talk on being a composer. Not a lesson – not telling them *how* to compose. Just describing what it's like as a career.'

It took Ilsa only a few seconds to consider the request and reject it. 'Composing music is a vocation, not a career,' she said. 'My kind of music, at least. None of your pupils, Asha, will ever have heard of me. They will never have listened to my music. They won't want to be like me, so how can I inspire them? You need someone who writes pop songs, or television jingles. Start with the music which the children would like to compose before introducing them to a man who does it.'

'That's half the point. All the composers I know about are men. Except you. I want a woman. It's part of the process of jolting the children's ideas. For at least three of next term's talks I want to produce a woman who's the tops in her own field – to stop the boys believing that women are no good at anything serious, and to show the girls that a woman can make a success of almost any career.'

Ilsa laughed sympathetically, but did not change her mind. 'I understand that you hope to make your pupils ambitious – but I suppose they will all have to earn their own livings when they leave school.'

'Yes.'

'Then I'm the worst possible example. No one can earn a living by composing works for the concert hall – which is all that I do. Well, perhaps half a dozen people in the world: not more. If you studied a list of contemporary composers, you would find that one or two had a private income, others earn money as conductors or instrumentalists, or teach, or write scores for films or television.'

'And you?'

'I live as a parasite on my husband's income,' Ilsa confessed. 'His earnings give me the time I need to do exactly what I like. I'm not expected to contribute to the family expenses – if I were, we should have had some hungry days! I'm not ashamed of being so dependent – I'm grateful. All through history creative musicians have looked for patrons. Mine happens to be Richard Laing. I suspect that isn't precisely the message you're trying to preach.'

'No,' agreed Asha honestly. 'Independence is the name of the game. The girls I teach take it for granted that there's always going to be someone else to tell them what to do. They don't realize that their ideas are out-of-date already. I want to put them in control of their own lives.'

'You can't imagine yourself being dependent on anyone, then?'

'Oh yes. One day I'd like to get married and have children, and I don't agree with those women who have a baby and promptly hand it over to a child-minder. But I think it's important to taste independence before you give it up. And anyway, I wouldn't think of marriage as dependence. My husband and I would be bringing up our children together: it would be his job to provide the money and mine to provide the care.'

'How delightfully old-fashioned of you!' laughed Ilsa. 'And speaking of children – ' She had heard the slamming of the front door, followed by whistling on the stairs, and waited for Michael to appear. 'Let me introduce Michael to you. Michael, this is Asha Lorimer, one of my new cousins.'

Asha looked surprised as she shook hands with Michael and chatted for a few moments about the chess tournament in which he had just been playing. 'You didn't tell us you had a son,' she said to Ilsa. 'Well, of course, we didn't ask you – too busy pushing the names of strange relatives at you to spare time for the ones you had already. It makes it even sadder that Aunt Kate never knew what happened to you. It was the thing that upset her most, believing that she hadn't got any descendants. If she'd only known that there was not only you, but that she had a grandson as well!'

'Except that actually,' began Michael. He caught Ilsa's eye as though uncertain whether it would be in order to continue; and Ilsa, interpreting his look although almost unable to accept its implication, felt herself pale with shock. Asha, looking from one to the other as she waited for Michael to continue, could have had no idea what the matter was; but Michael himself realized that he had given too much away.

'If you'll excuse me,' he mumbled. 'I'm supposed to phone the match result through.'

He disappeared at speed, and Asha stood up. 'Well, I've failed in my mission, so I'd better be off. Don't bother to come downstairs – I can see myself out.' She stepped towards Ilsa, preparing to kiss her goodbye, and then checked herself. 'Sorry,' she said.

Ilsa was still concerned with what Michael had unintentionally revealed. She needed a moment to remember that at their last meeting she had stepped back from Asha's embrace. 'You're very observant,' she said. 'I'm the one who should say that I'm sorry.'

'Not important.' Asha was smiling. 'Some families are kissing families and some aren't. As an orphan, I got a lot of fussing when I was a little girl, so I developed the kissing habit young.'

'I suppose we're all conditioned by our childhoods. You were an orphan brought up in a loving family. I was a loved daughter brought up in an orphanage. My mother couldn't favour me in front of the other children, so she only kissed me in private. It was a special treat, not a normal gesture. But that's not so important. I would really like to feel myself part of your family, to adopt your habits. What stops me' – Ilsa paused, glancing at Asha to guess whether she would want to hear, and collecting her strength to go on.

'The day that the British troops came to Belsen,' she said, 'I was following Richard through the camp. I had just met him for the first time. We passed some soldiers who had dug a pit and were pushing bodies into it with their shovels. Richard was horrified – he was horrified by everything he saw that day. He tried to prevent me from seeing. And he was horrified again to realize that I wasn't shocked – because this was a familiar sight to me. At least, I believed at the time that I wasn't shocked. It was later, after I came to England, that the nightmares began. At night, I would see again the people I'd met during the day. Fat, healthy, smiling people. But in my dreams they would be naked, and when I touched them – '

She stopped abruptly, unable after all to describe how it had felt, even in imagination to reach out to firm flesh and feel her fingers breaking through into rottenness. Nor could she confess that it was not always a nightmare – that sometimes even by day, confronted with real people, she had hardly been able to control her terror that she might reach out and find herself shaking a fleshless hand.

'Is it still like that?' asked Asha.

'No. Michael cured that part of it. Seeing him as a baby, watching him grow, *knowing* that his body was healthy, I could never have nightmares about him. As he grew up, I was able to accept other people for what they seemed. But never myself.' The nightmare had changed direction. Now she recoiled from the touch of strangers in case they should discover the rottenness within herself. And yet she was perfectly healthy. It was all an illusion.

'Was there no one who could help you?'

'If I'd met my mother again . . . To be held by the one person . . . but it's too late for that now. Richard wanted me to see a psychiatrist. Since I'd allowed him, as a doctor, to restore my body, he didn't see why I should object to letting someone else heal my mind.'

'And did you?'

'It's hard to explain. When you've been near to death,

or in pain, or in danger over a long period, you learn to put yourself somehow outside your own body – so that you don't care what's happening to it.' Ilsa wondered whether it was possible for someone so young and safe to understand. 'By the time the war ended, I was living only in my mind – my mind was myself. And the music came from my mind. I couldn't afford to let anyone meddle with it.' She gave a gasp, half of laughter and half of dismay. 'I've never put that into words before. How self-centred it sounds!'

'You really are a Lorimer,' Asha told her.

'What's so distinctive about Lorimers?'

'Single-minded determination. Devotion to whatever talent they may possess. Aunt Alexa had a daughter once: Frisca. She was a marvellous dancer. But during the war she had to have a foot amputated; and when she found out it had gone, she just died. Not because she was so terribly ill, I gather. But because living and dancing were the same thing for her. Lorimers are only contented in terms of success in what ever field they've chosen. You're a composer, and you don't care about being happy as long as you can compose. Or rather as long as you're composing, you *are* happy. Is that right?'

Ilsa was taken aback by the speed with which her young cousin had summed her up. 'Are you telling me that every member of my new family is so single-minded? Yourself, for example?'

'Oh, I'm a freak by family standards,' Asha said cheerfully. 'Devoted to the pursuit of happiness, you might say. Ordinary happiness. I enjoy teaching and one day I shall enjoy being married. But I'm never going to be best in the world at anything. Quite different from you. You're the genuine article – a hall-marked Lorimer.'

'I wish that were true. I'd like to feel that I belonged.

122

But it's not easy. I've already had to discard everything I thought I knew about my parents. To go further, to become part of your family, I feel that I'd need to let go of everything I take for granted in my present life – to be born again. Do you understand?'

'Yes, I do. And why should you want to try? I'm only suggesting that in one sense you belong already. The Lorimer genes have an identity of their own. Without knowing anything about your son, I'd guess that there's some sphere in which he's determined to succeed.'

'That's true. He wants to be an astro-physicist and reorganize the universe. But – ' Ilsa hesitated and then made up her mind. 'But he's not a Lorimer. My husband's son, but not mine. That's what he was going to say a few minutes ago – that he's not my mother's descendant by blood.'

'Oh.' Asha considered this for a moment. 'Perhaps that makes it less sad that Aunt Kate never knew about him. Ilsa, I mustn't keep you any longer. I'm sorry you won't inspire my fifth form to write symphonies! 'Bye for now.' She moved towards the door, raised her hand in cheerful farewell and ran lightly downstairs. Ilsa stood still in the middle of the room, waiting for Michael to return.

4

'I'm sorry about that,' Michael said. He appeared so quickly after Asha's departure that he had obviously been watching for it. 'I mean, to start with I wasn't sure whether it was all right to tell Asha, since she's part of the family. And then I realized – I didn't know before – I mean, I thought you knew that I knew.'

'No,' said Ilsa.

'I didn't mean to upset you, but I could see that I had. And yet nothing's different, is it? Obviously you can't ever have pretended to yourself that you were my real mother.'

'But I wanted *you* to believe – '

'I was thrilled when Richard told me,' Michael interrupted earnestly. 'It seemed an enormous improvement on the usual system. I mean, when you're born as somebody's son, she's responsible for you, isn't she? She started you off and so she's jolly well bound to look after you and be fond of you. It's a sort of duty. But you had a free choice. You didn't have to have me here, you didn't have to pretend that I was your own son, and any time at all that you'd regretted having me you would only have had to say one word and the whole arrangement would have smashed. And you never said a thing. It was a tremendous compliment.'

'But Richard – '

'That's different. He *is* my father, so nothing changed there. He was just telling me how lucky I was. You were the only one who could have spoilt it.'

Ilsa, lighting a cigarette, noticed that her fingers were trembling. 'How long have you known?' she asked.

'About three years.'

'One of the facts of life, was it, that a father is supposed to reveal to his son? What exactly did he tell you?'

'I should think probably the whole thing. I gather that my real mother wanted to marry Richad, and I was allowed to arrive because she thought that would happen. But he was married to you. And you stuck by him even when you knew about me. He said you were marvellous about it.'

'That gives a quite wrong impression,' Ilsa said. 'It was Richard who was marvellous.' Michael deserved the truth, she decided, pulling nervously on the cigarette. It was the history of his own life which had been distorted. Within the last few weeks she herself had suffered the trauma of learning that throughout her childhood the truth had been concealed from her. She should have known better than to expose Michael to the same risk of shock.

'Sit down, Michael,' she said, although she remained standing. 'I must tell you. In that television interview a few weeks ago I talked about how I met my husband. A romantic story, I said. Well, in a way, I suppose – ' She took a grip on her vagueness and spoke more firmly, beginning from the beginning.

'Some of it was true. Richard and I did first see each other through the wire at Belsen. I was the first prisoner he saw – a scarecrow figure with huge head and huge eyes – and he could hardly believe it. All that day he kept repeating, "We didn't know!" as though he were somehow responsible. There were so many men and women in Belsen on the point of death that it wasn't possible for Richard to see them as individuals. They needed mass feeding, mass nursing. He didn't like the

125

impersonality of that. He needed some one individual to observe, and he chose me. He watched over my diet, he saw me growing stronger, and he asked me to help in nursing the others. It was his personal triumph when I began to look less like a skeleton and more like a woman. You could say I was the symbol of his work for hundreds of others. I shared his pleasure in my own improvement. And I was grateful for small kindnesses he did me. One day, I remember, he gave me a lipstick.' Rich now, and always perfectly groomed, Ilsa still remembered her pride in that lipstick: the symbol of femininity, her sole personal possession.

'So it's true that affection grew between us,' she continued. 'But it wasn't a romance. That wouldn't have been possible. We were too different. A comfortable man who had never known what it was to be poor or hungry or desperately afraid. And a woman who had forgotten how it felt to be loved and secure. We had nothing in common.'

'You mean you didn't fall in love then?' asked Michael.

'No. We became friends. Even that was unlikely enough. But as soon as I was well enough I was moved out of Belsen to a Displaced Persons' Camp. It was the first step towards returning home. Richard gave me his address – an army post office number. To use if I was in trouble, he said. It was kind of him; but when we said goodbye I didn't expect ever to see him again.'

She was silent for so long that Michael gently pressed her to continue. 'So what happened?'

'For four years I'd dreamed of going home again. But when I applied for repatriation, I discovered that my home didn't exist. Not just the orphanage but the whole village was a pile of ruins. My mother had disappeared. I was told that she was dead. I know now – because Lady

Glanville told me – that she had been put on a train with all the children, to take them somewhere safe; at such short notice that even the driver of the train didn't know the final destination. So it's not surprising that all my attempts to find her met with no success. It all took a long time. I was in despair. I was free, in a way, but I had no home, no family, no work or working skill, no money or friends, and very little strength – and winter was coming. It seemed that I was going to starve again. I wrote to Richard. The post office number gave me no idea where he was. In Berlin, it turned out.'

'And he answered?'

'He sent me a travel pass.' Ilsa laughed wryly to herself at the memory. 'You can't imagine what it was like travelling in Europe then. Even a short distance. So many trains and railway lines had been bombed, and coal was short. Every carriage was so packed that we could hardly breathe, and we didn't know where diversions might take us. It was slow, dirty – oh, you tease me sometimes about my passion for baths, Michael, but I have a lot to make up for. By the time Richard saw me again I was almost as weak as in Belsen; but mentally much worse. In the camp I'd sunk into a kind of acceptance. But to be given a glimpse of hope and then to see it snatched away – I was distraught.' She smiled at Michael, reassuring him that now he had heard the worst. 'So for the second time Richard was horrified by my appearance. You know how easily his emotions are stirred. He was determined that the life he had saved shouldn't be wasted. So while he built up my strength for a second time, he offered me a new future: a life in England.'

'You mean he asked you to marry him?'

'He offered to marry me. Not precisely the same thing. He promised to give me a British passport, a settled

127

home for a little while, some training for a new career, and an allowance until I could support myself. Again, it wasn't a romance. We were still friends, and now we were becoming fond of each other. But what he proposed was so kind, so generous, that I shall be grateful to him all my life – because he already had someone he loved, in England. Tess, your mother. She would understand, he said: and he would make it clear that the marriage was formal and temporary. What he didn't know was that Tess was already pregnant. She was going to tell him as soon as he returned to England, and expected that they would marry at once.'

'Couldn't he have divorced you when he found out?' Michael asked.

'Not for two years under British law. He could have had the marriage annulled, because it hadn't been con-summated. But then I should have had to leave the country – with nowhere to go. It must have been a hard choice for him to make, and very hard for Tess. But he kept his promise to me. For four months we all lived in the same house. Then you were born – and Tess died.'

'So you took me over.'

'You needed care at once, and Richard was too upset to make any other plans. I was glad of a way to repay him. And so, gradually, we became what we seemed – a married couple with a little son. To find myself with a baby, when I knew I couldn't have children myself, was a most marvellous gift. I had to learn to love Richard, and it took a little time; but I adored you from the moment you were born.'

'That's all that matters then, isn't it?' suggested Michael. 'You adore me and I adore you. I'm at a notoriously difficult age, you know. Under any normal family set-up you and I would be at each other's throats by now, instead of indulging this mutual admiration.'

'Oh, Michael!' Ilsa stubbed out her cigarette and hugged him. Michael had always been able to make her laugh. But something had disappeared from her life. She would never again be able to treat him as a son, or pretend to herself that she was a mother. They would be friends, but that was not the same. Was it only half an hour ago that she had told Asha it would be hard to let go of her old life in order to embrace the new family which was on offer? Already, it seemed, she had been forced to abandon the illusion which was dearest to her heart.

'You're all right, are you, Ilsa?' asked Michael, unconcerned by any change in their relationship. 'I know it was tactless of me to start blurting things out, but for a moment you looked as though you were going to faint. And you really are getting terribly thin.'

'I'm perfectly well.' The words seemed truthful as she spoke them. Later that day, though, Michael's question prompted her to stare critically in the glass and then to step on to the weighing machine in Richard's bathroom. Richard was a big man who weighed himself every week in order to diet or exercise away any extra ounces. But Ilsa's weight had not changed for years – or so she had thought. Now, as the marker steadied, she saw that she had lost twelve pounds. And she had not been overweight before.

It was not important – but it reminded her of the letter which Dr Mason had pressed into her hand at Blaize. She had done nothing with it because her temporary collapse had been an isolated incident, explicable by the unusual circumstances. But the doctor – like Michael – had clearly wondered whether something was wrong. And it was true that she had found her cough more troublesome since Dr Mason drew her attention to it. She looked for the letter.

Dr Simpson, it appeared from the address on the envelope, was a hospital consultant; and the letters after his name revealed that he was a surgeon as well as a physician – not the sort of man to be interested in a patient who needed only a bottle of cough mixture. Ilsa spent a moment considering the significance of this.

How should she best assuage her growing uneasiness? She could go to her general practitioner and take his advice. Or she could wait for Richard to return and recommend the best man in the field for a private consultation. But which field? That was the first thing to discover, and it suited her mood that she should be in a sense anonymous – not Dr Laing's wife, but an unknown woman on the out-patient list of a National Health Service hospital. Quickly, before she should change her mind, she telephoned to make an appointment.

5

At Ilsa's first visit to the hospital Mr Simpson had been jolly as he read her letter of referral, asked the routine questions and made the routine tests before despatching her to the X-ray department. At the second visit his manner was more serious, but still reassuring. There was, it appeared, yet one more test to be done, under anaesthetic, requiring her to come into hospital for a day. At the third consultation Mr Simpson was jolly again. Ilsa suspected that he was about to lie to her.

'I hope,' she said, 'that I can trust you to tell me the truth.'

'Truth implies certainty,' he answered. 'Not everything in medicine is clear-cut. And most people distrust opinions which allow of no argument.'

'What I distrust is evasion,' Ilsa told him. 'I wouldn't have come to you in the first place if I had wanted not to know. You wrote to my husband, Mr Simpson, asking him to see you. As it happens, he's abroad at the moment.' Because Ilsa had been kept waiting for her first appointment, it was June by now and she expected Richard home the next day: but she saw no reason to reveal this. 'I deal with his personal correspondence when he's away. I was upset to discover that you proposed to talk to him before you saw me again.'

'What do you want to know, Mrs Laing?'

'My husband is a physician,' Ilsa told him. 'He doesn't specialize in diseases of the chest and he doesn't specialize in cancer. But he's kept all his medical textbooks. I spent an hour in his study after I'd read your letter to him.'

'If I may say so, Mrs Laing, that was an unwise thing to do.'

'Perhaps.' Ilsa shrugged her shoulders. 'But it's too late for me to forget what I read. So nothing you tell me will be more alarming than what I'm already suspecting.'

'And what is that?'

'I think that in the X-ray you were looking for carcinoma of the bronchus. And in the biopsy you were testing for metastasis.' She had memorized the terms as she checked through what Richard's book called the presentations with a mixture of recognition and incredulity.

'Almost anyone reading a medical dictionary can convince himself that he's suffering from some illness or other. It's usually quite imaginary. Your self-diagnosis is incorrect, Mrs Laing.'

'Then what is the correct one? It's my body that we're talking about. Must I return to the books?' She could read in his eyes that his reluctance to answer was because he believed that she did not genuinely wish to know, and became impatient. 'I know that the English like to pretend that death doesn't exist, Mr Simpson. But I'm not English. I'm Russian. I acknowledge death as a part of life. It's not the recognition that I must die that makes me angry, but the feeling that other people know more than I do about my own life. I want to be in control. I need to know the facts.'

There was a short silence: but probably, she thought, he had decided to believe her.

'Let me ask one more question first, Mrs Laing. I ought to have put it to you earlier, but the possibility it raises is not often found in a professional woman like yourself. Have you ever in your life had any contact with asbestos?'

'I don't think so.'

'It could be a very long time ago. Think right back.'

'I don't even know what it looks like.'

Mr Simpson opened a drawer of his desk and passed across two sealed glass jars. 'Have you ever been near any fibres like this?'

Staring at one of the jars, Ilsa searched the past with her memory – so successfully that she shivered with cold on the warm June day. 'Not that colour,' she said slowly. 'More grey. But – ' She paused until the picture was clear in her mind. 'When I was in Auschwitz, I helped to lay a length of railway track. And after, when it was finished, to unload wagons which came along the track. They were building a waiting room next to the crematorium. There were sacks of building materials. Cement and other things.'

'They were sealed?'

'Yes. But dust came through. And sometimes they fell and split. They were too heavy for us, you see.'

'And some of the split sacks contained fibre like this?'

Slowly, unbelievingly, Ilsa nodded. 'But Mr Simpson, that was twenty years ago! And only for a few weeks!'

'It's a time bomb,' the consultant told her. 'And your smoking has made the clock tick a little faster. Sometimes it's as long as forty years before the effect of exposure becomes obvious.'

'So what *is* the effect?'

'There's a pleural tumour. It is, I'm sorry to say, malignant.'

Ilsa had asked for the truth and had promised to believe it. But this particular truth was impossible. Surely.

133

'That can't be right,' she protested. 'I don't believe – I'm perfectly fit. I don't feel ill at all.'

'What you mean is that you haven't felt any pain,' Mr Simpson said. 'One of the problems of treating mesothelioma is precisely the absence of pain for such a long period. There's none of the early warning which we can hope for with other illnesses. But you have had warnings, you know. Your coughing is one. And perhaps you've forgotten how it feels to breathe really deeply. You say you don't feel ill, because any change has been very gradual. But it may be almost twenty years since you were truly well.'

Ilsa stared at him for a long time without speaking. Her face still registered disbelief, but in her stomach she was afraid. 'Can you operate?' she asked at last.

'I'm afraid it's too late for that.'

She gave a sigh of reluctant acceptance. 'So I would have been just as well off if I had never come to you.'

'A moment ago you said that you wanted to hear the truth.'

'Perhaps I only meant that I didn't want to know I was hearing a lie.' She tried to laugh at herself. 'I don't want you to tell my husband or anyone else, Mr Simpson. I'd like to choose the time myself.' She prepared to stand. 'Well – '

'You can't walk away yet, Mrs Laing. I can do a lot to help you – to get rid of the cough and to ease your breathing. I shall want to see you regularly; and if you have any discomfort I want to know about it at once. There's no need for you to suffer any pain. I'll prescribe some tablets now, though it may be a long time before you need to use them. Later on you can have something stronger.'

There was one more question to be asked. For all her

earlier strength, Ilsa could not put it, but Mr Simpson was experienced and sympathetic enough to guess what she did and did not want to know.

'You can do a lot to help yourself,' he told her. 'Keep out of smoky rooms and streets full of traffic fumes. Don't go out in fog. And I'll make two specific recommendations. Every cigarette you smoke helps to shorten your life. Most doctors nowadays would agree with that statement. I personally would go further and say that if you stop – not cut down, but stop – you can add a little time, recover some of what you've lost.'

Smoking had been one of Ilsa's pleasures as a young woman, one of her deprivations during the years of imprisonment. And after the war cigarettes had represented freedom and a form of wealth. Since her marriage to Richard she had never needed to be without a pack. Nevertheless, she felt confident that her will was stronger than her addiction. If she decided to give up the habit, it could be done. She reserved the decision for later consideration.

'It's less easy for me to be dogmatic about my other belief,' Mr Simpson confessed. 'Over the years I've had to give this prognosis, or something like it, to a good many patients. Some of them give up on the spot. I try to persuade them that they have years of good life ahead, but it almost seems as though they want to move straight into hospital and die. And because they want it, it happens. But there are others who have unfinished business. There's no valid medical reason why a mental determination to achieve something should slow down a physical invasion of the body. But it often happens.'

'Determination to live, do you mean?'

'That's how it may present itself. But the cause is usually more specific. A scientist has set his heart on finishing a piece of research. A young mother needs to care for her children until they're a little older. An old lady knows that her husband is dying and won't leave him to do it alone. Don't go back to your husband's books, Mrs Laing. Don't start studying all those charts which pretend to show expectations of life. It's too easy to forget that every average has to have a top figure as well as a bottom one. Remind yourself that you're exactly the same person that you were an hour ago. The facts haven't changed. Only your knowledge of them.'

That was not, in the circumstances, a very comforting statement. But the consultation was not over. There was more advice to be given, prescriptions to be written and explained. Controlled again after her outburst of disbelief, Ilsa listened, accepted, expressed polite gratitude, queued at the hospital pharmacy, departed.

Outside her house she paid off the taxi but did not go inside at once. Instead, she crossed the road and walked through the park at a pace brisk with anger. 'It's not fair!' How often, as a little boy, had Michael flung that accusation at her, his small body bursting with resentment. Ilsa, consoling him, had never contradicted the statement. From the moment of conception, life was unfair to everyone. But it was difficult to resist a feeling of bitterness now. She was in the prime of her life. It was hard to be brought up short just when her talent was gaining recognition. Had she not already suffered more in her lifetime than most people? Surely she deserved a little longer to prove that her survival had been worthwhile.

Calming herself, she turned into the rose garden. The June roses were at their best, still firmly shaped and delicately coloured, their petals not yet staining or twisting or falling. Ilsa paused in front of a formal bed of Peace and marvelled at the perfect form of each blossom and the subtle variations of colour – from cream to crimson, from primrose to peach. Had she ever properly appreciated the beauty of a rose before?

On this warm summer day, the scent of the roses was as soothing as their shape and colour. The better to appreciate it, Ilsa drew in a deep breath and at once found herself coughing uncontrollably. Passers-by – men and women who had already enjoyed twenty or thirty years more of life than she could expect – stared curiously or sympathetically as she clutched at the back of a park seat for support and gasped her way through the attack. Only after several moments was she able to breathe normally again.

She sat down, waiting to recover, and remembered another day when she had breathed deeply. At the age of twenty-three she had been hauled out of the cellar in which she had been sheltering a group of Jewish children. After three months with no sanitation and little ventilation, the atmosphere was foul, and there had been a few seconds in which the relief of filling her lungs with cold, pure air had kept at bay her fear of what might happen next. Then the German officer in charge of the orphanage had pointed his pistol at her head.

'I could shoot you,' he told her. 'Now. Here. I have the right.'

Ilsa had stood straight-backed in front of him, refusing to be afraid. Terror came later, as she was dragged away to join the children on their journey into the unknown – a terror not of death but of a life no longer under her own control. There was a sense in which she ought to think of herself not as unfortunate in hearing a death sentence now, but as lucky to have lived so long. She had had twenty years of borrowed time.

Another memory – triggered perhaps by the need to recall her past for Mr Simpson. This time she was lying on a bunk in Auschwitz, dying of typhus and dysentery – too weak to recognize that a brusque order to report to another hut and accept a change of work represented a chance of survival. The girl on the bunk above – Sigi Holzer, now long dead – had bullied Ilsa back to life, her voice reverberating inside an empty head. 'If you've given in, you might as well go on the fence, choose your own death. But if there's someone you love, something that you've dreamed of doing with your life, you've got to stay alive. For as long as it takes.'

'Going on the fence' meant flinging oneself against the electrified wires: it was the only means of escape from Auschwitz. Ilsa, painfully, had remembered her mother and the music which was already creeping into her mind. She had chosen to live – and for a little while, before better working conditions could have their effect, nothing but that choice had kept her alive.

What she had been told in Mr Simpson's consulting room was not dissimilar to the urgent words with which Sigi had urged her into activity. She still possessed the will to survive, for there was so much to be done: music to be written, friendships to be left in good repair. Her mother was dead: it was too late to weep over that final parting. But there were other relationships which needed attention. Richard had served notice before he left that he was not happy with things as they were. Ilsa resolved without hesitation that he must be given whatever he wanted. This was no time to bear grudges. With Michael, too, she must establish a new kind of friendship now that their true relationship was openly acknowledged between them.

Ilsa glanced at her watch and stood up. The immediate

138

timetable of her life was not changed by Mr Simpson's verdict, and Leo would be arriving at her house very soon. Three months earlier, curious to know why her friend's photograph should stand in Lady Glanville's drawing room, she had left a note for him at the Connaught Hotel, knowing that as soon as he was in England he would read it and get in touch with her. He had telephoned the previous evening.

There was one gesture to be made before she returned home. She felt in her handbag for the two packs of cigarettes which she always carried and tossed them into a litter bin. She was making a bargain with fate, following the doctor's advice and expecting a reward, to be measured in weeks or years. But now it was time to put her clouded future out of her mind and discover how much Leo knew about her new family, the Lorimers. In particular, there was one question to be asked. Had he ever met her mother?

139

6

'The Glanvilles saved my life,' said Leo. 'If it hadn't been for Pirry Glanville, I should have died. And if it hadn't been for Alexa Glanville, I should have gone mad.'

'You need to explain that.' Ilsa, while mentioning that she had seen her friend's signed photograph at Blaize, had given no reason for her unexpected interest in Lady Glanville and her family.

'I was living in Vienna at the time of the Anschluss,' Leo reminded her. 'My wrist had healed, but I had no money or work or reputation.'

Ilsa already knew of the hard times which Leo had faced in his teens. Born in Russia, he was a boy prodigy on the violin. But before his fifteenth birthday, his Jewish mother disappeared in one of Stalin's purges. His father, being a Georgian, must have believed himself safe; but the motor accident in which he died a few weeks later was hard to explain. Whether or not it had been expected that Leo would also be in the car, at the age of fourteen he found himself the orphaned son of disgraced parents, with a hand and wrist so badly injured that it seemed unlikely he would ever play the violin again. His homeland had ceased to be proud of him, and he in turn no longer felt safe in it. Vienna provided a refuge; but not for long.

'My papers were unconvincing,' he continued. 'The one thing they showed clearly was that I was Jewish. To be a Jew in Vienna in 1938 . . .! I was to be sent to a labour camp on my eighteenth birthday. Pirry smuggled

140

me out of Austria three weeks before that. He took a big risk for me. If you've met Pirry, you may think he looks soft. Such a charming man! Always smiling, as though nothing is important. But underneath – well, he saved my life. And took trouble afterwards to make sure that I could stay in England.'

'And Lady Glanville?'

'I shall never forget Alexa's face when Pirry asked if I could stay at Blaize.' Leo rocked with laughter at the memory. 'So thin I was in those days – half starved. Shabby. Anxious. And sea-sick – there had been a storm in the Channel. A miserable specimen. And Alexa, of course, thought I must be Pirry's latest lover.' He gave Ilsa a sideways glance. 'Do you know about Pirry? That he's a queer?'

'I didn't, no.' Ilsa had little interest in sex. She lacked both instinct and curiosity about the inclinations of the men she met. In any case, Pirry had been introduced to her as a relation, not a potential partner. 'It's not important. Go on.'

'Well, Alexa was horrified at first. But if you know her, you'll realize she's not one for half measures. Once it had been explained, she let me stay at Blaize. Gave me a practice room. Understood that what I needed was time and a lack of interruption. Soon I was able to play again, as well as before. But then the war began and I was declared to be an enemy alien! No one was sure whether I was Russian or Austrian – but what matter? In 1939, either way I must be an enemy. So I was interned.'

'And the Glanvilles rescued you again?'

'Pirry was already in the army. It was Alexa who made a fuss on my behalf, pointing out how ridiculous it was to suppose that a Jewish refugee would do anything to help Hitler. And why should the British taxpayer keep someone who could support himself if he was allowed to go off to New York? Luckily I already had a United States quota number. But it was Alexa who made it possible for me to go.'

'So when you came back to play in England after the war, did you sometimes visit her at Blaize?'

'Yes, of course.'

'And did you ever meet a relative of hers there – Dr Kate Lorimer?' According to Alexa, Kate had spent several years in residential work; but between appointments she had stayed at Blaize for weeks at a time.

'Once or twice, yes. She may have been there more often, but she usually stayed in her own suite when Alexa had visitors.'

'But you saw her?'

'Yes, in passing, from time to time. An old lady in a ginger wig. And now, Ilsa my dear, it's your turn to answer a question and explain why I'm undergoing this interrogation. What's your interest in the Glanvilles?'

'The old lady in the ginger wig was my mother,' said Ilsa.

'Ilsa, my darling!' More quickly than might have been expected in a man who had left his thin days far behind, Leo moved to sit beside her on the sofa, his arm holding her close. 'How cruel of me! I'm so sorry. I didn't know.'

'Nobody knew.' Ilsa felt drained by the mere fact of revealing what she had discovered.

'I'm so sorry,' he repeated. 'Your mother! And you never saw her in England? I know how much it would have meant to you. If only Alexa had told me more about her niece's background. Or if Dr Lorimer herself had been willing to talk. But I suppose it was painful for her. And it would never have occurred to me that an Englishwoman might be your mother.'

142

'Nor to me, of course. Well, it's too late now to be upset.'

'But you *are* upset.' His grip tightened round her shoulders. Ilsa, suffering from the shock of the consultant's news as well as from Lady Glanville's earlier revelations, allowed herself to sink into the comfort of his embrace. Comfort was all she needed, and all Leo was offering – but it was unfortunate, all the same, that this should be the moment when Richard came unexpectedly into the drawing room. Unfortunate, too, that Ilsa should be startled by his arrival into jerking away from Leo as though she felt guilty.

'Richard! We weren't expecting you back until tomorrow!' But that was a mistake as well; a tactless greeting to a husband returning after so long an absence.

'I left Melbourne early to avoid a strike. Don't let me disturb you. I've been on the move for thirty-six hours, given too much to eat and too much to drink, and I'm never any good at sleeping on planes. I'm going straight to bed now. By breakfast-time tomorrow I'll have my body-clock in sync. with British Summer Time. Give Michael my love when he comes in, Ilsa, but persuade him that I'd rather not be disturbed.' He nodded pleasantly at Leo and went upstairs.

'Richard!' Ilsa, dismayed, hurried after him. It was less than an hour since she had resolved to welcome her husband home with the warmth he wanted. Richard waited for her on the landing.

'I really am very tired,' he said. 'Completely flaked out, in fact. Pretend I'm not here. Coming home tomorrow, as planned.' He bent to kiss her lightly on the lips and then went into his bedroom and closed the door behind him.

In the drawing room Leo, unworried, was smiling. 'I hope Richard isn't a jealous man,' he said. 'It would rile me to be suspected of something that I've never in fact been allowed to enjoy. I'll leave you to make your peace with him. But I have two tickets for Glyndebourne on the last day of June. Will you join me?'

'I'd be delighted.' She held out her hand, expecting him as usual to raise it to his lips, but instead he took her in his arms, and his kiss comforted her for a second time.

Leo Tavadze was the man whom Ilsa might have loved, had she only known him earlier in her life. They had met soon after the war, introduced by music. Seeking an interpreter whose reputation could carry the burden of her unknown name and difficult music, Ilsa had sent the score of a violin concerto to the famous soloist in New York. On his next visit to London he asked her to call at his hotel, and they found themselves immediately in sympathy.

On the face of it, they were very different. Ilsa's sufferings at the hands of the Germans had left her tightly controlled, while Leo had celebrated his escape from a concentration camp with laughter and good food and wine in pleasant company. He had grown plump, while Ilsa was thin; his expression was good-natured where Ilsa's was cool; his eyes shone with enthusiasm while Ilsa's neutrally observed. When he fell in love with her – and it happened very quickly – he pressed his suit with exuberance, followed by over-acted despair. When Ilsa found herself beginning to love him in return, her defence was to withdraw, to force coldness into her voice as she reminded him that she was married. At the time she had seen this as an example of fidelity, and only later wondered whether she had genuinely resisted temptation, or had never felt it. Leo had been her closest friend for the past thirteen years, and he provided the second exception to her dislike of physical contact. She could accept

Michael's hugs because she had known his healthy body from babyhood. She was equally at ease with Leo but for a different reason. They had both been refugees: they had both suffered. In a smug, safe world they had in common the memory of insecurity as well as the veneer of success.

As he held her in his arms that afternoon, Leo must have believed that he was comforting Ilsa only for the loss of her mother. He could not have guessed at the other void which had just opened beneath her feet. That night she lay awake for a long time, keeping very still, as though listening to her body and taking it unawares she could find some evidence that Mr Simpson had told her the truth. But it seemed that only one of his statements was immediately confirmed: she felt no physical difference from the day before. Only her mental state had changed. She saw the future as a clock out of control, its hands whizzing madly round and round while her mind raced to keep up with it. From now on, everything would be either unimportant or urgent.

Building her bridges with Richard was one of the urgencies, yet she was unprepared when he came into her bedroom early in the morning. Refreshed by more than twelve hours uninterrupted sleep, he was ready to begin the new day with the sunrise – whilst to Ilsa, who had been awake until three in the morning, it was still the middle of the night. Feeling the side of the bed tilt beneath his weight as he sat down, she struggled to open her eyes. Her chest was heavy and her throat thick: she needed to sit up and establish her diurnal pattern of breathing. But Richard, looking seriously down at her, was demanding her full attention.

'Too early for a night bird like you, I know,' he said. 'But I've got something important to tell you. While I was in the States, I was asked if I'd set up an allergy clinic – a new Laing clinic – in Oregon. There's a lot of investment money around for private medicine. It's an attractive offer – giving me a share in a custom-built clinic equipped to my specification – in return for the use of my name and methods and my own presence there for the whole of the first year and three months in each subsequent year.'

'What about your work here?'

'I've got good people on the staff; people I've trained myself. Like any sort of detective work, most of my treatment depends on a meticulous routine of tests rather than the flair of one man. I could leave the clinics here in sound hands while I'm establishing the same routines over there. I believe I could make myself useful in the States. And it would be highly profitable.'

'So you've decided to go?'

'Yes. That makes it all the more important for me to ask the question which I put to you before I left. You've always said that you could compose in a cupboard if you needed to, so there shouldn't be any problem about a mountainside in Oregon. I hope that you'll agree to come with me. But first of all, we need to have a talk.'

Ilsa had had three months to consider the ultimatum he had put to her on her birthday, but it was the hour in Mr Simpson's consulting room which had concentrated her mind. Richard had been so good to her in the past, and she was so grateful to him, that she must repay her debt now by giving him whatever he wanted – whether that proved to be a divorce or a new beginning to their marriage – without reserve.

'I know you were hurt when you found out about Penny,' he said. 'I apologized to you then, but you haven't been able to forgive me, have you? For three

146

years. Well, now I'll say again how sorry I am that I upset you. But this time – '

'I'd like – ' Ilsa paused to clear the huskiness from her throat. 'I'd like to explain *why* I was hurt. It wasn't just jealousy. It was the humiliation of being deceived. I think I could have lived with the discovery if Penny had been a stranger. It was thinking of her as a friend – looking back afterwards and remembering all the times when I'd chatted and smiled without guessing. To be kept out of a secret has a curious kind of hurtfulness. But you're right that three years is too long to bear a grudge.'

'Are you saying – ?'

'I'm saying that I'm sorry for over-reacting.' She was almost tempted to laugh as she saw the astonishment in his eyes. This was not the answer he had expected. But after only a second, surprise was banished by tenderness.

'So can we start again?' His hand touched her cheek softly, stroking it as though to test whether she would shrink away.

'Is that what you want?'

'Of course that's what I want.' He leaned down and began to kiss her, gently at first but then with a sudden passionate force. Ilsa willed herself to relax the tenseness which so often in the past had spoiled their love-making. She needed to breathe deeply, but the weight of Richard's body was pressing down on her congested chest while his tongue filled her mouth. So important did it seem for her to give herself to Richard without reserve that for a moment she managed to resist the panic of suffocation. But her muscles tightened: she felt herself choking, unable to breathe at all. It was necessary to push him away as she began to cough.

This was the most violent paroxysm she had yet experienced. Gasping for breath whenever she could she got

147

out of bed and, supporting herself against the wall, staggered into the bathroom where the linctus which Mr Simpson had prescribed was waiting. By the time Richard followed her in she was sitting on the bathroom chair with her head buried in her hands and her breath coming in short, wheezing gasps. 'Sorry,' she said. 'Terribly sorry.'

Richard's smile was disappointed but affectionate as he looked down at her. 'You really should cut down on your smoking,' he said, as he had said often before.

'I've given up. I stopped yesterday. It seems unfair that such an effort shouldn't be rewarded by immediate relief. Sorry, Richard.'

'Come back to bed.' He piled up the pillows so that she could sit with their support at her back. Then for a second time he sat down on the bed. 'We'll wait until tonight. What do a few hours matter? And perhaps in any case it would be tidier if I were to speak to Penny first. Finish everything off neatly.'

'Penny? You've still been seeing Penny?'

'Not since I went off in February. But before that, yes, of course. You may have found it easy to behave like a nun for these last three years, but you didn't imagine that I'd been living like a monk, did you?'

'But – ' Ilsa found herself stammering with the need to adjust her earlier decision to a situation which she should have anticipated. A few hours earlier it had been incontrovertible that gratitude should express itself in the restoration of a loving marriage relationship which would offer Richard pleasure now, and later would comfort him with the thought that before she died they had ended the coolness which had grown between them. But it would be no kindness to let him end a love affair which might last him for the rest of his life for the sake of only a year or two with a sick wife. 'That's not necessary, Richard. I told you,' it was the humiliation before. If I know about it, that's different. I want to give you something, not take something away. I'd like to feel that you had her love as well as mine.'

'I'm a one-woman-at-a-time man,' Richard said. 'And you'd hardly suggest that I should invite Penny to follow us to America for the pleasure of watching you and me settle in together. She knows that I want to make my peace with you. She knew before I went away. I think, as a matter of fact – ' Richard hesitated before deciding to continue. 'I think she'd like to find a husband now, and have children. She's not getting any younger.'

'Does she want to marry you?'

'Obviously she sees that she can't.'

'I should put it the other way.' Ilsa got out of bed again and put on her dressing-gown. 'Do you want to marry *her*, Richard?'

'I don't care to live alone. I want to live as a married man. Well, I *am* married. To you. This is what I want – to live with you again, as we did before.'

'But I'm not sure – '

'Only a moment ago you said – '

'I thought you were lonely.' Ilsa began to pace the room. 'I felt a responsibility. I wanted to end this coldness, as you asked, so that we could be friends again. For the rest, I'll try, but – I don't think you ought to send Penny away.'

'For Christ's sake!' In his working life Richard was endlessly patient. Perhaps because such control did not come easily to a man who by nature was emotional, his temper was quick to flare outside the clinic. 'Can't I have a mind of my own? First you refuse to share me with

149

Penny and then you insist on it. What do you want, for God's sake?'

'I want you to be happy. You've been so generous to me. I'm looking for a way to be generous in return.'

'Your generosity presents itself as something very much like rejection. Have you ever loved me, Ilsa? Not just waited to do your duty as a wife, but longed for me to hold you? God, you're so beautiful! But why do you think I needed Penny in the first place? Because you've never behaved with any warmth or shown any passion. You gave me what you thought I wanted because you were grateful, I suppose – for being helped back to health, for being rescued from Europe, for having the time and money to indulge in an unprofitable profession. Well, gratitude is a very cold emotion. And I never asked you to be grateful. Only to love me. Do you love me? Show me. Now.'

He snatched her fiercely into his arms and pressed her head back with the force of his kiss. The position was uncomfortable, but this time it was not a fit of coughing which made it impossible for Ilsa to respond. Instead, her body stiffened with a pain in her chest which increased as though a band of steel, encircling it, was being steadily tightened. Only a day earlier she had told Mr Simpson that she had felt no pain. When he gave her the tablets he had known, she supposed, that this would come, but she was unable to move to reach them. She needed Richard now as a doctor; but the pain was so intense that she found herself holding her breath, and could not speak.

Aware of her rigidity, and misunderstanding it, Richard pushed her away with a mutter of exasperation, so that she staggered and fell on her knees beside the bed. A little time passed before she was able to exhale and then, with a series of exhausted grunts, begin to breathe normally again. She expected Richard to speak, perhaps understanding what had happened: but when at last she was able to raise her head, she saw that he had already left the room.

For some time, collapsed on the bed, she was unhappy, needing someone in whom she could confide. But Richard was a compassionate man, and the truth would hold him at her side. Rather than leave his wife to be ill alone, he would send Penny away. However comforting that might be for Ilsa herself, it would not be fair to tie him in such a way – and this unfairness, unlike the other, she had the power to prevent. As her strength and courage returned, she recognized that she must let him go.

7

Leo was too fat and Ilsa, these days, too easily tired. They laughed at each other as they struggled up the slippery grass of the downland. Leo had booked two rooms in a hotel near to Glyndebourne, so that they could avoid the long drive back to London after the opera. This arrangement held another advantage: they would be able to change in comfort before the perform- ance, while other opera-goers were struggling into their dinner jackets behind some Sussex hedgerow or arriving at Victoria station in mid-afternoon wearing evening dress. There was nothing wrong with that part of the plan: but in addition they had agreed to spend the whole day in the country.

'Such an expedition makes it appear faintly possible that I'm not in the peak of condition,' Leo admitted, mocking himself. 'If one leads the life of a decadent townsman, one should lead it consistently. Whose ridicu- lous idea was this, that we should *walk*? And I an American now!'

Ilsa joined in his laughter. She never thought of herself as temperamental, but nowadays could hardly keep up with her own changes of mood. Today she was euphoric, putting out of her mind everything Mr Simpson had told her. Since Richard's departure there had been no return of the terrible pain in her chest; and, as the surgeon had promised, abstinence from smoking had combined with the linctus he prescribed to effect a dramatic reduction in her coughing. There were times – and this was one of

152

them – when she felt sure that there was nothing wrong with her.

'I hope Richard doesn't mind you deserting him for the night like this,' said Leo – taking for granted, no doubt, an answer quite different from the one he received.

'He doesn't even know I'm here. He deserted me first, rather more permanently.'

Why had she told Leo that? His surprise at hearing the words could not be any greater than her own at speaking them. They had emerged without premeditation, but to Leo her statement must have sounded like a significant declaration. His silence suggested that he was seriously considering implications which she had not intended.

'I shouldn't have said that. I don't know why I did. It's only happened since I last saw you, and perhaps I haven't come to terms with it yet. The official story – for Michael's benefit – is that Richard has gone back to America to start a new clinic; and I have to keep a home going in England for Michael himself while he's still at school. He's taking his A-levels and the Cambridge scholarship examination this year. That version's true enough – but it implies a reunion which isn't likely to happen.'

'Does that upset you?'

'As a marriage, it ended three years ago. One must always feel sad, I suppose, to fail in a relationship. But I hope – ' She and Richard had had two meetings in the past three weeks. They had both been businesslike and polite. There was no reason why they should quarrel now and perhaps, if there was time, they could become friends again. Anxious to end this conversation, she turned to lead the way down the hill towards Leo's hired Daimler.

At the door of her room in the hotel, Ilsa looked at her watch. They must be in their seats at Glyndebourne before half past four. 'I shall take a bath,' she said. 'But I'll be very quick.'

'No rush. I'll come for you in about forty minutes.' Leo went to his own room, further down the corridor.

Ilsa unpacked her evening dress and hung it up before going into the private bathroom. Above the sound of splashing water a few minutes later she heard the door of her bedroom open and close. She went back to find Leo standing there.

'Ilsa my dear.' He sat down on one side of the bed, stretching out his hand so that she also had to sit in order to reach it. 'Is it really necessary for us to go to the opera? *The Magic Flute*, after all! What is it, when all is said and done? A Masonic publicity stunt. A fantastic vehicle for a few extravagant displays of vocal pyrotechnics. All very well to pass the time when no more satisfying experience is to hand, but – the evening will be interminably long. And it's not as though we can't imagine it all, is it?'

Ilsa hesitated. But why not, she thought; why not? How could she pretend to be surprised, when she had given him what he must have seen as an invitation? Although she felt no passionate excitement, Leo might not expect this of her. He probably saw it as an opportunity for them both to demonstrate the love they had felt for each other as friends for so long. Why not? 'Then let us imagine it,' she said, smiling at him with gaiety in her eyes.

Leo flung himself backward on the bed, pulling her with him.

'You're wearing your beautiful dress.' His free hand waved toward the gown of emerald silk hanging on the back of the door. 'You are the most beautiful woman at Glyndebourne today, as I am indubitably the most

154

distinguished man. I begin to see the advantages of imagination over reality. Everyone stares as we step with dignity from the Daimler. We wander through the gardens. The wilderness is especially attractive today. The salvia, though, I find out of keeping.'

'Ah, but the delphiniums!' exclaimed Ilsa. 'The wonderful shades of the blue garden! Have we time to walk round the lake?'

'I think not now. The first warning is about to sound. Our seats are upstairs, in the front row. The young man next to you will be seeing the opera for the first time, I suspect. He is reading the synopsis of the plot with great attention. A wise precaution, if I may say so, sir.'

'Ssh!' said Ilsa. 'Whatever happens afterwards, the overture at least makes sense.'

'Um pum pum pum pum pum diddle diddle, *um* pum pum pum pum pum,' began Leo, and Ilsa joined in lightly, faster and faster until she ran out of breath. 'Quiet!' she commanded, and they were happily silent for a few moments.

'The supper interval,' announced Leo at last. 'I left the hamper so generously provided by the Connaught in the sunken garden. So! Caviar, cold duckling and orange salad, and – naturally – strawberries and cream. Even a refrigerated ice pack for the champagne. A simple meal, but I trust it suffices.'

'Even an hour and a half has been hardly long enough. There's still no time for that walk round the lake.'

'Back to our seats. The plot grows even more preposterous. But Pamina has completely won my heart. How delightful that at last a slim waist is regarded by opera directors as being almost as important as a beautiful voice.'

'Except perhaps at Covent Garden,' said Ilsa.

'Any statement about opera implies the qualification, except perhaps at Covent Garden. Here comes the conductor.'

They were quiet again until Leo gave the signal to applaud. Ilsa stretched lazily on the bed. 'There's no point in hurrying to the car. We shall still have to wait before we can get out of the field.'

'But this is still part of the evening,' Leo reminded her. 'This snake of expensive cars, nose to tail along a country lane. As we wait for our turn the leader is climbing out of sight, over the hills and far away. Soon he will be racing along the empty roads to London, whilst we need make only this short journey to Lewes. The night porter lets us in, and we walk up the stairs together.' He turned his head to look at Ilsa.

'The evening is over,' she said. 'We're back where we started. My bath is running. And unless I turn the tap off soon, the manager will be knocking on the door, complaining of a flood.'

'Be very quick.'

Ilsa nodded her head and went into the bathroom. Just in time, she pulled out the plug and turned off the tap. The two actions took less than a second, but that was long enough for a doubt to be born in her mind. She took off her bathrobe and used it to wipe the condensation off the full-length mirror. With critical eyes she studied her own body.

She was too thin. Perhaps that had also been true when Leo first fell in love with her years ago; but then, covered by expensive clothes, her thinness had disguised itself as elegance. Without their concealment she looked bony. Her thighs, not sufficiently firmed out by flesh, were unhealthily pale; there was a gauntness in the hollows beside her collar bone; and the skin of her shoulders and breasts, whose whiteness had always been part of her cool beauty, was becoming somehow grey. No, surely, that could not be true – it must be only the new condensation of the steam as it blurred her image on the glass. But nothing could explain away the scrawniness of her long body. How could Leo possibly love a woman like this – and by daylight, now, in the afternoon? Could she bear to see disappointment in his eyes.

And there was something else: a deeper doubt. How often in the past had her old nightmare come between herself and Richard – the irrational terror that he would somehow break through the superficial skin of her beauty and touch the rottenness and decay within. At the time it had seemed merely a fantasy, but now it was true. Her body was indeed unhealthy and imperfect, and she could not bear to offer it to Leo. There could be no question about the depth of her affection for him. But they had missed their chance of loving each other thirteen years earlier: it was too late now.

Leo was still lying on the bed when, once again wearing her bathrobe, she came back into the room and stood still, not knowing what to say.

'Leo, my darling,' she began, and then shook her head helplessly, trying to laugh at her own incoherence. 'Leo, I'm so sorry – I just don't feel – I can't – '

He held out his hand and she went over to sit on the bed beside him – just as she had sat, laughing, only a short time earlier.

'You don't love me?' he asked.

'I love you as much as ever – oh, more than before. But perhaps that was never in this way. I'm frightened of changing whatever it is that we've shared. I want to stay as I am with you. To be not less, but not more either.' She could feel his hand squeezing her own and then

157

releasing the pressure, although perhaps he was not conscious of the movement. Then he drew her down to kiss him. It was the moment when he might have held her fast, refusing to accept her reluctance. But instead he was gentle, stroking her hair and neck: and when he allowed her to sit up again she saw that the smile in his eyes was understanding.

'You don't mind!' she exclaimed. 'You're not angry at all. You didn't really want me, did you?'

'I wanted exactly what you wanted, and to find that you want it too is the most wonderful thing. I want us to stay as we are.'

'Then why – ?'

'You told me that Richard had left you. It was something you might have kept secret, and so I knew that the news must be important. I misjudged the type of importance, that's all. I thought I must choose either to advance or to retreat. I couldn't bear to lose you – to think that you might look elsewhere for comfort. And of course – ' he laughed aloud – 'the prospect of making love to you was extremely pleasant. I'm only confessing, since you've given me the lead, that I'm just as comfortable not making love.'

'What a lazy man you are, Leo!' It was a measure of her relief that she dared to tease him.

'Well, you see, Ilsa, there's no one else like you in my life. If you were to become one of the women I've slept with, something would certainly have been gained, but also something would have been lost.'

'Then you shouldn't have pretended.'

'There was no pretence. One can prefer one course of action without necessarily regarding the alternative as anything but delightful. I know what you mean, though.

158

Perhaps the best thing about this delightful day is that you trusted me enough to be honest.'

Ilsa was silent. She had not, after all, been completely honest. In the three weeks since she heard the doctor's verdict on her health she had longed to confide in someone: to tell the truth – to say directly, 'I'm dying.' Michael was too young, and Richard had not waited. She would never be able to tell him now, for fear that pity would bring him back against his true wishes, or that guilt at abandoning her would turn his new life sour. She had hoped to look to Leo for comfort, since he had been her confidant for so many years. But when it came to the point, she saw that she could not disturb his comfortable life with such a confession. It was the end of another illusion. She had already recognized the limitations of her own love for Leo. Now she was forced to acknowledge that Leo's love for her had its own restrictions: he would not want to be burdened with the truth.

'I love you, Leo,' she said. It was curious, and sad, that she should speak the words for the first time now, just as they ceased to be of importance.

Leo kissed her. There was no passion in the kiss, no desire and there never would be again; but they were both happy with it. He looked at his watch.

'You know,' he said, 'if I dispense with an extra shave, I could be dressed in ten minutes. Could you step into your magnificent gown in the same time? Because it might still not be too late for the opera.'

8

The message from Asha Lorimer was brief and surprising. 'Can you come to tea on Saturday? Please try. Four o'clock.' Ilsa, curious, decided at once that she would go.

The address was in the Portobello Road, whose antique shops and stalls were thronged with tourists and browsers. Recognizing that it would be quicker to walk the last hundred yards, Ilsa dismissed her taxi at the end of the road. She rang the bell on a shabby door squeezed between two shops. Inside, footsteps hurried down a flight of stairs and the door was opened by a young man with a dark skin and an intelligent face. 'I am Ranji,' he said.

As they shook hands, Ilsa remembered the name from her first visit to Blaize, when Alexa had nagged Asha about her young Indian protégé.

'Shall I lead the way?' he suggested. In any case, there would hardly have been room for Ilsa to squeeze past him. She followed him up the dark, narrow stairs and through a second door, and was agreeably surprised to emerge into a large and very light living room. Perhaps the brightness was due to the absence of curtains – and the impression of size to the paucity of furniture.

'We were given possession only yesterday,' explained Ranji. 'And we thought it would be sensible to redecorate before moving our furniture in.' Like Ilsa herself, he pronounced each syllable with more precision than a native-born Englishman and there was in his intonation a very slight lilt, resembling that of a Welshman; but apart from that he spoke English perfectly. Ilsa was just working out the implication of what he had said when Asha appeared to confirm her conclusion.

'My dear, how lovely you look!' Ilsa's compliment was sincere. Asha's long and very fair hair gleamed as though each strand had been individually polished, and her pale face for once was flushed. She wore a dress of silky turquoise which clung round her slim waist before flaring out into a swirling skirt which seemed to crackle with an excitement of its own. She laughed with a mixture of delight and disappointment as she saw Ilsa look at her left hand.

'Oh! You've guessed! Yes, Ranji and I were married this morning.'

'Congratulations!' Was this an occasion for kissing the strange young man as well as her cousin? Yes it was, although he was shy about receiving the gesture as she was in making it. 'And to you, Mrs – ?'

'Mrs Ranjidambaram. Isn't it a mouthful?' Asha giggled happily. 'My pupils will never get their tongues round it. I shall go on being called Miss Lorimer at school. Like an actress with a stage name. Ilsa, I want to explain straightaway why we didn't invite you to the wedding itself. The thing is, I'm afraid Aunt Alexa isn't going to approve. She'll come round to it, of course, but for the moment . . . So we didn't tell her in advance, in case she got worked up. And if we didn't tell her, we couldn't tell anyone else in the family. Because she'll phone everyone up and ask why she wasn't warned. We didn't think that would be fair on people. This way, you can all truthfully say that you didn't know. Well, when I say all, I mean you and Bernard and Helen. I don't really know my cousin John, and Paula's working on a story in New York and Pirry lives in France. Look, do sit down. The last people left this enormous sofa behind because they couldn't get it down the stairs. Heaven knows how they got it up.'

Asha was chattering out of nervousness as well as excitement, Ilsa realized as she accepted the seat. 'Remind me about Bernard. You did tell me, I know, but I was so worked up about my mother at the time that I didn't take it in.'

'Bernard's a Lorimer, like I was, not a Glanville like Pirry. His mother – Aunt Alexa's daughter by her first marriage – married a cousin, which is how the Lorimer name got back to Bernard again. When he was still a boy he inherited a baronetcy and a shipping line and some docks and a mansion in Bristol. Some of the property was nationalized and he sold the rest and put the money into a research laboratory near Cambridge. He's clever as well as rich. He hires all the brightest chaps coming out of the university and works with them himself, and he's got his own factory so that whenever they come up with some wonder drug they can churn it out themselves and put the profits back into inventing something else.'

He arrived at that moment, a tousled, bright-eyed man in his late thirties. Whatever he spent his money on, it was certainly not clothes, Ilsa thought – but their crumpled, casual style was appropriate to the rest of his appearance. His red hair was curly, and any attempt which he might have made to control its springiness was wrecked by his habit of running his fingers upwards through the curls. His face – soft and friendly – was almost as crumpled as his clothes, etched with deep lines in unexpected places. They were lines of thought rather than worry, Ilsa decided, watching as he hugged Asha affectionately and then turned to acknowledge the introduction to herself.

162

'No Helen?' asked Asha. She had naturally invited Bernard's wife to her party as well.

'She's in hospital for a couple of days, I'm afraid.'

'I'm sorry. Nothing serious, I hope.'

'"Observation" is the word. Hoping to clear up something that's been dragging on. No, not serious, just a nuisance. Women are very complicated, aren't they?' He addressed this remark to Ranji. 'Asha, you haven't finished the introductions.'

'I was just coming to that. This is Ranji. My husband.'

'My God! Have you really done it! Grandmother will be furious! Oh, not about you, I don't mean,' he said, shaking Ranji's hand vigorously. 'It's just that I'm sure she was longing to give Asha a real send-off. The last of the great country-house weddings. Borrowing back the school's part of the house for a day during the holidays. I can see it now – the ballroom back in use, with half the county invited, and the banqueting hall laid out with expensive presents, and photographers and bridesmaids, and the bride sweeping down the aisle of the village church, wearing the family jewels and hundreds of yards of white tulle. A cake to be cut and lots of speeches full of almost-dirty jokes. Confetti and champagne and tin cans tied to the car. How could you rob her of all that, Asha!'

'You're making a very convincing case for this morning's registry office affair,' Asha said. 'And cake and champagne at least we can have. Sit down, Bernard, while I fetch a few things.'

He sat next to Ilsa and talked about her mother, guessing that this was what she would like to hear. Ranji hovered nearby, smiling to indicate that he was part of the conversation despite knowing nothing of the subject.

The party appeared to be complete and they were all surprised when the doorbell rang.

'Ranji, will you?' called Asha from the kitchen. 'It can't be anyone for us, because no one knows we're here, so send them away.'

As Ranji disappeared down the stairs, Asha pushed in a laden trolley, on which a home-made wedding cake held pride of place. She had made cucumber sandwiches as well, delicately thin triangles with their crusts trimmed off; and scones still warm from the oven; and jam tarts; and brandy snaps filled with cream; and a chocolate cake layered with butter icing. 'Good heavens!' exclaimed Ilsa, who never ate tea. 'What a feast!'

'I can't cook anything sensible,' Asha explained. 'Aunt Alexa let me go into the kitchen and pester the cook for a lesson whenever I liked, but I always asked to be taught sweets or cakes. My real speciality is fudge.' She turned in surprise as Ranji returned with a companion. 'Pirry!' Asha flung herself into her cousin's arms. 'I didn't know you were in England. What marvellous timing! You've arrived just in time to celebrate my wedding. The first champagne cork is about to pop.'

'Wedding? Did you say your wedding?'

Ilsa and Bernard smiled at each other as Pirry recovered from his astonishment and was introduced to Ranji. His nature appeared to be a placid one, for by the time he had murmured all the right phrases and turned to Ilsa, his startled expression had been replaced by the warm smile which she remembered from their first meeting.

'I'm delighted to see you here, Ilsa. I was intending to get in touch while I was in England because I have a request – but later, perhaps.' His expressive face revealed anxiety as he watched Ranji preparing to open the first bottle of champagne. 'The world,' he murmured sotto voce to Ilsa, 'is divided into those who were born with a champagne cork between their fingers and those who were not. Ranji!' he called more loudly. 'I must insist now on being regarded as the bride's father. Allow me to take charge of the drinks, in order that you and Asha can hold hands bashfully while we drink to your future happiness.'

'Now you see why we didn't want to be married at Blaize,' laughed Asha as Pirry's practised hands set the champagne flowing. 'We knew we shouldn't be allowed to organize anything for ourselves.'

'Never do anything for yourself if you can find someone else to do it for you. Here's to you, then, Asha and Ranji. Health and happiness. No, you can't drink to yourselves. You have to wait until you toast the guests.'

Only a few moments earlier, Ilsa, like Bernard, had felt sorry that Asha should have deprived herself of a party that she could remember all her life. But Pirry threw himself with such gusto into the role of life and soul of the party that the tiny gathering was magically transformed into the right social occasion. Appropriating the roles of bride's father and best man, he and Bernard told the kind of stories that Asha had hoped to escape, laughing at their own jokes while they ate a hearty tea. Their boisterousness was kindly meant, and Asha, flushed with happiness as she shared a cushion on the floor with her husband, joined in the laughter out of gratitude for their tact in turning the tea-party into a celebration. It was left to Ilsa, herself an outsider in the family group, to realize that Ranji was not only excluded from their family references but shocked by some of their jokes. But he did his best to share in the fun, smiling at each of them in turn.

When they had emptied the plates of scones and

sandwiches, eaten token slices of rich fruit cake and finished off the champagne, Pirry stood up to leave.

'But you haven't explained how you come to be here!' exclaimed Asha.

'That's easy. I called at your old chummery and was given your new address.'

'But why today? I mean, it's marvellous to see you. But you couldn't possibly have known it was a special day.'

'Well, I happened to be in town and I wanted to have a chat. To make some plans for Mother. But it can wait.'

'It doesn't need to wait. We're all family here.' Asha's arm tightened round Ranji's waist.

Pirry looked round the room and then sat down again. 'Yes, of course,' he agreed. 'All family. Well, I've come to look for somewhere Mother might live. Not now, but some time in the future.'

'Why does she need anywhere?' demanded Asha. 'The wheelchair business isn't serious, you know. She can potter about the house and garden perfectly well. And she's had one of those chair lifts installed to take her up the stairs on her bad days. She'll never leave Blaize.'

'Unfortunately, there are some circumstances – highly remote, but needing to be considered – in which she might have to leave.'

'Only if – ' Asha checked herself and stared, startled, at her cousin. 'Pirry, you're not ill, are you?'

'Definitely not. Fit as a fiddle. It's because Mother would ask exactly that question that I need to move with circumspection.'

'But if there's nothing wrong – '

'I'm not ill, but I'm prepared to recognize that I'm not immortal, either. A few weeks ago, the chap I was swimming with suddenly had a heart attack in his own

166

pool and sank like a stone. Only forty-six – four years younger than I am. I couldn't help thinking that if it had been me instead, it would have left Mother in an awful mess. I may believe – I *do* believe – that I'm good for another thirty years. But I don't propose to give up any of the things I enjoy. I shall continue to eat good meals and drink good wine, occasionally in excess, and I ought to recognize the possibility that the clock might suddenly stop. Put it this way. It can't do any harm for me to take a few precautions, and I shall feel easier when it's done. I do have a responsibility to Mother, after all.'

'Yes.' Suddenly Asha did not look happy any more. She turned to Ilsa to explain. 'Blaize is entailed, you see. And Pirry hasn't got any children. There's a branch of the Glanvilles hovering up in Scotland, just waiting to move in.'

'You mustn't believe everything Mother tells you,' Pirry said mildly. 'They're an ordinary decent lot. The one she hated so much died years ago and his son doesn't even know that there was ever a quarrel. However, that's beside the point. It's true that he will eventually inherit Blaize. Not only the house, but the whole estate, and the rents that go with it. Also a capital fund which was set up after the Park Lane house was bombed. So there would be two separate problems over Mother. The money problem and the housing problem.'

He looked round the room, smiling pleasantly. 'You shouldn't have asked me about this, you know. Weddings and funerals bring together the same people and very much the same food and drink, but their atmospheres aren't compatible. Even when the funeral is as hypothetical as this one. Are you sure you want me to go on?'

Nobody spoke; but Ilsa, watching Asha's face, saw her nod.

'Well then, I've dealt with the money. I've bought Mother an annuity. It came quite cheaply for someone who's already eighty-six – how is a mere actuary to know that she's indestructible? And I have a life assurance policy going in her favour. She could invest the proceeds to provide more income, or spend the capital a bit at a time – at five thousand a year, say, it would last her till her hundredth birthday. That should do, I hope. I don't want her to have any anxiety. But I have responsibilities in France as well.'

'So are you going to buy her another house?' asked Asha.

'Not a whole one. I don't see the point. Agreed, Mother's managed marvellously until now, but it's bound to get more difficult. She won't want to deal with staff, and she won't want so much space. Have you read about these country mansions which are being converted into homes for elderly people? You buy a couple of rooms, good-sized rooms, and put your own furniture in them. There's a manager to see that they get cleaned, and you can eat in the dining room and enjoy the grounds and it's only a question of money, not responsibility. In a place like that, Mother could feel that she was still living in some kind of style, but there'd be someone around to notice if she was ill. This is really why I came today, Asha. To ask whether you thought it would be a good idea for me to buy into something of that sort – and whether you'd come with me to inspect a suitable place. Because if the situation were ever to arise, I should rely on you actually to deal with it. You haven't quarrelled with her, have you, about this marriage?'

Asha shook her head. 'She doesn't know that it's happened. She may be angry at first, but I expect she'll accept it when she realizes that it can't be changed. She

168

may cut off from me for a bit, but I shan't ever cut off from her. After all, she's been almost as much of a mother to me as she has to you.'

'That's my girl!' Pirry stood up again. 'And having thus effectively put a damper on the conversation, I'll leave you to share the first washing-up of your married life. Ranji, my dear chap, I do apologize for flinging you into a cauldron of family affairs like this. But the feeling of being stifled by in-laws is an essential ingredient of any wedding day. I hope the other essential ingredients prove rather more enjoyable.' He hugged Asha warmly and left her to start her honeymoon. Ilsa and Bernard followed him down the stairs.

9

Down in the Portobello Road, Ilsa automatically looked round to estimate the chance of finding a taxi, but Pirry put one hand on her arm and the other on Bernard's. 'One more drink,' he said. 'The pubs will be open now. And I feel the need to dissipate the gloom.'

'If you're genuinely as fit as you claim, what is there to be gloomy about?' asked Bernard suspiciously.

'Oh, it's nothing to do with myself. But that marriage! A mistake, don't you agree? You'll come with us, won't you, Ilsa? The quickest way to feel part of a family is to join in the post-mortems.'

Ilsa was not by nature a gossip, but the circumstances which had precipitated her into this unknown family were bound to make her curious. 'Why are you so sure it's a mistake?' she asked, after they had settled themselves at a table with their drinks. 'I hardly know Asha and I've never met Ranji before, so I can't make any judgement myself.'

'None of us – except my grandmother – has met Ranji before,' Bernard told her. 'That's a bad sign in itself. A girl who felt confident about her choice would want to show him off, surely.'

'I'd find it simple to describe the kind of man Asha *ought* to have married,' said Pirry. 'She was only six when she was orphaned, and my mother was already seventy when she took charge of her. So Asha has had no experience of normal family life. She should have married the son of two happily-married parents so that she could

170

adopt his way of living. One has to learn from observation how married people cope with each other. Instead, she's picked a man whose relations are thousands of miles away – a man from a different culture. She probably doesn't know what he expects of a wife, and in a foreign country he may not know himself.'

'That means that they'll have to work harder at their marriage than most people,' Ilsa agreed. 'But won't it be easier, in the circumstances, that neither of them has a pattern to which they must conform? They'll make their own pattern.'

'Possibly. But there's another thing. Asha's parents were cousins. She's a Lorimer through both sides of her family. Bernard will agree with me that all the Lorimer women seem to have certain characteristics in common. Different talents, but always a great deal of determination.'

'I remember Asha telling me that herself,' Ilsa agreed. 'Positive achievers, I think she called them all.'

'Yes. Well. Because Asha's been brought up by a woman – my mother – who was genuinely famous in her youth, she may feel that she can't, doesn't *want* to live up to whatever is expected of her. But she's an intelligent and efficient girl. What she does, she does well. At the moment she may believe that she isn't ambitious and that it's enough to show her independence by escaping from Mother. But one day the Lorimer genes will prove too strong for her. She'll start to organize her own life. And then – in my opinion – she'll need to have a husband whose own life is sufficiently well-organized for him to stand up to her; otherwise he'll just go under. And what has she chosen? Someone younger than herself. Still at university, so he hasn't got a job or much money. Someone who may or may not meet prejudice on account of his colour, but who certainly hasn't got the kind of contacts to give him a good start. In other words, an insecure young man.'

'You're assuming that Ranji isn't a strong character,' said Ilsa. 'Do we know him well enough to be sure of that? As you said yourself, *any* young man may be overwhelmed by a mass descent of his wife's relations. And you seem to be assuming also that in a happy marriage the husband must always dominate the wife. Is it so terrible if the wife should prove to be the stronger of the two?'

Pirry looked startled, while Bernard burst out laughing. 'You're forgetting that our cousin Ilsa is a Lorimer female as well.'

Pirry joined in the laughter against himself. 'And also forgetting that the nature of my own domestic arrangements hardly qualifies me to pontificate on the holy state of matrimony. I met my own life-partner in a prisoner-of-war camp,' he explained to Ilsa. 'His name is Douglas and he represents the responsibilities in France I mentioned earlier, because I've lived with him ever since the war. Minds are broader outside England.' He was watching to see how she reacted. Leo had already revealed Pirry's inclinations and she felt no disapproval. It was none of her business how he chose to live. Her own family life might be crumbling about her, but she did not yet have any feeling of belonging to this one.

Bernard was the first to leave, and once again Pirry put out a hand to hold Ilsa back.

'There's something I want to ask you. And I shall be so desolated if you say No that I hardly dare put it into words.'

'What is it?'

'Have you ever thought of writing an opera?' he asked.

172

'Not a grand opera, a Covent Garden affair. But something suitable for television. That's a new medium which ought to be creating its own art forms. An opera which was a mixture of studio singing and film background could be exciting.'

Ilsa had never considered such a project and allowed her face to reveal the fact.

'I wonder whether we might collaborate,' Pirry continued. 'You may or may not know that I earn a little pin money from my translations of various gloomy Scandinavians and Germans. And as my mother's son, I've been brought up with opera. I do know about some of the technical problems. It seemed to me that *The Lady From The Sea* would have possibilities – Ibsen's play. The two kinds of water, the sea and the fjord, could be part of a television production in a way which would be impossible in an opera house. At the moment I'm still organizing the structure, to make sure that it would work technically and dramatically. Before I start on the actual libretto, I need to know whose music I'm writing for. Yours would be exactly right. Leo gave me his recording of your violin concerto as a Christmas present ten years ago, and since then I've bought everything of yours that's on disc. Even before I knew of our relationship I was wondering whether I might approach you.'

'I don't know the play.' Ilsa was neither encouraging nor discouraging.

'It's about freedom of choice. The heroine, Ellida, has to choose between two kinds of life – calm water life and open water life, you might say, with two men tugging her in different directions. You'd need to use two styles of music which in the end could be reconciled – as though the sparkling introduction to your piano concerto were dancing about on top of the adagio theme from the

173

Cradle Symphony and gradually becoming absorbed in it. I'm quite sure you could express all the variety of moods which would be needed. If I were to send you the scenario when I've finished it, perhaps with the libretto for a specimen scene, would you consider the project?'

At their first meeting, overwhelmed by the news about her mother, Ilsa had paid little attention to Pirry, assuming him to be a well-to-do dilettante, pleasant enough but possibly shallow in his tastes. His businesslike concern for his mother's welfare had already altered that impression. Now he was inviting her to consider him as a fellow-professional, and his knowledge of her work was flattering.

'No need to answer at once,' he said. 'I'll give you a ring before I leave England. And you needn't commit yourself to more than a look at the scenario even then. Now, may I drive you home?'

'Would you like to come in?' Ilsa asked ten minutes later as they drew up in front of the Nash terrace.

'If it isn't an intrusion, I would very much like to see the room in which you work. Because if this opera project were to take off – I hope I'm not pushing too hard, but I really have set my heart on it – we'd need to develop a kind of telepathic communication. I'd want to be able to imagine you at work.'

'You'll be disappointed.' Ilsa led the way in. 'You may expect something grand, looking over the park. But I like to have no distractions at all. I could work best in a prison cell without a window.'

Pirry looked round the small, dark room. 'Will you sit as though you were working?'

Ilsa sat down not at the piano but at her draughtsman's table, and tilted its surface to the angle she preferred.

'Does your house in France have a music room?' she asked.

'Yes. Very large. Some friends and I play chamber music there, so we need the space. One wall is all glass, opening on to a terrace with a view of the sea. *Very* distracting, I'm afraid you'd find it. But I hope you'll come to see it one day, all the same.' He was still staring intently at every detail of the room.

'I'd like to see your scenario,' Ilsa told him impulsively. 'It's a new idea, writing an opera. But it could be exciting.'

'Marvellous!' Pirry's eyes lit up with such enthusiasm that he seemed to be not older than Ilsa, but far younger. He took hold of her by both hands and raised her to her feet. 'Marvellous!' he repeated.

'I'm not promising anything. Only that I'll consider it. But, Pirry – ' She stopped, astounded by the realization of what she was going to say. 'I would need to see it quite soon. I may not have very long to work on it.'

'You mean that you're expecting another commission?'

'No. I mean that I'm ill. I have a kind of cancer.'

Pirry was still holding her hands. Ilsa, who normally so much disliked being touched, had not freed herself because his mood of excitement transmitted itself to her through the contact. Now, through the same channel, she felt his exhilaration changing abruptly to shock and sympathy. 'My dear Ilsa! I'm so sorry!'

Ilsa gave a short, surprised laugh. 'I've been keeping it a secret. Even my family doesn't know. Nor Leo, although he's my closest friend. But I suddenly wanted to tell someone.'

'Thank you.' His grip on her hands became painfully tight, and he used it to pull her closer, so that by their nearness they shared a moment of sadness. His voice was quiet as he asked, 'Does it frighten you?'

Ilsa shook her head. 'Not now. For a little while when I was first told, yes. Although even then it was anger more than fear. I suppose one always asks, Why can't I have a little longer? But it has to happen sometime, so . . . I told you because I wouldn't like to begin something and then – '

'No,' said Pirry. 'You told me because we are going to be friends. You knew that we must start with honesty and trust. It must be important to you, if there's a time limit, to believe that whatever you do should be worth doing. Are you sure – ?'

'I can't be sure until I see what you have in mind,' Ilsa told him. 'I need to find out whether I'm in sympathy with it. But I have a feeling that whatever inspires you will be inspiring to me as well. I shall look forward – very much – to hearing from you when you're ready.'

10

Less than a week after Pirry mooted the idea of an opera, Ilsa was commissioned by the BBC to compose a brief choral piece – for a concert to be televised on St Cecilia's Day in honour of music's patron saint. The invitation was accompanied by five poems, chosen in the hope that one of them might provide inspiration.

'Who is Humbert Wolfe?' asked Michael, reading the poems while Ilsa considered the invitation. Since Richard's departure she was making an effort to appear at breakfast every morning.

'I don't know. I haven't heard of him.'

'He wrote one of these. It's a conversation between a fiddle and a bow about the fiddler. I like the way it ends:

> "And if of dust he shapes this brittle
> lift of the wings, this song's one petal
> that shines and dies, is it not just
> to suffer for song, O singing dust?
>
> His was the choice, and if he wake us
> out of the wood, but will not slake us,
> thus stirred with the stars, at least we know
> what pain the stars have," says the bow.

Neat. Do you suffer for song, Ilsa?'

'For me it's the other way round,' she said. 'I suffer when the song is silent.'

'Will you take the commission?'

'Yes. But I shall have to move fast – November's only four months away.'

177

She chose the Wolfe poem, not only because Michael liked it, but because the words gave her the excuse to slash through the choral texture with dramatic phrases played on a violin. She worked hard in the next few weeks, and was pleased with the result.

'Will you come with me to the concert, Michael?' she asked on the morning of St Cecilia's Day: she had been sent two tickets for the studio performance.

'I can't really spare the time, if you don't mind.'

Ilsa was disappointed – yet while the final rehearsal and the concert itself were in progress she would not have been aware of having a companion; and by the time the performance ended she was too tired to talk. She should have been hungry, because she had stayed in the studio between rehearsal and performance to scribble down ideas. But the thought of the canteen was unappealing. A more attractive way to restore her energy would be a refreshing bath at home. As soon as she had thanked the performers, she made her way up the stairs from the underground studio and straight out of the lobby.

A single step outside showed her that no taxis would be on the road that night. A dense wall of fog pressed against her face, irritating her eyes and throat in only the brief second before she turned back through the swing door to consider what to do. But the distance from the studios to her home was not really very great – Michael had frequently teased her with the statement that she could walk it in half the time she spent waiting for a taxi. She gave a little sigh, a small grimace, and then pulled her scarf across her mouth and nose before stepping outside for a second time.

The air was very cold and surprisingly wet. This was not an old-fashioned pea-souper, not darkened by smoke or made poisonous by chemical effluents as in the first years after the war; but it was dense enough to be stifling. Breathing through the scarf, Ilsa felt that she was suffocating; but when she pulled it aside she at once began to wheeze and cough.

She covered her mouth again and tried to hurry; but so closely did the fog press against her eyes that she experienced all the anxiety of a blind woman lost in unknown territory. At first she could feel her way along the walls or railings of the street, but then she had to cross the wide road which lay between her and the park. She strained her ears as well as her eyes, but the fog muffled sound as well as obscuring vision, and the few vehicles which were still on the road appeared without warning out of the silence. Inside the park the problems were greater, for there were no walls to guide her. To take a short cut across the grass was to risk losing all sense of direction. With one arm extended in front of her to warn of obstructions or other pedestrians, she made her way cautiously round the outer circle.

Long before she reached the house she was coughing. She closed her mouth, trying to control the irritation; but then it shook and rumbled inside lungs which were panting for air. When finally she leaned against her own front door, she surrendered to the violence of the attack for a few minutes while summoning the strength to turn the key in the lock. Staggering inwards with the opening door, she was only just able to push it shut before collapsing on the stairs to rest. It had taken her almost an hour to cover the short distance home.

The hall light was on, but the rest of the house was in darkness. Presumably the Rundles were asleep in their own flat. Michael might be asleep as well, or perhaps still working at his books. Ilsa drew on her remaining strength and hauled herself up the first flight of stairs to the drawing room. Sitting down on the sofa, she huddled inside her fur coat and brought her noisy, shallow breathing gradually under control.

For those first few minutes she was glad to be alone, but soon she became resentful of the silence. Where was everybody? The Rundles should have stayed up, anxious for her safe return. And Michael – why did Michael never come to her concerts? It was unforgivable of him to take so little interest in her work. She should be discussing the music with him now: the house should be full of light and warmth and friendly conversation. If she had company, she would not feel so ill.

Allowing anger to overcome her exhaustion, she stood up and turned on all the drawing room lights. At once, as though she had rung a bell, Michael appeared in pyjamas and dressing-gown.

'I was listening for you,' he said. 'I was worried about how you were going to get home, but I couldn't think of anything to do.'

'There wasn't anything. It was lucky I was in walking distance. But the fog's given me a tickle in my throat. Would you fetch the bottle of brown medicine from my bathroom?'

After she had taken a strong dose of the Brompton's mixture she was able to relax. Her breathing came more easily and her heart, which had been pounding with anxiety and exertion, gradually steadied.

'How did the concert go?' Michael asked. 'I've been feeling mean all evening about not coming. It's the scholarship exam next week that's the trouble. All the time when I'm not working for it, my brain keeps asking me questions I can't answer, so that I have to dash straight off and look up my notes. I couldn't have listened

180

to the music properly. But I should have gone, all the same, shouldn't I?'

Ilsa smiled at him, affection driving away her fear of collapse. Michael was as tall as herself, but in his camel dressing-gown he looked as cuddly as a four-year-old, with the same expression of earnest perplexity. Except in school work, he was young for his age.

'I would have liked your company,' she admitted. Breathing was still an effort, but she could control it well enough to talk. 'Concerts are like coffee: an acquired taste. If you go regularly, you'll begin to enjoy them one day. And then you'll be cross with yourself for not starting sooner. Tonight, of course, you needn't have pretended that you expected to appreciate the music. It would only have been a gesture of family solidarity.'

'Sorry,' he said.

'Well, I hadn't realized the Cambridge exam was so close. I thought it was at the end of term. So we each have our own dragons to fight. I have to listen to a first performance in a concert hall, while you'll face your crisis in an examination room with nobody to applaud. All the worry and none of the fun. Never mind. The day you know enough to send the world spinning into a black hole, I'll take my turn to stay away.'

'You're cross about my not going, aren't you?'

'Not cross at all. I could have pressed you harder to come, but I thought it was better to let you decide. You decided wrongly and you studied your decision and saw that you were wrong. That's one mistake you won't make again. It's all thoroughly satisfactory.'

Michael's worried expression gave way to a boyish grin. 'How appallingly lazy you are, Ilsa! You even make me bring myself up.'

'And a very good job you're making of it. Michael,

181

you're not worried about this scholarship exam, are you? It's only a trial run. You're still young. You'll have another chance next year.'

'The school calls it a trial run because they don't like to muck up their percentage of honours with failures. As far as I'm concerned, it's the real thing. I want to start at Cambridge next October.'

'Why are you in such a hurry to grow up?' asked Ilsa, smiling.

Michael sat down on the arm of the sofa. 'Almost all the important discoveries in science nowadays are made by people under thirty,' he said earnestly. 'It's as though after that one's brain loses the ability to make – what would you call it? – the creative leap. Intelligence starts going downhill from the age of about seventeen. So it's a kind of race, you see, to acquire as much knowledge and good judgement as you can while you've still got the brains to move on from what's already known. Does that sound cocky? I don't mean it to. But if I turn out to be any good, there may not be much time.'

'If you turn out to be any good, you may end up by making time run backwards for you.'

They laughed together, but Ilsa began to cough again. Michael's cheerful company had distracted her but now, as she tried to stand, she was once again conscious of her exhaustion. Michael, however, had remembered something he wanted to tell her and did not notice.

'Ilsa, I tried to watch the concert on the box and it wasn't on.'

'What do you mean? It must have been.'

'No. No picture at all. Just a blank screen and music. Not your music, either.'

'Wasn't there any announcement?'

'There might have been at the beginning, but I didn't switch on until I thought they'd have reached your piece.'

'I suppose there was a technical fault. Or perhaps someone important has died. Churchill, it could be. How infuriating.' It was not often that Ilsa could hope for a large audience for her work, so she had reason to be annoyed by this lost opportunity.

'Yes. Rotten luck. Well, goodnight.' He gave her a smacking kiss on the cheek and went up to his bedroom at the top of the house.

It took Ilsa longer to reach her room. The effect of the Brompton's mixture had worn off more quickly than usual and as she climbed the stairs she was only able to take a series of quick, shallow breaths. Her lungs were full of fog which bubbled up, filling her throat, drowning her from within. 'We are the water people,' Pirry Glanville had said. Now water was choking her, dragging her down into an invisible ocean. She sat on the edge of the bed and bent down, trying to force out the fog. The effort triggered off her coughing again.

To the turbulence in her lungs was added the agonizing pain which she had experienced once before, when Richard was in the room. It tightened across her chest, pinching her heart and knotting her muscles in spasm. She heard Michael rushing down the stairs from the floor above and thought that he must have heard her groans – but as he burst through the door it was clear that his arrival was a life-saving accident.

'I put the radio news on,' he said breathlessly. 'President Kennedy's been shot. He's – Ilsa, are you all right?' He did not need to wait for an answer. Ilsa heard him lift the telephone receiver to summon the doctor and allowed herself to collapse.

When she opened her eyes again, Michael was still

next to her bed, but everything else had changed. There was a mask over her face, and tubes dripped into an arm which was tightly strapped down. When she stared at him, he seemed oddly out of focus. He said something that she could not hear, and a uniformed nurse appeared at his side. Their two faces blurred and faded again.

This must have happened several times, for sometimes Michael was not there and sometimes there was a different nurse. Once she thought she recognized Mr Simpson, and more often, more certainly, their family doctor, Dr Wainwright. It was Dr Wainwright who gently drew her out of the twilight and back to full consciousness. Without remembering the intermediate stages, she found herself one day propped up against a mound of pillows and breathing without the help of oxygen.

'You'll be all right now.' Dr Wainwright was studying the record of her pulse and temperature. 'Back to normal quite soon.'

Did he know what 'normal' meant? 'What happened?' Ilsa asked. Her voice, out of practice, emerged as a croak.

'A bad bout of bronchitis is what I told Michael.'

'True?'

Dr Wainwright sat down. 'No. But according to John Simpson, you didn't wish your family to be informed about your health.'

'He told you.'

'There are rules about specialists passing their findings on to GPs. Or etiquette, at least. How could I treat you without knowing? I was sorry to read his notes. We've been working on this together. You can thank him for pulling you through.'

'Through what?'

'A pleural embolism. It could have killed you.'

184

'Will it happen again?'

'You'll have to be careful. As soon as you're well enough to travel, I'd recommend you to go somewhere warm and dry. Now, do you feel up to seeing Michael? He's been worried.'

He came into the room as soon as the doctor had left, and gripped her hand tightly. 'Shouldn't you be taking your exam?' she asked.

'I finished that ages ago. The results came out last week.'

'How did you get on?'

'Trinity offered me a place. I'll be starting in October.'

'Oh, darling!' He had hoped for a scholarship. 'That's my fault. You must have been worried all the time you were doing the papers.'

'You're supposed to congratulate me! Most people don't get accepted at all. As for the scholarship, that's not important. Cambridge has a civilized system of offering extra awards to people who do well in their first year. I'll pick up something then, you'll see.'

'But Michael, if it's all settled, how long have I been ill?'

'Five weeks,' he told her. 'Dr Wainwright kept you sedated to stop you coughing. He explained it to me so that I wouldn't think you were in a coma. Now he thinks you're stronger, so he's cut down on the drugs. That's why you've woken up so suddenly.'

'Five weeks!'

'Yes. You've missed Christmas. Would you like your presents now?'

'Just yours,' she said, and allowed him to dab her wrists with the scent he had bought.

'I'll tell you who sent the others. Then you can look forward to seeing them tomorrow, when you're strong enough to enjoy them.' Neatly cutting string and paper, he took off the outer wrappings of the parcels and discovered one that was not a Christmas present, but a typescript. 'From Pirry Glanville,' he reported, reading the signature on the enclosed letter. 'It looks like a play.'

'He wants me to write an opera,' Ilsa explained.

'Are you going to?'

'I don't feel up to it.' There would not be time. All the same, she asked Michael to leave the libretto within reach.

The next day she was a little stronger and found it easier to talk.

'I phoned Richard, of course, to tell him you were ill,' said Michael. 'He asked if he should come back. I don't know whether I said the right thing. He'd explained to me before he left how important it was for him to stay out of England for a whole year. Something to do with tax. He was ready to dish that, but I thought you wouldn't notice whether he was here or not while you were having all those drugs, so I suggested he waited until you could talk to him on the phone yourself.'

'You said I had bronchitis?'

'Yes. I explained about the fog.'

'You were quite right not to bring him back. In fact, you should have gone out there for Christmas.'

'He did invite me. But I didn't want to leave you.'

'Why not go now?' suggested Ilsa. 'If you've won your place at Cambridge, there's no point in staying on at school. You could have an interesting six months in America. Richard might set you a research job to do at his new clinic. Or at least give you some lab. work.' Most seventeen-year-olds might choose to fill a gap between school and university in more frivolous fashion, but Ilsa knew that Michael was only happy when he was working.

'No. I'm going to stay with you.'

It took Ilsa only a moment to decide what to say. 'Lord Glanville has invited me to stay with him on the Riviera, so that we can work together on the opera. That will take a long time – a year, at least. If you were away at the same time, we could close up the house.'

'I thought you weren't going to do the opera.'

'I was still dopey when I said that yesterday. Dr Wainwright has told me to spend the rest of the winter in a warmer climate. Pirry didn't know I'd been ill, but his invitation is perfectly timed. If I accept, you and Richard will know that I'm comfortable and well looked after. And as soon as I'm strong again, I shall want to get back to work.' She could see that he was tempted, but still doubtful. 'Go on,' she urged. 'It will take a little time to get an American visa, and you'll need a letter from Richard to guarantee your support. Phone him up today and tell him that you'd like to come, and that I'm better. Too croaky to talk on the phone, but better.'

'Sure?'

'Sure,' she said; and to prove it she opened the libretto of *The Lady From The Sea* and began to read.

At their two brief meetings she had found Pirry's personality attractive. He had charmed her into expressing enthusiasm for his project, but the excitement of a new commission soon after their last encounter had taken the edge off her interest. Would his work prove sufficiently professional to tempt her again? The fortunate timing of his invitation was not enough in itself to make her uncritical.

On her first reading of the typescript she was concerned only to judge whether the story was sufficiently dramatic, the characters inspiring and the production technically possible. But even at that stage the conflict between the wild strength of the seafarers and the more placid lives of those who lived on the fjord excited her with its musical possibilities – just as Pirry had promised. When she opened the folder for a second time she could already feel herself retreating into the state of mental isolation which invariably preceded the first stirrings of creativity. This was, after all, a challenge she could accept. She had the ability to do the work. All she needed was time.

On the last day of December Mr Simpson visited her. 'I warned you about fog, you know,' he said.

'Yes. I'm sorry.' Earlier, she had intended – if she ever saw him again – to ask why he had bothered to save her life. What was the point, she would have asked, of dragging me back just to go through it all again before too long? But the question remained unspoken because an answer had already presented itself. There was still something she wanted to do. She was going to write an opera. She was going to write it with Pirry and in the process, she felt sure, she would find her place in the family she had discovered less than a year earlier. She had let both Michael and Richard go, but there was still somewhere she could belong.

11

Ilsa found it easy to understand why Pirry had chosen *The Lady From The Sea* for his first libretto, for the sea was his own natural element. Sailing was his passion and swimming his regular exercise. From every window of his villa on the headland of a small cape there was a view of the Mediterranean. He owned no beach, for the promontory was high and rocky; but a zig-zag stairway led down to a jetty from which he could dive directly into deep water, and also to a large sheltered boathouse. Here was moored his two racing yachts, the much smaller single-handed Snipe which he kept for relaxation, and the motor boat which he and Douglas used for workaday trips to Nice or Monte Carlo during the summer months when the coastal road was choked with tourists.

When Ilsa first arrived from England, weak from her illness and tired by the journey, there was no question of her joining her host on the water. In any case, the weather was blustery and she had been warned to keep warm. But as the spring sunshine began to sparkle on smoother water and little by little her energy returned, she accepted his invitations to go out for an afternoon when there was no racing. As a girl she had sailed in the Gulf of Finland and, although she now lacked the strength to control a boat, or even to crew, her body instinctively knew how to lean and balance as Pirry gybed or turned close into the wind.

On racing days it was Douglas who went out with Pirry, while Ilsa watched – if the course was near enough

– from the gazebo on the tip of the headland. The two men had been living and sailing together for almost twenty years, and Ilsa wondered at first whether Douglas might be resentful when she arrived for a long stay. But his protective attitude towards Pirry made him pleased that the long-planned opera was to take shape at last, and she found him friendly and welcoming. He was a sturdy, straight-backed man in his early sixties, with iron-grey hair and a thick moustache: he spoke little and was always busy.

'Duggie doesn't appreciate our sort of music,' Pirry had said at their first introduction. 'He raves about some pop group called the Beatles and is deaf to the charms of Beethoven. But he can tune any kind of engine to sing a sweet song. And he understands all these new-fangled electronics. He's longing to set up a multiple tape deck – whatever that may be – in the music room for you, so that you can build up layers of sound and judge the effect.' Douglas had smiled, glad to have his sphere of interest delineated and making it clear that he would not interfere in Ilsa's work.

Her days quickly constructed their own timetable. In the early evening she discussed details of the opera with Pirry over the champagne cocktails which he had prescribed to cure her lack of appetite. After dinner he would sometimes come into the music room with her for an hour, but for most of the night she worked alone, with only a single spotlight to pierce the blackness and only the steady surge of the sea against the rocks to disturb or inspire her. Morning was her time for sleeping, in the guest cottage a short distance away from the villa. After-noons were for relaxation – although even then she was still thinking about the opera, her mind alert to recognize and remember any new ideas. Never far from her thoughts was the fear that she might not have long enough to finish the work.

There were good days and bad days in these months which she spent as Pirry's guest. Mr Simpson had kept his promise to see that any pain was controlled. Approving of her move to a better climate, he had provided her with a liberal first supply of drugs and instructions, and a long letter to be passed on to Pirry's medical adviser, Dr Lequesne. Her ill health had been clear enough when she first came out to France – clear even to Douglas, who was not told the truth of it. But the spring restored her strength to such an extent that sometimes she wondered whether Mr Simpson could have been mistaken. She allowed herself to hope, but was never tempted to slacken the pace of her work. The summer was hot, and she was well enough to accept a visit from Michael in September. When she waved him goodbye for the start of his first term at Cambridge, she was confident that he suspected nothing.

With the coming of winter, though, her sense of wellbeing began to fade. Although she coughed less violently than a year earlier, there was a thickness in her chest which made breathing a painful struggle. Her neck, too, had become stiff, making it difficult to sleep comfortably. Not that she cared about sleep any longer. Finishing the opera was all that mattered.

As the end of the year approached, it was possible to be optimistic. By now Pirry had nothing to contribute but encouragement, for she had completed the setting of the libretto. What remained was the orchestration of a storm scene and the composition of the overture – left until last so that it could incorporate the themes which were to follow. Christmas Day came almost as an intrusion, and as soon as it was over she returned to the score.

Pirry and Douglas had planned a party for New Year's Eve. They would use the music room for dancing and, because Pirry had ambitious plans for decorating it, Ilsa worked in the guest cottage for the three days before the party. The change of routine disturbed her concentration and she could feel the pace of her work slowing. Her brain seemed muddy and confused: she could no longer hear the music clearly in her head. Perhaps, she thought, the drugs she was taking were dulling her wits. In order to test whether this was the case, she abandoned them.

The regime laid down by Mr Simpson and continued by Dr Lequesne was designed to anticipate pain rather than merely relieve it after it began, so only when she ceased to take the medication did she realize what she had been spared for the past twelve months. The drugs had laid a flimsy veil over her mind, but a far more potent block to inspiration now was the tightness in her chest. It began as a dull ache but gradually increased in strength. She was unable to eat, unable to work, unable to think of anything but the pain. As she crouched in agony over the desk at which she had been working, her muscles locked themselves into rigidity and her brain had lost the key to unlock them. The telephone, directly linked to the villa, was only a few feet away. She could see it, but was unable to move a hand to reach it.

It was Pirry who rescued her, calling at the cottage half an hour before his party was due to begin and needing only a single glance to see what was wrong. Like a baby, Ilsa felt herself first picked up and then set down on the bed. Pirry kept his arms round her while she struggled to speak. In brief gasps she explained how idiotically she had deprived herself of her drugs.

'What will work fastest now?' he asked.

'Injection. Pethadine. Bathroom.' Until now she had

192

been taking diamorphine by mouth, but the stronger drug had been waiting for just this kind of emergency.

He unfastened her dress and helped her off with it. By now the pain in her chest was so intense that Ilsa was finding it difficult not to cry. Pirry's expression, as a rule pleasantly easy-going, was grim with sympathy as he hurried into the bathroom. She heard him washing his hands before he came back with the hypodermic syringe and an ampoule. 'I'll do it for you,' he said, studying the dosage and checking it with her. 'I'm used to giving Duggie jabs for his asthma.' Sitting on the edge of the bed he swabbed her skin, slid in the needle with a smooth firmness and pushed the plunger home. Removing the needle, he pressed down on the spot for a few seconds, and even after relaxing his grip did not move away. Ilsa guessed that he was going to wait until the drug took effect, and was grateful.

'I brought a bottle of champagne so that you could see the new year in over here if you didn't feel like company,' he said. The casual note had returned to his voice: by a friendly chattiness he was reassuring her that the emergency was over. 'But pethadine may not be an approved ingredient of a champagne cocktail. So perhaps you'd better let the old year slip away without celebration.' He took hold of her hand, squeezing it gently. 'But I hope you'll remember 1964 as one of your good years, Ilsa. It's been marvellous for me, and all because of you. My cousin from a cold climate.'

Ilsa tried to smile, and Pirry looked down at her as though perplexed by his own thoughts. 'It's odd, you know.' He was still chatting inconsequentially, to pass the time. 'I was brought up by women. My father died when I was only five or six, and after that the household seemed to be entirely female. My mother, my aunt, my

193

sister, a host of female cousins. The Lorimer ladies. I wouldn't have minded them being so successful themselves if they hadn't been so determined that I should be talented as well. I was to do something worthwhile with my life, and do it energetically. But I never was energetic, I fear. The world is divided between those who see life as the raw material for achievement and those who regard it as a finished product. I admired them all, the Lorimer ladies – but collectively, as a family, they've always terrified me. I'm not a misogynist – a lot of my best friends are women. All the same, I feel as though I've been frightened of women all my life.'

'Not your mother, surely.'

There was a long silence, as though he were putting the question to himself for the first time.

'There's a special feeling about inheriting a title,' he said. 'You do sometimes wonder why you were born. My mother's always made it clear that she would accept any kind of wife for me, if only the marriage would produce – not just a baby, not just a son, but an *heir*. It makes me wonder about myself. My father was in his fifties when I was born. His first wife had been an invalid. When he married Mother – oh, I'm sure they loved each other. But it's difficult not to believe that the wish for an heir came into the contract somewhere. I wasn't born for my own sake. I was born so that I could be the next Lord Glanville and cut out my Uncle Duncan. The world is divided another way as well – between those who simply live and those who inflict life on others. My mother had that power over me: the most terrifying power of all.'

'But you love her.'

'Oh yes, I love her dearly. But then there's this ridiculous business of the entail, which adds a certain guilt and resentment to the package. Not only did she give me life,

194

but she makes it essential for me to go on living, because my death would diminish her in a very literal way. And just suppose – sometimes I have a nightmare. I love Duggie as well, you see. But suppose something happened – the house on fire, perhaps, and I could only save his life at the cost of my own. What would I do, Ilsa? Somewhere along the line I've lost the right to love anyone more than my mother.'

He sighed, and for a few minutes neither of them spoke. Then Pirry returned to the thought from which mention of his mother had diverted him. 'But it *is* odd, you know. You're a Lorimer lady, aren't you, Ilsa? Quite as talented as any of the others. As formidable, even. How does it happen that I'm not frightened of you?'

'It's because I'm cold. Self-centred. Interested in nothing but my music.' Ilsa was quoting what Richard had said – without bitterness, because she believed it to be true. She added her own contribution for good measure. 'And not possessive. I'm no threat to you.'

The pethadine was taking effect now, flowing through her body. Pain receded, leaving behind a blissful weightlessness. Pirry's fingers, moving delicately over her skin, soothed her towards sleep, but a new thought startled her into alertness again. It was true that there was no way in which she could threaten Pirry, and perhaps it was because he did not threaten her that she felt so much at ease with him. From their first meeting she had known that he would never desire her body, never wish to explore it, probing its rottenness. Yet when he had pressed the needle into her body – a body invaded by a real and not an imagined malignancy – he had shown no embarrassment and she had felt no disgust. And now he was stroking her almost like a lover, and she found only comfort in the contact. From Richard, all too often, she had shrunk away; but Pirry's touch in this dozy, happy twilight of the mind filled her with a kind of love. 'Pirry!' she said, her voice incredulous with the discovery.

With the empathy which had made their working collaboration so sensitive and successful, Pirry understood what she meant. 'I don't understand it either,' he said. Briefly his hand tightened on her bare shoulder and he leaned over to kiss her on the forehead. 'Happy New Year, Ilsa,' he said. 'Go to sleep now. I'll see you again in 1965.'

12

Now a sense of urgency possessed Ilsa. She had been given a warning. Her body might withstand the attack of the disease for some time yet, but for how much longer would the clarity of her mind survive? She worked all afternoon as well as through the night, sleeping only for three or four hours each morning. Meals were brought in, but she had little appetite. Dr Lequesne, summoned on New Year's Day to approve the injections which she now needed regularly, had offered to find a private nurse: but Pirry, with only a quick glance at Ilsa, turned the offer down and himself provided the care she required.

The need for haste drove Ilsa to abandon her usual method of working in the music room. She moved from a writing table to the piano and made use of the recording devices which Douglas had installed. If she failed to complete the composition herself, a competent orchestrator would be able to understand her intentions from the tapes. Pirry, too, was drawn into the work. As she wrote one line of music she dictated another to him. He was in any case determined to stay close at hand, ready to give her an injection every three hours.

And then, at nine o'clock one morning, the opera was finished. Pirry jumped to his feet, exclaiming with excitement, as Ilsa signed her name on the score. After sitting for thirteen hours almost without moving she was unable to straighten herself at once. Her hands climbed from his waist to his shoulders as though she were pulling herself up a ladder; but when at last they were standing face to face, neither of them could speak for laughing.

Beneath the excitement she was very tired. She allowed Pirry to help her back to the cottage and then, unusually, slept right through the day, waking in the evening with a dry mouth and a head which spun dizzily as she sat up in bed. It was hunger, no doubt – she had eaten nothing for twenty-four hours. Moving carefully, she bathed and dressed and made her way across the lawn to the villa. Even before reaching the drawing room she could hear the sound of hysterical laughter. She arrived at the glass door and stared inside.

To the music of the radio, Pirry and Douglas were dancing. Since Ilsa had known them, their behaviour together had never been anything but dignified, but now they seemed to be caricaturing themselves – flirting, mincing, giggling. Pirry was wearing the maid's frilly white apron tied round his waist. When they caught sight of her Douglas collapsed, still laughing, into a chair, while Pirry – showing no embarrassment – came over to slide open the door and help her inside. He opened a bottle of champagne which was waiting in the ice bucket and filled three glasses.

'Time to celebrate! To *The Lady From The Sea*!'

Ilsa was too happy to worry about whether it was wise to drink on an empty stomach. But after the toast she looked at the men in mock disapproval. 'I have the impression that you two started celebrating some time ago.'

'That was something quite different,' Pirry told her, laughing. 'Your husband turned up while you were asleep.'

'Richard! Here?'

'Yes. Tell her, Duggie.'

'Pirry was out sailing,' said Douglas. 'He'd told me that you weren't to be disturbed after working all night, so it seemed simplest to say that you were out as well. I was changing the oil in the Porsche – wearing my dirtiest overalls – and Dr Laing obviously thought I was the chauffeur. He started pumping me about what went on here. Not quite the gentlemanly thing to do, in my opinion, gossiping to servants! He made it pretty clear what he was after. He'd been expecting you to divorce him, apparently, but you hadn't; so he'd come to find out whether he had grounds for divorce himself. After all, you appeared to have been living with Lord Glanville for the past year.'

'So what did you tell him?' But Ilsa could already guess.

'He heard Pirry come up from the boathouse. "Is that Lord Glanville now?" he asked. "Yes," says I. "I'll fetch her." So I nip over and put Pirry in the picture, and he grabs Jeanne's apron and the pan that she's stirring and out he prances and within five minutes Dr Laing's got the message that he'll have to look elsewhere for his guilty party.'

'If you *want* him to divorce you, we can go back on it, of course,' said Pirry more seriously. 'It would really set my friends chattering if I were to be cited as a co-respondent. But since there aren't any genuine grounds, it seemed simplest to make that clear, and even to exaggerate just a little.'

'Just a little,' agreed Douglas happily. Both men began to giggle again.

'But he wants to talk to you,' said Pirry, refilling Ilsa's glass. 'There's something about his girlfriend hoping to have a baby. I didn't like to ask whether there was any urgency. I suppose you were going to divorce him for desertion after two years and not for adultery, were you?'

If Ilsa had thought about it at all, she had dismissed the subject of divorce as unsavoury, and unnecessarily upsetting to Michael. It would be humiliating to undergo questioning about her private life. But behind that distaste had lain her belief that the tumour in her chest would end the marriage more decisively than any judge. 'Is Richard coming back?' she asked.

'Tomorrow evening. Of course, if you don't want to see him . . .'

'I'll see him. He's right: it's time to be businesslike.' She shrugged the matter off as the celebration continued. But later, when Pirry had seen her back to the guest cottage, she returned to the subject. 'When Richard comes back, I don't want him to know that I'm ill.'

'Why not? It would stop him bullying you.'

'He won't do that anyway. You don't know him, of course. He's a kind man. Sentimental. He may be angry with me now, but that's my fault. If he ever learns that I was already ill when he walked out – and that I knew it – he'll never forgive himself for going.'

'Why should you worry about his feelings?'

'Because I owe him so much for his kindness – and his love – in the past. So don't say anything, will you? Not tomorrow, or ever.'

'Just as you like,' said Pirry. 'But – '

'But what?'

'Nothing. Sleep well.'

Ilsa's puzzlement lasted only for a few seconds after he had left. As she brushed her hair she stared at her face in the glass and the reason for Pirry's doubts stared back at her. Even were Richard not a doctor he would know as soon as he saw her that he was looking at a dying woman.

Make-up could perhaps camouflage the black sockets of her eyes and the unhealthy colour of her skin, but she would not be able to conceal her hollowed cheeks or the lines which pain had etched above her nose and at the corners of her mouth. Richard would look at her and be first of all dismayed and later, when he had had time to think, guilty.

She could refuse to see him, of course, or go away. But that would be cowardly – and already an alternative solution was insinuating itself in her mind.

For the second time since her illness had revealed itself she remembered a conversation in Auschwitz, the fervent whispering from the bunk above her head. 'Choose your own death,' Sigi had urged. Ilsa herself, many years later, had spoken the truth in demanding truthfulness from Mr Simpson. 'I want to be in control.' No amount of self-control could now keep her alive for very much longer, but this one power still remained – she could choose her own death. She could go out to meet it in a place and at a time of her own appointment and make of it a positive act rather than a suffering.

The satisfaction of holding that power, as throughout a wakeful night she approached a decision, was the only argument which carried weight. To consider Richard's feelings, to leave undisturbed Michael's memory of the cheerful, busy woman who had brought him up, to spare herself physical pain and the mental anguish of knowing that she could no longer create music, to save Pirry from having to watch as she became weaker – all these were trivial points, relevant only because there was nothing on the other side to balance them. Brought up in a godless society, she had never felt any need of religion. Her life was her own, to live as she could or end as she pleased. She could make a kindness out of her death, and she would be doing no one any harm. Why should she deny herself this last pleasure of choice?

It must seem to be an accident. Her bathroom cabinet was full of the drugs she had been prescribed, and the villa's private bar was well stocked with alcohol. But Pirry had been giving her injections for the past three weeks, and to take an overdose might expose him to trouble. In such a case, too, the nature of her illness would be revealed to Richard at an inquest. How could she contrive that Pirry would be able to keep his promise and guard the secret of her condition?

It was easy to think of an answer. For a little while she explored it with her mind, and saw no objections. She lay on the bed without attempting to sleep, deliberately recalling all the most vivid memories of her life and from time to time shivering with delight and excitement like a young girl on the night before her wedding. Every moment now was to be savoured.

The next morning Pirry came to give her another injection. 'I'm driving into Nice,' he told her. 'Shall I take the last pages of the score to be photo-copied?' Throughout the year he had taken this precaution with previous batches, in case the original sheets should be lost or damaged.

'I'll sort them out for you,' Ilsa said. 'One or two discarded pages may be mixed up with the final version.' She led the way to the music room, walking more easily than for several days. Pirry commented on this.

'Well, the pressure's off. It was a strain, getting it finished.'

'Does it leave you feeling sad or happy, now it's done?'

'Oh, happy. Yesterday I was too tired to be sure, but now – I think it's good, Pirry. You know, I should

202

never have thought of attempting an opera if you hadn't persuaded me. I'm very grateful.'

'Grateful! I can hardly believe my luck that you agreed. Can we do it again, Ilsa? This has gone to my head. I'd like to write a libretto from scratch, instead of adapting someone else's story. A modern plot. How about an opera in which the main character is a house? Families move in and out, there are squatters, and terrorists holding hostages. There could even be a ghost.'

'A singer to represent each wall.' Ilsa entered into the spirit of the fantasy. 'The four walls acting as chorus while the inhabitants change. Oh, Pirry!' Recognizing the desperation of his attempt to provide her with a new incentive for survival, she hardly knew whether to laugh or cry. 'Dear Pirry!'

'Dear Ilsa!' He stepped forward and took her in his arms. As they stood close together, Ilsa could feel the comfort of his affection and concern warming her body. She hoped that her own excitement was communicating itself to him in turn.

When the moment of closeness was over, Pirry looked at her with mischief in his eyes. 'If Richard was peeping through the window then, all his suspicions – or hopes – will be confirmed,' he said. 'Well, I'll be back in time for lunch. Goodbye.'

'Goodbye.' That was perfect, Ilsa thought as Pirry left the music room – to part, not quite casually, with love and laughter. There would be nothing for Pirry to regret.

She sat down and began to write to Michael at Cambridge: a cheerful letter which would give no hint of her intention but would make her love for him obvious. Her pen moved with more generous strokes than usual as she described her pleasure at completing the opera. 'And now the sun is shining, tempting me to an hour on the sea in Pirry's yacht,' she wrote. 'I expect to see Richard this evening, so I'll finish this later and add his news as well as the rest of mine. Goodbye for the moment.' She addressed the envelope and left that and the letter untidily visible. Then she went back to the cottage to change.

By the time she was ready, Pirry had driven off in the estate car and Douglas was working on the Porsche again.

'I'm going to take the Snipe out,' Ilsa told him. 'An appropriate treat to celebrate finishing the opera.' The Snipe was the only one of Pirry's boats which she could hope to manage single-handed; and, because he sailed it every day that he was not racing, she could hope to find it already rigged.

'It'll be cold in the wind.' But Douglas could see that she was sensibly dressed, and it was not in his nature to tell other people what was best for them.

It took Ilsa a little while to make her way down the zig-zag steps to the boathouse, and the effort of pulling on the fixed rope which drew the little yacht out of the protected water was almost too much for her. But as the Snipe emerged from shelter and reared up under the attack of the wind, she gave a gasp of triumph.

Almost at once, though, she realized that she lacked the power to control the yacht on a day of such blustery weather. It would be an accident after all! She laughed aloud at the discovery and felt her body flooding with excitement more passionate than either love or life had ever aroused in her. To prolong the ecstatic anticipation, she determined to hold a safe course for as long as she could. The wind carried her across the bay and she was able to make one successful gybe to turn back towards the cape. But now it was necessary to tack. Her arms began to ache and her breath panted into the chill January wind. The Snipe, tilting dangerously, raced back through the icy black water. With a correct instinct, Ilsa threw her weight outwards. But her strength was draining away fast: she would not be able to hold the little yacht close to the wind for very much longer.

At this distance from the headland she had a view of the villa and its gardens. She saw Pirry appear from the side of the house and run to the top of the steps – Pirry, whom she had never known to hurry! He searched the bay with his eyes, looking for her, and even at this distance the attitude of his body revealed his anxiety.

Intoxicated with self-induced exhilaration, Ilsa let go of the tiller for a moment to wave; but Pirry, dashing down the steps, did not see the gesture. She began to lower her arm, but something had knotted in her chest and she could not move, or even breathe. A pain fiercer than anything she had previously experienced squeezed her heart – but it was not important, for now a wave surged against the rudder which she no longer controlled, pressing it in a new direction. As the Snipe hesitated, tossing its head in the spray, rearing over each wave and smacking down again into the trough which followed, the wind seized its chance to snatch at the far side of the sail. Doubled up in agony, Ilsa lifted her head and saw the boom sweeping towards her.

As cold as the snow on the day of her birth, the icy water snatched at her breath and pressed a freezing finger on her heart. The pain exploded and died. Without any struggle, Ilsa released her hold on life and disappeared.

13

It was on the morning of Sir Winston Churchill's funeral that the telephone call came from France to the flat in the Portobello Road. Considerate in all his arrangements, Pirry had made sure that should there ever be bad news, Asha and not his mother would be the first to hear. He had been efficient as well. For many months a folder had been lying in a drawer of Asha's desk, listing addresses, telephone numbers, details of the emergency plan already drawn up for Alexa. The international operator made the connection and Asha listened in silence as Douglas, tearful but straightforward, told her what had happened. Pirry was dead. He had died, it seemed, in an attempt to save Ilsa's life.

Hardly able to believe the news, she repeated it to Ranji. 'I must go to Blaize,' she said, and he nodded in sympathy. 'I'll take a bag. I shall probably need to stay the night with Aunt Alexa.'

'Then I should come also.' They had not spent a night apart since their marriage.

Asha shook her head. 'It's not the right occasion, darling.' Under the disguise of peremptory orders for some errand to be performed, recent telephone calls from Blaize had suggested that Alexa was preparing to forgive Asha for her secret and unsuitable marriage. But she had not yet brought herself to mention Ranji's name. She was pretending that he did not exist; and Asha had been equally well able without using words to make it clear that she would not visit Blaize again until she could bring her husband with her. Still, this was not the right moment to stand on principle. 'You go and watch the procession, as we planned, and tell me about it tomorrow.' They had been intending to join the thousands who would be lining the funeral route to St Paul's.

Asha could tell that Ranji was not happy with the arrangement, but the need to arrive alone at Blaize was so clear to her that she gave him no chance to argue. Instead, she turned back to the telephone and made a call to ensure that the suite of rooms bought by Pirry would be ready for Alexa as soon as she chose to move her furniture in. Only when that was settled did she kiss her husband lovingly and set out for Blaize.

The curtains of the drawing room were closed when she arrived and for a moment, as she waited for the door to be opened, Asha wondered whether the news of Pirry's death had preceded her. But it was only that Alexa preferred to watch television in darkness. The state funeral, with its many stages of ceremonial, was scheduled to fill the screen for most of the day.

'Sit down,' Alexa commanded, showing no surprise at the visit. 'You haven't got television in that flat of yours, I suppose.'

'No, we haven't.' Thus provided with an excuse for coming, Asha saw no need to be abrupt in breaking the news. As she sat down, she looked to see what was happening. Inside St Paul's the coffin had been set in position for the service; there was a momentary pause, filled with the sound of organ music, whilst the pallbearers moved away.

'You've missed the procession,' Alexa said. 'And the arrival. There was a nasty moment on the cathedral steps when we thought we were going to lose another ex-prime minister. Attlee must be almost as old as I am. Over eighty, anyway. Too old to be carrying coffins about. And Winnie was no lightweight, either. All's well, though.'

The words were flippant, but her voice was husky with emotion. As the service began, Asha found herself sharing the same mood. The sentiment engendered by the occasion was so intense that it seemed to burst out of the black and white picture, filling the room. The camera's eye rested silently on kings and presidents and generals inside the cathedral, or searching the crowds outside for the faces of weeping women and men whose eyes were fixed on distant memories.

The service ended; the procession re-formed; the dignitaries scattered. The coffin was carried on its way again; this time, down to the river. In the distance, as the launch which now carried it drew away from the bank, a row of tall dockland cranes dipped in tribute to the occasion. The silent movement and elegant line of their dark silhouettes provided an unexpectedly poignant moment of beauty. Alexa abandoned the pretence that she was not affected.

'Turn the sound down, will you?' she said. 'But keep the picture.' She blew her nose and took off her spectacles so that she could dab her eyes.

'It's not just the man, you see,' she tried to explain as Asha obeyed. 'After all, to someone your age, what was he? A party politician who drank too much and lived too long? Or a page out of a history book? But to anyone older he represents a time and a mood. Those dockers who dipped their crane jibs just then – Bolshies to a man, I wouldn't be surprised. Saw him as their class enemy. Voted him out of office after the war. Quite prepared to use their industrial power to bring him down again after he got back, even if it brought the country down with him. But those same dockers fought for the same country in 1940. What we're burying today is a reminder of the time when everyone in England was on the same side as everyone else. You hear people say sometimes that the best years of their life were in the war, and it seems sad that that could be true. But I can understand it. I expect almost everyone in England has been watching this today – on television if they can't get to London – or listening on the radio. And I can remember the last time that happened – a whole nation sharing a single emotion, concentrating on a single event.'

As though she had spoken a cue, there was a change in the picture on the screen. Presumably the coffin was out of camera range: it was possible to deduce that the interval was being filled with recordings of Churchill's most famous wartime orations, illustrated by the events which had occasioned them. The picture now was of the beach at Dunkirk, with its long lines of soldiers stretching into the sea, waiting to be rescued while German planes swooped over them.

'That was the time,' said Alexa. 'We didn't have television then – at least, I didn't. We all listened to the radio. Every moment we could, for six days. The hottest days of summer. Pirry was there, you know, at Dunkirk. He almost got away. But the ship sunk under him. That's how he was captured. Five years in a prisoner-of-war camp. I often wonder if things would have been different if . . .' She stood up, stiff and unsteady after her day of viewing. 'I must phone Pirry. Now. He calls me every Sunday evening, but I'm not going to wait. I want to talk to him.'

She was turning towards the telephone. Asha, moving quickly, stood in her way.

'You've been crying too,' said Alexa. 'I didn't notice,

in the dark. You shared the feeling, then, in spite of being too young to remember?'

'I shared it, yes. But that's not why I was crying. I didn't come here just to watch television, Aunt Alexa. I've brought bad news.'

'About Pirry?'

'Yes.' Asha had had all day to rehearse it, but still found it difficult to say the words. 'Pirry – he's dead, Aunt Alexa.'

'Pirry! Pirry! He can't be. How?'

'In the sea. After a sailing accident, Douglas said.'

Alexa sat down, suddenly, as though her legs had ceased to support her. Asha held her hand tightly, not daring to speak. The old lady who had wept for Churchill's passing sat dry-eyed and stiff-backed as she tried to believe that her son was dead.

'It's not possible. That idiot Douglas must have made a mistake. Pirry's been sailing all his life. He doesn't have accidents. And he's a marvellous swimmer. After being sunk at Dunkirk, he swam for hours back to land. Tell me, it isn't true, Asha.'

'Douglas said the sea was terribly cold. He didn't actually see the accident. But he thought Pirry might have got cramp. Or else that he died from shock when he hit the icy water. Oh darling, I'm so sorry.' Asha searched for words of comfort, but could find none. She sat in silence, gripping Alexa's hand, while a long time passed.

Meanwhile the television screen continued silently to record the day's events, and in the end it was a change of scene which distracted Asha's eyes. Churchill's coffin was on a train now. The camera followed the train out of the station, through a deep cutting, over a bridge, between rows of small, smoke-blackened houses, on and on until it was so far away that the railway lines seemed on the

210

point of converging. She knew that in fact it was on its way to the family resting place in the village of Bladon; but without the commentary to interpret the picture it seemed as though the train were disappearing into a symbolic infinity. The rituals of mourning were coming to an end. She released Alexa's hand for a moment and turned the set off.

Alexa's voice pierced the darkness of the room with a chilling calmness. 'I'd like to walk round the house. Will you phone through and tell Mr Jamieson?' For the past twenty years Alexa had made her home in only the west wing of Blaize. She had the right at any time to visit the school which occupied the rest of the mansion, but always as a matter of courtesy gave notice of her wish to do so. 'And make an appointment for me to see him tomorrow. Pirry got those people up in Scotland to agree to the lease. The school will be given good notice. But it may have to go in the end. Mr Jamieson will want to start looking round.'

Both women blinked as Asha turned on the light before moving to the telephone. 'It's a holiday weekend,' she reported after the call. 'Mr Jamieson's away until Sunday evening. The caretaker said to give him a minute while he switches the lights on at the mains for you.'

'Where will they go?' Alexa wondered aloud. 'And where shall *I* go?' At last her self-control shattered. 'Asha, what am I going to do?'

In 1947 Alexa had led a five-year-old girl through the door which led from her private wing to the school building. The journey had been intended as a treat, the offer of a new kingdom to explore. But Asha, frightened by such an expanse of unknown territory, had cried for her dead mother: it was the first clear memory of her life.

Alexa, on that day, had promised to look after the

211

orphaned child and had kept her promise faithfully. Now it was time for the debt to be repaid. It was Alexa, eighty-seven years old and devastated by bereavement, who was lonely and afraid; and Asha who must take the responsibility for her happiness.

'There's a place waiting for you,' she said. 'A sort of country flat. Terribly nice. It's all arranged. I'll take you to have a look at it. You can move in whenever you choose – the day after Pirry's funeral, if you want to.' The elderly gentleman on his Scottish estate who had already, unwittingly, become the sixteenth Lord Glanville, was unlikely to play the part of a Victorian villain and turn a helpless old lady out into the snow. But if Alexa was determined not to be beholden for a moment to the new owners of the title and estates, Asha intended to relieve her mind of any fears. She brought Alexa her stick and took her other arm. Together they passed through the door leading to what had once been the state apartments.

The building was cold, and empty with the special hollowness of rooms from which a community is temporarily absent. Still supporting Alexa, but careful not to intrude on her thoughts by speaking, Asha allowed herself to be taken to the ballroom. It had been used for a concert before the school dispersed, and no one had yet tidied away the rows of chairs or the violin stands on the low platform.

'We had such marvellous occasions,' sighed Alexa. 'I remember the very first ball I attended here. It was in 1905, long before Pirry was born. Before I had any thought of ever living at Blaize. Piers already wanted to marry me, but I was in love with someone else. You won't remember Matthew. We danced together here. I was beautiful in those days. But that's dead as well.'

Had the shock induced a sudden rambling senility in the old lady? Perhaps, Asha decided, this period of reminiscence was an essential part of mourning. It was necessary for rituals to be observed. For Churchill the ceremonies of state; for Pirry the memories of a mother in a house peopled with ghosts.

'And the banqueting hall.' Alexa was moving on. 'That was used for supper when we had a ball. I remember the telegram coming here. It was Brinsley's twenty-first birthday, in 1914. Pirry was just a baby then. Brinsley was summoned to the Front. One more dance, he called for. I remember him shouting, "Lord Kitchener won't begrudge us one last waltz!" Margaret and I watched from the gallery. They were so handsome, the three cousins: Brinsley and Robert and Kate. All a generation younger than me, and all dead now.'

She shook her head sadly as she moved on and began slowly to climb the wide oak staircase up to the long gallery at the top of the house. It was the school library now; but apart from the clutter of bookshelves, hardly changed since Tudor days.

'Your father used to play here,' she told Asha. 'As a little boy he was lame. After the operation, Robert often brought him up here to play games on crutches, until he could walk again.' Asha had heard the story before, but she did not interrupt Alexa's memories.

High along the panelled wall hung a row of portraits, of thin-faced men with long noses. 'The Glanvilles belong with the house,' said Alexa without regret. 'Except for these two. These are mine.'

It was late in his life that she had commissioned a portrait of her husband, for he was already silver-haired when they married. Like his forebears he was tall and thin, but showed none of their superciliousness: his eyes

213

were kind and intelligent. The portrait was a conventional one of a man in formal clothes. Beside it, Matthew Lorimer's painting of Pirry on his twenty-first birthday seemed at first glance to be not so much a portrait as a burst of sunlight. The young man's red-blond hair and fair skin emerged from a golden background so subtly that the final truth of the likeness was startling by comparison with the first impression of random brush strokes.

'He was such a pretty boy.' Alexa stared at the picture. This was what she had come to see. 'He and Frisca, both beautiful children. And both dead. Both my children, dead before me. It's not supposed to happen that way. You promised, Pirry. You promised to stay alive.'

She was weeping at last; but after a few moments she gave a deep sigh, seeming to bring herself under control.

'Pirry always thought that I was afraid of leaving Blaize,' she said. 'But it was never my house. Always his. I wasn't brought up here. I looked after it because I hoped he'd come to live in it himself. I wouldn't have minded moving out then. But now – ' She shivered. 'I don't like things to change. I wanted to go on as I was. What's going to happen to me, now that that man's got his hands on it all at last?'

'That man', the younger brother of Alexa's husband, had been dead for twenty years; and his son – himself no longer young – probably knew no more than Asha did how the young Alexa had been the cause of a quarrel between the two brothers. But on this subject Alexa had never been rational.

'I'll look after everything, Aunt Alexa. You don't have to worry.'

'It was never the house,' Alexa repeated. 'Not the bricks and mortar. But Blaize was a home – the heart of the family. Not the Glanville family, after Piers died: the

214

Lorimers. They all came here, to live or stay. Well, what's left of the family now? Ghosts, that's all. A house full of ghosts. So many deaths, and no births any more. When are there going to be babies in the family again? Why should I want to stay here? I can entertain you all in a bed-sitting room. You and Bernard and Ilsa and – why didn't Ilsa telephone? She was staying with Pirry. She ought to have phoned directly, to tell me what happened.'

'Ilsa died as well, Aunt Alexa. In the same accident.'

Alexa was silent for a moment, but then looked up again at Pirry's portrait. Asha could tell that she did not really care about this second piece of news. She had lost a son and a great-niece at the same time, but had only tears enough for one of them.

Even Asha had been too deeply affected by Pirry's death to think of anyone else until now. In silence she remembered the woman who had appeared almost from the dead in such an extraordinary way to take her place amongst the Lorimers. Until today, it had seemed that she had no part to play in the history of the family, that they had not loved her enough to make her feel that she belonged. She would never be one of the ghostly memories of Blaize. Yet Pirry must have cared for her; and her death had set in train a series of events which she could not have anticipated. As Alexa continued to stare broken-heartedly at the picture of her son, Asha thought about her pale, cold cousin and shivered in the unheated gallery. She took the old lady's arm again.

'Let me take you back into the warmth, Aunt Alexa,' she said.

PART THREE

Asha
Ancestors
1975–77

1

Looking back, when it was all over, Asha saw the Ancestor as a harbinger of trouble, so closely did the bad times follow on his arrival in her life. But as she abandoned the taxi at the end of the pedestrianized street and began to carry the old man's portrait home on a sultry July Saturday in 1975, she saw the gift from her great-aunt only as an inconvenience, not as a malign influence. It was heavy, and awkward to carry: nothing more.

Never before had the Portobello Road seemed so long or so crowded with tourists. They clustered round the stalls of the street market, fingering souvenirs, and enthusing without discrimination over silver or pinchbeck, rare books or fairground relics. They sat down in the middle of the road to rest their poor feet. In a score of different languages they complained of the heat. Because they were not looking for anything in particular they wandered aimlessly without caring whom they jostled. One of the nurses who looked after Lady Glanville had as a kindness wrapped the heavy Victorian painting in brown paper, and this – without offering any great protection against a swinging handbag or aggressive elbow – made it almost impossible to carry. Hot and bad-tempered, Asha retreated down a side street to rest for a moment.

Much of her ill temper was directed against her husband, Ranji – unfairly, since he could not have foreseen that she would return so heavily laden. She had asked if she could have the car for her visit to Alexa's nursing home and was told that the Loiterers would be playing away this Saturday. Whenever their cricket match was outside London, Ranji gave a lift to three of his team-mates. It was natural that they liked to travel together – but two of the others were car-owners, so Asha didn't see why Ranji shouldn't be a passenger occasionally, instead of always the driver. Besides, only that morning some kind of government snooper had turned up at the flat, claiming that he needed to check the car's registration documents to see who owned it. Ranji had told him firmly that it was his wife's property – which was in fact the case. Asha, never possessive about objects, had forgotten how pointedly her great-aunt had insisted that the vehicle was a gift to her personally. Reminded, she felt that she should be able to use it when she chose. It had been feeble of her not to insist that Ranji should at least ask whether his arrangement could be changed.

Asha recognized that the real cause of her irritation had less to do with the use of the car than with the amount of time which Ranji devoted to sport. From Monday to Friday they were both out at work all day. Asha's hours were shorter, but the strain of teaching was greater – and she more often had to work in the evenings. It would have been pleasant to relax together each Saturday, or even to share a little of the week's neglected housework. But Ranji's cricket and tennis seasons began as soon as his hockey and squash seasons ended.

She tried to be fair. Thirteen years ealier she had fallen in love with a graceful, athletic student. She had loved the glossy health of Ranji's shining brown skin, and the firm strength of his muscles. The body she still adored required exercise to keep it in trim – and temperamentally, too, Ranji needed regular opportunities to practise the sports in which he excelled. A rainy Saturday, washing away a match, could make him tetchy for the whole weekend.

Asha herself had been born thirty-four years earlier as a premature baby with a heart defect, and the oxygen which saved her life had permanently affected her eyesight. Wearing glasses, she had no problems in her professional and domestic life; but on a tennis or squash court a fast-moving ball could arrive only inches from her eyes before she would be aware of it. It was impossible for her to share Ranji's pleasure in playing games. But of course he had a right to his recreations – it was her own fault that she had no week-end hobby of her own. Ranji could not be blamed for her present grumpiness.

All the same, if only she could have had the car today it would have cut an hour each way off her journey to the country and relieved her of this uncomfortable piece of furniture-removing. Asha gave a loud sigh and stooped to pick up the Ancestor again.

'Carry your bag, Miss?'

'Chris!' Any friendly face would have cheered Asha at this moment and the appearance of Chris Townsend, who taught art at her comprehensive school, lifted her spirits immediately. He was wearing nothing but a smile and a brief pair of swimming trunks – appropriate to the temperature if surprising for a street in the middle of London.

'I saw you from my sun-bathing roof,' he said. 'No one else in the city has such fair hair. Paler than blonde. I recognized its shimmer even though I couldn't see your face. There's a refrigerator full of cold beer only twenty yards from here. Come and sample it. Then I'll put some clothes on and lug this object back to your place.'

Ranji would not be home for hours. Asha accepted the offer gratefully. 'I didn't know you lived here,' she said.

'I squat here. A man with a salary on the Burnham

Scale and no working wife can't afford to live anywhere.' He led the way into a terrace house which from outside appeared derelict, its ground floor windows covered with sheets of corrugated iron. A tiny front garden was littered with empty Coke tins, broken glass and the red boxes of a take-away chicken shop, whilst all the exterior paint-work of the building had peeled away to reveal rotten grey wood. The stairs inside were dark and musty. Then he opened the door of his room on the first floor.

For a moment Asha stared in astonishment. Then she began to laugh. Chris had painted three walls of the room in a dazzling white. The fourth wall was covered by a bright mural of stylized flowers and butterflies. As though in a jungle, tiny men and women wandered naked amongst the stems of the flowers. Asha examined the wall with delight while Chris disappeared into his kitchen for the beer.

'I thought squatters were all hippies,' she said when he returned.

'The hippies get the publicity. People like me, who want to be left alone, keep rather quieter.'

'How safe are you?'

'It's almost foolproof. The council bought the whole terrace, scheduled it for complete modernization and then found that it had run out of money. If it put tenants in from the housing list, they'd sue for essential repairs. It can't even afford to demolish. A caretaker like me is just what's needed. No one recognizes my existence officially, in case vacant possession should ever be required, but a considerable number of blind eyes are turned. What have you got?'

'A flat above a shop. Oh, this is what I needed!' She took a long drink of the cold beer and then sipped more slowly.

'What are you carting about here?'

'The portrait of an ancestor. I have an immensely elderly relative who brought me up after my parents died. I call her Aunt Alexa, but she's really a great-aunt on my father's side and a great-great-aunt through my mother. She's getting on for a hundred. Until a few months ago she lived in a country house specially converted for elderly people and was incredibly spry – up and about every day. But now she does seem to be getting frail at last. She's had to move into a nursing home. And she can't have her own furniture there, as she did before. So when I visited her today, she gave me this.'

'May I see?'

'Of course.' Together they tore off the brown paper. Chris leaned the portrait against one of his white walls and they both stepped back to look at it. Although Asha had seen the picture often enough on the wall at Blaize, this was her first chance to study it with the possessive eye of an owner.

The effect was one of weight. The wide frame was black, with only a touch of gold on the innermost beading. The subject wore black as well, and the background was little lighter. What saved the picture from deadness was the appearance of the sitter. He had a great deal of white hair – yellowed now by varnish and the passing of time – which curled on his shoulders and joined with sideburns and full beard to frame his face. Greenish-blue eyes pierced out commandingly from beneath bushy chestnut eyebrows. Asha stared at the portrait with a slight uneasiness, not sure that she wished to share her flat with such an autocratic personality.

'Who painted it?' asked Chris.

'No idea. Can't you tell me?'

He fetched a magnifying glass and went down on his

223

knees to study the canvas before announcing that it was unsigned. Moving it away from the wall so that he could look at the back, he found a small label attached to the frame. '1877. J.J. Lorimer, it says here.'

'That's the sitter, not the artist. John Junius Lorimer, merchant prince, of the city of Bristol. Aunt Alexa's father. He died in 1879. Can't you tell from the style of the picture who painted it?'

'I might if it were someone well-known or idiosyncratic. No clues here though. Probably a provincial artist.'

'Pity. I hoped I could make my fortune by discovering that I owned the 1877 equivalent of a Giorgione.'

'No such thing. 1877 wasn't exactly a vintage year in Bristol. Have you ever had *your* portrait painted, Asha?'

'No.'

'You must let me have a go one day. That dazzling hair! And your complexion is so fair as well. Translucent. A technical challenge. I'd like to do a series. Asha by Renoir. Asha by Bonnard. Asha by Picasso. We could storm the Academy together.'

'What about Asha by Townsend?'

'You've put your finger straight on to my Achilles' heel,' said Chris sorrowfully. 'I haven't got a style. If I had, I shouldn't be wasting my time at a crummy old comprehensive school. I have an enormous talent for imitation. That's quite useful for a teacher. I can show my pupils how to achieve any result that's ever been achieved before. But apart from that – ' He shrugged his shoulders; and Asha, not liking to pay compliments out of ignorance, evaded the subject.

'It's not a crummy old comprehensive,' she said.

'I withdraw the phrase. A progressive, well-organized, well-equipped, friendly comprehensive school which is four times as big as it ought to be and lacks both discipline and academic standards but otherwise is in every respect perfect.'

'Given the system – ' began Asha; but Chris interrupted her.

'And who gives us the system? Why should a handful of politicians who don't live here and would never dream of educating their children here have the right to say that we must have two thousand children in our school? Have you ever met a single working teacher, Asha, who genuinely believes that a school the size of ours is any good?'

'The range of subjects – '

'Was never a problem in a school of five hundred until one reached A-level courses. A sixth-form college would deal with that, and allow our sixteen-year-olds a bit of responsibility in what's left of the school. And then, instead of altering the exam grading system so that nobody exactly fails, we might be able to improve our teaching so that a few kids actually pass.' He checked himself, smiling at his own indignation. 'Asha, I haven't seen you since your appointment was announced. Congratulations. I was glad it was you. Promise of higher things later as well, I imagine.'

'Thanks.' Three days earlier Asha had been appointed deputy head of Hillgate Comprehensive School. The promotion – as Chris suggested – implied that she would be well-placed in two years' time to apply for the headship when its present holder retired. But the governors had not formally mentioned such a possibility and so it had not seemed necessary for Asha to volunteer the fact that her own plans for the next three years included a baby.

Somehow there had never been a convenient time for starting a family. Ranji – younger than herself – had still been a student at the LSE, when they married. By the time he was earning a reasonable salary Asha had been promoted to be head of the history department and was anxious to consolidate her new position. She would have been willing to take a break from work in 1971 – but that was the year in which Ranji gave up his salaried employment in order to start and run his own business. It was a necessary precaution then to hang on to the one job which guaranteed a monthly pay cheque.

Now, at thirty-four, she was aware that the risks of motherhood would increase with every year that passed: she must not wait much longer. Three terms as deputy head would let her put into effect plans which a weak headmaster had been dodging for too long. But if she were to start a baby next March, say, she could leave in July. The thought gave her pleasure, but she kept it to herself.

'Another beer?'

'No, thanks. I must get back.'

'Why?'

'Just as I was leaving for school yesterday morning,' said Asha, 'a bookcase fell over. None of our walls or floors is truly vertical or horizontal. The bookcase had probably been doing a leaning tower of Pisa act for months, and one more book on the top shelf was the last straw. I didn't have time to cope with the mess before I went out, and when I came home again I was absolutely whacked. You know that end-of-the-week feeling.'

'I know precisely the feeling,' Chris agreed.

'So all the mess is still there. But weighing heavy on my conscience by now.'

'Hang on, then.' Chris dressed himself in shorts and sandals. He picked up the portrait as though it weighed nothing and followed her out. Asha noticed the care with which he locked the door behind him.

'You can't trust anyone these days,' he explained. 'Turn your back for a moment and somebody's squatting in your property.'

'Disgusting!'

'Yes. Absolutely disgraceful!'

Asha went ahead, forging a path up the middle of the road. The crowd was thinner now, although tourists were still posing for photographs with monkeys or parrots on their shoulders, and two young men with guitars and a collecting hat were the centre for a sing-song. Freed from her heavy load, she was able to move more quickly than before, and they soon reached her home.

The shop beneath the flat was divided into half a dozen tiny booths. The woman nearest the door, a specialist in sporting prints, looked at the portrait with interest as Asha felt for her key.

'Going into the trade then, dear?'

'No. Strictly private. How are things?'

'Tricky. Easy to buy these days, but hard to sell. All those banks and companies collapsing – it's made people nervous. I saw Ranji on Thursday when I was on my way to a sale; but not to speak to. We must have been on the same train, but I didn't catch sight of him until we arrived at Cambridge.'

'Cambridge?' Asha, her key now in the lock, tried to keep the incredulity out of her voice. On Thursday Ranji had gone off to work at his regular time and had answered her evening query about the day with his usual 'Nothing special'. But her surprise was nobody else's business. 'I hope you found something worthwhile at the auction,' she said instead, and led the way up to the flat.

'I have some beer too,' she said as Chris propped the picture against a wall.

'Actually, I wouldn't say no to a cup of tea. And before

227

you put the kettle on, why shouldn't I help you get these books back?'

'Why should you?'

'Because any chore is less choring with two people than with one – right?'

'Right!' said Asha, pleased. Ten seconds while I get out of my aunt-visiting clothes.'

'What sort of a person is your great-aunt?' Chris called through the open door as she changed.

'She was born in a slum. Became the most famous opera-singer of her day – her day being somewhere around 1900. Marched with the suffragists. Married a peer of the realm and lived in aristocratic comfort for fifty-odd years. Lost almost all of it when her only son died without an heir. When you live to be ninety-eight, you can pack in several different lives.' Asha returned to the living room wearing jeans and a T-shirt.

'Talk about different lives!' exclaimed Chris. 'You look about sixteen. Don't let the sixth form ever see you dressed like that, or discipline will shatter. Now tell me, is this to be a botch job or shall we do it thoroughly? We can put everything back as it was before, and one day it will tip again. Or we can slice a bit off the bottom of the bookcase so that it leans back on the wall.'

'I've got a plane,' said Asha. Chris, trained to handle a variety of tools and materials, did the job with speed and neatness. When he had set the tall bookcase up again she fetched a cloth and cleaned it.

'You know where everything goes,' said Chris. 'I'll bang the dust out of the books and hand them up to you.'

It was a dirty task. As the dust flew, Asha was ashamed to think how long it was since she had done any spring cleaning. Not this spring, certainly. But because they

228

chattered as they worked, the shelves were re-stocked in an amazingly short time.

Two hours later Chris stood up to leave. 'That was good,' he said. 'Not just the tea. Those terrible staff rooms are like railway stations. Always people coming and going. And even for an innocent cup of coffee, you have to decide whether to patronize the southern line or the western region, so to speak, facing Bransby the Bore or Miss Charles the Chirruper. One never properly converses.' He paused, staring at the portrait he had carried in. 'I could clean that, you know. It mightn't make the old boy look any more handsome, but at least he wouldn't be dark yellow.'

'I hardly think he's worth it.'

'There'd be no charge. It wouldn't need much more than patience. And a room to work in. Nothing at school is vandal-proof.'

'We have an attic.' Asha took him up the narrow staircase which led to the top of the building.

'It's a studio!' exclaimed Chris. 'Here's London full of desperate artists searching for anything that would serve to paint in, and you let a real studio stand empty.'

Asha saw that he was right, although it had not occurred to her before. As well as an ordinary window, there was a large skylight in the north slope of the roof. But she had her own plans for the future of the empty, spacious room. One day it would be a nursery.

'Sorry,' she said. 'I mean, certainly you could use it to clean the Ancestor, if you're really prepared to do that. But I'm not going into the landlady business.'

'Oh, well!' He shrugged his shoulders. 'Anyway, this would do fine for giving the old chap a scrub. But not while this sun-bathing weather lasts, and then I'll be away for the holidays. The first rainy Saturday morning next term, I'll be round.' He moved across to the window and stared out. 'You'd have a lot more sun if that tree came down,' he pointed out. 'It's far too close to the house.'

Asha came to stand beside him. 'Its doom is already written.' She opened the window so that they could lean out, and showed him that the tree was one of a long line of elms. Although this was full summer, the arms of the three trees furthest away stretched bleakly upwards, bearing no foliage at all, and on the boughs of the next two the leaves had turned brown and begun to curl. 'It's the Dutch Elm Disease,' she said. 'They're all dead or dying except ours, and that can't last long. We had the Parks Officer round to see whether there was anything we could do and he said it was hopeless. They're touching root and crown. The beetles which cause the trouble don't need to fly – they can just step from one branch to another. There could be two million tiny beetles on the move out there – terrifying thought! Our tree is the end of the line, so it may be good for one more season; but after that it will be for the chop. I find it sad. They're more than a hundred years old, those elms – they were here before the houses.'

'It's a mistake to believe that everything should go on for ever,' Chris said. 'A mistake to which the British are especially prone. It's necessary to let some things die – institutions, buildings, systems, trees – in order that something new may be nurtured. And better to plant a new tree in a suitable position than to keep alive an old one which should never have been allowed to remain so close to a building. I'm surprised to find that you're sentimental.'

Asha was surprised herself, when she thought about it. She clapped her hands cheerfully. 'You're right. Let the axe fall. Let the sun flood in. I shall paint the whole attic

230

white, like your beautiful squat, and then invite you to put another marvellous mural on one wall – to be paid for in beer and frivolous chatter.'

'Done!' Chris held out his hand to seal the bargain. It was odd, Asha thought, that although they had been colleagues for three years, this was the first time they had ever enjoyed a sustained conversation alone together. The good humour which his company had induced in her survived his departure by at least an hour. Had her husband returned within that time, she might never have remembered what the seller of sporting prints had told her.

But Ranji was late, and selfish in his demands for supper when he came, so that what should have been a simple question became the beginning of a quarrel.

'Where were you last Thursday, Ranji?' she wanted to know.

2

Although this was the most serious tiff to disturb her twelve-year-old marriage, Asha did her best not to be unreasonable. During the hours of waiting for her husband's return it had crossed her mind that he might be having an affair – that he might have been travelling to a rendez-vous in Cambridge. But she did not think it very likely: Ranji had never in the past shown any inclination to chase after other women. She would have accepted almost any explanation of his movements on the previous Thursday except the one which she now knew to be untrue: so it was foolish of Ranji not to recognize that she would not ask such a specific question without knowing part of the answer.

He repeated his claim that he had spent the day as usual in his office; and even before she discovered what facts it concealed, the lie by itself upset her. With determined eyes and tight lips she turned against her husband, a technique which over the years had reduced a succession of thieving, bullying, truant or lying schoolchildren to sullen confession and, by her refusal to discuss anything else until she had learned the truth, force from him at last a sulky explosion: 'Well, if you must know, I was looking for a job.'

The unexpected answer turned her aggressive questioning to puzzlement. 'Why do you want a job when you've got your own firm?' For the past five years Ranji had run a contract cleaning business. He employed a predominantly Indian workforce to provide regular office cleaning and

232

also – more lucratively – to clear up new properties after the departure of the builders and maintain them in immaculate condition until a tenant had signed a lease. Sometimes, when he recognized a bargain, he took over the lease himself and sub-let at a profit, but this kind of gamble was only a side-line: it was the service he offered which provided his main income.

'I *used* to have my own firm,' Ranji corrected her. 'That was three months ago. The property market collapsed last year. Perhaps you didn't notice.'

'What difference – '

He sighed before beginning a patient explanation. 'As soon as prices slumped, the banks got cold feet and called in the loans they'd been almost forcing on people a year or two earlier. The loans were secured on properties which couldn't find a buyer and weren't in any case likely to realize the inflated values placed on them – but they were put on the market anyway, and so prices fell again. Two of my most important customers went bankrupt and most of the others had to cut down on their expenses. I was left with bad debts and no new work coming in. And *I* had a bank loan as well. My bank manager didn't have the sense to work out that he was more likely to get his money back from a going concern than from a man on the dole. He read my balance sheet and saw that it didn't balance. So he demanded repayment of the loan. I couldn't pay, of course. He put a liquidator in to discover what assets I had.'

'That man this morning . . .' said Asha slowly.

'While you were at school on Wednesday the bailiffs came to inspect our furniture. I told them that it all belonged to you and I think they accepted that – just because you're a native and I'm so obviously a foreigner. Anyway, they could see that we owned nothing valuable.

But when I said the same about the car, that it was yours, they didn't believe that. I didn't know where you kept the documents. The man came to check with you that I'd told the truth.'

'Ranji, does all this mean that you'll be made bankrupt?'

'Yes, indeed. And since half my assets are claims on other companies which are now bankrupt themselves, it's difficult to see how I can earn my discharge.'

Asha took his hand and squeezed it sympathetically, wondering if there was anything she could do to help. 'Do you think Aunt Alexa – ?'

'No,' said Ranji. 'This isn't the sort of amount she might keep in her piggy bank. Even after I've handed over everything I've saved in the past five years there'll be thousands of pounds still owing, and if I borrowed it, I might never be able to pay it back. Besides, she doesn't even like me. You can forget that idea.'

'Darling, I'm so sorry about this. But why didn't you tell me? You must have been worrying about it for weeks.'

'Oddly enough,' said Ranji stiffly, 'confessing to one's wife that one has made a mess of things is not the most morale-raising of occupations. I agree that I ought to have told you. But I was waiting for something positive to put against it. Such as, "I'm afraid the business has gone bust but I've landed an absolutely super job, so we'll be back to living on two steady salaries again and isn't it simply marvellous!"'

'That's fine as far as other people are concerned. But I'm your wife. Anything that happens to you is happening to me as well. I want to share everything with you. Even the bad days.'

'Well, you know now.'

Asha kissed him affectionately, understanding that the deception which had sparked off their argument could be explained by his shame. Yet even as she forgave him for the small untruth she was aware in the back of her mind of a niggling annoyance, too petty to be put into words. Instead of leaving the flat at his usual time every morning during the past few weeks, and keeping away during his normal working hours, could Ranji not have contributed rather more time to the running of the household – taking over some of the chores, or at least sharing them, instead of leaving them to a woman who was still doing a tiring day's work? The bookcase, for example. Ranji, like herself, had been in the flat when it toppled over. But only Asha had genuinely needed to hurry off to work that morning, and only Asha had been genuinely worn out in the evening.

She had enough sense to know that this was not the moment to criticize him. 'Did you get the job?' she asked.

'Which job? I've applied for dozens. Nowadays, no one's allowed to put "white skin preferred" in a newspaper advertisement, but that doesn't stop the preference from existing. And running your own business isn't the best qualification for becoming an employee. People are afraid you may not be able to fit into a team. In any case, with so many firms going out of business, there are dozens of chaps with better qualifications floating around.'

Worried and helpless, Asha could only kiss him again. 'Ranji, darling, I'm so terribly sorry,' she repeated. 'From now on we must discuss everything together. I do hope it won't be long before you find something. And at least we shan't starve while you're looking.' Too late she recognized that this was the wrong thing to say.

'Yes, indeed. It's just as well that I'm married to a successful career woman.'

Asha did her best to ignore what seemed almost a note of grievance in his voice, and applied herself to the task of cheering her husband up. He was in no mood to discuss his job prospects any further, so she asked instead about the cricket match. It proved to be a tactful question. In return for Ranji's description of the wickets he had taken, Asha might have pointed to the neatly-stocked bookcase, clean, upright, secure, as a token of her own achievement. Instead, she waited for him to notice it, and was disappointed. Nor did he enquire about her visit to the nursing home. Her niggling feeling of resentment returned and she held back her news until he should be interested enough to ask. Chris had carried the portrait up to the attic to await its cleaning, so there was nothing visible to prompt a question about her ancestor.

The last ten days of terms were, as always, hectic. In school hours there were tests to be given and marked, books to be collected and all the special events which marked the end of the school year to be organized. In the evenings there was the usual last-minute rush of reports to be written. It was difficult for Asha – still working busily at nine o'clock one evening – to hear without irritation Ranji's enquiries about when she was going to get supper.

'Couldn't you?' she asked.

'If you'd thought to provide any food, no doubt I could try to cook it.'

'Isn't there – oh, I'm sorry. I was on dinner duty, so I couldn't get out to the shops. But we've got cheese and onions and tomatoes and plenty of eggs.'

Ranji made a Spanish omelette and burnt it. Asha, picking at the meal without appetite, sighed. 'Did you spoil this specially so that I'd never ask you again?'

'Don't be ridiculous. I have to eat it also. Although I

do think you might organize yourself to allow time for looking after your home. I noticed this morning, the bedroom is dusty.'

'And did you dust it? Listen, Ranji.' Asha was too tired to be tactful. 'I've got a very full week ahead. In the holidays I'll play the little housewife as perfectly as you like. But just for this week, when I'm busy and you're not, couldn't "organizing myself" include asking you for help? If I give you a list, will you do some shopping tomorrow?'

'I have an interview tomorrow.'

'All day?'

'Do I have to account to you for every minute of my time?'

'Ranji, I understand how you feel. But it seems silly not to recognize that your commitments have changed. Why can't we adapt to the change – and adapt again when you get a job?'

'*If* I get a job.'

Asha made no further comment. But that night she lay awake for a long time, unhappy with herself. For twelve years she had prided herself on her ability to do her work as a schoolteacher well and at the same time to be a good wife. Now she saw that she was only a good wife to a husband so much absorbed in his own business that he was glad to think of her standing on her own feet, having her own interests and responsibilities. In this changed situation her hard work was a reproach to him. What he needed now was the support of a clinging, fussing homemaker.

Paradoxically, though, he could only afford that kind of support when he was working. A few days earlier, in the empty attic, Asha had allowed herself to dream of babies in a nursery: but that dream could not be fulfilled until Ranji became a breadwinner again. So for the sake of their future family Ranji's period of unemployment must be as short as possible: and for the sake of his pride they must together do their best to earn his discharge from bankruptcy. There must be no more of the suppressed resentment which had spoiled the evening for them both. Asha saw that she must make it her responsibility to build up her husband's self-respect again – and, if possible, she must help him to find a job.

3

The school holidays began, and at once the atmosphere was lighter. Now Asha had time to clean and cook with a thoroughness which Ranji could not criticize. Now, too, with his lack of occupation admitted, they could spend whole days together, walking in the country or exploring the city like tourists. They were friends again. But beneath their happiness, Ranji's unemployment ticked away like a time bomb which might at any time explode to shatter his good temper and plunge him into gloom.

Since there were no longer any secrets between them, Asha was allowed to read her husband's file of advertisements and letters of application, and the discouraging replies clipped to each sheet. She sympathized with his resolve not to take unsatisfactory work just for the sake of working. He was determined to be a successful businessman and would consider only openings which led in this direction. But all over the country companies were cutting down on staff rather than taking on new employees. What could he do?

One way of earning a living was on view every Saturday from the windows of the flat. 'How about renting a stall in the Portobello Road Market?' Asha suggested. 'Or a cubicle in one of the arcades? I could find out from the tenants downstairs whether anyone's thinking of giving up.'

'Not a practical idea, I think.' Now that the first humiliation of confession was over, Ranji did his best to show appreciation of Asha's suggestions and to control

239

the easy reaction of sarcasm – but that did not prevent him from demolishing her ideas with decisive logic. 'In the first place, I have no knowledge of the antique trade. In the second place, I have no capital with which to buy an initial stock. And in the third place, a bankrupt person is forbidden to borrow or to accept any kind of credit.'

His tone did not allow for argument. Asha changed the subject – but the idea must have lingered in the back of her mind. It was Chris who indirectly tempted it back to the surface in a new form.

Chris arrived at the flat without warning towards the end of the summer holiday. 'I've come to give Mr Lorimer his bath.'

'Come in.' Asha was delighted to see him. 'But what on earth have you brought with you?'

'If you remember, you promised that I could paint your portrait as a reward for cleaning your great-granddaddy.'

'Did I? No, I don't remember.'

'Well, you did. Not just one portrait, either. Asha by Bonnard, Asha by Renoir, Asha by Vermeer. What I have here is a perfectly frightful portrait of some Georgian squire, complete with a decent frame, which I was able to buy for less than the cost of a new canvas. I propose to obliterate the old codger with some tasteful background and substitute a portrait of Asha by Gainsborough. And with that in mind I've persuaded one of your neighbours downstairs to lend you a dress.' He was in the drawing room of the flat by now, unpacking a long gown of pale grey silk shot with pink, and an over-skirt of silvery lace. 'The dress was made for someone so thin or so tightly-laced that no potential customer has yet been able to make it meet round the waist. But since you're only going to stand still, no one will know that the bodice is held together at the back with tape and safety pins. Will

240

you try it on straightaway, so that I can work out the pose?'

'I'm being hustled,' said Asha; but she was smiling. The long holiday had enabled her to relax. Although her new responsibilities as deputy headmistress included such tasks as the drawing up of a complicated timetable, she had disposed of these early in the vacation and could feel the next few days to be truly free.

Slim though she was, she found that Chris was right about the dress. What he had not thought to mention was the extreme lowness of the *décolletage*. The tight cut of the bodice imposed its own line, pushing up her breasts in an authentically revealing eighteenth-century style. She flushed in slight embarrassment as she studied her appearance in the glass before making her way up to the attic.

'Gorgeous!' exclaimed Chris, taking the almost topless style for granted. 'Absolutely super! Now. Stand as straight as you can, here. Head right up. You're a duchess at the very least. This chair is a parasol. Rest your hand on it languidly. One toe forward. Now look into the distance, over my head. Oh Asha, marvellous!' He began to sketch the pose. 'Thank goodness you haven't acquired a tan. All the way here I was wondering whether I might have to do Asha by Gauguin first. If I leave photographs with you, could you practise putting your hair up, dressing it round some kind of pad? Gainsborough's sitters wove their hair into a sort of bird's nest and then didn't wash it for a year, but all I need is an approximation. It will alter the shape of your face. I'll copy a balustrade and a couple of steps from one of the genuine pictures. Keep your chin up. No smiling. Haughtiness is the name of the game. Complete confidence in your own beauty and elegance.'

His non-stop chatter made it clear that Asha must not

241

reply, lest an everyday conversation should tempt her to relax the stiffness of her back, the tilt of her head. When at last she was allowed to move she stretched her muscles before taking a look at his work.

'You can't tell anything from a pencil sketch,' he warned her. 'This is only to help me plan the background.'

'Will you really be able to make the picture look genuine?'

'I'm not attempting deception,' Chris pointed out. 'I'm using modern paints, and although I can produce the same texture and finish I shan't be as meticulous about brush strokes as a forger would. Let's say that if you were to hang the finished picture on the wall of a stately home which didn't happen to possess any real Gainsboroughs, the casual visitor – not the expert, of course – might just think he was seeing one. And if you put it in your sitting room when it's finished and claim that it's an ancestral portrait – like old Mr Lorimer, but prettier – I doubt if anyone will challenge you.'

'I'm surprised you don't take that up as a second career,' Asha laughed. 'Painting mock ancestors for people.'

'No business sense, that's my problem. I could paint them, but I'd never be able to sell them. And anyway, there'd be competition in the mock ancestor field.' He gestured towards the painting which he had set down next to that of John Junius Lorimer – a primitive, two-dimensional portrait of a wooden-faced country squire in hunting pink. 'Ugly old chap, but he must have been somebody's great-great-grandfather, and he was up for grabs. Anyone who was more concerned with inventing a past than acquiring a work of art could have claimed him as an ancestor.'

'Was it very expensive?' asked Asha thoughtfully. An idea was germinating in her mind.

'Dirt cheap. If he'd had a fancy gold frame, that would have been a different matter. These dealers who go round knocking on doors, offering to buy pictures for the value of the frames – they may hope to pick up an unrecognized Rembrandt: but to be going on with they're buying what they claim to want. The pictures are mainly junk, and the countryside is full of them.' As he talked, Chris began to dab the portrait of John Junius Lorimer with pads dipped into three bowls of strong-smelling liquids. Asha watched in silence, developing her inspiration, trying to find the snags.

'I often watch the tourists in the Portobello market,' she said. 'Sometimes they only want a souvenir. But often I have the feeling that they're looking for a past. An American buys a Georgian silver teapot, and it links her personally with some stately drawing room. Buyers like that might be in the market for ancestral portraits – if only it could be made easy. The Old Masters in the auction houses are too expensive. But suppose – ' While Chris continued to rub and dab, Asha pulled up the skirts of her long dress and sat cross-legged on the floor. The idea was taking shape.

'None of us has any capital.' She was thinking aloud now. 'So we couldn't acquire a large selection of old portraits. Not enough, anyway, to fill a gallery and attract buyers who wanted a choice. But suppose we did it the other way round. Collected orders first and filled them afterwards. Asking for a deposit with each order. Cash flow, that's what Ranji says is the most important thing in running a business.'

'You're going too fast for me. What are you talking about, and who do you mean by "we"?'

'You and me and Ranji. Ranji because he knows how to run a business. You because you know about pictures. And me because it's my brilliant idea.' And because if we need to borrow money to start with, the loan will have to be to me and not to Ranji, she thought: but there was no need for Chris to know about the conditions of bankruptcy.

'And what precisely is this brilliant idea?'

'Well, just suppose. Suppose we were to print a leaflet and get it distributed in some WASPish part of the States. The leaflet would invite the reader to order an ancestral portrait. It would be clear from the start that it couldn't possibly be his real ancestor. But we'd take some trouble to find the right kind of picture. And if he bought it, he could say whatever he liked about it afterwards.'

'It seems to me that we should be provoking terminological inexactitudes for profit,' Chris said solemnly. 'But go on.'

'Well – ' Asha was still thinking aloud – 'to get into the scheme, the prospective buyer would send us information about what country his family originally emigrated from, and when. And he could send family photographs, so that we could look for a vague likeness. He'd pay a fee with his application. We'd call it a search fee and it wouldn't be refundable; but if he actually bought one of the pictures we offered him, his payment would be deducted from the cost.'

'So you'd hand me a photograph of some Russian Jewish grandmother and send me out to scour the Home Counties for some face that could have been her father!'

'Don't be negative, Chris! This could work. We'd make it clear in the brochure that we'd mainly be drawing on British portraits. And in exchange for their search fee, we'd send people photographs of possibilities – three,

244

perhaps, at different prices, to choose from. Seriously, wouldn't that make a nice little business? It would cost a bit for the publicity and the first half dozen pictures, but after that it ought to be self-financing.'

'I see two prospects,' said Chris. 'Either the idea would be a complete flop and we'd lose any money we'd put into it: or it would be a success, and we wouldn't be able to cope with it. It's one thing to pick up a country squire like this just for the sake of the canvas. But to scour country sales and private houses with special features in mind would be a full-time job. Not to mention packing and insurance and all the filing and book-keeping and registering as a company if one has to do that and paying taxes and God knows what else.'

'Ranji could do all that. It would have to be Ranji's business. You and I would be consultants, taking a commission or charging for our time. If Ranji bought cheap pictures, they might need to be cleaned or restored, for example. You could do that, couldn't you?'

Chris had ceased to look doubtful and instead appeared to be considering some new proposition. 'You mustn't think that I'm in any way encouraging this folly,' he said after a long pause. 'But I could fling one more mad idea into the pool. Earlier on you suggested that I could paint mock ancestors for people. Well, it's true: I could. If you sent out three photographs to a prospective buyer, two could be of portraits which were genuinely old but unlikely to show any resemblance to the buyer. The third could be of a picture painted by me, showing a face with a family likeness to any photographs the buyer submitted, plus period costume. Instead of Asha by Gainsborough, Mrs John D. Doe by Gainsborough. Of course, it would have to be made clear from the start that that portrait would be painted by me now, in the twentieth century. No false pretences.'

'Absolutely not. Could you really do it, Chris?'

'You'd better wait and see how this one turns out. But yes, if I have any talent at all, it's for this. And as a matter of fact – ' now it was Chris's turn to express enthusiasm – 'it would be possible to build up a stock in advance. In America, you know, before photography, there were itinerant portrait painters. Primitives. They'd call at the richest-looking houses offering to paint the children of the family. And to save time, they'd carry with them pictures of children of various sizes in party clothes, finished except for the head. So Mama would order a four-year-old boy and little Junior's face would be added to a white satin suit. If I bought myself a couple of shop-window mannequins, I could have a few headless costume-pieces ready by the time your first brochure drew blood.'

'Is it possible, Chris? I mean, am I completely raving, or could we make it work?'

'I don't know whether a market exists,' said Chris, more seriously than before. 'I certainly don't know how we find it if it does. I have no capital to contribute, though I could run to the frames and canvases of my first offerings. I have a job, so for thirty weeks of the year my free time is limited. You also have a job, more demanding than mine. So *I* can't make it work. *You* can't make it work. It would all depend on Ranji.'

Asha sat for a long time without speaking. Ranji must not have a second failure, and with such a speculative idea the risk of failure must be high indeed. It would be better if he could find himself secure employment. But then, every week which brought him only letters of rejection represented a failure – of a different kind, but equally hard to bear.

Holding up the skirt of her long dress she stood up and crossed the room to study the progress of Chris's cleaning work. He had just reached her great-grandfather's hair, which beneath the dark yellow varnish proved to be white and curly. This was the portrait of a real person, with his own eighty years of history. Her aunt Alexa, no doubt, had tales to tell about the dramas of his life, his loves, his successes and failures. In her childhood at Blaize Asha had often begged for stories about the generations of Glanvilles whose portraits lined the long gallery. Their rich clothes and aristocratic features had spread a romantic aura round the family into which her great-aunt had married and Asha had given little attention to the sombre Victorian whom alone she could claim as her own ancestor. Now she was interested, excited.

'Could you find another canvas to use for your mock-Gainsborough?' she asked Chris. 'Leave the squire as he is, wooden face and all. With John Junius next to him – not to be sold, but as an example. And then the fancy-dress picture of me when it's ready. We'll show all three to Ranji at once – to let him see the possibilities. After that, as you say, it would be up to him.'

4

Ranji considered Asha's suggestion for setting up a cottage industry more seriously than she had expected. No doubt what appealed to him most was the possibility of running his own business again, on however small a scale. Asha suspected that he felt no great enthusiasm for the prospect of working as a subordinate in a large company. He spent less time reading job advertisements and writing letters of application, and instead devoted much of the day to all the formalities which Chris had rightly guessed to be necessary at the start of a new venture.

Everything had to be done in Asha's name: her husband was not allowed to own a credit card or even a cheque book. In any case, Ranji was determined to earn an honourable discharge from bankruptcy by paying everything he owed, but was clear that this could only be done from the profits of a thriving concern; so the precarious income of the new venture must also be Asha's to start with. Inevitably there was a period of several months in which no receipts could be expected at all, while money had to be spent on printers' bills, postage, registration fees and Ranji's first buying expeditions to country auctions. Asha was careful never to show anything but confidence in his handling of the project – although sometimes, as she signed the documents and blank cheques he put before her, she felt uneasy at the speed with which their savings shrank and their commitments grew.

It was just as well that nothing more than encouragement and signatures were required of her, for her first year as deputy headmistress was a punishing one, and as the end of the summer term approached she could feel herself wilting as visibly as the geraniums in her window boxes. The summer of 1975 had been hot enough: but the summer of 1976 rapidly carried England to an officially recognized state of drought. The huge panels of glass which chilled Hillgate Comprehensive School in winter had during the past six weeks transformed the building into a greenhouse in which pupils and teachers alike drooped listlessly over their desks. When the four o'clock bell rang on the last Friday in June, Asha – needing to reach the district health centre before it closed for the day – had to force herself into briskness.

With her case full of sixth-form essays to be marked, she hurried across the playground and along the street, overtaking small groups of her pupils as they dawdled their way home. During school hours there was little racial separation between the children. Black and white, yellow and brown – they talked and played together or picked each other for sports teams without consciousness of colour. But as they made their way now towards their homes, Asha noticed how homogeneous each group was.

Hillgate was probably the most multi-racial school in London. Civil wars, revolutions, government repression and natural disasters all over the world were reflected in its register. There were Lebanese children, Arabs and Iranians: Greeks from Greece and Greeks from Cyprus: Turks, Irish, Vietnamese, Chinese and Pakistanis. There were Indians from India and others – a quiet separate group – who had never lived in the sub-continent but had arrived, penniless, in England after being expelled from Kenya or Uganda. Many of them had been prosperous in

Africa and had taken a surprisingly short time to succeed in their new country. Their children, intelligent and hard-working, were Asha's most rewarding pupils.

A far larger group – almost half of Hillgate's pupils – was of West Indian descent. Asha saw few of these as she walked towards the clinic, for as they came out of the school gates they had turned in the other direction, towards the large houses built round the former race-course. This part of Notting Hill had been developed a hundred years earlier to attract wealthy families to an area less fashionable than Mayfair – but now each of the spacious properties housed up to ten families in conditions which prompted sanitary inspectors and fire officers to write anxious reports.

There had been a time – and not so long ago – when slum landlords had flourished here, evicting protected tenants and cramming in immigrants who were too des-perate for shelter to complain about the conditions. But by now most of the houses had passed into the hands of the West Indians themselves, who painted the once-stately facades in dazzling shades of daffodil yellow, shocking pink or royal blue and no longer complained about discrimination in the housing lists. Most of them were happy to remain in an area where an all-night reggae party would be greeted by the neighbours with enthusiasm rather than with complaints to the police.

By contrast, the council estate in which the health centre was situated had a bleak, unfriendly atmosphere. In winter the wind howled along forlorn concrete corri-dors and staircases, but the drought had brought a differ-ent kind of desolation. Dust hovered in the windless air and the sound of babies' crying came through a score of open windows. Large notices forbade the playing of ball games on the grass, but there was no longer any grass.

250

Half a dozen boys, for lack of any more interesting activity, were kicking an empty beer tin around on one patch of the baked mud, whilst two girls in bikinis stretched themselves out nearby to improve their sun tans. Asha recognized the girls as Hillgate pupils, gigglers who were sitting out the days of their compulsory education until free to leave.

To leave for what, Asha asked herself as she walked briskly on. It was a question which often worried her as she taught her least intelligent pupils. In a few months' time these girls, no doubt, would be shampooing hair or serving in a shop; spending their evenings at discos; doing their best to entice some poor boy away from his mates and his football matches in order that as soon as possible they should be able to escape from their parents, put their own names down on the council housing lists and end up – where? In another flat on this terrible estate? Could that really be anyone's ambition?

The trouble was that few of her pupils had ambition of any kind. The white children were almost as apathetic as the blacks, who took it for granted that they would fail their exams and be offered the worst jobs. Unlike the bright-eyed, competitive Asians, most of these children – to use their own tired phrase – couldn't care less.

Asha had decided long ago that the difference must lie in the attitude of the parents. The Asians from Kenya and Uganda who had struggled back to prosperity in England knew that it was possible to succeed by hard work. They were determined that their children should do well and offered not only encouragement and discipline but also the example of achievement.

By contrast, the mothers of those two sunbathing fifteen-year-olds had probably thought school a waste of time themselves, and accepted the same attitude in their daughters without wondering whether a little more enthusiasm for education might not pay dividends in the form of a more interesting life. Asha wondered where it would ever be possible to break through the habit of apathy. For the giggling girls it was already too late; and they – no doubt very soon – would be the equally unsupportive mothers of the next generation of school-children. The circle seemed closed.

With this discouraging reflection Asha reached the health centre, a low brick building which changed its function according to the day of the week and the time of day. Room Four had been an ante-natal clinic in the morning but was now the family planning clinic.

Dr Clarke did not, as usually happened, scribble a prescription while asking a few routine questions about Asha's general health. 'Let's see,' she said thoughtfully instead. 'How old are you now, dear?'

'Thirty-five.'

'And you've been taking the pill for – what? – thirteen years? I think I must advise you that it's time to stop.'

'But why?' Asha was dismayed. Although she was anxious to start a pregnancy as soon as it became practicable, the time was not yet ripe for her to abandon the regular salary which was supporting Ranji as well as herself. The first enquiries about ancestral portraits had begun to arrive in the spring, and the search fees which accompanied them made a welcome contribution to the new balance sheet; but Ranji had yet to make his first actual sale.

'As you grow older, the pill can produce a dangerous side-effect of clotting in the blood. And although it hasn't been finally proved, the risk is thought to be greater for women who've been taking it for a considerable period. At thirty-five you're approaching the risk area on the first

252

count; you've already reached it on the second. I'd be happy to discuss it with you again in a year or so. But for the time being I think you should consider the alternatives.'

'But – '

'There are plenty of contraceptive methods which are nearly as reliable as the pill. We can see which suits you best. Or, of course, there's one completely foolproof way. If you've decided not to have a family, your husband might consider a vasectomy.'

'We haven't decided that at all,' exclaimed Asha. 'I want to have children. It's just rather awkward at the moment. If I could keep on as I am just for a few months – '

'If you seriously plan to have a child, then I would in any case recommend you to come off the pill for a few months first; so that wouldn't affect my advice. And I do think, dear, that you ought not to stretch that "few months" too long. I don't want to be alarmist, but with every year that passes there's a slightly higher risk of problems with a first pregnancy – risks both to you and to the baby.'

Asha, aware of this, did not argue further. She allowed herself to be examined and was thoughtful as she walked home.

Ranji greeted her with good news. 'We have our first orders! Two on the same day. A family in Virginia wants something like the mock-Gainsborough which Chris did of you. And a Dutch woman from Pennsylvania has fallen for the hideous Pothoven family group which has been in the gallery across the road for a year. I took a four-week option on it before I sent the photographs, and told her we could offer a genuine Old Master if she made up her mind quickly.'

253

'I'm surprised she recognized Pothoven as being an Old Master.'

'As well as the photograph of the picture itself, I sent the good lady a copy of Pothoven's page in our encyclopaedia of art. It spoke most highly of the gentleman. So we have two customers.'

'I'm so glad. Congratulations, darling.' Asha sat down, encouraged by his satisfaction to raise the matter which troubled her. 'Ranji, I've been to the family planning clinic.' She told him what the doctor had said. 'She was right. If we're going to have a family, we ought to start now. Or very soon.'

'Soon, perhaps, if you wish to; but not now. How could we?'

'Well, if the ancestors are taking off – '

'We have two customers, that's all. And from the money they send I must buy the Pothoven, pay Chris to paint a Gainsborough, and pack and insure and despatch the pictures. We're only acting as an agency, Asha. The client may seem to be paying a good price, but not much will stick to our fingers. And we must pay off the starting expenses first.'

'But as more and more orders come in – '

'*If* they do. It's still a speculation. We need your salary.'

'We'd have it for the first seven months of pregnancy: I'd go on working. Then I'd get maternity benefit when I stopped. And my job would be protected by law – I could go back three months after the birth if we found we couldn't manage.'

'It's all very well to have a job kept open. But how could you work with a young baby?'

'He could stay with you. It would only be in term time.

254

You'd be working from home anyway; and babies sleep most of the day.'

'That's an absurd suggestion,' said Ranji. 'I know nothing about looking after babies.'

'Nor do I. We could learn together.'

'We must be clear on this.' Ranji's voice was stiff. 'I don't agree with the modern idea that not only the woman should be the mother but the man also. If you wish to have children, I am not against this – when we can afford it. But it would be your choice and your responsibility. Small children should be brought up by their mothers. Of course I would be a good father to my son. But you must not come to me in a year saying that you rely on me to give baby his bottle and change his nappies, because that is not my task.'

'It's a question of time, Ranji, don't you see?' said Asha earnestly. 'If I were still in my twenties, of course we could wait until we were more secure. But I'm not young any more and time's running out and soon it will be now or never.' Her voice trembled, revealing how much the doctor's warning had upset her. She needed to be angry if she were not to cry. 'If you don't accept modern ideas about sharing the care of children, then I suppose you believe in the old-fashioned way of organizing a family. If I make the choice you kindly allow me, and accept the responsibility for caring for a baby, I ought to be able to leave you with the responsibility of supporting your family.'

'Yes, you ought.' Like Asha herself, Ranji was only partly successful in controlling his anger at this attack on his pride. 'But before you make such a choice, you must think it through. Where would we live, for example, once your baby was past the cradle stage?'

'*Our* baby.' Asha made the correction icily.

'Our baby, then.'

'The attic would make a marvellous nursery and playroom.'

'Chris must have the attic for painting the pictures which would feed the baby, and for storing those I buy. We would need a bigger place to live. I can't get a mortgage until I'm discharged from bankruptcy. You wouldn't get a mortgage without a regular job.'

'Perhaps Aunt Alexa – ' A year earlier, Asha had been quick to recognize that her great-aunt could not be approached to settle Ranji's debts. It would be a different matter, though, to ask for support at the time of starting a family. But even as she spoke, Asha was doubtful. The rise in the cost of living during the past two years might at last be adding substance to the complaints of poverty with which Alexa had greeted every income tax demand for the past thirty years. Asha stood up and began to wander thoughtfully about the flat. It was true that there would be no room for a baby unless the attic could be used. She went up the stairs to the top floor.

The attic was lighter than she remembered it. Crossing to the window, she saw the reason at once. The Dutch Elm Disease had reached the end of the line of elms and brown, curled leaves were falling unseasonably in a steady, rustling shower from the nearest tree. Well, no doubt the extra light was good for Chris's painting. He had set up his easel in the centre of the room, surrounding it with a clutter of reference books and jam jars full of long-handled brushes. A dummy, bald-headed and bare-legged, wore a cravat of which Beau Brummel would have been proud, with a brocade coat which Asha recognized from the school production of *The Rivals*.

Round this central area the pictures bought by Ranji on his country expeditions were neatly stacked, with empty frames stacked in one corner. And all this was quite apart from the space in the dining room which had been taken over by filing cabinets and a desk. Ranji was quite right. They would need to find either a new nursery or else a new studio, store room and office.

It could do no harm to find out what Alexa's financial position was. Asha had never asked for anything before – and she did not intend to ask now if it seemed that the request for a loan would cause anxiety. But if it should prove that her ninety-nine-year-old relation was nursing a small fortune – well, at least she could test the water. Asha went to find Ranji again.

'I'll be taking the car tomorrow,' she reminded him. 'You remember, it's my Oxford Gaudy weekend.'

'There's a good train service to Oxford,' said Ranji. 'I'm playing cricket at Bexley. I shall need the car myself.'

'There's a perfectly good train service to Bexley as well. Or you could get a lift from Mike or Alex. I did warn you of this date a month ago.' She resisted the temptation to remind him that the car was her own and that she had paid for its MOT test, service and road tax, and for the petrol in the tank. 'I'm not going straight to Oxford, you see,' she said instead. 'I want to call on Aunt Alexa on the way, and the cross-country journey would be hopeless. So I shall take the car.'

5

Alexa's home for the past twelve months had been a
country mansion, converted into a nursing home for the
elderly infirm. Its fees were high, but patients received
good value for their money. The ground floor room in
which she would spend the rest of her life was spacious
and light. From her bed she could look at the grounds of
the manor, whilst inside the room, on a wide shelf
beneath the window, house plants clustered in a thriving
indoor garden. The shelf continued along the wall which
faced her bed, supporting a remote-control television set
and Alexa's own record player and stereo speakers, as
well as her large library of records. There had been room
for very few of her personal possessions in the room
which now constituted her whole world: she had chosen
to fill the space with music.

Little in Alexa's surroundings changed from visit to
visit. The room was always clean and sweet-smelling, the
flowers were always fresh and the bedside table stocked
with whatever drink was appropriate to the season. Today
a jug of fresh lemon juice stood beside a thermos flask of
iced water. Asha gratefully accepted the invitation to
pour herself a drink, for the day – like every other in the
past two months – was blisteringly hot, unrefreshed by
any breeze. As she handed a glass to her great-aunt, her
eye was caught by a change in the scenery.

'What's this?' she asked, crossing to the window. In
the middle of a group of house plants stood a bronze
statue of a dancing figure.

'Turn it away from me,' Alexa commanded. For many years the tone of her voice had been imperious, and this effect was heightened by the breathlessness of old age, which clipped her speech into a series of staccato statements or instructions. 'Nasty sly face. I don't like it looking at me. Let it look out of the window. That'll give a nasty shock to anyone who stares in!'

'But what is it?'

'Siva dancing, Bernard calls it. A nasty heathen god.'

'Were you too polite to tell him you didn't like it?'

'He didn't bring it as a gift. Asked me to keep it as a favour. So I didn't have to pretend. Wouldn't have let it stay if I'd known it was going to annoy me. But it's all right like that, I suppose.'

'I still don't understand – '

'Bernard bought it from some sculptor. And Helen can't stand it. Won't have it in the house. He doesn't want to sell it. So he asked if it could lodge here. Hopes Helen will come round to it later, I suppose. They've been going through a bad patch, those two. Seem to have made it up now, though. I'm glad about that. Especially for Helen. Bernard's got his work. But when a woman doesn't have children and doesn't have a job, she needs a husband. Just to talk to, you know, as a friend, even if the rest isn't so important any more.'

'Do you think she's sorry she didn't have children?' From the earliest years of her childhood Asha had been on affectionate terms with her cousin Bernard, in spite of their difference in age. But she had never been intimate with his wife. Helen, calm and elegant, seemed content with a life devoted only to gracious living: the smooth running of a country house and a London flat. Asha, always busy, found it hard to imagine how Helen spent

259

her time. The two women had little to talk about when they met.

'Of course she's sorry,' said Alexa without hesitation. 'But she can't start now. Not after a hysterectomy. So there's no point in her weeping about it.'

'How old were you, Aunt Alexa, when you had your first baby?'

'Thirty when Frisca was born. Thirty-six for Pirry.'

'And it was all right, was it, having a baby at thirty-six?'

Age had robbed Alexa of mobility but had had no effect on her intelligence. 'Thinking of starting, are you, dear?' she asked, bright-eyed with interest. 'Yes, thirty-six was all right. Pirry was a beautiful baby. Something you should remember, though. Nobody tells you at the time. Then they say you should have known. This pill you all take. Makes you feel you're in control. You can decide when you don't want a baby. So you think you can decide when you *will* have a baby. Not always so easy. I used to think it unfair. Girls who didn't want babies were landed with them. Those who did want one sometimes couldn't manage it. You young ones, you've only cured half the problem. Remember that.'

'You mean that you can't always start a pregnancy straight away? I know that.'

'That's part of it. The other part is that pregnancies go wrong. No one warns you. They don't want to frighten you. But it happens. It took me three years to have Pirry. One baby died. Then a miscarriage. And you always have to wait in between. So allow for things to go wrong. Don't leave it too late.'

'Were you glad you had children, Aunt Alexa?'

'Frisca was an accident – wouldn't have been born in the age of the pill. I was upset at first. It was inconvenient.

Later – she was a very special person, Frisca – I was proud. She gave people so much pleasure. But then she died. When you have to bear that kind of sadness, you wonder whether the pleasure was worthwhile.'

'And Pirry?'

'Pirry was the price I paid for a happy marriage. Piers wanted an heir, and I was in love with him. Whatever he needed, I wanted to give him. But in a different marriage I could have been happy without children. Had my own career, you see. Like you. It seemed worthwhile to me. Does yours?'

'Yes,' said Asha. 'Yes, it does. Most of the time, at least.'

'I know how you feel,' said Alexa unexpectedly. 'Time passing. This year, you still have a choice. In five years' time, not. You're tempted to do what's possible now just because it won't be later. You need to be very sure, dear. And clear about *why* you want children, if you do. If I'd chosen to have Pirry to look after me in my old age, I'd have lost out, wouldn't I? But I had him to make Piers happy, and that was all that ever mattered.'

There was a quick tap on the door. A nurse looked in, smiled at Asha and closed the door again.

'They're good girls,' Alexa commented. 'I'll say this for the Brownlows.' Mr and Mrs Brownlow were the owners of the nursing home. 'They charge the earth, but they pay well. So the nurses stay. I like that. No chopping and changing just as you've got used to someone. Every afternoon one of them pops in for a chat. When you get to my age, you don't have many friends left to come visiting.'

'You can manage the charges all right, can you, Aunt Alexa?' Asha had hoped for a lead of this kind. 'You're not worried about money?'

'Always worried about money since that wretched socialist government after the war. But it was Pirry who played me the worst trick. Promised that he'd survive me, and then died. Only fifty-two. And he knew what it would mean.'

'Yes, it was rotten for you, having to leave Blaize.'

'It wasn't just Blaize I lost. You wouldn't remember. There'd been Glanville House as well. Bombed in the war. We had compensation, and a good price when we sold the site for a hotel. But the lawyers said all that money was the equivalent of the house. Part of the entailed property. Pirry and I, we could use the income from that capital. But when Pirry died, it all went with the title.'

'Did you never have any capital of your own?'

'Not before I married. I was born in a slum. Earned a lot later, of course, but we all lived extravagantly in those days. On my wedding day, Piers made a settlement. My little opera house was expensive, though. Cost a lot to get it going. More again after the first war, to convert it back from being a hospital. And it never made a profit. Too small. However much I charged for the tickets, there couldn't be enough. I only engaged the very best singers.'

'But you've got enough left to pay the bills, have you?'

Alexa's bright eyes sparkled with triumph. 'I did well there,' she boasted. 'Bought an annuity when I was ninety. Dirt cheap. They didn't think I'd live so long. It was enough until I came here last year. Now I'm dipping into my savings, a little every quarter. But there's enough to last me until I'm a hundred and two. After that, I shall have to throw myself on your mercy.'

'I'll start saving now,' Asha promised her. 'The Aunt-Alexa-hundred-and-third-birthday fund.' Alexa had answered the question which could not be directly asked.

She had done far more than her duty in bringing Asha up, and nothing more must be expected. Asha bent over the old lady and kissed her with affectionate gratitude for all the love which had warmed her childhood. 'I must go now, Aunt Alexa. It's my Gaudy weekend.'

'Gaudy? What's Gaudy?'

'Old girls' reunion for Dame Eleanor's College. It happens every year, a week after term ends at Oxford. I've never been before. But if I stay on at Hillgate, I have a chance of being Head next year. It's one of the things I've got to decide in the next three months, whether to apply. If I do, I need to make contact again with the dons. We've never sent anyone to Oxford or Cambridge. It's difficult for us to compete with schools which give special coaching for the entrance exam. But we've got one or two clever children coming up. I need to establish a little general goodwill. So in a way it's a working weekend. Would you like something on the record player, Aunt Alexa?'

Alexa could switch on the radio and television herself, but relied on others to operate what she still called the gramophone. Usually she asked for an opera or symphony, so today's request came as a surprise. 'Put half a dozen of Frisca's records on, will you, dear.'

The records which Frisca Glanville had made in the 1930s were seventy-eights. Asha made the necessary adjustment to the control and glanced anxiously back at the bed. 'I didn't upset you, asking about your children, did I?'

'No, dear, of course not. Past history now. But when I feel sad about Frisca, I like to hear her, alive and young. She always said that she wanted to die before she was forty, and she did. Perhaps it was best for her. I have to

263

think that. She was never any good as a singer, of course. But I like to hear her, all the same.'

Asha paused for a moment as the music filled the room in a curiously distant fashion, as though the passing of many years had in some way come between the recording and the listener. At its brightest the band was tinny, and in quieter moments the sound surged forward and back like a wave pulled away by the tide before it could break. Alexa, the opera-singer who had always striven for perfection, was right to claim that Frisca had no great singing talent. It was as a dancer that she had become famous, known wherever films were screened for her blonde beauty and vitality. But the musicals in which she appeared had required her to sing as well as to dance and her voice, although it lacked power, was clear and tuneful. Alexa, absorbed in the sound, did not notice as Asha quietly left the room.

6

Dame Eleanor's College – standing sturdily aloof from the contemporary fashion for co-residence – was still an all-female institution. Its red-brick walls had a no-nonsense look to them, possessing none of the mellow stone charm of the men's colleges. It had no tradition of history to be trapped in peaceful quadrangles. But as though in compensation, the architect had set the building's widespread wings in landscaped grounds which had grown to become one of the most beautiful gardens in the university. Pausing only to unpack the evening dress which she would wear for the formal Gaudy dinner, Asha left the room allotted to her and stepped outside on to the terrace.

The summer drought had attacked Oxford as fiercely as London, but with a different effect. The Portobello Road, dusty and dirty and littered with empty Coke tins and half-naked bodies, had been made sordid by heat: but here the shimmering sunshine created an idyll. Summers of the past were preserved by memory in just such a state of perfection, but had perhaps at the time proved more disappointing. The college lawns, although parched, were smooth and tranquil: thirsty roses bloomed extravagantly over pergolas or against walls; dry terraces were dotted with the silver or scented leaves of Mediterranean bushes. The heat had hurried forward the autumn flowers, so that michaelmas daisies mingled their blues and purples with those of wisteria, delphinium, buddleia and lavender. Large specimen trees provided cool circles of shade; and

265

quiet corners, gardens within a garden, offered a restful privacy, whether to undergraduates and their books or to the older women who today might choose solitude to remember how they had been young here.

A chattering of voices and clattering of tea cups drew Asha towards a less peaceful area: trestle tables round the Principal's lawn were stocked for the occasion with plates of egg sandwiches and cream cakes. Amongst the crowd of white faces was a familiar black one. Surprised and delighted, Asha hurried forward. She had not seen her Jamaican cousin since Paula had returned to her homeland shortly after her husband's death a few years earlier.

'Paula! How marvellous to see you! I didn't know you were in England.'

'Asha, hi! I tried your room earlier, but you hadn't checked in. I've come over to visit a few of the classier travel agents and tell them in person where their clients can find the best holiday in the Caribbean. You know that Bristow Great House is a hotel now, don't you? I signed up for the Gaudy as soon as I knew that I'd be within striking distance of the old alma mater at the right time' – Paula had been a Scholar of Dame Eleanor's College in the nineteen-fifties – 'and they promptly invited me to make one of the speeches tonight. Why don't we grab ourselves a seat?'

They settled themselves on a garden bench from which they could observe their fellow senior members.

'Don't they all look old!' commented Asha, when they had exchanged some of their own news.

'The young ones don't come. When they first go down they've had enough of college life. And then they're tied down with babies. And then they feel nervous and out of touch. As soon as they start doing well in their jobs, that's when they come.'

'How do you know? Have you been making a survey?'

'I talked to my old tutor, to find out what kind of audience I'd have tonight. The answer was that it would be exuberant, because only the successes come back. Anyone who feels she's failed the college by not making good use of her degree stays away. As for the preponderance of oldies, there's always a special reunion for everyone who matriculated fifty years ago. That brings back a clutch of sixty-eight-year-olds, retired headmistresses every one.'

'They can't *all* have been successes – in the way you defined it.'

'Sure they can. A girl who chose to go to university fifty years ago in England was pretty well making a statement that she didn't intend to get married. Because if she became a teacher or a civil servant or anything like that she'd have to resign her job on marriage. Ergo, most of these grey-haired ladies will be spinsters who devoted their whole lives to their careers and were almost bound to do well in them. Since the war – I'm still quoting from my tutor – it's a different ballgame. Almost all the graduates get married nowadays. But they can still become headmistresses, because there aren't many spinsters left to challenge them.'

The statement reminded Asha of her own situation. Without caring what she would be revealing, she put a direct question. 'Paula, did you ever regret not having children?'

'Have you come to the choosing time?' Paula was as quick to understand as Alexa had been. 'A baby or promotion, is it?'

'It's a one-sided choice. I mean, if I don't have a baby

soon, I never shall. But if I let the chance of a headship go now, I can try again in ten years. I feel an idiot, not knowing what I want. But – ' She sighed, and was grateful for the sympathy in Paula's smile.

'It never bothered me,' her cousin said. 'I was always clear that the choice was between living my own life and living my children's lives. To have children and not devote yourself to them is selfish. Well, I believe that to have children at all is a selfish decision, but I know that not everyone goes along with that. I chose to be responsible for myself only, and I've never regretted it. But what was right for me isn't necessarily right for somebody else.'

'And Laker didn't want children either?'

For a moment Paula's confidence faltered. 'There was a moment, just before he died, when I wondered. Perhaps he *would* have liked to have had a son. But we made a bargain. I told him, when he first asked me to marry him, that I was never going to have a baby. I made him believe me and then ask me again. It was only fair to do it that way.'

'Aunt Alexa was just the opposite. She had to promise before she married that she *would* have children, to give her husband an heir.'

'That's what I mean by being selfish,' said Paula. 'Poor Pirry, brought into the world just to take his place on the family tree! But don't let me bully you. It's just that there's so much social pressure on a woman the other way – to have babies. As though she needs to prove she's a proper woman and a proper wife. Maybe for a lot of women that's genuinely the way to happiness. But not for everyone. For hundreds of years a married woman hasn't had the choice. Now she has. She can ask herself whether she wants a child – and *why* she wants a child – and it's a mistake for her to be influenced by all the centuries in which the question couldn't be asked. Or by all the women who've lost years of their own lives to the demands of their children and have to persuade themselves that no alternative could offer any satisfaction. The firm answer to your question is that it's easy to live a wholly adult life and do something worthwhile with it and enjoy it. End of speech.'

Asha noted with interest that although the practical results were different, Paula's argument had a good deal in common with Alexa's. She tucked the opinion away for later consideration, and took the cue for a change of subject. 'What will your speech be about tonight?'

'They wanted me to talk about discrimination. Sex and colour both, I guess. But it's not something I've suffered from much. Not in England, at least. At a certain level it actually helps to be black. But the theme I prefer may fit in with your suggestion. Expectation. Why do so few women reach the top in business and politics and the professions? Is it really discrimination? Or is it because they don't *expect* to succeed? Ability on its own isn't enough – they need a mixture of self-confidence and ambition and determination. But why should I waste my arguments on you now when you'll hear it all this evening?'

The evening belonged to Paula. Almost to a woman the senior members of Dame Eleanor's College proclaimed by their dresses and hair styles their lack of interest in personal appearance. Paula outshone them all. As an undergraduate she had been conspicuous by her elegance and wit. Now, in her late forties, her brilliance with words had not changed and her appearance was even more dazzling. Her personality sparkled as brilliantly as the sequins on her tailored jacket. Asha, laughing with the rest, felt a possessive excitement which took her to

Paula's room after the formal part of the evening was over.

Paula took longer to disentangle herself from the after-dinner conversation. When she arrived, she showed no surprise at Asha's presence.

'Have you been admiring the *décor*?' She waved a hand round the room, pausing with amused incredulity to indicate a particularly battered wardrobe. 'I can hardly believe it. Nothing's changed in twenty-five years. All this furniture so lovingly collected from junk shops! The army surplus khaki linoleum! And the porridge-coloured walls – how well I remember that shade of slightly-burnt porridge! Some provident bursar must have laid in a hundred years' supply of paint. When I left Jamaica as a starry-eyed eighteen-year-old I thought I was coming to a place of privilege. And of course I was – but I still remember my dismay at finding myself in a kind of slum.'

'There's something I want you to do for me,' Asha said. 'Will you come to Hillgate and give a talk to our school-leavers – see if you can put a few stars in *their* eyes? They've taken their O levels or their CSEs and they're killing time until they're allowed to escape from school. They're bored and they're unambitious. Someone like you could inspire them. Not just by repeating the things you've said tonight. But by being yourself – black and successful. It's an aspect of expectation you didn't mention. The exceptional boy or girl can construct a ladder to success in his imagination. But most children need to see someone standing on the top rung, to show them that it can be done. We've got a great many black children at Hillgate. But it's hard to find black achievers to show them. A successful journalist like you – '

'Why are they bored?' interrupted Paula. 'Why are they unambitious? What are you doing to our children in your schools, Asha? I see kids in Jamaica *longing* to learn. Not always clever, but full of enthusiasm. Their parents support them. I may not approve of a boy getting a whipping from his mother if he has a bad mark at school, but it surely does encourage hard work. If anything, Jamaican kids are *over*-ambitious, wanting to achieve more than their capabilities allow. And the parents who leave Jamaica for England must be those with the most initiative, not the dullest. What is your school doing for their children?'

'It's failing them.' Within the space of an hour Asha's incoherent ideas had fitted themselves together, pointing a way ahead. 'They've been defeated by good intentions.'

'Elucidate!' Paula, always ready for an argument, threw a pillow on to the floor and sat on it.

'You said earlier that Oxford was a place of privilege. In one sense that's not true of this college. But you could call it a centre of excellence. A place to be reached only by girls with more than just ability – with determination and ambition as well. Nowadays it may be easier, when most of the men's colleges admit girls. But every one of the women here tonight had to show her ambition and determination at the age of seventeen or eighteen to achieve her first success – a fiercely competitive success just to get a place here at all.'

'And what have the people with good intentions done about that?'

'They've looked at the losers instead of the winners. No one must fail – and so no one can win. It started reasonably enough, with a move towards equality of opportunity; but a little at a time it's changed into equality of achievement. All have lost, so none must have prizes. Nobody at Hillgate ever comes top in a school exam: the best few children get a good grade instead. The children

271

themselves have lost the urge to compete. They're almost ashamed if they turn out to be better than the others at something. And so the whole atmosphere of the school has begun to work *against* achievement, not for it. The teachers have given in, and no individual child is strong enough to fight the system.' Chris had said something like this only a few months ago; but it had taken the ambience of Dame Eleanor's, and Asha's memory of her own fierce ambition at seventeen, to convince her of the truth.

'Have you decided to change the system, then?'

'I can't do it from underneath,' said Asha. 'I'd have to be the Head. Even then it wouldn't be easy. I'd have to start unobtrusively, ready to fight the governors and the ILEA when they found out. We'd still have to take the children we were allotted – so many from each level of ability; always more duds than geniuses. But our eleven-year-olds arrive for their first day at Hillgate full of enthusiasm. We must keep that alive, instead of drowning it.'

'So you'll make them all compete with each other for seven years and then send them up to Oxford?'

Asha laughed ruefully. Hillgate pupils rarely achieved the A-level grades which qualified them even for the local polytechnic. 'Just to see *one* here would be enough to show that it can be done. But there are other goals. Music, for example. We have bands and orchestras; we lend instruments and arrange teaching. But we don't enter the children for the grade exams. *That* would be turning a pleasure into work – and they might not pass! So a child who turns out to be talented can't get into a music college because he hasn't got the right certificates. And then we have a good many natural athletes. They have training at school, but most of them stop when they leave. If they were prepared for national competition and introduced to adult clubs they might set their sights higher. Why shouldn't we produce Olympic swimmers as well as Oxford scholars?'

'Why not indeed?' Paula, already exhilarated by the success of her own speech, clasped her hands high in a champion's gesture.

'Nothing but the best!' Asha remembered. 'That was what Aunt Alexa used to say all the time she was bringing me up. It ought to be the school motto. When I think of the drab streets and narrow lives from which so many of the children come . . . We must open doors, all sorts of doors, so that they can step through and look up. But first, they need ambition.'

'It's a dangerous policy.' Paula, although sympathetic, was laughing. 'As your well-intentioned governors will undoubtedly point out. Once your whole sixth form is inspired with a passionate desire to become Olympic champions, concert pianists, Nobel prizewinners, those who end up collecting garbage after all may feel more resentful than if they'd never thought of anything else.'

'Ambition doesn't have to be tied to the hours of earning a living. A man can empty dustbins and still be a champion weight-lifter – or at least be good enough in some sphere to feel pride in himself. The lazy children and the stupid ones will dodge any attempt to help them anyway. Why should the others be sacrificed to them? All the silly girls who can think of nothing but boyfriends will troop off to their cash registers and typewriters to pass the time till their wedding day just as they do now. But we should offer a ladder to anyone with a head for greater height.'

'Never let anyone undervalue you, Asha,' said Paula, smiling. 'All those speeches about how women must use their legal rights and aim for positions of power! You're almost there already – you realize that? When men talk about power, they mean the power to make money or run the country. But as head of Hillgate you'd have the power to alter the lives of thousands of children. You're going to take the job, aren't you?'

'I'm going to apply for it.' Asha knew that success could not be taken for granted. But the governors had demonstrated confidence when they appointed her deputy head. She had a good chance.

That night she lay awake for a long time in her narrow student's bed and thought about her husband. Only rarely did they spend a night apart, and yet she did not miss him now. Indeed, she was glad to be alone where nobody knew him, where she had her own independent place. During the past twelve months she and Ranji had seemed to do little but bicker. What had happened to the joy she had felt throughout the first years they had spent together? Was it because they were both unsure of their careers that they had lost confidence in their marriage as well? It was not surprising that Ranji should be affected by his business failure, but Asha had been slower to realize that her own tetchiness had been caused by indecision. As recently as twenty-four hours earlier she had still been confused. Now she looked clearly into the future.

She enjoyed her work and she was good at it. She would enjoy even more a post with greater responsibility, and she would be good at that as well. She and Ranji would be friends again, with the slight distancing which friendship required, when there was no longer any suggestion that she should become dependent. It was too late to change the pattern of a marriage in which Ranji expected his wife to look after him domestically but in every other respect to stand on her own feet. More cheerful than she had felt for many months, Asha sank into sleep.

7

Bristow Great House was an unusual hotel. Its name was deceptive, for the eighteenth-century plantation house at the centre of the estate was neither large nor grand. Like most of the old planters' homes in Jamaica it was built in the hills, to catch the breeze, and so held little attraction for those tourists whose sole ambition was to roast themselves beside the sea. The guest bungalows, added at the time of the conversion, were scattered throughout the gardens. Each had its own rocking chairs on its own verandah, with a view of the hills or the lake, but each was secluded from the others. Bristow made no pretence of appealing to the gregarious.

To Bristow in the winter of 1976 came Ros Davidson, a thirty-one-year-old Californian from San Francisco. Needing a holiday after her divorce, she had chosen Jamaica because she had never been there with Lee: there would be no memories to disturb her. As she stepped from the airport car outside the Great House she sighed with a mixture of tiredness and satisfaction, feeling herself enveloped in the balmy evening air. The heavy scents of blossom mingled with a vegetative dampness to suggest decadence and decay. There would be no slick Californian efficiency here, she felt happily sure. Meals would be late, the electricity would fail, people would promise to do errands and would then forget, the whole place would be delightfully haphazard. 'Who owns the hotel?' she asked as she registered, signing herself as Ros Davidson after ten years of being Ros Jarvis.

'Miss Mattison.' The black girl at the reception desk was young and friendly. 'Leastwise, Mrs Laker-Smith she is by rights. But when her husband ben die, she come home and take up her old name again. The Great House, it belong in her family since wayback. Her people built it as a plantation house first of all. Then her daddy made it to a hotel, twenty-thirty years ago.'

'She's British, I guess.' Laker-Smith sounded a typical lah-di-dah English name.

'Born and raised here in Bristow, ma'am. Now then, Wesley here, he'll show you to your bungalow. Have a happy stay.'

Night had fallen by the time Ros had showered away the dirt of the journey and dressed again. For a little while she sat on the verandah of her bungalow, rocking the chair gently and savouring the sweet-smelling warmth. Then she strolled between hedges of hibiscus and croton and poinsettia towards the office. Holiday or not, she would need to telephone California during her stay, and it would be wise to seek local information on possible delays.

Her questions were quickly answered, but she lingered by the desk, eavesdropping. Two of her fellow-guests were arguing about some leaflet they had picked up.

'It would be interesting.' The fading of the woman's voice recognized that she had already lost the argument.

'Look honey!' Her husband was patient but definite. 'It may be interesting for people who are lonely, but we have relations! With eight sisters and three brothers and God knows how many nephews and nieces and cousins, who the hell needs ancestors?'

He put the leaflet back in the rack and led his wife away. Ros, curious, took the paper out again. 'Hang an ancestral portrait on your wall!' it commanded in Gothic type, with a selection of illustrations to indicate the possibilities. It was like an advertisement for a marriage bureau, she thought in amusement: tick the great-grand-father who most appeals to you. She took the leaflet away to read later.

As she sat down in the open-air bar the barman came smiling towards her. 'Your welcome drink, Miss Davidson.'

'Thank you. Thank you very much.' It was a rum punch of some kind, cold and fruity and refreshing. A smartly-dressed woman sitting at the bar turned at the sound of her voice and came across.

'Everything all right, I hope?' Her skin was as dark as the barman's, but her voice was that of an educated Englishwoman.

'Everything's just fine,' said Ros. 'Are you Miss Mattison?'

'That's right.'

'Won't you have a drink with me?'

Paula Mattison smiled. 'I'd be delighted to chat, but this – ' she lifted her glass – 'will see me through, thank you very much.'

'I'm going to be just plain nosy,' Ros said. 'I want you to tell me how you came to own this wonderful place. Your girl at the desk said it had been in your family right from the start. But the hotel brochure claims that the original house is almost two hundred years old.'

'And you don't quite see a plantation slave building himself a Great House?' Paula Mattison laughed as she completed Ros's thought. 'Well one of my ancestors, Pastor Lorimer, was a white man whose family had owned Bristow since about 1790. He bequeathed the estate to his illegitimate son, Duke Mattison – my father. The agricultural land was sold off before my father died, because he didn't think I'd be able to run a whole plantation. But a hotel might be a woman's work, he reckoned, so he held on to the house and built the bungalows. As for my grandfather's legitimate descendants – I see you picked up the Ancestors leaflet.'

'Yes. I haven't read it thoroughly yet. This is an odd place to find it.'

'The man who runs the business is married to another grand-daughter of Pastor Lorimer: a cousin of mine, as blonde as I'm black. Mostly the leaflets are distributed in the States, but I was in London last June and brought a few back here for fun. It may be something you can do without – but if you *do* want to try it, I can guarantee that it's an honest enterprise. Will you excuse me now? I see some more new arrivals.'

'Sure.' Ros herself was hungry, ready to move to the candle-lit restaurant. Sitting beneath the stars she enjoyed the unfamiliar tastes of pepperpot soup, pumpkin stuffed with shrimps, spiced chicken and Tia Maria cream cake, all served by a smiling waitress who identified unfamiliar items of food before leaving her to enjoy them. The friendliness of the place was as delightful as the warm and sweet-scented air. Ros's mood was mellow when, over coffee, she looked more closely at the leaflet which she had put away in her handbag.

It was amusing to imagine the contrasts which would have been displayed if Paula Mattison had been able to hang pictures of her own forebears on the wall – black and white side by side. In comparison, Ros's own ancestors would make a dull display. Her father and grandfather had been alike in many ways. Clever with their fingers and inventive with their minds, they both had lively eyes and curly dark hair. She knew little about her Scottish great-grandfather except that he had been

279

blinded in the Crimean War and as a result had developed the delicate touch with clocks and locks on which the family fortune was based.

On the distaff side, Ros's knowledge of her ancestry was incomplete. Until she was nine she took it for granted that her father's wife was her own mother. Only when the two adults divorced did she learn that she had been born, before their marriage, to an English mother.

'Tell me about her,' Ros pleaded then; but her father shook his head.

'She loved you very much,' was all Brad would say. 'We were all so happy together. I met her in London, during the war; that was where she died. It was a sad story. I try not to think about it. We'll have to look after each other from now on, hey, honey?' He never mentioned her mother again. But after his death, Ros had found in his desk a photograph crumpled from much handling – a snapshot of a young woman smiling down at the baby in her arms, while a blonde three-year-old girl tugged at her skirt. On the back Brad had written 'Barbary at Blaize, with Ros and Asha.'

If anything, the photograph only served to deepen the mystery. Barbary must be her mother, but who was Asha and what had happened to her? And where was Blaize? Ros had looked it up in a world gazetteer but could find no town of that name. So all she knew for certain was that her mother was English, and dead. There would be little information to offer the enterprising businessman who was prepared to find an ancestral portrait with a likeness which could be considered probable. All the same, Ros did not throw the leaflet away.

That night she slept soundly, alone in a four-poster bed. Lee had removed himself from her bed at home, of course, some time before the divorce proceedings started;

but it remained the bed they had shared, and it was difficult to escape there from memories and regrets. Although in the end it was Lee's behaviour which had provided the legal grounds for divorce, Ros knew that much of the fault for the break-up was her own.

Her father had warned her, as soon as he realized that she was serious about a young man for the first time. 'You're a beautiful girl, honey, and every man who sees you wants you. But this one has his eyes on your money as well.'

'Then you could shake him off by disinheriting me.'

But they both knew that Brad was devoted to his only child. She was certain one day to enjoy his fortune. To Ros, who was willing to share, Lee's attitude promised security in the marriage. If he wanted money, it would be there for him to have long after the rosebud beauty which had earned Ros her name faded away.

Both Brad and Ros had misjudged their man. It was not money that Lee wanted, but power. While his father-in-law was still alive, the young husband indulged his wife's curious determination to work full-time in her family business as a whim which would be cured by the arrival of the first baby. But no baby appeared and when Brad died, two years after the wedding, Ros took over not only her father's stock in Davidson's Security Systems, but also his presidential chair.

Even then, Lee assumed at first that she would only be a figurehead. There were a good many people in the company as alarmed as he at the prospect of a young woman assuming executive control, but the fears of the others were gradually assuaged. Only Lee's resentment remained. Ros gave him his own sphere of the business and the vice-presidency that went with it, but she would not surrender the final authority – and this, it soon transpired, was what he had wanted all the time. If Lee had taken his revenge by running after one eighteen-year-old girl after another – and he had – it was from a need to show who was master. But he had lost that battle, too, on the day Ros decided she would rather be lonely than either tolerant or angry.

Now she revelled in the peace of being alone. On the first morning after her arrival, as she carried a book into the hotel grounds, she was looking for nothing but solitude. Rocking gently in a hammock slung between a magnolia and a breadfruit tree she relaxed lazily in the heat and humidity but was kept alert by the richness of the garden's scents and the variety of its sounds. Small birds chattered unseen in the thick foliage of the trees, peacocks and peahens screamed and hooted at each other in the distance and were answered by the gabble of a turkey nearer at hand. In the background, water splashed in a man-made cascade. She swung gently from side to side, luxuriating in the self-indulgence of doing nothing at all.

A humming-bird distracted her, hovering with its tiny wings whirring as it fed from a hibiscus blossom beside the hammock. As it flew away up the hill she followed it with her eyes and was struck by the beauty of the landscape. The gardens were far older than the bungalows – as old, presumably, as the original plantation house. They clothed the hillside in a series of green terraces, each layer brightened by the blossom of hibiscus and poinsettia, begonias and climbing lilies, orange and avocado trees and by the bronze leaves of hostas and crotons. A line of ackee and breadfruit and African tulip trees had been planted to conceal a new tennis court and swimming pool, but the lake was part of some original plan, fitting into the curve of a grassy avenue.

It was an *English* garden, she was suddenly sure, for all its humming-birds and palm trees. An English eye had planned it, using the ingredients provided by Jamaica. Ros tried to laugh at her own certainty. Although born in London, she had been taken from England while she was still a baby, and never returned. Even if an English garden did possess some inherent characteristic by which it could be recognized through all its variations, she had no idea what that would be. And yet she was sure. The broad avenues of grass which meandered between groups of shrubs or curved round specimen trees to reveal new vistas must have been laid out in the eighteenth century by the Englishman who established the plantation and cared for by his descendants ever since.

Lucky Miss Mattison, to live in her ancestral home, thought Ros – and for the first time since the divorce, her aloneness frightened rather than contented her. With Lee gone, she had no family left. Her parents were dead, and so was the only aunt she had known. Her one Davidson cousin had been killed, unmarried, in Vietnam. It was possible, she supposed, that she had some living English relatives on her mother's side, but she did not know how to set about finding them. It was a pity. She would have liked to know what had happened to that blonde three-year-old, Asha.

It must have been the Englishness of the garden which led her thoughts lazily on. As soon as she returned to California she would have the whole house redecorated, so that it should no longer be the home she had shared with Lee. She had a Spanish *décor* at the moment. It might be amusing to try an English style, if such a thing existed.

Ros laughed aloud as she realized where her musings were leading her. The sales pitch of the Ancestors leaflet had hit its target. Why shouldn't she have ancient portraits hanging on her walls? She wouldn't pretend that they were really her ancestors, but she would enjoy making up histories for them, inventing their descendants. She had slipped the leaflet into her book to act as a bookmark, and now she read it again, mentally drafting the information she could give. After all, she had British ancestors on both the maternal and paternal sides of her family. She could send photographs of herself and of her father. She could even have a copy made of that smiling snapshot: Barbary at Blaize. Yes, she would do that. She would write to London and ask for an Ancestor.

8

The photograph caught Asha's eye as soon as she arrived home from school on a miserable February afternoon. At first she was merely curious as she looked down at the picture – which Ranji must have placed on the table especially for her to see – but then she studied it with puzzled intensity. A young woman with a baby in her arms was smiling at the camera, while a fair-haired little girl tugged at her skirt.

'Where did you find this?'

'Do you recognize anyone?' Ranji came to stand beside her. 'My goodness, you're soaking. Take your mac off before you drip all over my documents.'

'That's me in the photograph,' Asha said, obeying his instructions. 'And my mother. I've never seen this particular snap before, but there are others of us together when I was about that age. But who is the baby? Where did this come from, Ranji?'

'It's one of three photographs sent by a potential client. Does the name Ros Davidson mean anything to you? Or Brad Davidson, her father?'

'No.' Asha turned the photograph over and read a typed slip stuck to the back. 'The original of this was labelled "Barbary at Blaize, with Ros and Asha."'

'Ros Davidson, of San Francisco, is the baby in that picture. And she says that the woman holding her, Barbary, is her mother. Barbary, Asha, Blaize – such unusual names! There can't be any doubt. Ros Davidson's mother must be your mother.'

'It isn't possible.' Asha was hardly able to speak.

'It must be so. The photograph . . . What happened to Ros, Asha, after your mother died?'

'I don't know.' She sat down, numbed by shock.

'You must remember having a baby sister.'

'I don't remember anything.' Without warning Asha burst into tears.

Ranji took her hands to comfort her. 'Tell me,' he said gently.

She needed a moment longer before she could control her voice, and the tears were still running down her cheeks as she spoke. 'One day when I was five or six my mother took me to school. Just in the ordinary way – there was nothing special about it. When we reached the corner she kissed me goodbye as usual. I ran on to the gate. Then I turned round and we waved at each other, as usual. I went into school and – and I never saw her again.'

For a second time she began to sob uncontrollably. Ranji's arm hugged her shoulders. 'You'll feel better if you tell me the whole story,' he said.

Asha gave a single deep sigh and dabbed her eyes dry. 'Just before playtime the headmistress sent for me. She said that my grandmother had come to fetch me. I'd only met my grandmother once before. I didn't want to go. But the headmistress said that my father had sent a letter and it was quite all right. I thought someone must have had an accident. I went with my grandmother to find out what had happened – but she didn't take me home. I was frightened and wanted my mother. My grandmother told me that I should never see my mother again. I think I must have become hysterical. I can remember screaming and screaming until in the end my grandmother locked me into a room and said I could come out when I was quiet. She *was* my grandmother: there was no doubt about that. But as far as I was concerned, I'd been kidnapped. And I never saw either of my parents again. I can remember every minute of that day, Ranji. But nothing, nothing at all about my life before it.'

'You remember your mother, surely?'

'Not as a real person. I've seen photographs of her, and so I know what she looked like. But I couldn't tell you anything that we ever did together. All I know about my first five years is what Aunt Alexa told me.'

'How did she explain your "kidnapping"? What happened to your parents?'

'They both died. My father first. He'd been in a Japanese prisoner-of-war camp and by the time the war ended he was desperately ill. After his death my mother was ill herself. She died because she was unhappy, Aunt Alexa said.'

'That can't be the whole story. One of them might have died while you were at school that day, but not both. Do you really not remember anything at all about a baby called Ros?'

Asha shook her head. 'It's not a selective forgetfulness. All those years have disappeared. I don't suppose many people remember much of their first three or four years, do they? I may only have lost a few months. Important months, that's all. If Ros was my younger sister, I suppose she could have been adopted by someone outside the family after my mother died.'

'She was born in May 1945.' Ranji pointed to the date in Ros's letter. 'Your father would still have been a prisoner then. Brad Davidson must have been her real father, not her adoptive one.'

Asha stared at one of the other photographs which had been sent with the application. Brad Davidson, pictured

287

with Ros when she was eight or nine, looked a jolly man; heavily built, with dark hair which curled at the back but had receded from his forehead. Asha could not remember that she had ever seen him before – and yet almost certainly it had been into his camera that she had smiled that day on the terrace at Blaize. 'I think I need to have a chat with Aunt Alexa,' she said.

Alexa was not alone when Asha arrived at the nursing home on the next Saturday. A young man holding a notebook sat beside the bed. His clothes – a T-shirt, gym shoes and the bottom half of a track suit – were more appropriate to an athletics stadium than to a nursing home: but Alexa, usually quick to criticize slovenly dress, appeared to have established a cordial relationship with her visitor.

'This is Peter Langley,' she announced in a businesslike way. 'Peter, my great-niece, Asha. She's far too young, of course, to be any help to you.'

'What sort of help?' asked Asha as she shook hands.

'Peter works on the *Bristol Evening Post*. He's helping me to prove when I was born.'

'But surely you know.'

'Yes, of course I know. But the Queen doesn't know. You do realize, don't you, dear, that I shall have my hundredth birthday in March. The Queen is supposed to send me a telegram. Matron wrote off some weeks ago to give her warning. But a secretary wrote back asking for my birth certificate. It's not as simple as they seem to think. A hundred years ago people didn't always bother with birth certificates. Even if they did, you couldn't expect a poor orphan to keep such a thing.'

'How on earth have you managed all these years without one?' asked Asha, laughing.

'You poor child! Brought up in a bureaucratic age.

288

Without papers you don't exist. When I married Piers, I was allowed to decide for myself whether I'd ever been born or not. And since then, the certificate which shows that I'm Lady Glanville has been enough for most people. But not for Her Majesty, it seems. Well, I know *when* I was born, so I had to find out where, to get a copy of the certificate. Bristol seemed the most likely place. I wrote to the editor of the *Post* and asked if one of his young men could look into it for me.'

'It's fascinating,' said Peter, his voice conveying a greater sense of awe than seemed likely from his appearance. 'Lady Glanville has been telling me all about her parents. I did a series of pieces on local history a year or so ago, so of course I knew something about the collapse of Lorimer's Bank in the 1870s. But to meet someone who was indirectly responsible for it . . .!'

'That's going it a bit, surely!' exclaimed Asha. 'Aunt Alexa, what *have* you been saying?'

'Well dear, my father was John Junius Lorimer. There's no denying that. And I was born only eighteen months before the crash.'

'That hardly makes you responsible for it!'

'There was a lot of gossip at the time,' Peter said, 'about what had happened to all the bank's assets. John Junius Lorimer was accused of embezzlement. One fact which emerged out of all the rumours was that he'd spent a lot of money on some jewellery which couldn't be found when his possessions were sequestrated. Lady Glanville's just been telling me what happened to the jewels. I hope you'll let me write about all this, Lady Glanville, as well as finding a birth certificate. Reporters always hope to find themselves writing history – history in the making. Mostly, though, it turns out to be school fêtes and court reports. What you've been telling me really *is* history – and I don't think anyone's known it before.'

'Write anything you like, dear boy. And come back if there's any more you need to know.' She held out her thin hand in dismissal.

As the door closed behind him, Asha looked suspiciously at the bright-eyed old lady. 'You're not having him on, are you, Aunt Alexa? Bribing him with juicy tit-bits so that he'll do the dull slog for you?'

'The jewels are real enough,' Alexa said indignantly. 'Rubies and diamonds. I keep them in the bank. I'll wear them on my birthday, if you like. Then you'll see how people dressed for parties a hundred years ago. Still, you don't want to talk about old family matters, do you, dear?'

'As a matter of fact, I do.' Asha managed to keep her voice steady. 'I want you to tell me about Ros. And Brad. And my mother.'

Alexa was not easily disconcerted, but the directness of the request made her pluck at the edge of the sheet with nervous hands. 'What do you want to know?' she asked at last.

'Everything. The truth. And the reason I wasn't told before.'

Alexa thought for a moment before nodding. 'Yes, it can't do any harm now. Pull me up a little, will you, dear?' Asha arranged the pillows to give her more support. 'Well, then. Your parents lived in Malaya, but your mother came back to England when she was pregnant. She'd had trouble before. Wanted to be near a good hospital. You were born in London – well, you know that. And before Barbary – your mother – could take you home, the Japanese invaded Malaya. So she stayed in England with me. Brad Davidson was someone I'd known when he was a boy, in San Francisco. He came to England during the war. Visited me and met Barbary. They fell in love. But she wouldn't live with him, not then; she thought her husband might still be alive. She sent Brad away. A very high-minded woman, your mother. Poor child. Poor child.'

'And what happened to my father? You've always told me that he was taken prisoner by the Japanese.'

'We learned that later, after the war. But a couple of soldiers came to Blaize before then. They'd escaped from Malaya. Made your mother believe she was a widow. She wasn't the only one to make that kind of mistake. The Japanese wouldn't give any information. And thousands of their prisoners *did* die. You mustn't blame your mother for what happened, Asha. She tried to do what was best. In a way, that was what killed her.'

As though she had come to the end of the story, the old lady fell silent. Asha prompted her. 'So she thought my father was dead.'

'Yes. Then she met Brad again. They thought they'd be able to marry when your father's death was confirmed after the war. So they set up house together and Ros was born – on VE Day, I remember. You all went off to America.' She made a helpless gesture with her pale hands. 'Then your father came home.'

'I don't remember him at all,' said Asha.

'He was very ill. He'd been treated appallingly by the Japanese. Barbary came back to England with you as soon as she heard the news. He loved you – he was very possessive about you – but, well, nothing was normal. He couldn't stand the kind of noise that any little girl makes. Barbary sent you to Blaize for holidays and weekends. You'd spent the first four years of your life there: it was your home.'

'So what happened?'

'Your father found out about Brad and Ros. A normal, healthy man might have been able to understand and forgive. But your father had been – well, damaged. He was vindictive. Stole you from your mother.'

'At school,' said Asha. 'He sent my grandmother.' They had reached the beginning of her own memory.

'That's right. Not that Eleanor was your real grandmother, of course. She married your grandfather, but she didn't have any ties of blood with you or your mother. All the same, she was the one your father chose to help him. Then he died. He'd been dying all the time, in a sense. His will left us in a terrible muddle. He didn't want your mother to have you back, you see. So then it was her turn to become ill. She couldn't find out where you were, not at first. When she did, she had to go to court for custody. She was a sweet girl, Barbary, and very honest. Determined to do whatever was right. But not tough. Not a fighter.'

'What happened to Ros?'

'Barbary had to leave Ros in America when she came back here. Brad wouldn't let his baby go. He hoped that if he held on, Barbary would come back to him. That was part of the reason for your mother's breakdown, that she seemed to be losing both her little girls at once.' Alexa fell silent, perhaps remembering that time. Not wanting to tire her, Asha refrained from putting any more questions – but the story was not yet complete. 'So Ros stayed on in America,' the old lady said with a new briskness in her voice. 'She wouldn't remember her mother. I was sorry for her, the poor little girl. I left her the rubies.'

'The rubies?'

'The Lorimer jewels. We were talking about them earlier. After Frisca died I had to make a new will. I left

292

the rubies to Ros and the money to you. I'd forgotten about that. I must change it. Ros doesn't even know who I am – and there may not be much money left. You've been a good girl to me, Asha, dear. You deserve to have anything I've got. I'll wear the rubies for my hundredth birthday. But you can have them after I've gone. Or even after the party. If I just slip them to you, perhaps we could dodge these terrible taxes. I'll ask my lawyer.'

'You're very generous, Aunt Alexa. But I've made you tired. Have a good rest.' Asha kissed her goodbye. As she drove thoughtfully back to London she gave no further thought to the rubies. Instead she probed her memory, endeavouring to mesh her own recollections of childhood with what she had just learned.

Ranji was interested to hear her great-aunt's revelations. 'While you were gone, a thought occurred to me,' he said. 'Just for once we could sell a real ancestor if we chose.' He pointed to the portrait on the wall. 'I remember you telling me that you were descended from the old gentleman through both your mother and your father. So Ros Davidson must have a line back to him as well through her mother – *your* mother. I think Miss Davidson is not exactly on the breadline. She wrote on the note-paper of Davidson Security Systems Inc., a company of which she appears to be executive president.'

'She's my half-sister! I'm not going to let you – '

'Ssh, ssh. Don't get so indignant. I'm not going to rip her off. We can send her all the usual possibilities. You have better photographs of her mother, so Chris could produce a lifelike costume piece. I'll try to find her a swash-buckling seventeenth-century slave-trading sea captain. But – unless you feel sentimental about it and don't want to let it go – we could also offer her a genuine 1877 portrait of John Junius Lorimer of Bristol. I am only suggesting that it would hardly be unreasonable to charge a stiffish price for something which would be exactly what we claimed it to be – a contemporary portrait of Ros Davidson's true ancestor.'

Asha stared at the portrait of her great-grandfather. It was true that the nineteenth-century autocrat of Lorimer's Bank with his sombre clothing and imperious gaze was out of place in their flat. And this would not be the same as selling John Junius to a stranger. Ros had almost as much right to provide a home for the portrait as herself. 'We ought to ask Aunt Alexa, though,' she said.

'Why? She gave the picture to you. She doesn't expect to see it again. We don't need to tell her that we're selling it.'

Asha considered for a moment longer. 'After the party,' she said at last. 'There's going to be a party for her hundredth birthday. I've been told to invite all the family. Not that there are many left. She might want John Junius brought back for the day. But after that, I wouldn't mind.'

'It would take that long to arrange, in any case.'

'Aunt Alexa will probably want me to invite Ros,' Asha suggested. 'I took her by surprise today. When she thinks about it, she'll want to find out how I knew the right questions to ask.'

'The timing could fit neatly. I send the usual portfolio for a new client, plus a photograph of the genuine article here. In view of its high price, I ask if she'd like to inspect it personally. In the meantime, while I'm putting everything together, you'll be writing Ros a personal letter, telling her who you are and everything you know about her place in the family. And asking her if she'd like to come to the party.'

Asha nodded in agreement. 'I should think she'd be

294

thrilled. Aunt Alexa knew her father, Brad Davidson, at the time of the San Francisco earthquake, apparently. All those years ago – isn't it incredible!' She looked again at the portrait of the Bristol banker. 'I think of John Junius as existing way back in history. He was born in 1800. He must have cheered the news of Waterloo while he was still only a schoolboy. But he held Aunt Alexa in his arms when she was a baby. When she first started getting excited about this centenary birthday I only felt that I should humour her by making the arrangements. But I'm beginning to understand her feelings. Not that it's anything to be proud of, living to a hundred. But it's certainly *interesting*. Yes, I'll write to Ros.'

She smiled to herself as she sat down at once to compose a letter of introduction and invitation. Ros would be as thrilled as she was herself to learn that she had a sister, and just as sorry as Asha was that they had not grown up together. But it was not too late for them to become friends. Asha felt no doubt about the answer she would receive. Ros would come to England for the party.

9

'The rubies,' said Alexa. 'I shall need the rubies on the day before the party. Will you collect them for me, dear? They're in the bank. For safe keeping. Tell the manager I want them out for two days.'

'I doubt if he'll take my word for it.' Asha added yet another note to her list of final instructions. It was fortunate that the date of the celebration fell within the school's Easter holiday. 'You'll have to give me a letter of authority. And the bank receipt.'

'I put those jewels into safe deposit in 1913. You don't expect me still to have a receipt, do you? Young Dangerfield will arrange it.' Three generations of Dangerfields had handled Alexa's legal affairs since she married Lord Glanville. Asha had met the current representative of the family firm, a pleasant young man, when Alexa's move to the nursing home was under discussion. 'And ask him to come with you when you bring them here. So that I can arrange for you to have the rubies instead of Ros. If anything needs to be signed, he can bring it the next day. I've invited him to the party.'

'Where are you holding this party – in the Albert Hall?' As the date approached, Alexa had become generous with invitations. 'Why do you want the jewellery a day early, Aunt Alexa? Wouldn't it be safer if I brought it actually on your birthday?'

'That nice young man from the Bristol paper is bringing a few of his friends along on the day before. They want to ask questions and take photographs, ready to appear on the eighteenth. He put in a lot of work, you know, finding out where I was born. This will do him good in his job. And I shall enjoy reading what they say. He'd like me to be all dressed up, as if the party had started. So I need the rubies.'

'I'll fix it.' Asha's mood was one of brisk efficiency. Her appointment as Head of Hillgate Comprehensive School from September had been confirmed, and her head was full of plans for changes. Compared with the problems involved in taking over an unwieldy educational establishment and setting it on a new course, Alexa's requirements were child's play.

On March 17th Asha and Mr Dangerfield met at the City bank in which the jewel case was kept and together went through the formalities of extracting it from the strong room.

'Lady Glanville was hoping to slip this to you after the party tomorrow,' said the lawyer as he drove the valuable cargo towards the nursing home. 'She thought she could avoid Capital Transfer Tax. If she'd made the gift fifteen years ago it would have been perfectly legal. But I'm afraid I can't be a party to what she has in mind now. And the bank records of ownership can't be changed retrospectively. I'm sorry to be unhelpful. If I'd known that the jewels existed, I would have given her advice earlier. But as it is . . . She's going to instruct me today about changes in her will. I'll do my best to have the codicils ready for signature tomorrow.'

'I didn't know the jewels existed any more than you did, until a few weeks ago,' Asha told him. 'Are they insured while they're out of the bank?'

'Special cover for two days, and they have to go back to the strong room overnight. I won't tell you what value I've put on them in case it makes you nervous. One of the conditions, incidentally, is that Lady Glanville mustn't be left alone while she's wearing them. Either you or myself must be in the room all the time.'

Asha nodded. She was still thinking of the birthday itself as the big occasion, so the scene which greeted them on arrival took her by surprise. Peter Langley's 'few friends' proved to be a squad of reporters and photographers large enough to cover a royal tour. Matron, anxious, was lying in wait for Asha.

'I wouldn't let them in until you came,' she said. 'You must make it clear to them what it means to be old. Just because Lady Glanville is bright and able to talk doesn't mean that she's strong. You know how quickly she tires. And she's over-excited already about tomorrow's party. I've asked the nurses to play it down, but they're excited themselves.'

'I'll see that this doesn't go on too long,' Asha promised. 'Let me have a word with her first. Then I'll make a timetable for the interview.' She tapped at Alexa's door and went in. Mr Dangerfield was closing his notebook as she entered, so presumably he had been given his instructions. Asha bent over to kiss the old lady. 'You look marvellous,' she said.

It was true. The soft waves of her snow-white hair made it apparent that a hairdresser had come to her room that morning. And he must have brought a beautician with him, for the nurses would not have been able to create such a delicately smooth complexion on the face of a woman about to celebrate her hundredth birthday.

'White of egg.' Alexa could read her great-niece's thoughts. 'Old stage trick. Only good for a couple of hours. But I didn't see why the photographs should show me looking like an old crone.'

'You've never looked anything but beautiful.' As she

paid the compliment, Asha's eye was caught by the jewel case. Its three velvet-lined drawers had been unlocked and pulled out to reveal their contents. She stared in astonishment at the rich display.

The main piece was a necklace which at the front divided into three tiers of rubies, from which hung a pendant in the form of a rose: a single large ruby, surrounded by petals made of smaller stones, was set in silver and edged with diamonds. This rose design, on a smaller scale, was repeated in a pair of delicate drop earrings. In the third tray of the jewel case was a tiara. Yet another rose of rubies in its centre was surrounded here by trembling leaves outlined in diamonds. Asha had learned that the Lorimer jewels were valuable. She had not expected them also to be so beautiful.

'Will you help me put them on, dear?' Alexa asked. It took a little time. Asha had never handled a tiara before and she and Alexa were equally nervous about disarranging the newly-created hairstyle. The necklace was more easily fitted. Alexa had chosen a bed jacket of pale pink chiffon, so sheer as to be almost transparent. Fitting into the décolleté lines of her lace-edged nightdress, the necklace appeared from a distance to be resting on smooth young skin. Alexa had always known how to make the best of herself.

'Five minutes' rest now,' commanded Asha, when the earrings were also in place and the final effect had been approved. Leaving the lawyer to fulfil the insurance condition, she went out to talk to the waiting journalists. She told them firmly that Lady Glanville would become confused and quickly tired if they all crowded into the room at once. It was agreed that the photographers should go in first and leave without arguing when Asha told them that their time was up.

While the cameras were flashing, she chatted to the reporters and was amused to find that Peter Langley had appointed himself Alexa's press agent, issuing his rivals with a *curriculum vitae* to guide their questioning.

'What have you left out?' Asha whispered to him when the others were not listening. 'What's the revelation which your readers and no other will discover tomorrow?' She could tell from his grin that her suspicions were well-founded.

'The Bristol bank crash,' he confessed. 'It's not part of her career. But it's an interesting piece of social history, and the birthday is a peg to hang the story on.'

'I hope you're not still arguing that her birth was responsible for a financial collapse a hundred years ago!'

'Well, it might have been, you know. At this distance of time, who can tell what really happened? Now if only her father had kept a diary! He must have been a fascinating character. On the face of it, so eminently respectable, so fabulously rich – model husband, solid banker, connoisseur of art, city benefactor. And beneath it all, the secret life – the Italian mistress, the illegitimate daughter, the valuable gifts, the cooking of the books. Then the collapse of the bank, the ruin of the community, the disappearance of the jewels – it's a marvellous story.'

'Which you've already sold.'

'Naturally. With your aunt's full approval. I've persuaded her, incidentally, to let me ghost her memoirs. Her memory is incredible, and it's important that people who've been famous should set the facts down. They owe it to their descendants.'

'She'll never have any descendants, I'm afraid.'

'Well, posterity, then.' He looked at his watch. 'Time to change shifts?'

Asha had intended to allow her aunt another rest

before the questions began, but Alexa's eyes were bright with excitement. As she recalled her youth, she almost seemed to be young again in reality, and her pleasure in the occasion was infectious. She had long ago mastered the art of being interviewed and her reminiscences poured out without any great regard for the questions which prompted them. It was she as much as the journalists who protested when Asha at last announced that the session must end. An actress to the last, she kept the bright smile on her face until the door closed on the last of her visitors. But her fingers were fidgeting with the sheets in a sign of tiredness and her exhaustion was evident as she allowed her head to fall back on the pillow.

'You were marvellous, darling.' Asha bent over her with a kiss of congratulation. 'May I just take the necklace off?' She undid its fastenings and then gently eased out the delicate ear-rings and removed the tiara, marvelling at the value of the stones she was handling. How impossible it was to visualize a world in which rich women had worn such fortunes round their necks each evening as a matter of course – a world of which Alexa was a survivor. 'May I try them on?' she asked. 'Just for a second, before I put them away?'

'No.' Alexa softened the sharpness of her answer with an affectionate pat of the hand. 'No dear, I don't want you ever to wear them. Tomorrow I'll sign the new will, and then they'll be yours one day; but you're to sell them. Send them straight from the bank to an auction house. Promise me you'll never put them on. They bring bad luck, these rubies. I don't want you touched by it.'

'Aunt Alexa! I never knew you were superstitious!'

'I'm not with anything else. Not with these, even; not superstitious. Just stating a fact. They've always brought bad luck. People have died because of them. I've only

301

worn them once myself. For a ball – and before it was over, the man I loved had left me.' She sighed, and was silent for a long time, perhaps remembering the occasion.

'Then why did you choose these particular jewels to wear today, Aunt Alexa? You must have lots of others.'

'Most of the others went when Pirry died. Glanville family heirlooms. The lawyers said I couldn't keep them, I've sold all my own. Except these, because I'd forgotten all about them. Until you talked about Ros. As for wearing them today . . .' She was silent for so long that Asha thought she had forgotten the question. 'When I was young, Asha, I had great ambitions. Didn't someone once define hell as the place where you find all your wishes have been granted? It wasn't like that with me. I got what I wanted – my career, my husband, my son, my little opera house – and I enjoyed having it all. But now – what does an old lady look forward to? Celebrating a hundredth birthday. A bunch of grapes and a telegram from the Queen. Ridiculous ambition! It's served, though, for the past few months. Tomorrow, it's over. Achieved. What then? I'm not saying that I want to die. Certainly not. But if I try to look forward . . .' Again she fell into silence.

'I accuse you of being a sensation-monger,' Asha said cheerfully. 'You sent for the photographers and you put on the jewels and you hoped that you'd drop dead on the spot through some kind of magic. That's what you wanted, wasn't it? A sensation on the front page of all the newspapers. Well, it hasn't happened. You're going to go on bullying these poor nurses here until you're the oldest living person in England. After that, you'll have to take on the Georgian peasants who claim to be a hundred and forty. *There's* an ambition for you. I shall tell Matron to put you on a yoghurt diet at once.' As she spoke, she

302

arranged the rubies in their velvet-lined drawers. Closing the case, she bent over the bed to kiss Alexa goodbye.

'Have a really good rest this afternoon,' she said. 'This has only been a preview. You'll need all your strength for the real thing. I'll be back at three tomorrow, ready for the party.'

'Ah yes,' Alexa murmured. 'The party.' Her eyes were already closing in sleep as she squeezed Asha's hand. 'Thank you for arranging everything, dear. You're a good girl. I'll see you tomorrow , then, at the party.'

10

'I'll escort you back to the bank.' Peter Langley made the offer as Asha closed the door of her great-aunt's room.

'There's no need,' she began; but then remembered that she had come in Mr Dangerfield's car and required transport if not protection.

'Lady Glanville's insurance company would see a need,' Peter suggested. 'You and that little box are an invitation to muggers.'

'No one's ever mugged me before,' Asha claimed cheerfully.

'Perhaps you've never been in possession of something so much worth stealing.'

'Who would know that I am now?' She answered the question in her own mind. 'You're not suggesting that one of your journalist friends . . .?'

'Certainly not. A more honest bunch of chaps you'd never find. All the same, it *is* faintly possible that they may have adjourned *en masse* straight from here to the nearest pub. It would only take one loud voice commenting on Lady Glanville's sparklers to make some local villain prick up his ears. There's no point in arguing. Mr Dangerfield and I have agreed that you must have protection. And he's decided to trust me, since he's got an appointment to keep.'

Asha, pleased, responded with vivacity to Peter's enthusiastic chatter as he drove her to the bank, and laughed at his exaggerated sigh of relief when she had exchanged the jewel case for a receipt.

'Five past one,' he said. 'Marvellous timing. Lunch?'

'I'm afraid I can't. Ranji will be expecting me.'

'You mean that at this moment he'll have the soufflé rising for you, the casserole bubbling, the zabaglione whipping?'

'No such luck. I mean that at this moment he'll be looking at the clock and muttering because I promised to be home before one. To get lunch for *him*.'

'You've been delayed,' said Peter. 'The press conference went on longer than you expected. You can't possibly get back before three. So he'd better boil himself an egg and you'll make it up to him at suppertime. There's a telephone on that corner.'

Asha hesitated for a moment longer and then succumbed to temptation. She dialled her own number, but found it engaged. A quarter of an hour later she tried again from the restaurant. Ranji accepted the lie in silence – probably he was already sulking over her lateness. Asha sighed to herself at the thought of arguments to come, but resolved that since she would have to pay for her outing later, she would at least enjoy it now.

'Your great-aunt really was quite a girl, wasn't she?' said Peter. 'She showed me her scrapbooks. All the reviews of her performances. And the photographs! She seems to have taken the whole of Europe by storm at the turn of the century.'

'That's an odd phrase, isn't it?' suggested Asha. 'Taking Europe by storm. I don't suppose there were ever more than a few thousand people who went to the opera then – and not all of those bothered to listen to the music: they were simply following a social fashion. Aunt Alexa's daughter, Frisca – the film star – was much more truly an international success: she appealed to all classes in any part of the world where there was a cinema.'

305

'I've seen some of those old films. Frisca Glanville was a marvellous dancer. And she was pretty, I'd agree. But there are lots of pretty women, and styles of prettiness are a social fashion as well. Lady Glanville had something extra. In every generation there seem to be a few women who are outstandingly beautiful. She was one of those, wasn't she – quite apart from her singing. There's one photograph in the scrapbook that I remember in particular, from her twenties. She's wearing a long pale dress of some satiny material. Cut very low – you can see what lovely breasts she had. And very tightly fitted at the waist: such a slim waist. Long hair swept up and coiled like – like a crown, with jewels in it. It's a posed photograph, of course: artificial, you might say. But she looked like a princess. Perfectly, absolutely beautiful.' He was silent for a moment, indulging his admiration. Then his eyes twinkled as he looked up at Asha. 'You could look like that if you wanted to.'

'Don't be silly.'

'Oh, I realize that you don't want to. You like to appear businesslike, efficient, competent, because your professional success depends on that look – just as Lady Glanville, when she was an opera singer, needed to be glamorous. But – while she was wearing those rubies, I imagined how good they'd look on you, with your marvellous complexion. Your hair's as beautiful as hers must have been once. You're as tall and as slim as she looks in the photograph. If you took your glasses off – sorry for the cliché – and wore a dress out of Lady Glanville's Edwardian wardrobe and posed for a photographer, you could produce as stunning an effect as she did. It's a question of style. Some generations have it. Ours hasn't. But you're beautiful in a way which would fit into a good

306

many of the old patterns. Hasn't anyone told you that before?'

Asha felt herself flushing. Chris had said something of the sort when he first asked to paint her. But even the success of his mock-Gainsborough portrait had not made Asha think of herself as a beautiful woman, and nor did Peter's compliments now. 'You're embarrassing me,' she said.

'Sorry.' He accepted her wish to change the subject. 'What did surprise me in Lady Glanville's scrapbook was her support for the suffragettes. I mean, of course, the suffrag*ists*.' Asha guessed that he had received the lecture which Alexa invariably delivered to those who used the popular newspaper term. 'Have you inherited Lady Glanville's feminist principles as well as her beauty?'

'I can't have inherited anything at all from her,' Asha pointed out. 'I'm not a direct descendant.'

'But you must have an ancestor in common somewhere.'

Asha thought of an elderly Victorian gentleman whose portrait would soon be on its way to the United States. 'Yes,' she agreed. 'That Bristol banker who interests you so much. I'd guess, though, that Aunt Alexa's beauty must have come through her mother, not from John Junius Lorimer. As for his attitude to women – I should think he'd have had a fit at the thought of letting them vote. He would have expected the females of his family merely to do good works and practise amateur talents and display his wealth in their clothes.'

'Without ever having to worry about money. Don't you sometimes regret that those days are gone? Wouldn't you like to sit back and feel that your husband or father was entirely responsible for your comfort?'

'We're talking about a very small section of society,'

307

Asha pointed out. 'And although the men may have been financially responsible for their wives and daughters, it was the servants who actually provided the comfort. What I do regret is that, as the servants disappeared from the middle-class scene, it was the women who took over their jobs. So that now we work outside the home as a matter of course, we're still left with the responsibility for the domestic support system. I'm generalizing madly, but you know what I mean. Husbands nowadays are happy to take on the chauffeur's chores – to wash the car and tinker with the engine. But in most families it seems to be the wife who's replaced the cook, housemaid, gardener, interior decorator, laundrymaid, nanny, governess and housekeeper – and all in her spare time.'

'That's changing, surely.'

'Is it?' Asha thought of Ranji's pained expression whenever she suggested that he might prepare a meal or help her change the sheets. It was possible that his was a special case – that his upbringing in India had made it difficult to change his view that housework was demeaning for a male. But from many staffroom conversations she suspected that the pattern of her married life was not unusual. And if she were to be honest with herself, she would have to admit that it was with Ranji's helplessness – as a young student confused by Western ways – that she had fallen in love. 'Well, I'm glad to hear that a young man thinks so.'

'Women are so formidably efficient,' Peter suggested. 'It's hard for a man to tackle the wallpapering when his wife has demonstrated that she can do it better. You need to look incompetent occasionally. And the other side of it, of course, is up to you as a teacher. Do you give your boys a chance to learn cookery, for example?'

'It will be one of next year's innovations.' Asha was

pleased that she could give a positive answer. 'Cookery classes for all first-year pupils. And no sex segregation in the options later. Boys and girls alike can choose to type or sew or cook or do carpentry or metalwork.'

'And will you – ' Peter's face shaded with apology. 'I ought to warn you that I seem to be interviewing you. That wasn't the idea when we started talking, but we seem to be moving that way. Do you mind?'

'I'm not worth a page in your notebook,' laughed Asha.

'Oh, but you are. You're about to become a very powerful woman. The lives of more than a thousand children in your hands. Their futures, their ideals, their happiness. Did that Bristol ancestor of yours ever have as much power as that?'

'He had enough to ruin a whole community,' Asha reminded him wryly. 'As you've already discovered, when Lorimer's Bank went bust, the whole of Bristol went bust with it. I hope I shan't achieve quite that effect.' But she was interested to hear Peter repeating almost word for word the opinion with which her cousin Paula had encouraged her to apply for the headship.

'Different kinds of power, agreed. All the same – you know what I mean. You'll be able to impose your philosophy of life on the impressionable young. It's a matter of public interest to know what that philosophy is.'

'I'm afraid I'm not feeling philosophical today.' Asha turned the conversation away from herself, asking Peter about his work. Only at the end of the meal did he return to the subject of her family.

'I hope you don't feel that I've – well, "used" Lady Glanville,' he said. 'When her letter came in, asking if someone could trace her birth, the editor gave me the time to do it because of her title, really. He thought the hundredth birthday might rate a paragraph if she was a local girl. Discovering that she'd been so famous was a piece of serendipity and I have rather battened on to it – making Fleet Street work through me, until today. It's done me a lot of good professionally. All quite deliberate. But all rising out of the fact that I thought she deserved it. I wouldn't like you to think – '

'She's loved every minute of the fuss,' said Asha. 'Talking about the days when she was young and famous. I don't remember her ever being as excited as she was this morning. And knowing what will be in all the papers tomorrow is the best birthday present she could have had. I should have thought of it myself. I'm grateful to you, so I'm glad if you found it useful.'

'I gather you don't like compliments,' said Peter. 'But she's lucky to have you – you realize that? So many old ladies find themselves alone in the world. All their relations are dead or don't want to know.'

'It's the other way round,' Asha told him. 'I've been lucky to have her. Peter, I must get home. I'll see you again tomorrow. The great day. Thank you so much for the lunch.'

Ranji's lunch had been baked beans on toast. He had left all the debris in the kitchen to prove it.

'I'm sorry about that.' Asha realized guiltily that it was half past three. 'I'll do something special tonight.'

'Have you had anything to eat yourself?' Ranji asked.

'Yes. Peter Langley took me out, since I was so late anyway.' Admitting that her meal had been less frugal than Ranji's helped to ease her bad conscience at the pretence that she could not have returned to the flat at a reasonable hour.

'Where did you phone from?' he asked.

310

'When I spoke to you, it was from the restaurant. I tried before, at about one o'clock, but the line was engaged.'

'That would have been while I was talking to Matron. She said you'd left some time earlier – she expected to find you here.'

'I had to take the jewellery back into safe deposit.' The defence was true, but she noticed that Ranji showed no sign of the irritation which might for once be justified. 'What did Matron want?'

'She had some news for you, Asha. Really, she wanted to tell you herself. When the nurse went in to get Lady Glanville ready for lunch, she found her dead.'

Asha had been running water into the pan to soak away the burnt layer of baked beans. She set it down and turned, speechless, to stare at Ranji.

'Over-excitement and over-tiredness, Matron said. It would seem she was trying to shift blame from her own shoulders. Though why she should need to make excuses after keeping the old lady alive for so long, I can't imagine.' He came into the kitchen and stretched past Asha to turn off the tap. 'It's a shock, darling, I know. Sit down for a minute.' He offered a handkerchief to mop up the tears which were flowing down her cheeks. 'She'd had a good run, Asha. Ninety-nine years and three hundred and sixty-four days. Nothing to cry about.'

'But she was so much looking forward to her party tomorrow.'

Ranji smiled affectionately as he put an arm round her shoulders, hugging her. 'You make her sound like a five-year-old in a frilly birthday frock, wondering about her presents.'

'That's how it was, in a way. When I was a little girl she looked after me. But these past few years, when she

311

couldn't manage, I've had to look after her, or arrange for someone else to, just as though she *were* a child. And like a child she'd set her heart on enjoying all the fuss. Seeing what the papers say, getting her telegram, blowing out the candles on the cake. She'll be so disappointed.'

'Asha, sweetheart, she's *dead*.'

'Yes. Yes, of course.' The first shock of hearing the news was succeeded by the desolation of believing it. Ranji, sympathetically, did not disturb her thoughts until with a last sniff she indicated that, although unhappy, she was ready to talk again.

'I promised Matron you would call back to discuss the funeral.'

Still shocked and distressed, Asha moved towards the telephone. But before she rang the nursing home, she dialled another number. Alexa's birthday, had she lived, would have been reported in style in the national press. Now the birthday party would not take place, but that was a news story in itself – and the journalists and photographers who had crowded her room would not let their material go to waste. Had she died six months earlier the fact might have been reported only briefly, because she had reached the pinnacle of her fame so very many years ago and few people still alive would remember Alexa Reni's voice and beauty. But tomorrow, if Fleet Street were alerted in time, she would receive the kind of obituary afforded normally only to royalty. Asha would not now be able to hand over the centenary present which she had already gift-wrapped; but instead she could give her great-aunt the reviews of a lifetime.

Alexa would have appreciated that.

11

Ros Davidson slept late on the morning after her flight from San Francisco to London. It was half past ten before she rang room service for breakfast, and not until eleven o'clock did she unfold the morning paper which came with the tray.

England had lost the Centenary Test, whatever that might mean. This fact – apparently the most important item of world news – was recorded by a heavy headline and a large photograph of a man called Lillie bowling a man called Knott in Melbourne, Australia. Ros passed her eye quickly over it and concentrated instead on another photograph, lower down the page. Above the caption *The Singing Suffragette* it showed a beautiful young woman in the dress of 1912, carrying a Votes for Women banner. Ros nodded approvingly to see that her relative's hundredth birthday rated the front page – until her jet-lagged eyes focused more clearly on the small print and she learned with dismay that Lady Glanville, who had once been Alexa Reni, was dead.

Stunned by the news, Ros read the front page story and then turned at once to the obituary columns. Asha's invitation to the birthday party had explained Lady Glanville's relationship to Ros's mother but had only briefly mentioned how famous the old lady had been in her youth. With increasing frustration at the discovery that she had arrived too late, Ros read the exceptionally full account of Alexa's life from the moment of her illegitimate birth in Bristol in 1877, and of a career which had begun with her first appearance on the stage at the age of nine.

On the obituary page there was another photograph. Alexa, in costume, was singing Carmen with Caruso in San Francisco – the photograph had been taken only a few hours before the earthquake and fire which destroyed most of the city in 1906. Incredulously Ros discovered Lady Glanville's connection with her own home town and – even more amazingly – with her own family.

How tantalizing it was to have missed by such a very short time the opportunity to talk to Lady Glanville. Worst of all, she had lost her best chance to learn about her own mother. Asha would probably not remember much from her infancy. Ros had been relying on the old lady to recount the whole of Barbary Lorimer's life history.

The deep disappointment which swept over her as she pushed the newspaper aside made her briefly angry that her father had never told her the truth while he was alive – had never mentioned that she had a great-aunt and a half-sister living in England. It was all to do with trying to forget the heartbreak of her mother's death, she supposed: but her ignorance made her feel curiously lonely – and, at this moment, affected by a greater sense of bereavement than would normally be caused by the death of a stranger. She sighed to herself and considered what she should do now that the day could not adhere to its original programme. The first thing was to make a telephone call to her half-sister.

Asha's voice was both friendly and businesslike as she made clear her wish to arrange a meeting as soon as possible. 'I know I oughtn't to make a visitor do the travelling,' she said. 'But I'm tied to the telephone. Would you mind?' She gave detailed instructions about

Tube lines and the way to walk from Notting Hill Gate station. Ros listened politely and took a taxi.

It set her down in a scruffy street, outside what appeared to be a shop. Ros checked the address doubtfully; but even before she had time to ring the bell a door opened at the side of the shop and a tall, slim woman with long, pale hair was holding out both hands in welcome.

Not even for the first moment were they strangers. Each of them separately had longed to have a sister and their delight in finding each other was mutual. As they went up the stairs together they held hands like friends reunited after a long parting.

The rooms of Asha's home were more spacious than the neighbourhood suggested. If Ros had expected something grander, that was probably because of the connection with Lady Glanville. The furniture was not stylish, but it was comfortable; and the coffee she was offered at once was freshly-ground as well as freshly-made.

'You're upset,' she said, looking more closely at her sister's pale face as the tray was set down on a coffee table. 'You and the old lady were close, I guess.'

Asha nodded. 'I keep reminding myself that she was so very old, that this was bound to happen. But all the same . . .'

'It hit me too,' Ros told her. 'Sure, I can't weep for someone I never met. But even before I left the States there were so many questions I had in mind to ask her: and reading the obituary this morning made me think of a whole lot more. It's all churning around in my mind. She married my uncle, it said, in San Francisco, just before he was killed in the earthquake! No one ever told me that before.'

'It was because of that connection that your father

came to call on her when he was in England during the war – and that was how he came to meet our mother. Mind you – ' Asha managed to smile – 'there's always been a certain doubt in the family as to whether any legal wedding took place in 1906. It was planned, certainly. And Aunt Alexa had to claim that it happened, because she had a baby. In those days illegitimate babies were not yet in fashion.'

'A baby! My cousin, then!' Every new fact she learned left Ros more astounded and bewildered.

'She's dead now, I'm afraid. But while you're here, you'll meet her son, Bernard Lorimer.'

'I've always wanted to be part of a big family,' said Ros. 'I was raised rich and pampered, but that one thing was never on offer. I want to meet you all. I want you all to think of me as kin. But most of all I want to hear just everything about you, Asha. Right from the beginning. And especially how we came to lose each other. Your letter didn't explain that.'

'I only found out recently from Aunt Alexa,' said Asha. Ros listened intently as her sister passed on the details she had learned, and then asked questions to bring Asha's career up to date.

'So we're both boss-women,' she commented as she heard about the promotion to headmistress which would take effect in September. 'You're going to run a big school, and I already run a company. Only because my father gave it to me – but that doesn't alter the fact that I'm in charge and that's how I like it. With different fathers, it must be from our mother that we've inherited the taste for being in control.'

'According to Aunt Alexa, she was shy,' Asha said. 'But of course she was still young when she died. And it's

316

true that the Lorimers as a family are pretty strong-minded. Come upstairs, and I'll show you our great-great-grandfather – a boss-figure if ever there was one.'

Ros stood up to follow, but her eye was caught by a picture on the wall – a full-length portrait of an aristocratic young woman in a gown of grey lace and pink satin. 'Is that another ancestor of ours?' she asked. 'There's a likeness to you, although not to me. It's beautiful. And so clean.' She wondered why Asha did not answer, and tried to interpret the mischief in her smile. Puzzled, she studied the portrait again. 'You?' she said incredulously.

Asha's smile broadened as she repeated the pose. With her head held unnaturally high she pointed a neat toe forward and turned the knuckles of one hand to rest on her hip while the other was supported by an invisible parasol. 'Ranji told you, didn't he, when he answered your letter, that one of the alternatives on offer was a painting of yourself in period costume. This is the proto-type – we show it to give clients confidence that the result will look good. And just up these stairs is the man who painted it.' Asha led the way up into a very large, light room. 'Meet Chris Townsend. Chris, my sister, Ros Davidson.'

The young artist was not standing at his easel but sitting astride a painter's donkey with a canvas propped in front of him at a slight angle. He turned his head to smile at them and set down the brush he was using.

'Please don't get up.' Anxious not to disturb his paint-ing, Ros moved to stand behind him. 'May I look?' She studied the photograph of a bespectacled sixty-year-old businessman which was fastened to the unfinished paint-ing. Then she compared it with the kilted figure striding mistily across the canvas. 'I don't believe it! It's impossible – but it's exactly him.'

317

'He reckons that he's descended from one of the ancient kings of Ireland, and who am I to argue?' said Chris. 'He only sent a profile, so a profile is all he can have. But the costume is genuine, at least. And I feel like being Turner this week.'

'Will you paint me?' asked Ros. She was not normally impulsive, but this unusual day was proving to be both exciting and frightening. People died, people lost touch – even relations as close as sisters. Perhaps it was still the effect of jet lag, but she felt her life to be shadowy and shifting. A portrait would put her on record as having existed, would fix her in one period of her life. And this young man was good. If he would allow her to commission him she could feel all the pleasure of being a patron and perhaps later enjoy a second pride in watching him grow famous.

Chris twisted round to stare at her more closely. Ros, never shy, lifted her chin and flashed brightness into her eyes.

'Certainly I'll paint you,' said Chris in a businesslike manner. 'I'll need half an hour's camera session with you before I start: and then three four-hour sittings, with a gap of at least three weeks after the first one – unless you want a run-of-the-mill effort just from the photographs. What period have you in mind? And have you a favourite artist?'

'The period is now,' Ros told him. 'Me now by you now.'

'There's no such thing as me,' said Chris. 'Asha would have warned you of that if you'd given her advance notice. My talent is for appearing to be someone else.'

'I don't believe you.' Ros studied the mock-Turner again and thought of the 'Gainsborough' downstairs. 'Sure, you have that talent, but you could do it straight.

318

Could I have Blaize in the picture, do you think? Is it still standing, Asha?'

'Oh yes, Blaize is still there,' Asha assured her. 'Aunt Alexa will be buried in the churchyard on the estate. If you come to the funeral, you'll see the house.'

'I've no rights in Blaize,' Ros admitted. 'So it mustn't steal the show. It's been a kind of dream castle, that's all, ever since I was nine. I knew I was a baby there because I'd seen a photograph: but I didn't know what or where it was. What I'd like is Blaize in the background, misty like the moor behind your Irish king. With me in the foreground, very clear. Not a photographic style, but in modern dress and recognizable.'

'I can tell you're sisters.' Chris pretended to be gloomy, but he was smiling. He was an attractive young man – and he found Asha attractive: Ros, whose intuition in these matters was immediate and usually accurate, was sure of that. 'Bullies, the pair of you. Everything to be just the way you want it. Well, when I look at the Ancestor I can see where you both get it from.'

Ros turned at the reminder and saw that the picture of John Junius Lorimer had been set up an on easel for her to inspect. She had already seen a photograph of it, but that had not prepared her for the imperious eyes which stared directly into her own.

'I see what you mean. A strong picture of a strong man. Will you be able to give me a family tree, Asha? Your husband's letter just said that he was the great-grandfather of my mother. I want to know everything you can tell me about my mother's family.' She gazed at the old man's face for a few moments longer. 'Think of all the things he must have done in his lifetime – all the people he must have loved or hated.'

'Everyone's life is a story, isn't it?' suggested Asha.

'Right. I was thinking just that this morning when I read the sentence in the obituary about my uncle, Frank Davidson. How he and Alexa must have loved each other – how she must have cried when he died in the fire! That's a book in itself. Oh Asha, I truly do wish that I'd had time to meet her. To miss it only by a day! That's really tough. All my life I've been starved of ancestors and relations. You'll never be able to shake me off.'

'I don't want to. I may have a full head of ancestors but, like you, I'm short of relations. And especially of sisters. Are you interested in buying John Junius, then?'

'Oh yes,' said Ros. She put an arm round her sister's waist, hugging her close. 'If you're willing to sell, I've come here to buy. I'm going to refurnish my house as an ancestral home. And I shall hang my Lorimer ancestor in the place of honour.' She stared into the old man's piercing green eyes, giving as good as she got. 'I guess not everyone would want a personality as strong as that in the room. But I can cope with him. I'm a Lorimer as well.'

12

Alexa had expressed the wish to be buried in the little
churchyard at Blaize. The parish church had been built
by the Glanvilles many centuries earlier for their own
convenience – a fair distance from the village but very
close to the house. Asha thought it would be tactful to
telephone the present head of the family before making
arrangements for the service; and was invited to Blaize to
discuss her plans.

The Lord Glanville who greeted her proved to be a
plump and pleasant young merchant banker. He made it
clear that he welcomed an opportunity to bring to an
end the obscure feud between the two branches of the
Glanville family. 'I'm sure my father-never intended Lady
Glanville to leave Blaize so precipitately after her son
died,' he said. 'Her belief that she needed to vacate the
house immediately was all of her own making. Father
found himself cast as the ogre of the piece without being
given any opportunity to discuss the situation.'

'Aunt Alexa and your grandfather had a bitter quarrel,'
Asha told him. 'Over eighty years ago it must have
been, but she never forgot it. I don't know exactly what
happened.' And now I never shall know, she thought.
There would be no further chance to explore the remote
history of Alexa's life.

'I imagine you often visited your aunt while she was
living here,' Lord Glanville said. Asha had not quite
been able to control the movement of her eyes as she
noted the changes which had taken place since she was

last at Blaize. The drawing room itself looked far larger now that it no longer contained a grand piano. The room had formerly been crowded with photographs of Alexa in her various operatic roles. Now the only display was of silver cups and medals and trophies in the shape of horses. A large Stubbs hung on the wall which once had displayed the portrait of Alexa's father.

'I did more than visit,' Asha told her host. 'I was brought up here. This was my home until I married.'

'Then welcome home. Let me give you a drink. I asked the vicar to drop in so that you could fix everything up in comfort. We spend a small fortune every year on heating that church and it's never anything but arctic. What kind of funeral are you planning?'

'A very small one. While she was alive, Aunt Alexa made plans for a memorial service to be held in London. More of a concert than a service. An opera singer will sing one of her favourite arias. And the violinist, Leo Tavadze, was a protégé of hers once: he'll play something. She thought some of the ex-pupils of the school might perform as well. But I was only to choose the good ones. "Nothing but the best." It was always her motto. That service will be a public occasion. But the funeral itself will be very nearly confined to family. I imagine that some of the old tenants here may want to come. And one or two of the nurses who were looking after her when she died asked to be told the date. But that's all.'

'I'd be glad to offer any members of the family a drink or a meal or whatever's appropriate to the time after the service. Will you bring them back here?'

'That's very kind of you. It will be most welcome. There won't be many. The family has almost died out.'

'If it hadn't, I shouldn't be here now.'

'I didn't mean just the Glanvilles,' Asha said. 'There

are hardly any of Aunt Alexa's own family, the Lorimers, left. My husband will come with me, of course, and my half-sister who's over here from America. There's Aunt Alexa's grandson – from her first marriage, nothing to do with the Glanvilles. And some sort of cousin who turns up on family occasions like this. If he and Bernard bring their wives, that would carry the family party up to seven. And except for one more cousin who lives in Jamaica, that's all the family that exists. It's odd.'

Lord Glanville waited for her to explain the oddity, and Asha gestured towards the Stubbs.

'There used to be a portrait of Aunt Alexa's father hanging there. He had four children, thirteen grandchildren. In any normal progression one would have expected the number of his descendants to increase in each generation. But – well, there it is: there are only five of us left. It *is* odd.'

And something else was even odder, Asha thought to herself three days later as she introduced the survivors to Lord Glanville after the funeral. There were no children in the family. No Lorimer babies had been born since Ros, who was now thirty-two.

Would there be any in the future? John Lorimer, the cousin who was almost a stranger to Asha, had only recently – in his mid-fifties – married for the first time; and his wife did not look young enough to start a family. Paula, in Jamaica, was also over forty by now: whilst Helen Lorimer, Bernard's wife, was only a little younger and had had a hysterectomy. Ros was not too old to become a mother. But she had made it clear to her sister that her greatest satisfaction came from the successful running of her own business. Children would be an interruption to her work and would tie her to their father with a degree of permanence which she found unacceptable. Since she had chosen to be childless while she was married, it was unlikely that she would change her mind now that she lived alone.

That left only Asha herself. The survival of the Lorimer family might not be her sole responsibility: but in practical terms she alone would decide whether it lived or died. Without formulating the thought so precisely, she must have been aware of this for a long time already. It was hard to understand why she should suddenly feel overwhelmed by the burden now as she looked round at the small group of people in their black funereal clothes.

Perhaps it was because the sight of the family assembled in Lord Glanville's drawing room made its contraction clearer than a mental count could ever do. But even as she persuaded herself of this, a second emotion swept over Asha: a desolate loneliness triggered off not by the smallness of the group but by the place in which it was reunited. As though it were yesterday, she remembered her arrival in Blaize when she was five years old. She had tried to be brave, but the tears streamed down her face as she cried aloud, 'I want my Mummy!' Her mother was dead. It was Alexa, already seventy years old, who had gone down on her knees beside the orphaned child and promised to look after her. In every sense except that of giving birth Alexa had been Asha's mother, and now Alexa was gone. Asha put up both hands to cover her eyes, but was unable to press back the tears which repeated a thirty-year-old memory in a present sadness.

The others were chatting over their drinks with as much animation as if this were a cocktail party: they did not notice her sudden distress. Only Ranji, quickly sensitive to her feelings, excused himself to the vicar and came across the room. He did not speak, but took her in

324

his arms and held her tightly so that her hands, still flat over her face, pressed against his chest.

'Sorry,' she said at last, sniffing herself under control. 'Silly.'

'Not silly at all. Absolutely natural. Stay here just a minute while I tell everyone we're going.'

Asha dried her eyes and said her goodbyes. Ros had already been invited to drive back to London with Bernard, who remembered her as a baby. She kissed Asha sympathetically and promised to call her next day.

In the car Ranji did not speak but took hold of Asha's hand and placed it on his knee, stroking it gently from time to time as he drove. When they drew up in front of the flat she tried to explain something of what had upset her.

'When I was a little girl, Aunt Alexa was all I had,' she said. 'And in these last few years, she's really only had me. When I'm ninety-nine, I shan't have anyone.'

'You'll have me,' said Ranji. 'I shall be ninety-six only. I'll drop you here. You can be getting into bed while I park the car.'

'Bed? I'm not ill. When I cried, it was only – '

'Other things can happen in bed beside being ill,' Ranji reminded her. 'I love you very much, and especially when you cry. That beautiful woman needs comforting, I say to myself. Go and make the sheets warm for me.'

Asha watched him drive away. It would take him a few moments to find a space in the residents' parking area and to walk back. She went upstairs to the flat and into the bathroom. With one hand already stretched towards the cupboard in which she kept her contraceptives, she stopped to think. Did she really care that the family was dying out? Was she truly afraid of being lonely, of having no one to love her as she had loved Alexa? If so, this was the moment when she could take a chance. Ranji, in romantic mood, would not stop to check that she had taken precautions. And if, later, he learned that she was pregnant and accused her of not consulting him, it would be easy to say that she too had been excited – that after all the years of taking the pill and not needing to worry, the more recent routine had been forgotten at this less usual time of day.

No. That would be cheating – and there was no need to lie. She had told Ranji a year ago that she wanted a child and he had left the decision to her. Since she had not made any definite statement of her choice then, there was nothing to reverse now. In any case, this would be an isolated occasion, a gamble of a sort, nothing more. Too much of her life was predictable, running to a well-organized timetable. It was necessary once in a while to open the door to the unexpected. Her knowledge of the possible consequences would add a touch of danger to their lovemaking and change it from a routine to an adventure. She could feel herself flushing with excitement as she closed the bathroom cupboard. Smiling, she moved towards the bedroom, unfastening her clothes as she went.

13

On a warm evening in June Ros flew into Heathrow for the second time. For her first visit in March she had allowed only the few days needed to make the acquaintance of her sister, attend Lady Glanville's birthday party and inspect the picture of her ancestor. A business meeting in San Francisco made it impossible for her to extend her stay by more than a day on that occasion – just long enough to allow Chris his first sitting – but before she left she made arrangements to return in the summer for a real vacation. Now Chris could finish the portrait and she would give herself time to explore London as a conscientious tourist.

Even in the bustle of Terminal Three's crowded arrival hall Ros recognized at once what had happened to her sister. She hardly waited until Asha had welcomed her with a kiss before producing a laughing accusation: 'You're pregnant!'

Asha's expression of delight at the reunion changed to amazement. 'How can you possibly tell?' Automatically her hand stroked her smooth, unbulging skirt.

'You have the radiant look that writers of magazine stories describe in such gooey detail.' That was not wholly truthful. It was a mixture of triumph and secretiveness in Asha's smile which aroused suspicion. 'I notice you're not about to deny it.'

'I make no comment,' said Asha primly. Then she grinned. 'In other words, you could be right, but I haven't broken it to Ranji yet.'

'Because you're not sure? Is sisterly intuition speedier than pregnancy testing?'

'Oh, I'm sure enough. Waiting for the right moment, that's all. What sort of flight did you have?'

'The best sort: uneventful.' Ros took the hint to drop the subject of pregnancy. She had no wish to spoil the pleasure of the reunion by stumbling into some kind of marital minefield.

For this visit she had made arrangements to rent a service apartment, more spacious than the guest room offered by her sister and more comfortable than a hotel. Asha drove her there from the airport. The luxurious building was almost unnaturally silent, with double-glazed windows to insulate all its rooms from the noise of traffic. The door of the lift made no sound as it opened and closed, and the thick pile of the carpet stifled their footsteps as they followed the receptionist along the third-floor corridor, turning two corners before they reached the door of the apartment. Quietness had been Ros's primary specification when she made the booking, and her request had been honoured.

'There's something we have to talk about straightaway,' Ros said after the receptionist had shown them the apartment and left. She made herself comfortable on a sofa in the sitting room and gestured Asha to do the same. 'Lady Glanville's rubies.'

'What about them? They're your rubies now. You've been told that, haven't you? I ought to have let Mr Dangerfield know in March that you were here in England. But your visit was so short, and there was so much to be done after Aunt Alexa died. I didn't think about it until he wrote to find out whether I had an up-to-date address for you.'

'The rubies should have gone to you,' said Ros. 'Mr

Dangerfield told me that. If Lady Glanville had lived just one day longer they would have been yours. And you knew it.'

'It was extremely unprofessional of Mr Dangerfield to say so. The law doesn't take any notice of "ifs".'

'He only told me because I asked him right out. We had a long talk on the telephone. It didn't seem right that something so valuable should go to me, a stranger, when you'd been so close to Lady Glanville. I reckoned that she must have forgotten what she said in her will – and that she'd have changed it if she remembered. When I put that to Mr Dangerfield, he admitted that she was just on the point of altering the will. Why didn't you challenge it, Asha? An old lady on the eve of her hundredth birthday – a court might well have considered that the will didn't represent her true wishes.'

'Aunt Alexa was never senile,' Asha pointed out. 'To the very last minute of her life she knew exactly what she wanted. Besides – ' she seemed for a moment to be struggling for a clear understanding of her own feelings. 'I only saw those jewels for the first time on the day Aunt Alexa died. I didn't even know they existed until a few weeks before that. So they aren't some kind of heirloom that I'd been expecting to get. And there's another thing. She lived as a rich woman for a lot of her life, but by the time she died she hardly had anything left. Whatever I did for her in those last years was because I loved her, not because I hoped to inherit anything. She knew that, and I knew it, and that was the right way for things to be. If I'd tried to dispute the will, I'd have spoiled that relationship – even after it was over. Do you understand? The rubies, as jewellery, mean nothing to me. I couldn't ever wear anything so valuable. And as a token of love I don't need them either, because I know what she felt.'

'I get all that,' Ros agreed. 'But they have a third value that you don't mention. Hard cash. I'm not asking you what I should do, Asha. I'm telling you what I've decided. When I called Mr Dangerfield I first of all asked him to find a way of making you the heir. Some of what he told me I could hardly believe. If I got it right, he was saying that so long as all the beneficiaries agree, they can carve up the estate any way they like and shucks to what the person who's dead wanted.' Ros allowed her face to reveal what she thought of such an unbusinesslike arrangement.

Then she continued more briskly. 'At first I thought we could deal with it that way. But one more point came over loud and clear. If you had inherited the rubies directly from Lady Glanville you would have had to pay some kind of tax – was it capital transfer tax? – on their value. And it wouldn't have been peanuts. So because the money she *did* leave to you didn't come to much, you would have had to sell the jewels before you could pay the tax which entitled you to own them. Well, that's what Mr Dangerfield said. I won't tell you what I think about such a crazy system – he got me to believe it in the end. So it wouldn't help for me simply to sign away my rights. OK then, we agreed another plan. I accept the legacy. I put the whole set of jewellery up to auction – in London, because if it got round California that I owned that kind of property I'd have gunmen queuing up for the right to break into my safe. Once the rubies have turned into cash, I pay off any British taxes and then I make a money present to you. Mr Dangerfield said the tax law wouldn't catch a gift from a foreigner.'

'Ros, I can't possibly – '

Ros silenced her with a wave of the hand. 'You don't get to have a choice,' she said. 'Look at it this way, honey. I'm a very rich lady. I don't need more money. If I knew I was going to die tomorrow, I wouldn't know what to do with what I have. Well, my employees would find that they owned a co-operative and a couple of charities would clap their hands. Lady Glanville wanted you to have a gift of money in memory of her. I intend to see that her last wishes are carried out. Now then, when is Chris going to let me sit for him again?'

She was amused to see how completely her eloquence on the subject of the rubies had silenced Asha. Ranji, she guessed, would have no sentimental doubts about accepting the offer: and Asha, realizing that, had no choice but to give in with a helpless, affectionate laugh and kiss of thanks.

It was as well that Ros had arranged a leisurely visit, for disposing of the rubies proved to be a protracted business. Mr Dangerfield – moving with what in legal terms was lightning speed – had already negotiated the tax liability on an agreed valuation, but Ros had to establish her identity as well as her claim. On the day that probate was granted she acquired theoretical ownership of her legacy. The actual hand-over took place later, towards the end of her stay in England. Escorted by Mr Dangerfield to the bank manager's office, she signed a set of papers to release the jewel case from the strongroom. Its contents were displayed to her while she compared the pieces with the written specification. A second set of papers arranged for the valuables to go immediately back into safe keeping until they were auctioned in the autumn.

'I shan't see these jewels again,' Ros said. 'Someone from Sotheby's will come to photograph them and prepare a description, but I'll be gone by then. I'm going to ask you both to wait a moment longer. Just once, I want to wear them.'

She took the necklace from its velvet-lined drawer and fastened it round her neck. Slipping from her ears the thin gold rings which she wore by day, she replaced them with the delicate drop of ruby roses. Only when it came to the tiara did she hesitate. It was the lawyer who unexpectedly offered to help.

'I remeber how Lady Glanville wore it,' he said. 'May I?' Ros felt him slide the tiara into her hair and settle it firmly. 'I held a mirror for Lady Glanville as well, but – '

The bank manager, without speaking, opened a coat cupboard which proved to have a looking glass fixed inside the door. Ros had expected English professional men to be stuffy, but these two were taking obvious pleasure in her child-like enjoyment of dressing-up. She produced a camera from her handbag.

'Would you?' she asked Mr Dangerfield. 'Something for the family album. Well, two or three. The flash is automatic.'

The lawyer glanced at the banker and received a nod of permission. Within a few moments the jewels were back in their case and a security guard had returned them to the strong room.

'Crazy, isn't it?' commented Ros, describing the incident to Asha a few hours later. 'My father falls in love with a married woman in a foreign country and thirty-five years later I'm wearing a set of precious jewels given me by someone who never saw me after my first birthday.'

'You didn't wear them!'

'Just once. Why not?' Ros looked curiously at her sister, whose expression displayed a momentary alarm. But Asha did not explain. 'As soon as they're printed, I'll show you the pictures to prove it. Talking of rubies, I had a call from someone called Peter Langley, who said you knew him. He's working on a biography of Lady Glanville, right?'

'Yes. She asked him to help her write her memoirs, but she didn't leave herself time. Now he plans to do a kind of family history. A hundred years of the Lorimers. He knows a lot about Aunt Alexa's father – the man in your portrait.'

'First he's writing a newspaper piece about the rubies. I guess that's faster money than the book. He'd read Lady Glanville's will when it was probated, so he wanted to interview me as the current owner. I said he could call round. This is to check him out with you.'

'He's a journalist, yes. And honest, if that's what you're asking. If he'd wanted to steal the rubies he could have knocked me down and run for it in March. All the same . . .'

'All the same?' For a second time Ros noticed a doubt in her sister's eyes, but again was given no explanation.

'Oh, I'm sure it's all right. I don't like that kind of publicity myself. I've told him not to mention me in any of his articles, though I don't suppose I can keep out of the book. But in four days' time you'll be gone, so I don't suppose it can do any harm.'

The phrase was a curious one to use about a simple newspaper interview, but Ros did not press the matter. She had other business at Asha's home, for her portrait was finished. Chris was clearly nervous as she and Asha appeared in the attic to inspect the painting, but Ros found no difficulty in expressing enthusiasm. He had painted her sitting on the ground, as though on a hill top. Blaize – misty, as she had asked – stretched across the background: but Ros herself, her hands clasped round one knee, had been depicted in strong browns and reds. There was nothing wistful in the pose to suggest that she was pining for Blaize. Instead, Chris had perfectly caught in her expression the firmness with which she was accustomed to take important decisions. 'I like it,' she said.

That, of course, was not enough. It was necessary to praise every aspect of the work, to exclaim over details, to assure Chris that he did indeed possess a distinctive style. As he accepted her compliments she became aware that he was waiting for Asha also to express an opinion. For a second time Ros wondered whether her sister realized that the young artist was in love with her.

'How soon can it travel?' she asked Chris, dismissing the thought.

'It should really have time to dry. But I'll put it in an air-tight crate together with John Junius so that it can't get knocked or dusty.' Ros had left the Victorian picture behind after her earlier visit so that it could be packed together with this new one. 'I'll bring the crate round to your apartment the night before your flight.'

That time was not far off. On the day that Peter Langley's article appeared – illustrated by the photograph of Ros wearing the jewels – she took Asha and Ranji out to dinner before returning to the apartment to pack. This was not a task which demanded much time or thought at the end of a trip and she was in bed before midnight. Her flight was booked for the next morning. She had enjoyed her vacation – but she looked forward to returning home and was in a contented mood as she slipped easily into sleep.

Ros did not consciously hear the noise that woke her in the middle of the night but, once disturbed, had no doubt that there had been a sound. With wide-open eyes she stared into the darkness, holding her breath and listening. The silence was so complete as to be almost unnatural. Was someone on the other side of the door listening as

334

intently as herself? Could mere imagination be enough to make her skin prickle with uneasiness?

It was not imagination. There was a second sound, so faint that it would have been inaudible had she not been waiting for it: the sound of a well-made, well-oiled door whispering over the thick pile of a carpet. From the bed, set into one end of the L-shaped bedroom, Ros could not see the door, and its opening admitted no light: but she was quite sure that someone had come in from the sitting room. Moving as stealthily as the intruder she began to move a hand towards the bedside telephone, but then changed her mind. The instrument had an old-fashioned English dial instead of a speedy press-button face and she had already noticed that the emergency number was, ridiculously, the one which took longest to dial. Long before she could complete a call she would be heard and interrupted.

So instead she lay still. Her mouth was dry – too dry to scream, even had there been any chance of anyone hearing – and her heart pounded so loudly that it must surely be audible. But she did her best to control her breathing, exaggerating it slightly in the hope that she would give the impression of being deeply asleep. The burglar would soon discover that all the drawers were empty and then, please God, he would creep out of the room as surreptitiously as he had entered. His quietness, suggesting that he hoped not to disturb her, was the only reassuring factor in a terrifying situation.

The wait seemed interminable. In San Francisco Ros kept a loaded pistol in her bedside chest. But knowing that to carry a weapon would be illegal here and on the plane, and believing England to be a less violent country than her own, she had brought nothing with which to protect herself. In any case, she had once in the past

335

been robbed at gunpoint, in her own car, and believed that passivity, although humiliating, was often the safest policy.

A drawer was slammed back into place and a man's voice swore violently. In spite of her attempt at self-control, Ros could not resist a gasp of alarm. She grabbed at the telephone, knowing that her pretence of sleep would no longer be accepted, but before she could lift the receiver she was seized from behind. One hand covered her mouth, pressing her head back so roughly that she felt her neck must break, whilst the other grabbed an arm and twisted it painfully behind her back. She tried to struggle, kicking out frantically, but her attacker was too strong. Still kicking, she was turned face downward on the bed. A knee on her neck pressed her head into the pillow so that she could not breathe. As she struggled – not now to escape but to avoid suffocation – she was hardly aware of the wire being twisted round her wrists. But a sharp tug brought her feet up behind her back to be tied to her hands, stretching all the muscles of her body. By the time the pressure on her neck was released she was trussed like an animal, unable to move her arms or legs. Her gasps for breath mingled with sobs of pain.

A hand covered her mouth again as she was turned on to her side and the bedhead light was switched on by a man dressed in a black sweater and jeans. A dark stocking over his face flattened his nose and thickened his lips but was not sufficiently opaque to dull the glitter in his eyes.

He held a knife for a moment in front of her face. When he was sure she had seen it, he lowered it until the blade touched her neck. Ros lay still, not daring even to swallow the lump in her throat.

'Keep quiet,' said the man. 'Or else.' He pressed the

knife against her skin as he took his other hand away from her mouth. Ros kept quiet.

'The jewellery,' he said. 'That's all I want. Tell me where it is and I'll take it and leave you alone.'

'What jewellery?' As soon as she spoke Ros realized that the question was a mistake.

'Don't play games. The rubies.'

'I don't have them. They're not here.'

'I saw the picture in the paper. They were round your neck. Where are they? I'll find them anyway, but it'll be better for you if you tell me.'

'I wouldn't keep anything like that in a rented room. They're at the bank.'

'You're packed for travelling and it's Sunday tomorrow. You must have taken them out. Come on. Where are they?'

'I promise you – ' But the man was too angry to listen and Ros, seeing how short was the fuse of his temper, was even more frightened than before. She watched apprehensively as he felt in a pocket. Did he mean to torture her? But what he produced was a wide piece of sticking plaster which he pressed firmly over her mouth. Then, muttering under his breath, he left her and went into the sitting room.

Now that he no longer troubled to be quiet, Ros could follow his actions in her imagination as he broke open her suitcases and flung out the contents. There were pauses, when perhaps he was opening a toilet bag or discovering her jewel roll which did not in fact hold any valuable jewellery. She could hear him muttering, as well, and the fear that his anger was a form of madness pumped through her body with each beat of her heart. Her stomach was turning, and that in itself terrified her, for if she were to be sick with her mouth so firmly sealed she would choke on her own vomit.

Without warning he was back, pulling her on to the floor so that he could strip the bed. He tore the cases off each pillow and lifted the mattress to see what was hidden beneath it. The wire cut into her flesh as, half lifting her and half dragging, he carried her into the sitting room and tugged the plaster from her mouth.

'For the last fucking time. Where are they?'

'Waiting to be sold.' It was urgent that she should tell him everything before he silenced her again. 'They're going to be auctioned. The bank's keeping them until the sale.' If only she were able to show him the receipt – but she had given it to Mr Dangerfield, with authority to hand the valuables over to Sotheby's. 'You have to believe me. Why should I let you kill me for a few jewels if I could hand them over? They're in the bank. That's the truth, God help me.'

'They're in the crate, aren't they?' Ros felt sick again as she realized that he refused to believe her. The wooden crate in which the two pictures had been sealed up for the journey was the only container left unopened. He held up a small axe which she recognized by its red blade. She had last seen it in a case at the end of the corridor, kept ready for emergency use in the event of fire. 'You think I won't dare use this because of the noise. But there's no one to hear. I shan't ask again. Where are they?'

'In the bank. Please. Please. No, please.' As the plaster was pressed back again Ros tried frantically to persuade herself that the man had nothing to gain by harming her. But somewhere inside the panic which now overwhelmed her was a small cold centre of recognition that she was going to die as certainly as if she had been sentenced to

338

execution. To die for no good reason. Part of her mind seemed to be outside the scene and watching it, as though this could not possibly be happening to herself. Murder victims were always other people. But her body knew the truth, voiding itself on the carpet and jerking convulsively as she strained against her bonds.

She heard herself moaning and made one last effort to bring her terror under control, to reach a calm acceptance of whatever was going to happen to her. But it was impossible. The man had abandoned his first attempt to prize the crate open and now, crazy with frustration, brought the axe crashing down into the wood. Surely someone must hear. Surely someone would help. But there could not be much time. The trembling of her body grew more violent as he twisted the axe out of the wood and raised it to chop downwards again. And again. And again.

And then, reaching the limit of fear, she became still, no longer shuddering, no longer conscious of her stretched muscles or the tightness of the wire which trussed her. All the bones in her body seemed to have dissolved. As though her throat were already cut and her blood already drained away she felt herself sagging down into the thick pile of the luxury carpet. The crazed blows continued to beat down on the splintering wood. Ros closed her eyes and waited.

14

At seven o'clock on Sunday morning London was lazily relaxed. There was no traffic on the streets and the few pedestrians who had risen early to choose their Sunday newspapers strolled at a leisurely pace as they studied the headlines. Asha, on her way to Ros's apartment, moved more briskly, although there was no hurry. Ranji would not be bringing the car round until nine to drive Ros to the airport – this earlier walk was only to give the two sisters time for a last chat and a cup of coffee together.

There was no one about in the silent entrance hall of the apartment block. Part of the service it offered was the impression that there was no one else alive within several miles. Remembering the racket of the Portobello Road and the perpetual yelling of children in the school playground, Asha felt briefly envious of the peace that money could buy.

Stepping out of the lift at the third floor, she walked along the carpeted corridor, reached the door of Ros's apartment and put out her hand to ring the bell. But her arm fell back to her side as she saw that the door was not quite closed; and its frame was damaged.

Asha froze. Common sense told her that she should turn away at once and hurry to find help or at least company. Her brain gave instructions and her body, numbed by alarm, refused to obey them. Instead, she held her breath, listening for some faint sound which would speak of danger or need: but all the suspense was in her own mind and not in the heavy, undisturbed air. If she were to ring the bell, would there be a cheerful shout from Ros, an apologetic explanation of how she had locked herself out of the apartment and forced her way in? Asha tried to make herself believe in the possibility; but failed.

Like a puppet controlled from above she lifted her arm again. This time it seemed far heavier than before. The door opened silently as she pushed it: the curtained room was still and dark. Without moving her feet she leaned forward to feel for the light switch.

What she saw did not surprise her, because she already feared it; but that did not reduce the shock. Still without moving she forced her eyes to survey the chaos of the sitting room. The chairs and sofas had been overturned, and their cushions scattered on the floor. The drawers of every piece of furniture lay face downward on the floor. Ros's three suitcases – no doubt placed neatly near the door after being packed for the journey – had been opened: their contents were strewn over the carpet. The wooden crate containing the two portraits had been hacked open with an axe, which was still embedded in the wood. Asha gave a small cry of anguish as she saw that there was blood on the blade.

Sure by now that no living person was waiting for her in the apartment, she forced herself to step inside. Her feet crunched on cosmetic jars or stepped softly on clothes. Behind one of the upturned sofas she found her sister's body.

Her muscles tensed as she tried to contain her horror, recognizing that a single groan, a single shudder would be enough to trigger off a total lack of self-control. One reaction, though, could not be controlled. With an irrational reversion to childhood rules she turned away, trying to leave the room before she was sick – as though it were possible to inflict any greater contamination on the bloody scene. But there was no strength left in her legs, and in the doorway of the apartment she fell forward on to her knees, vomiting and sobbing for breath. How was it that no one heard? Long after her body had, surely, emptied itself, she continued to retch, doubling up in spasms which became steadily more painful. She tried to crawl away from the mess and found that the carpet of the corridor, like that of the sitting room, was stained with blood. Had she trodden too near to Ros and brought a trail out with her? No. The blood was her own.

The spasms continued and the pain grew until even her distress was not great enough to shield her from it. And the distress itself took on a new dimension, because now another life was at risk. 'Ranji!' she called, between each agonizing contraction of her muscles. But Ranji was not due to arrive for more than an hour. Unable to move, Asha watched her blood soaking into the thick pile of the luxury carpet and knew that he would be too late to save his child.

She must have fainted, because when she next opened her eyes she was in a hospital bed. One arm lay stiffly by her side, attached to tubes dark with blood. On the other side of the bed Ranji held her hand with both his own, kneeling on the floor with his head bowed so that his forehead touched her wrist. She called his name faintly and at once he was kissing her. He had been crying, she saw as after a little while he pulled himself up to sit in a chair.

'Oh my God, Asha, I was so frightened. When I saw what had happened, I thought you were dead as well.'

What had happened? Asha did not remember. She stared into Ranji's eyes as though she could read in them the history of how she had come to be here. Dead as well? As well as whom?

No sooner had she asked herself the question than the answer imprinted itself on her eyes. As vividly as though she were back in the apartment she saw again the white satin nightdress stained with blood, the wrists and ankles so swollen that they almost concealed the wire which bound them, the half-severed head of the sister who had been unknown to her for so many years and now was lost for ever. As strongly as though she were seeing that picture for the first time she felt her stomach muscles contract, and cried out not only because of the hideous memory but from the pain of her involuntary retching.

Ranji must have been warned, because he held some kind of dish ready as she hung her head over the side of the bed. Only a little dark green bile emerged. He wiped her mouth gently clean as she collapsed back on the pillows, exhausted.

'Don't think about it,' Ranji pleaded – but she could not think of anything else and even as he tried to comfort her he must have realized that. When the ward sister stepped through the curtains which screened Asha's bed from the rest of the ward and announced that a police-woman wished to speak to him, he refused at first to leave.

'It's really your wife she needs to talk to,' Sister told him. 'I said she'd have to wait a bit and she agreed to that if she could get some immediate information from you about Miss Davidson.'

'I'll be all right,' whispered Asha. 'Come back again.'

He squeezed her hand as a promise and rose to his feet. The nurse was about to follow him when Asha called her back. 'Sister! I'm pregnant. Will this – ?'

The nurse looked down sympathetically. 'I'm sorry, dear. I'm afraid you lost the baby.'

Asha's eyes flooded with tears – and yet she had guessed even before she asked.

'It was early days, wasn't it?' Sister said. 'This won't stop you trying again. You'll need to build up your strength. But in two or three months . . .'

Asha dabbed at her eyes with the sleeve of the white hospital nightdress. 'Does my husband know?' she asked.

'He saw that you lost a lot of blood before he found you. After we'd examined you here, we told him that you'd had an internal haemorrhage.' She gestured towards the transparent tubes which continued steadily to feed their contents into Asha's arm. 'People get alarmed if they see the drips without any warning. He was so concerned about you that he didn't ask about the baby.'

'He didn't know. I'd meant to tell him today, after my sister – my sister – ' She began to cry again. 'I don't want him to know now,' she managed to say at last. 'It will only upset him more.'

The nurse nodded neutrally. 'Could you cope with the policewoman?' she asked. 'If you felt able to get it over, we could give you a sedative. A really good sleep is what you need now.'

'All right.' Asha waited, numb with unhappiness, until the policewoman arrived, accompanied by Ranji. 'I can't tell you anything that you didn't see for yourselves,' she said. 'It was all over before I got there.'

'What time was that?'

'About quarter past seven.'

'Did you meet anyone inside the building? In the hall or corridor? Or did you hear any movement, as though someone might be keeping out of your way?'

'No. Nothing.'

344

'And in the street outside. Was anyone moving unusually fast, behaving suspiciously, wearing blood-stained clothing?'

Asha shook her head.

'I'm sorry that I have to ask this kind of question, but did you touch your sister's body? It would help if we knew whether it was still warm then.'

'I didn't touch anything except the door and the light switch. I just looked.' Unbidden, the picture of what she had seen returned. Her eyes seemed to flood with blood. In a room which suddenly darkened she did not hear the next question and was only aware that one had been asked because of the anxious expressions of her two visitors when she drifted back into consciousness. 'Sorry. What was that?'

'If you could describe the room,' said the policewoman, reluctantly businesslike. 'The position of everything you remember.'

Asha did her best, while the policewoman checked the details against her own observation later in the morning. 'I've nearly finished,' she said when this was done. 'But can you suggest that the intruder might have been looking for? Would Miss Davidson have had a lot of money on her?'

'She used credit cards more than cash. And she was on the point of leaving England. She'd settled the bill for the apartment, and we were going to drive her to Heathrow. She'd hardly have needed any more sterling at all.'

'What about other property? Were the pictures in the wooden crate valuable?'

'Not to anyone outside the family. And they weren't stolen, were they?'

'The intruder might have been disturbed. But what attracted him to the apartment in the first place? This wasn't a casual break-in and a quick snatch of anything lying around. The search was thorough – and angry. There must have been something specific he expected to find.'

There was a long silence. Asha remembered the uneasiness she had felt at Ros's casual mention that she had tried on Alexa's jewellery. It could not be a coincidence that Peter Langley's article – illustrated by a photograph of Ros wearing her legacy – had appeared on the morning before Ros's murder. The jewels were in the bank and the receipt was in Mr Dangerfield's safe – but the article had not mentioned this.

'The rubies,' Asha said – so faintly that Ranji and the policewoman were forced to lean towards her in order to hear. 'Yes. He would have been looking for the Lorimer rubies.'

15

For two days already the scream of the chainsaw had pierced its way through to the living room of the flat. Asha and Ranji had learned to close their ears to it; but Mr Dangerfield, paying an unexpected call, reacted to the sound with startled alarm.

'There's a row of elm trees between this row of buildings and the next,' Asha explained. 'The last of them died of Dutch elm disease this summer, and now the council has realized that they're dangerous as well as dead. So they're all coming down. Coffee?'

'Thank you very much.' The lawyer sat down and opened his briefcase. 'I thought I might see you at the auction yesterday.'

Asha's hand trembled as she poured out the coffee. Three months had passed since Ros's death and her own miscarriage, but the mere allusion to her great-aunt's jewellery still made her shudder. 'Not interested,' she said briefly.

'But as you'll see, they've brought you in a very handsome sum.' Mr Dangerfield set two sheets of paper on the table in front of her. Glancing at the first, Asha saw that it was the printed form on which Sotheby's had typed the amount for which the lot had been sold. The other sheet was covered with handwritten figures. No doubt it contained Mr Dangerfield's calculation of the tax to be deducted. She did not bother to study it.

'I don't want anything to do with the rubies,' she said, setting down the cups and saucers so that their rattling should not betray how much the subject upset her. 'As far as I can see, they came into Aunt Alexa's side of the family dishonestly and they've brought nothing but trouble ever since.'

'No one's expecting you to have the jewels themselves,' Ranji reminded her. 'It's only money.'

While Asha continued to shake her head, the lawyer leaned forward in his chair. 'It's certain that Lady Glanville intended to bequeath the jewellery to you,' he said. 'It was unfortunate that her wishes should have been frustrated by a matter of hours, but at least Miss Davidson didn't make the same mistake. Her instructions were completely clear, confirmed in writing and signed. I was empowered to act as a trustee in putting the jewels into the auction, paying all charges and taxes out of the proceeds and handing over the balance to you. The legal transfer was effective before Miss Davidson's death and I am obliged to carry out her intentions.'

'But you can't make me accept,' said Asha. She turned to her husband, sitting beside her on the sofa. 'Ranji, I'm sorry if this seems unreasonable. But anything we did with the money would always remind me of Ros and what happened to her. No one can force me to take it, surely?'

'It's enough to buy a house,' Ranji pointed out.

'How could I ever be happy in a home bought with this money?'

'Or it could pay off my debts. I could apply for my release from bankruptcy. Then I would be able to put the Ancestors on a proper business footing.' There was a note of appeal in his voice which at last penetrated Asha's almost hysterical reaction to every mention of the rubies. How selfish she was to think only of herself!

The two men waited as Asha, without speaking, forced

herself to consider the question more rationally. Any money handed over to the Official Receiver to pay off Ranji's debts would be effectively removed from her control. It would disappear, bringing her no direct benefit. There would be no acquisition, no object or building tainted by Ros's death to act as a permanent reminder of unhappiness. And Ranji's creditors, innocent victims of the market collapse for which he in turn had not been to blame, deserved to be recompensed. 'I see,' she said slowly. 'Yes, of course.'

With her mind made up, she looked straight into the lawyer's eyes. 'Then will you draw up something for me to sign, Mr Dangerfield? I want to transfer my interest in the jewellery to Ranji, so that the auctioneers hand over the sale proceeds directly to him.'

'You realize, of course, that a very considerable sum is involved and that you have no legal liability for your husband's debts? As long as this money remains your property the Receiver can have no claim on it. But if it becomes part of your husband's personal assets . . .' Mr Dangerfield's voice expressed no disapproval. He was merely making sure, as a good family lawyer should, that his client understood the consequences of her decision.

Asha hardly bothered to listen to him. She was aware only of Ranji's hand squeezing hers in a tight grip of gratitude, of Ranji's brown eyes brimming with love as they looked down into her own.

She had been wrong to think that the gift would bring her no benefit. Her husband was an honest, honourable man who felt the shame of his debts keenly. Thanks to Ros, he could recover his self-esteem and these past two unsatisfactory years could be put behind them and forgotten. The heirloom which had touched so many of the Lorimers with misery would at last, in the very

349

moment of passing to strangers, bring happiness to the family. She smiled back at Ranji, mouthing the words 'I love you' in silence so that Mr Dangerfield would not hear.

'I shall be happy to arrange it,' the lawyer said. 'And to present the case for discharge from bankruptcy if you would like me to do that.'

'I'll leave you to fix it up together,' Asha said. The shriek of the chainsaw, nearer than before, drew her up to the attic to see what was going on.

She was greeted by the smell of oil and turpentine which had become part of the flat's atmosphere. The summer tourist season had brought a rush of orders to Ranji's fledgling business. People who had read the Ancestors brochure in the United States, but were reluctant to commit themselves by letter, had added the studio to their list of London sights. Chris had needed to spend the whole of the long summer holiday at work here to meet the demand for modern costume pictures. The most recently finished was drying in the rack. In its place on the easel a newly-primed canvas awaited the first touch of colour.

Chris, though, was not at work. Instead, he was standing by the window, watching the activity outside.

'Any minute now!' he said as Asha came into the room. 'They had terrible trouble with the first of the elms. No room to manoeuvre at all, so they practically had to chop it into matchsticks. But this last one's going to depart in style. They've trimmed off the side branches, so the trunk should fall into the space left by the rest of the line. There she goes!'

He put his arm round Asha's waist, pressing her close to the window so that she could see what was happening on the ground. As the saw was withdrawn and switched off the silence was almost audible, the anxiety of the tree surgeon's crew almost tangible. The old tree shuddered and gave a single wrenching groan. Then it began to fall. Asha would have expected it to crash to the ground but instead it appeared to float in delicate slow motion. Only at the last minute was there a rush and a thud and a flurry of dust and woodchips. She made use of the distraction to free herself from Chris's arm.

'Two million homeless beetles!' Chris exclaimed – but Asha, turning away from the window, hardly heard the words. She was amazed by the transformation of the attic. It had never been dark; but suddenly, as though a blind had been released, the whole room was invaded by light – a bright, intense morning sunlight which bathed the virgin white canvas with gold.

'Don't move,' said Chris. She heard the click of his camera and, as she looked up in surprise, he took a second photograph.

'It's Hockney,' he explained. 'Sunlight through an open window, the white rectangle of canvas, all those angles on the easel, and Woman Standing. When are you going to let me paint you again, Asha? The Asha-by-Gainsborough has become a brochure advertisement for selling other paintings. It's lost its magic. I need to do another, more private.'

'Asha-by-Hockney?'

'No. Too harsh a light. A Bonnard. I'd like to paint you taking a shower. With your arms above your head – twisting your hair dry, perhaps. That lovely pale body seen through a screen of water.'

'You mean you'd want me to pose in the nude!'

'Why not?' asked Chris. 'I sometimes wonder if you realize how beautiful you are.'

'Sorry,' said Asha. 'Not quite my line, I'm afraid. I

wouldn't pose like that even for a stranger. So you can't expect me to – to – '

'To sit for someone who's falling in love with you? For someone you might even – '

But Asha had moved away, evading the hand with which he tried to hold her back. She turned towards the door and came to a halt, startled. How long had Ranji been standing there?

His expression gave no clue to his feelings. 'Paula is on the telephone for you,' was all he said.

'Paula? In England?' Asha put Chris out of her mind as she hurried down to the living room. 'What are you doing here?' she demanded as soon as she and her cousin had exchanged greetings. 'Is this another trip to persuade travel agents that Bristow Great House is the best hotel in the West Indies?'

'Not this time. I've been invited to give evidence to a race relations commission. I'll tell you all about it when we meet. Can I see you this afternoon? For a walk in Hyde Park, perhaps, to blow away the jet lag?'

Asha hesitated. 'The new school year begins at two o'clock this afternoon, Paula. At least, that's when all the new children who are coming up from their primary schools to start at Hillgate have been told to arrive. I'm taking an Assembly at three, to give them a pep talk. But this evening – '

'Five minutes,' said Paula. 'Just five minutes between two and three o'clock, in your room at school. Could you spare me that?'

'Yes, but – '

'See you!' said Paula, and rang off before Asha could insist on some more leisurely meeting.

Ranji came into the room carrying two mugs. 'More coffee?'

352

'Thanks.' She pulled a cushion on to the floor and sat down on it. Years ago, when she had first known Ranji, this had been her way of indicating that she was ready for a serious conversation. His smile suggested that he remembered this.

'When Mr Dangerfield was here, I said that I couldn't bear to buy a house with the money from the rubies,' she reminded him. 'But all the same, we might consider moving, don't you think? The one thing to be said for an over-size school is that it entitles its Head to an over-size salary. We could afford a mortgage.'

'Why would you like to move?' Ranji was not opposing the suggestion.

'The Ancestors business is really taking off now, isn't it? All these people telephoning and ringing the doorbell! The attic is a studio and a store room and the dining room's more of an office than a place to eat in. This flat was fine as a home for two people, but now – it's not private any more.'

'And you think that you should remove yourself from temptation?'

Asha glanced up at Ranji, whose dark brown eyes looked steadily into hers. 'Until today,' she said, 'I haven't even been aware that there could be a problem. But now that I *am* aware of it, I have to make a positive decision, don't I? I mean, even to do nothing would be a reaction of a sort.'

'And you don't wish – ?'

'I don't want to spoil Chris's friendship with me by asking him not to work here – nor to disturb his partnership with you.'

'And so you wish to remove yourself from temptation!'

'Yes,' Asha admitted. She put down her mug as Ranji slid to the floor beside her. His kiss was long and loving.

'I'm a lucky man to have a wife I can trust so well,' he said.

Guiltily Asha remembered one secret she had kept from him. She considered it for a moment and then confessed. 'That day three months ago,' she said. They both knew what day she meant. 'I had a miscarriage. I'd been pregnant.'

'I thought so. So much blood. I didn't like to ask you then, to upset you again. But even earlier I'd been wondering. I'd been waiting for you to say something.'

'That very day I was going to tell you.'

'Was it an accident – the pregnancy, I mean?'

'No.'

'So do you want to try again?'

'No.' Asha's answer was definite. 'I made a misjudgement, Ranji. It was after Aunt Alexa's funeral. I was upset and – well, I can't explain in any way that makes sense. I felt that the family ought to be kept alive. And I seemed to be the only person who could do anything about it.'

'So you took a decision as though you were the head of the family. You ought to have asked me.' He spoke reasonably, without anger.

'Of course I should have discussed it with you. I'm sorry. On top of that, it was sloppy thinking. And a wrong decision.'

'So what do you think now?'

'I think now that to bring a child into the world for no better reason than to provide my ancestors and myself and you with descendants would be unforgivable. And I think also that I'm of more value to the world as a teacher than as a mother. I could bring up one or two children of my own well enough, no doubt. But as a headmistress . . . This afternoon, Ranji, I shall welcome more than three hundred children to Hillgate. Most of them come from poor homes, with narrow horizons. I'm going to open their eyes to new worlds – and open doors so that they can step through. I've been given the power to influence their lives, and I have a duty to use it. There are going to be a lot of changes in that school.'

'And if I were to say to you that I would like to have a child, two children – ?'

'I wouldn't believe you. If I did, I'd tell you it was too late. But you're *not* saying that, are you?'

Ranji did not answer at once, and for a moment Asha was anxious. Then he looked at her with the sweet smile which had won her heart fourteen years earlier. 'Just testing,' he said. 'You still see yourself as head of the household, I think. But I love you all the same.'

16

Asha stood at the window of the head teacher's study. Waiting for Paula, she watched the new children arrive at the school gates.

How young they seemed! They had all passed their eleventh birthdays, but expressions of anxiety or expectation gave each of them a look of vulnerability. A few more shabby clothes with an air of either shame or defiance, but most were over-dressed. In every family which could afford it the change of school had been signalled by the buying of new clothes – with an eye to long life. The sleeves of new blazers reached almost to fingertips, while some of the girls walked proudly in navy-blue raincoats whose hems flapped round their calves. Poor little things, efficiently water-proofed on a hot September day.

As well as being over-dressed, they were over-loaded, made lopsided by the weight of a bulging shoebag or over-stuffed briefcase. Unfortunately for posture, the old-fashioned school satchel was still out of fashion. But Asha was glad that this first arrival at a new school had been treated as a special occasion. It meant that the parents were on her side. Unconsciously she clenched her fists, silently promising not to let them down.

Some of the children were accompanied on this first afternoon by mothers or older siblings; but any nervousness on the part of the new pupil was less than the fear of being thought a baby. Goodbyes were swift and at some distance from the gate. And then there was no time

356

for loneliness. As each youngster stepped inside the playground, an older boy or girl moved forward from the reception group waiting by the door. The newcomer was led to a list pinned to a blackboard, where each name had a cloakroom number and classroom letter.

It was on Asha's own insistence that the school had been opened a half day early. In the past she had felt sorry for the eleven-year-olds who found themselves milling around amongst almost two thousand children in a huge building, and who spent the whole of their first day in a state of anxiety or panic about where they were supposed to be and how to get there. Now they would feel looked after as they hung up their clothes and found their desks and met their class teachers and the other children who would become their friends. After Asha herself had welcomed them all, they would have the chance to explore all the buildings, with guides to help them, and to learn a few of the school rules without being swamped at once by the whole burden of orders and prohibitions.

A taxi drew up outside the school gate, and a smartly-dressed black woman made her way briskly through the cluster of eleven-year-olds. Asha moved away from the window and opened the door of her study, ready to welcome her cousin. 'Paula!'

'Asha, hi! Great to see you. And special thanks for letting me intrude on your working day. Something's different. What is it?' Paula stared intently. 'You've put your hair up. Very elegant. Makes you seem older. But then, you never looked more than seventeen before, so perhaps that's the idea.'

Asha laughed her agreement. 'Right! I've even acquired an MA gown to add dignity and authority. Look at this! Not for everyday wear, of course. But in an hour's time all the new children will be waiting in the assembly hall, and I intend them to notice my arrival.'

'Good for you. It's one of the points I'm hoping to get across to the commission tomorrow. Jamaican children actually *like* authority and discipline in the classroom. One of the things that throws them when they come to England is to find school teachers saying matily, "Call me Charlie". I hope you're hiding a cane in that cupboard!'

'What is this commission, Paula?'

'Your government's latest effort to investigate race relations in England. We're due for a stormy encounter tomorrow morning, I think. *I* want to discover whether our people who've emigrated to England are being treated decently, but I suspect that the commission wants to find out how we in Jamaica would cope if any large repatriation scheme was put into effect. I may not have told you – I'm moving into politics. The hotel can more or less run itself now, and I've hired a manager. When I was sixteen I decided to be prime minister of Jamaica one day, and it's time to get going. I've done a lot of local broadcasting, so people know my name. But I mustn't hold you up now with my chatter. I've only come to ask a single question.'

'Why were you so keen to ask it here instead of spending the evening with us and having a proper talk?'

'I'm taking you both out to dinner this evening,' Paula said. 'I fixed that with Ranji before you came on the line this morning. But I wanted to see you first when Ranji wouldn't be around.'

'You'd better sit down.' Asha felt suddenly chilled. 'Is something wrong, Paula? Something affecting me?'

'It's tricky,' said Paula. 'I'm breaking a confidence, you see. Ranji specially asked me not to say anything to you. But then I thought, if I have to take sides between you and him, I'd always choose you. Naturally.'

358

'Why should you have to take sides?'

'I hope I don't. But I wondered whether perhaps you were splitting up.'

'No, of course not. We're very happy together.'

'Then that's all fine and dandy and I'm sorry I spoke.'

'You'll have to go on now,' Asha said quietly. 'What was it that Ranji didn't want you to tell me?'

'That he was offering me the portrait of old John Junius Lorimer – the one that used to hang in the drawing room at Blaize. He wrote to ask me whether I'd like it. But if I took the picture, I wasn't ever to tell you that I had it. My first thought was that maybe you'd walked out on him and he was disposing of everything that reminded him of you. It was a relief when you both seemed to be using the same telephone yesterday. Oh God, Asha, what have I done?'

Asha struggled to control the trembling of her body. She could feel the blood draining from her face. Something in her head was roaring as it had roared on the day she pushed open the door of Ros's apartment, and if she had not been sitting down her legs would have collapsed beneath her as they had collapsed then. She was staring in Paula's direction, but all she could see was a blood-stained axe half buried in a wooden crate.

It must have been a moment or two later that she was aware of a hand pressing her head down between her knees. 'Do you have a bathroom?' Paula asked. 'Cold water?' Asha indicated a door and a moment later her cousin came back with a wet towel. 'Crazy!' The coldness was pressed firmly down. 'I'm sorry, Asha. Why couldn't I do what I was told? I should have asked Ranji, of course, not you.'

'It's all right.' Taking a grip on herself again, Asha saw that it would be best to dispose of the subject. 'Quite

359

simple, really. That portrait was in Ros's room when she was killed, you see. It was damaged by the same axe . . .' She had to make an effort not to cry. 'When I saw Chris repairing the canvas afterwards, I remembered . . . I asked Ranji to get rid of it, any way he liked. I thought he'd sell it, to a stranger. But perhaps he felt it ought to stay in the family. If he'd given it to Bernard, I would have seen it when I visited. He must have decided that Jamaica was safe.'

'Until I put my big foot in it. I *am* sorry, Asha.'

'Ranji's very good about that sort of thing,' Asha said. 'He's sensitive. And kind. I must stop letting memories upset me. I'm glad if you're going to keep our ancestor in the family. Perhaps I'll be able to come over to Jamaica and say hello to him again one day.'

'I shall hang him in the lobby of the hotel and explain to guests that he's my great-grandfather. That should cause a double-take or two.' Paula hesitated, perhaps wondering whether she was about to be tactless for a second time. 'So as far as you and Ranji are concerned, everything is hunky-dory?'

'Yes. Fine.' But Asha remembered how she had confided in her cousin at the Oxford Gaudy a year earlier, and saw the need to explain. 'There *was* a bad patch. Ranji had problems at work. And I – I think it was all my fault, really. When I first met Ranji he was young and rather nervous and flat broke. He would never have dared to push me into marriage. I did all the pushing. Mostly because I was so much in love with him – but partly because Aunt Alexa went on about it so.'

'You held the purse strings then, I suppose. You were in a position to push.'

'I suppose so. But it didn't seem right to go on in the same way after he started earning. Perhaps I was still a bully, but I bullied him into being the boss instead, if you see what I mean. I thought that was what he'd expect – a supportive, Indian-type wife. Well, he did, of course – but at the same time I was working as hard as he was, and I needed a supportive "wife" as well. It was crazy of me to impose a pattern of marriage which was the opposite of what I really wanted. Talk about digging a trap for oneself! He was as much in love with me as I was with him, after all. He would have put me on a pedestal and gone down on his knees to scrub the floor all round if I'd told him on the first day of the honeymoon that that was how we were going to live.' She sighed in mock regret. 'Too late ever to get back to that, of course.'

'So for fourteen years you've been curbing your natural inclination to dominate – and now you're a headmistress! What does Ranji think about that?'

'I expect he hopes that I'll work out all my bullying tendencies in school hours and be especially sweet when I get home.' Asha laughed light-heartedly at the idea. 'Or perhaps he never really wanted to take all the responsibilities I pushed on him.' Only a few hours earlier Ranji had accused her of acting as though she were the head of the household. He had seemed to be asking for a denial – but he might not necessarily have wanted the denial to be true.

It was too complicated to explain: and Paula was still tentatively exploring. 'So – remembering our chat at Oxford – would I be right in deducing that you've decided to abandon your descendants as well as your ancestors?'

'You would be right.'

'You realize, of course, that in view of the shameful way in which Bernard and I have evaded our responsibilities, you're effectively sealing the doom of the entire Lorimer family. Killing it off.'

'As long as I'm alive, the Lorimer family lives. *La famille, c'est moi!* But I couldn't do this job properly if I were worrying about a baby at home. Why should I be held back by some nebulous obligation to the future?'

'Why indeed? You don't have to defend your dynastic decisions to me. I was there before you. Marriage is marvellous, but babies are a bind! Phrased more elegantly, that's the central thought of my political programme in Jamaica. Of which more this evening.' Paula stood up as a seventeen-year-old boy knocked at the door and announced that everyone was ready.

Asha put on her academic gown and hood and showed her cousin out of the school. As Paula left through one of the main doors, an eleven-year-old West Indian boy burst in through the other, panting with panic because he was so late for this important first day. Skidding to a standstill, he looked helplessly round the large entrance area at all the anonymous doors.

'Over there.' Asha indicated the way to the assembly hall. She moved in the same direction as he scuttled inside, but paused outside for a moment, allowing the disturbance of his arrival to subside before she followed him in.

There was a glass panel set in the upper half of the door. Through it Asha could see colour photographs of the school's previous headmasters, hanging on the wall which faced her. One day, no doubt, her own photograph would be placed beside them – just as in a wealthier age the oil painting of her Victorian forebear had been added to the line of ancestral portraits in Brinsley House, the Lorimer mansion in Clifton.

Beneath the photographs the new boys and girls, trying not to fidget, sat in rows under the watchful eyes of their class teachers. Asha's lips parted in a smile as she studied them through the glass. These children, starting their secondary school lives on the same day that she began her career as a headmistress, would be her special pupils.

Asha straightened her shoulders, nodded to the prefect who was waiting to open the door for her and walked with slow dignity up the steps and across to the centre of the platform. A hundred years earlier John Junius Lorimer, Chairman of Lorimer's Bank, had summoned his children and his domestic staff into family prayers in much the same way as she had called her new pupils to this assembly. But she intended to speak of enthusiasm and ambition and excellence, not of duty and service and faith.

Could he have seen his great-granddaughter today, John Junius would have been amazed at her calm authority and dismayed by the decisiveness with which she had cut herself free from the burden of dynastic responsibility. Yet one family tie could not be cut. From her Lorimer ancestors she had inherited the spirit which made her determined to succeed in her own ambitions while refusing to accept anything but the best efforts of others. Such a legacy was less easily renounced than a painting or a collection of jewels.

Forms scraped and feet scuffled as the year's new intake rose untidily to its feet. As Asha waited for the silence which would follow the moment of shuffling and fidgeting she looked down at the three hundred and twenty young faces in front of her and could not restrain a smile of love.

These were her children.

The best years of her life were about to begin.

Outstanding fiction in paperback from Grafton Books

Muriel Spark
The Abbess of Crewe	£1.95	☐
The Only Problem	£2.50	☐
Territorial Rights	£1.95	☐
Not To Disturb	£1.25	☐
Loitering with Intent	£1.25	☐
Bang-Bang You're Dead	£1.25	☐
The Hothouse by the East River	£1.25	☐
Going up to Sotheby's	£1.25	☐
The Takeover	£1.95	☐

Toni Morrison
Song of Solomon	£2.50	☐
The Bluest Eye	£2.50	☐
Sula	£2.50	☐
Tar Baby	£1.95	☐

Erica Jong
Parachutes and Kisses	£2.50	☐
Fear of Flying	£2.95	☐
How to Save Your Own Life	£2.50	☐
Fanny	£2.95	☐
Selected Poems II	£1.25	☐
At the Edge of the Body	£1.25	☐

Anita Brookner
A Start in Life	£1.95	☐
Providence	£1.95	☐
Look at Me	£2.50	☐
Hotel du Lac	£2.50	☐

To order direct from the publisher just tick the titles you want and fill in the order form.

Outstanding fiction in paperback from Grafton Books

To order direct from the publisher just tick the titles you want and fill in the order form.

GF1481

The world's greatest novelists now available in paperback from Grafton Books

J B Priestley

Angel Pavement	£2.50	☐
Saturn Over the Water	£1.95	☐
Lost Empires	£2.50	☐
The Shapes of Sleep	£1.75	☐
The Good Companions	£2.50	☐

Alan Sillitoe

The Loneliness of the Long Distance Runner	£1.95	☐
Saturday Night and Sunday Morning	£1.95	☐
Down from the Hill	£2.50	☐
The Ragman's Daughter	£2.50	☐
The Second Chance	£1.50	☐
Her Victory	£2.50	☐
The Lost Flying Boat	£1.95	☐
The General	£2.50	☐
The Storyteller	£2.50	☐
Key to the Door	£2.95	☐
A Start in Life	£2.95	☐
The Death of William Posters	£2.50	☐

To order direct from the publisher just tick the titles you want and fill in the order form.

GF581A

All these books are available at your local bookshop or newsagent, or can be ordered direct from the publisher.

To order direct from the publishers just tick the titles you want and fill in the form below.

Name _____

Address _____

Send to:
Grafton Cash Sales
PO Box 11, Falmouth, Cornwall TR10 9EN.

Please enclose remittance to the value of the cover price plus:

UK 55p for the first book, 22p for the second book plus 14p per copy for each additional book ordered to a maximum charge of £1.75.

BFPO and Eire 55p for the first book, 22p for the second book plus 14p per copy for the next 7 books, thereafter 8p per book.

Overseas £1.25 for the first book and 31p for each additional book.

Grafton Books reserve the right to show new retail prices on covers, which may differ from those previously advertised in the text or elsewhere.